"Karen Chance will _____ pires, mages, and a fair ma_____s."
—US_____York

Praise f_____

_____ the Night

"Cassie is a well-rounded character, and the intensity and complexity of the plot puts her through her paces physically, emotionally, and psychically." —*Publishers Weekly*

"If you thought *Touch the Dark* and *Claimed by Shadow* were action-packed, well, buckle your seat belt.... Lara Croft would have a hard time keeping up.... Once again, Chance has written an action-packed story with very few places to put the book down for a night's sleep." —*SF Revu*

"Quick pacing and imaginative use of some old mythologies blend into a captivating read that will leave readers clamoring for more." —Monsters and Critics

"Ms. Chance continues to expand her well-built world with time travel, fantastical beings, steamy romance, and the non-stop action her wonderful series provides. This is a fast-moving read that's hard to set down, and it will no doubt leave readers eager for future installments in the Cassandra Palmer series." —Darque Reviews

"Cassie is a great character.... As far as supernatural and paranormal series go, this is one of the best." —*The Romance Reader* (five-star review)

"Entertaining.... Subgenre fans who have not read Cassie's saga should take a chance as these are well-written horror-fantasy tales." —Alternative Worlds

continued ...

"A wonderfully refreshing step away from the cookie-cutter regime of the usual vampire novels . . . this novel has it all. Believable characters, descriptive settings, and thrills and chills kept this reader on the edge of her seat."
—Roundtable Reviews

"Fast-paced and filled with faeries, kids, vampires, mages, ghosts, incubi, gargoyles, magic spells, evil plots, backstabbing, and surprises—this one follows the lead of the first two and adds in a bit more of each to 'kick it up a notch,' so to speak."
—Fantasy Book Spot

"If you love vampires and you're looking for something a little different, then you definitely need to check out this series. Karen Chance is easily becoming one of my top authors."
—Literary Escapism

"Thrilling . . . each revelation adds intriguing twists to the already knotty plot. Highly entertaining." —*Romantic Times*

Claimed by Shadow

"A nonstop thrill ride from beginning to end, a wildly entertaining romp with a strong, likable heroine. The story is fast-paced and barely lets up from the word 'go,' lightened with plenty of wry humor and more than a dash of romance."
—Rambles

"Ms. Chance is a master . . . a series well worth getting hooked on."
—Fresh Fiction

"A great writer of supernatural fantasy that is on a par with the works of Kim Harrison, Charlaine Harris, and Kelley Armstong."
—*Midwest Book Review*

"Magic aplenty populates this fast-moving, rather dark tale of power, corruption, double-dealings, and painful attractions as Cassie comes to grip with her new role in this follow-up to *Touch the Dark*. It is nice to see a strong, capable heroine taking charge with a kick butt attitude while attempting to balance right and wrong in the face of impossible odds."
—Monsters and Critics

Touch the Dark

"Exciting and inventive." —*Booklist*

"Fast and heavy on the action, *Touch the Dark* packs a huge story. . . . A blend of fantasy and romance, it will satisfy readers of both genres." —Fresh Fiction

"A very promising start to a new series, and an exceptionally entertaining first novel." —*Locus*

"A grab-you-by-the-throat-and-suck-you-in sort of book with . . . sexy-scary vampires. I loved it—and I'm waiting anxiously for a sequel."

—Patricia Briggs, *New York Times*
bestselling author of *Bone Crossed*

"A wonderfully entertaining romp with an engaging heroine. Here's hoping there's a sequel in the works!"
—*New York Times* bestselling author Kelley Armstrong

"Karen Chance takes her place along with Laurell K. Hamilton, Charlaine Harris, MaryJanice Davidson, and J. D. Robb to give us a strong woman who doesn't wait to be rescued. . . . The action never stops . . . engrossing." —SFRevu

"[A] plucky heroine with special powers dealing with the supernatural . . . exciting and fun." —*Philadelphia Weekly Press*

"A fast-paced, entertaining adventure in the best tradition of contemporary supernatural fiction. . . . I look forward to seeing what Karen Chance does next." —Emerald City

"A fast-paced action novel that never lets up. . . . Karen Chance is one of the most original voices in paranormal fiction. . . . A 'do not miss' novel for fans of vampires or fans of great storytelling . . . compelling, heart-racing, [and] erotic."
—Pink Heart Reviews

"Sexy vampires and interesting magical powers set up a thrilling and suspenseful environment in *Touch the Dark* . . . combines humor, action, and the paranormal into a scintillating story that will leave readers begging for more."
—Romance Reviews Today

Curse the Dawn

KAREN CHANCE

AN ONYX BOOK

ONYX
Published by New American Library, a division of
Penguin Group (USA) Inc., 375 Hudson Street,
New York, New York 10014, USA
Penguin Group (Canada), 90 Eglinton Avenue East, Suite 700, Toronto,
Ontario M4P 2Y3, Canada (a division of Pearson Penguin Canada Inc.)
Penguin Books Ltd., 80 Strand, London WC2R 0RL, England
Penguin Ireland, 25 St. Stephen's Green, Dublin 2,
Ireland (a division of Penguin Books Ltd.)
Penguin Group (Australia), 250 Camberwell Road, Camberwell, Victoria 3124,
Australia (a division of Pearson Australia Group Pty. Ltd.)
Penguin Books India Pvt. Ltd., 11 Community Centre, Panchsheel Park,
New Delhi - 110 017, India
Penguin Group (NZ), 67 Apollo Drive, Rosedale, North Shore 0632,
New Zealand (a division of Pearson New Zealand Ltd.)
Penguin Books (South Africa) (Pty.) Ltd., 24 Sturdee Avenue,
Rosebank, Johannesburg 2196, South Africa

Penguin Books Ltd., Registered Offices:
80 Strand, London WC2R 0RL, England

First published by Onyx, an imprint of New American Library,
a division of Penguin Group (USA) Inc.

First Printing, April 2009
10 9 8 7 6 5 4 3 2 1

Printed in the United States of America

PUBLISHER'S NOTE
This is a work of fiction. Names, characters, places, and incidents either are the
product of the author's imagination or are used fictitiously, and any resemblance
to actual persons, living or dead, business establishments, events, or locales is
entirely coincidental.

The publisher does not have any control over and does not assume any responsibility for author or third-party Web sites or their content.

To MBB

ACKNOWLEDGMENTS

Thanks to Laurence P. Lehman for a fun conversation on voivodes.

Chapter One

Stalking a time traveler is hard work, even if you are one. Especially when said traveler totally has you made. "Can we talk?" I screamed as I dodged behind a column to avoid a spray of bullets.

The woman hunting me through the cellar slung her flashlight beam in my direction. "Sure," she said amiably. "Hold still for a second."

Yeah, right.

My name is Cassie Palmer and a lot of people think I'm not the sharpest pencil in the box. My strawberry blond hair, which usually resembles Shirley Temple's in a windstorm, is part of the reason. My blue eyes, slightly pudgy cheeks and tip-tilted nose might be another, except that most men's gazes never make it up that far. But dumb blonde or not, even I wasn't buying that one.

My own weapon—a new 9 mm Beretta—was crowding the waistband of my jeans and poking me insistently in the hipbone. I ignored it. Years from now, the woman with the gun would leave a little message that would save my life. I kind of wanted her to be around to write it. Not to mention that shooting people is a good way to ensure that they don't want to talk to you, and we really needed to have a chat.

"When did the Guild start employing women?" she demanded, getting warmer.

I stayed utterly still, pressed against the back of one of the wooden columns holding up the roof. As hiding places go, it pretty much sucked, but there weren't a lot of alternatives. The cellar's walls were stone, except for areas that had been patched with brick. The ceiling was wood and flat, I guess because it served as the floor of the building above. And that was it, except for a few old barrels, some mildew and a lot of dark.

Even empty, the place was big enough that she'd have trouble finding me if I stayed silent. On the other hand, it was going to be tough for us to have a conversation if I never said anything. "Look, you've obviously mistaken me for—" I began, only to have the wall behind me peppered with bullets.

Stinging particles of brick and old mortar exploded out at me, and a few must have grazed my cheek because I felt a trickle of blood start to slide down my neck. The stillness after the gunfire made my ears ring and my nerves jump, and my hand instinctively closed over my gun. I dragged it back. I wasn't here to shoot her, I reminded myself sternly.

Although the idea was growing on me.

"I thought you guys were a bunch of misogynistic assholes with delusions of grandeur," she taunted.

I stayed stubbornly silent, which seemed to piss her off. A couple bullets thwacked into the wood at my back, shaking the column. I bit my lip to stay quiet until I felt something like a firm pinch on my left butt cheek. A second later, the pinch blossomed into white-hot pain.

My searching hand came back damp and sticky with streaks that looked black in the almost nonexistent light. I stared at it incredulously. I hadn't been here ten minutes yet, and I'd already been shot in the ass.

"You shot me!"

"Come out and I'll make the pain stop."

Yeah—permanently.

She paused to reload and I scurried behind a nearby barrel. As cover went, it wasn't much of an improvement, forcing me to hunker down against the cold, filthy floor to stay out of sight. But at least vulnerable bits of my anatomy weren't poking out past the sides.

I explored the gash in the back of my jeans. The bullet had only grazed me—what Pritkin, my war mage partner, would call a flesh wound. He'd probably slap a Band-Aid

on it and tell me to stop whinging—whatever that meant—
after he finished shouting at me for getting shot in the first
place. But it *hurt*.

Of course, it would hurt a lot more if she shot me again.
I peered over the top of the barrel, hoping to talk some
sense into her while she was temporarily unable to kill me.
Instead, my attention was caught by movement near the
stairs. The dim glow of her flashlight gleamed off the barrel
of a semiautomatic that had reached out of the dark. That
was a problem since we were currently in 1605 and that
type of gun hadn't been invented yet.

Even worse, it was aimed at her head.

"Behind you!"

She didn't hesitate. The flashlight went skittering across
the stones, distracting the shooter, who blasted the hell out
of it while she disappeared into shadow. One of the bullets
went astray and hit a small wooden cask. It looked harmless, but it must have contained the equivalent of a few
sticks of TNT. Because a deafening explosion was followed
by a ball of orange flame smashing against the ceiling.

Fire rained down everywhere, including onto the shooter's hand and arm. The gun hit the floor and a man danced
out of the stairwell, beating at the flames with his bare
hands and shrieking. He also dropped a lantern that spun
across the stones in lazy parabolas, lighting him up inter-
mittently, like a strobe.

He was a tall, lanky blond, with horsey features half hidden by a floppy hat. He wore a long dark vest, knee pants
and a puffy shirt that was quickly going up in smoke. He
managed to get the flames out by flinging off the vest and
ripping open the shirt, revealing a pale torso and some
singed chest hair. He bent to retrieve his fallen gun, and a
bullet sheared off more hair, this time from the top of his
head.

He tore off his hat and stared at the hole in the crown as
if wondering how it got there. The woman demonstrated
by firing again, but he must have been a mage, because
he'd managed to get his shields up. Her bullets hit them
and hung there, a few feet away from his body, starfishing
out from the impact points. He stared at one that would

have taken him straight between the eyes and gave a little shriek.

It didn't look like he was all that accustomed to gunfights, because his concentration wobbled. His shields went with it, and the suspended bullets dropped to the floor, rattling against the stones like beads. He snatched up his gun with adrenaline-clumsy fingers and got off a few random shots in our direction before stumbling through a doorway near the stairs. He never stopped screaming.

The woman kicked a few burning scraps of wood aside and emerged into the dim puddle of light given off by the lantern. She retrieved her flashlight and clicked it a few times, but nothing happened so she sighed and stuffed it into a pocket of the coat she wore. It was camel-colored wool and looked warm, I noticed enviously. Underneath she was wearing a lavender silk dress with a wrapped top and calf-length flared skirt. She looked like June Cleaver out for a night on the town, if June had accessorized with firearms.

This was the first time I'd seen her clearly, and I took a second to adjust my mental image. Our last meeting had also been on a time shift, but she'd been traveling in spirit instead of in body and had chosen to appear as a young woman. She didn't look that different in the flesh. Her brown hair was streaked with silver now and there were fine lines around her eyes and mouth. But her body was as slim as ever and her current expression—exasperated amusement—was eerily familiar.

"Come out. I won't hurt you," she promised.

"You mean again?" I asked nervously.

"You're hiding behind a barrel filled with gunpowder. If I wanted you dead, I'd just shoot it," she told me with a deep under-note of *duh*.

She was tapping her foot impatiently and had lowered the weapon. That might not mean anything, but the fact was, I hadn't come here to cower in the dark. No matter how good that sounded. Besides, I didn't think she was kidding about the gunpowder.

I slowly emerged. "Where did I shoot you?" she demanded.

"In the butt." Her lips quirked. "It's not funny!"

"If you say so." She looked me over. My outfit was more

appropriate than hers for crawling around a damp cellar, except for not including a coat. I was wearing jeans, sneakers and a T-shirt that said "I Took the Road Less Traveled. Now Where the Heck Am I?" Yet for some reason, she looked perfect while I'd ripped the knee out of my jeans and had black stuff all over my arms. I held my wrist up to my nose and smelled it.

She hadn't been kidding.

"You're playing hide-and-seek in a cellar full of gunpowder?" I demanded incredulously, desperately brushing at myself.

"A cellar full of gunpowder that an idiot is trying to blow up," she corrected. "So I'm a little tense right now. Who are you and why are you here?"

Now that the moment had arrived, I didn't quite know where to start. "It's complicated," I finally said.

"It always is." She headed for the door where the mage had disappeared, gun in hand. "You aren't Guild."

"I don't even know what that is," I said, jogging to keep up. "Is that who we're hunting?"

"That's who *I'm* hunting. I don't know who—or what—you are." She snagged the abandoned lantern and shoved it at me.

I took it gingerly, worried about powder residue near an open flame. It was a weird little thing, shaped like a large beer stein, with a black metal body and a door that could be opened or closed to control the light. I opened it all the way, but it didn't help much. "I'm Cassie. And, uh . . . I'm sort of Pythia."

That stopped her. Her sharp blue gaze swept over me again. "Don't think so," she said curtly.

The Pythia was the supernatural community's chief Seer and, as a bonus, also the person charged with maintaining the integrity of the time line. It would have been a crappy job even if I'd had the faintest idea what I was doing. Since I didn't, it was also really dangerous.

My assailant was named Agnes, AKA Lady Phemonoe, the former Pythia. She was the one who had stuck me with this mess and then died before she could give me any training. As a result, I'd spent the first half of my first month in office trying to get out of the deal and the rest of it running for my life. So it had taken me a while to realize the obvious: I was a time traveler now, whether I liked it or not. Agnes' death didn't necessarily mean she couldn't train me. She just had to do it in the past.

I hadn't intended for it to be quite this far in the past, but she was always surrounded by people in her own time. And most of them were the types who might recognize and resent another time traveler. Getting her alone had been tough.

Probably not as tough as talking her into this though.

"Then how did I get here?" I demanded.

"My best guess is that you're some Pythia's newly appointed heir on a joyride, testing out the power," she said, stopping beside the black hole of the doorway. "Ooh, look. I can travel through time. Isn't that cool?" she mimicked.

"I'm not joyriding! And I don't find being shot at and almost blown up cool!"

"I did the same thing myself a few times when young and stupid," she said, ignoring me. "And almost got killed. Take some advice: go home."

"Not until we talk," I said flatly. "And we can't do that here. The explosion was loud enough to wake the dead. Someone is probably on their way to investigate right now!"

"I wouldn't worry too much about that," she said, slipping off little champagne-colored heels. "These cellars date back to the eleventh century. And when they built something back then, they intended it to last. The walls are seven feet thick."

I felt the muscles along my spine start to relax just as a barrel came bouncing at us out of the dark. Agnes slammed the door and scrambled back while I ducked behind another support column. I'd barely made it when a second explosion deafened me and a hail of former door parts exploded through the room, impaling everything in sight.

A jagged piece of iron from one of the hinges hit the floor beside me, burying itself into the stone an inch from my right foot. I jerked back and stared at it wide-eyed. "Why is it that everywhere I go, someone is shooting at me?" I demanded hysterically.

"Your winning personality?" Agnes offered. "And if you don't like it, you could always, oh, I don't know, *leave*?"

"I'm not going anywhere!"

Agnes didn't respond. I looked around the column to see her cautiously approaching what had been the door. Burning shards framed the opening in fire, and streamers of noxious fumes were swirling slowly outward. It looked like a portal to hell, but she nonetheless squatted to one side, peering into the darkness within.

"Who is the Guild?" I whispered, joining her despite my better judgment.

"An order of mages who play around with very dangerous spells. Unfortunately for us, once in a while they don't manage to blow themselves up."

"And that's a problem because . . . ?"

"Because they're time travelers."

She started forward, and I grabbed her arm. "Wait. You're going *in* there?"

"That's the job."

"The job sucks!"

"You're telling me." She threw off my hand and slipped echo across the threshold, her stocking-clad feet silent on the old stones.

"Agnes!" I hissed it after her, but there was no response. I stared into the dark for half a second, cursing softly, and then followed.

I'd closed the lantern's little door, but it must have gotten dented in the fall, and the sides didn't meet all the way. Thin beams of sepia light leaked out, gilding the stones around us and turning our shadows into hulking monsters. I stared into the darkness crowding the rest of the room and tried not to think about sharpshooters and easy targets.

When the attack came, the only warning was a flicker of red in the gloom. Agnes aimed for it, but before she could pull the trigger, a bloody snake of lightning flashed across the room and struck her shoulder. She spun around and collapsed against me with a choked cry.

I dropped the lantern and grabbed her and my gun. But I only managed to get a couple of shots off before her fingers closed over my wrist. "Not in here."

I didn't argue since I didn't have anything to use as a tar-

get anyway. I dragged her out of the puddle of light into the
shadow of a nearby support column. She peered around
the side, but unless her eyesight was a hell of a lot better
than mine, she didn't see anything. I listened, but there was
no sound except her ragged breathing.

"Maybe I hit him," I whispered.

"I'm not that lucky."

Her voice sounded strained, and something gleamed
wetly on the shoulder of her dress. "You're hurt."

"My own damn fault." She peeled violet-printed chif-
fon away from a nasty-looking burn. "I loaned my ward
to my heir for a training exercise right before she eloped
with some loser. Naturally, she didn't bother to give it back
first."

I bit my lip and didn't reply. The ward in question was a
pentagram-shaped tattoo the size of a saucer that currently
sat between my shoulder blades. It didn't guard against human weapons, but was pretty amazing when fending off
magical assaults. My mother, who had been Agnes' heir
before wisely running for the hills, had passed it on to me.
But somehow I didn't think this was a great time to bring
that up.

"Do you usually wear high heels to chase armed men
around?" I asked instead.

She wiggled the toes of her now bare foot, making the
ladder in one silk stocking creep up a little higher. "I was
called away in the middle of a dinner party."

"You could have brought a bodyguard with you."

"Yes, that's all this fiasco needs! Another mage. Probably
go off half cocked and blow up the whole complex, saving
the Guild the trouble!"

"And maybe saving your life!"

She leaned her head wearily back against the column. "I
can do that for myself."

I crossed my arms but said nothing. Her breathing was
still heavy and her color wasn't good, but I was in no position to give a lecture. She wasn't the only one who had left
a partner behind.

Pritkin hated my trips through time for the same reason I did—the conviction that, sooner or later, I was going
to screw up something we couldn't fix. I'd decided to save

myself some grief and just not mention this to him, but it was a decision I was starting to regret. He carried enough firepower for three people, if those people happened to be Rambo. He'd have come in pretty handy right about now.

After a minute, Agnes struggled back to her feet. She stood with one hand braced against the column, her head bowed, her forehead knotted in pain. "Can you make it back to your time?" I asked. "Because if not, I can—"

"I have a job to do," she repeated, straightening. Her slight shoulders squared. "We need more light."

"We need to get out of here!"

"Then go. Nobody's stopping you." I stared at her for a moment, really tempted, before cursing and scurrying back for the lantern. For a wonder, nobody shot at me.

It had a ring welded into the top, so I grabbed a long stick from one of the piles of firewood that crunched underfoot and hooked the light on the end of it. After opening the door as wide as it would go, I poked the contraption out into the room while remaining behind the column with Agnes. I'd been hoping to illuminate a crumpled body on the floor. Instead, the warm golden glow fell across dozens of casks and barrels.

Some of them were almost buried under the mounds of wood and coal that nearly filled the room. But a few were stacked nearby, as if the camouflage attempt had gotten to be too much work. Or maybe the problem was that these barrels were leaking.

The nearest one had a crack as large as my finger in the side. The floor around it was covered in tiny grains that sparkled in the light like black diamond dust. My hand shook as I realized what they were, and a couple sparks spilled from the open side of the lantern. I had time to think, *Oh, shit,* before flames leapt up from the floor and ran straight toward the heap of barrels.

I dove for Agnes and we hit the floor together as a wave of force swept over us. A roar of sound deafened me, fire bloomed behind me and a wash of heat flooded the air. Dead, I thought in a rush of nausea.

And then nothing.

After a stunned moment, I opened my eyes to see a room filled with what looked like red and gold glitter. It took me a second to recognize it as flaming bits of wood and powder thrown off by the explosion, frozen in the air like confetti on the Fourth of July. A small piece was resting beside my cheek and it was hot. I knocked it away, and it moved a few inches before stopping, hanging suspended and molten as a tiny sun.

"You know, you're a real pain in the ass," Agnes mumbled. I belatedly realized that I'd squashed her face against the floor.

"Sorry. I—"

"Get *off* me."

I rolled to the side and stopped, blinking. A couple feet away was a freeze-frame out of hell. A ball of fire hung in space, surrounded by burning bits of wood that had once formed the sides of a barrel. Sparks were everywhere, turning the dull old stones around us bloodred and highlighting the pissy look on Agnes' face.

"What happened?"

"What does it look like?" she snapped. "You almost blew us up!"

"You didn't tell me there was gunpowder in here!"

"There was gunpowder out there!" She waved an arm wildly in the direction of the other room. "And someone threw a barrel at us from in here! What the hell do you want, a diagram?"

"I want to know what's going on," I said heatedly. "All I know is that I followed you into a cellar—"

"Which you had no business doing."

"—and now some crazy man is trying to kill us!"

"At the rate we're going, he won't have to," Agnes said, staggering back to her feet. Her hair had come loose from its once neat chignon and floated down over her temples and cheeks. It moved delicately with her breath, giving away how fast her heart beat. She put a hand to her head. "I'm going to feel like hell tomorrow."

"You stopped time." I'd seen her do it once before; I'd even done it myself on one memorable occasion. Of course, in my case, it had been an accident.

She eyed the suspended fireball. "What gave it away?"

I decided to ignore that and retrieved my stick. I used it to push at the burning splinters. They were radiating outward from the blast in a concentric ring, like spores off hell's dandelion. They bent at my touch but didn't go out or fall to the floor. I stared at them for a moment, a strange echoing vertigo in my mind when I thought about the distance between this new life and everything I'd ever known.

"Look," Agnes said, pointing at the far wall. The mage stood pressed against the stones, caught midscream. "I told you we didn't get him."

As she spoke, she was starting to gather the wooden shards and bits of lit powder from the air. She looked pretty steady on her feet, but I knew from experience how much strain even a small hiccup in time could cause. "How long can you hold it?"

"Long enough if you help. And be careful—if we miss even one . . ." She didn't have to finish the sentence.

I swatted the stray sparks like fireflies, knocking them to the ground and stomping on them before I realized that it wasn't doing any good. Time had stopped, meaning that I could jump up and down on the damn things all I wanted, but they weren't going to go out. I settled for gathering them into the tail of my T-shirt while Agnes dug into the barrels closest to the explosion. Flaming shards of wood had penetrated their sides, causing fire to boil up around their edges as the powder caught.

The embers I held were uncomfortably warm. I finally resorted to stripping off my T-shirt and using it as a net to trap them without burning myself. I made a dozen glowing piles in the empty outer room before I had them all. By then Agnes had dealt with the barrels, and we turned our attention to the big boy.

She poked the fireball with a stick, but it remained frozen in place, like the shadows on the ceiling and the clouds of smoke in the air. "I can handle that," I told her, taking the stick. To my surprise, she gave in without a fight. From the little I knew of her, I guessed that meant we were running out of time. "If you want something to do, you could tell me what's going on."

"You really don't know about the Guild?" she asked, watching me whack at the ball like an oversized piñata. It wasn't elegant, but it seemed to work. The exploded cask and its attached flames slowly began to move through the air.

"I don't know anything. That's my problem!"

"They're a bunch of utopians out to create a better world through time travel. Stop plagues, wars and famines before they start—that kind of thing."

"Doesn't sound so bad," I panted as the explosion moved in fits and starts into the outer room.

"Maybe you should sign up. Except they don't like women much. Might have something to do with the Pythias thwarting their plans for the last five hundred years. Send it up the stairs," she added as I stopped to get my breath.

I eyed the staircase without enthusiasm. "Why? The other one exploded in here and nothing happened."

"The other one was a lot smaller. This could bring down the ceiling on our heads."

I sighed and started thumping the fiery thing again. "And you might want to check out their manifesto," she continued as I battled my way upward. "Not all of us like the idea of living in a Stepford world where if we do anything the Guild doesn't like, they go back in time and change it. Repeat offenders are to be snuffed out of existence. Couples are to be denied the right to reproduce if their child is seen as a future threat to the Guild."

"Okay. That sounds a little less enticing," I admitted.

"And it goes on and on. They aren't big on free will. They don't care that one person's utopia is another person's hell," she said as we emerged into a long room.

It was covered wall to ceiling in biblical-themed murals. The light of the explosion brought the colors to life, glinting off gilt paint and causing the jewel-colored glass in the high, arched windows to shimmer. I blinked, staring around like a tourist until Agnes poked me in the back.

"That way." She pointed at a door I hadn't noticed. "And hurry. I can't hold things much longer."

I gave up hitting the cask and started pushing it instead. It had a weird, spongy feel in the center, I guess from the ignited but not-yet-burned gunpowder, which didn't make for great leverage. But I nonetheless managed to maneuver my bomb-on-a-stick through the long, narrow room and outside. Three- and four-story buildings of stone and wood hemmed in a courtyard. Frozen smoke belched from their chimney pots, reaching pale fingers toward a leaden sky.

It was bitterly cold and the air hit my face like a wet rag. It took me a moment to realize it was raining. Sheets of water hung suspended in the air like a beaded curtain, gleaming in the light we threw off. Heavy drops dangled like cabochon diamonds from the edge of rooftops, spangled low-hanging limbs and congealed half-in, half-out of puddles. It was strangely beautiful.

"The river," Agnes gasped, from cold or exhaustion. "That way." She pointed toward the right, where a line of scattered trees blocked the view.

Mud squelched under my feet as I started forward. I kept my head down, but it didn't help. Soon water ran down my forehead and dripped into my eyes, its movement the result of my own forward momentum. The rain wasn't falling on us; we were running into it as we hurried forward, leaving a path of clear air behind us like the wake of a ship.

To make the going even tougher, there was very little light. Only a few stars were visible in the cloud-covered sky, and while we shed a glow, it didn't extend far in any direction. Everything beyond our immediate vicinity was lost in shadow.

That was a problem because the place was a minefield of carts, wheelbarrows and junky lean-tos. I kept running into things and slipping on slick paving stones, which became worse after we left them behind for dirt. But Agnes turned to glare at me every time I slowed down, so I hurried after her.

We navigated across a more or less open area, around a rickety-looking fence and down a path to an iron railing. Below us was undoubtedly a river. I couldn't see much, but the smell was unmistakable: a mixture of rotting fish, sewage, mold and damp.

Agnes gave me a shove. "Get rid of it!"

I looked around. A mass of dark buildings clustered along the water's edge in either direction, just waiting to be firebombed. The only safe place for an explosion was over the water. But the stick was too short to push the fireball far enough to do any good, and climbing over the railing wouldn't help. A stone retaining wall started immediately on the other side, flowing straight down to the water's edge.

But I had to do something. The explosion had begun expanding again in super slow motion. Agnes was losing her grip on time.

I pulled off my T-shirt again and draped it around the fiery mass. "What are you doing?" she demanded.

"Improvising!"

The glowing mass lit up the thin cotton, and a few brown spots appeared. The shirt was on fire, but with time still in slow mo, I thought I might have a minute before it disintegrated. I grabbed both ends, creating a big slingshot, and spun around in a wide circle until I got up some momentum. Then I let go, sending the entire burning mass spinning away into the night.

It made it almost to mid-river, a bright ruby ball of fire against the black of water, before splashing down. It went under, lighting up a school of fish as it slowly began to sink. Then Agnes gave a small sigh, time sped back up to normal and the underwater explosion threw a column of water twenty feet into the air.

Chapter Two

Most of the water fell on a nearby sailing ship docked for the night. But not all. I scooped fish guts out of my bra and glared at Agnes. She didn't notice, having already taken off.

"What's the rush?" I demanded, jogging to keep up.

"It'll be November fifth in another hour," she said as light erupted behind us. I looked over my shoulder to see lanterns being lit all over the ship. Sailors scrambled to the railing, staring alternately at the waves rocking them back and forth and at the mangled sushi that had splattered the deck and lay draped over the ropes.

I turned back to find that Agnes had almost disappeared up the path. I ran after her, rain slapping me in the face. "And?"

"Guy Fawkes, Guy Fawkes, 'twas his intent, to blow up King and Parli'ment," she singsonged.

Something clicked. "Three-score barrels of powder below, to prove old England's overthrow." She looked surprised. "I had a British governess," I explained.

"Then you know the score. Some English Catholics want to blow up parliament and James the First along with it. They don't want a Protestant king, and they think his death will return the country to Catholicism. It might have worked, if one of the members of the plot hadn't had a relative in parliament. He received a letter warning him to skip tomorrow's session and ratted them out."

"And Fawkes was found in the cellar surrounded by the evidence hours before parliament met."

"But the Guild is here to see that this time, he succeeds."

"Why would they care about that?"

She put on a burst of speed instead of answering, probably in response to the candles appearing in windows all around us. We ran, slipping and sliding over mud and water-slick grass, until we reached the painted room. I slammed the door on a few shouts from outside and leaned against it, panting.

"They don't. It's their own history they hope to help," she said, glancing at me and grinning, the adrenaline rush sparkling in her eyes. "They were just getting started in these days. But before they could grow their numbers significantly, the Circle found out what they were up to and hunted them down, almost to a man. It took them centuries to recover. I suppose they think that a massive civil war might give the Circle more important things to worry about."

She headed down the stairs and I followed silently. By Circle she meant the Silver Circle, the world's largest magical association and an umbrella organization for thousands of covens. To most people in the supernatural community, the Circle represented order, safety and stability.

I wasn't one of those people.

That had a lot to do with the fact that the Circle was currently trying to kill me in the hopes that a more suitable Pythia would take my place. Suitable in their view, meaning someone brainwashed from childhood to believe that they could do no wrong. They'd had a few thousand years of treating the Pythias as their personal errand girls and weren't happy to have a more independent-minded type in office.

"Speaking of the Circle—" I began, before Agnes clapped a hand to my mouth. We'd reentered the outer room of the cellar, and I guess she didn't want us alerting the mage that we'd returned. Just as well. I'd gotten the impression that a little tension between the Pythia and her magical protectors was normal, but the whole I-want-you-dead thing might freak her out.

What freaked me out was the reappearance of the mage, pale and wild-eyed, exploding out of the gunpowder room at a dead run. He crashed into me and I instinctively grabbed him, getting a fist to the stomach in return. I kicked him in the knee and he yelled and reared back, fist clenched, but stopped when he felt Agnes' gun beside his ear.

"Go ahead," she told him. "The paperwork for a trial is a real bitch."

"So are you!" he snarled.

I clutched my stomach and covered him with my gun while Agnes pulled a pair of cuffs out of her coat. "I have a problem," I told her quickly, before she could shift away. "I really am Pythia, but I don't know what I'm doing and there's no one in my time who can help me."

"That's a problem," she agreed, snicking the cuffs shut.

"Yeah."

"Good luck with that." She grabbed the mage by the collar.

"Don't you dare leave!"" I said furiously. "I helped *you*!"

"You almost blew this place sky-high! Anyway, even if I wanted to help you, there are rules."

"Screw the rules! You stuck me with this godforsaken position—"

"I didn't hear that."

"—and now you think you can just walk away? You have a responsibility here!"

I'd been waving the gun around in my agitation, and it accidentally went off and took a chip out of a brick over the mage's head. He blinked. "Uh, ladies? Might I suggest—"

"Shut up!" we told him in unison. He shut up.

Agnes tried to shift, but I grabbed her wrist, wrenching us back at the same moment that she tried to go forward. "Are you crazy?" she screeched, only it sounded like she was talking in slow motion.

Time wobbled around us: one second, we were back where I came in, with bullets whizzing around our heads; the next we were in the future, watching a party of cloaked men in funny hats examining the ruined door. One of them caught sight of us and paled, and then we were gone, bouncing backward once more.

Agnes somehow managed to put on the brakes, wrenching us out of the time stream with what I swear was an audible pop. For a moment, we stood there, white-faced and shaking, back where we'd started but a little worse for the wear. I don't know about the others, but I felt like I'd just stepped off a roller coaster—light-headed and a little sick.

"I need to go to the bathroom," the mage said weakly.

Agnes took a deep breath and let it out, glaring at me. "You're a lousy liar. If I'd trained you, you'd have known better than to pull a stunt like that!"

"Didn't you hear me?" I demanded. "You *didn't* train me. That's the problem. You gave me this lousy job and then died before—"

"La-la-la. Not listening." She stuck a finger in one ear, which didn't help much as the other hand still gripped the mage's shirt.

I stared at her. My last image of Agnes was her heroic death to keep a rogue initiate from laying waste to the time line. Somewhere in my hero worship, I'd forgotten how deeply weird she could be. Of course, if I kept this job as long as she had, I might not be too normal, either. It wasn't a comforting thought.

"What the hell is wrong with you?" I asked, honestly worried that my last chance for a mentor was headed down the toilet along with her sanity.

"What's wrong with *me*?" She took the finger out of her ear to shake it at me. "You're not supposed to tell me these things!"

"I haven't told you that much—" I began, only to be cut off with a savage gesture.

"You've told me plenty! I have an initiate in training and she isn't you. You said I got you into this, so what happened to her? Is she dead? Did she turn dark?" Her hands waved around, banging the mage's head into the wall. "I don't know!"

"Sort of both," I said uneasily. Agnes' second heir, Myra, had turned dark and began using her time-travel abilities for her own and her allies' gain. Agnes would be forced to kill her to remove the threat to the time line but would die herself in the process. And that would leave an untrained nobody in the Pythia's position—me.

"Don't tell me that!" she whispered, clearly horrified.

"You asked."

"No! I didn't! I was explaining how much information I could get out of this meeting if I thought about it, which I'm absolutely not going to do because I may have already learned too much. What if something you say causes me to change the way I deal with the present—*my* present—which then alters *your* future? You might shift back only to find out that you don't exist anymore! Hadn't thought of that, had you?"

"No," I said, working to keep my temper under control. "But that doesn't change the fact that I need training!"

"The early Pythias didn't have much in the way of training, but they managed to figure things out. So will you."

"Easy for you to say. You were trained. You never had to figure anything out!"

"Like hell." She put the hand not choking the mage on her hip in a familiar gesture. "No amount of training really prepares you for this job."

"But at least you know how the power works. I didn't get the manual!"

"There *is* no manual. If our enemies ever figured out everything we can do, they would be much more successful in opposing us. And time isn't all that easy to screw up any—"

She paused as, somewhere on the far side of the gunpowder room, a key turned in a lock. Agnes drew her gun and pushed it into the mage's temple hard enough to dent the skin. "Say one word—make one sound—and I swear . . . ," she whispered. He looked conflicted, ideology warring with self-preservation, but I guess the latter won because he stayed silent. Or maybe he couldn't talk with her fist knotted in his collar.

The three of us peered through the missing door and caught glimpses of fire. A dark-haired man stood at the far end of the room. He sat a lantern that looked a lot like the mage's well away from the casks, which he started shifting around. He was dressed like the mage, too, except for a long dark coat, and he had boots on. The spurs chimed softly in the quiet.

"Fawkes," Agnes whispered. She nudged the mage with the barrel of her gun. "Did you change anything?"

He stayed silent.

"Answer me!"

"That's not how it works," he said irritably. "You can't say you'll shoot me if I talk and then ask me a question!"

We froze as the man paused, looking our way but not seeing anything. It was pitch-dark at our end of the cellar. We'd left the mage's lantern behind when we took our stroll with the bomb and it must have gone out, because the only source of light came from Fawkes'. He paused, sniffing the damp air, where the acrid smell of the explosion still lingered. But after a moment, he went back to work.

"We've got to hurry this up," Agnes whispered. "Where was I?"

"You said time is hard to mess up. But hard isn't impossible. Some things *can* make a difference." On a recent trip through time, I'd accidentally changed one little thing, merely meeting a man a few hundred years before I was supposed to, and the results had been insane. The results had almost gotten both of us killed.

"Of course they can," she said impatiently. "That's why we're here."

"But how do I know what can safely be changed and what can't?" I asked desperately.

Agnes frowned. "What is this?" she demanded, her voice suddenly going flat and hard. It matched the icy color of her eyes. "Some kind of elaborate hoax?"

"What? No! I—"

She jerked the mage down to the level of her face. "Did you recruit a woman to try to fool me? Was that was this was all about?"

He glanced at me and then back at her. "Yeah," he said slowly. "You got me."

"I should have known! I knew the power wouldn't allow two Pythias to meet!" she hissed, and turned her gun on me.

I stared at her. "He's lying!"

"If he was lying, you wouldn't have asked me that!" she spat. "No Pythia would."

"Asked what? All I want is some help!"

"Oh, *I'll* help you!" she said, and lunged for me. The mage took his chance and ran into the gunpowder room while Agnes and I went down in a flail of limbs, her trying to cuff me while I attempted to get free without either of our guns going off. It wasn't easy. I swear the woman had an extra arm, because she somehow managed to hold both my wrists while a tiny fist clocked me upside the jaw.

"The mage is with Fawkes!" I gasped as another pair of cuffs clicked shut around my wrists. "They're going to set this whole place off and we're all going to die!"

"Yeah, and if I let you go, we'll die faster!"

"I'm not going to help them!"

"I know you're not. You're staying tied up here until I deal with this."

I glared at her. "I'm Pythia! I don't really need you to release me!"

She sat back on her heels, surveying me mockingly. "Okay, Pythia." She waved a hand. "Do your thing."

"Okay, I will!"

"Okay, then."

One of the few upsides of an otherwise hellish job is the ability to shift spatially as well as temporally. That's a fancy way of saying that I can pop in and out of places as well as times, something that's saved me on more than one occasion. I'd used the ability to move across continents; getting out of a pair of handcuffs was child's play.

I shifted a couple feet to the right, expecting to leave the cuffs behind. I'd pulled a similar trick once before and it had worked great. But this time, the cuffs traveled right along with me. Agnes demurely rearranged her skirts as I tried again. My body moved another couple feet to the left, but my hands remained as tightly bound as before.

"What the hell?"

"Magical handcuffs," she murmured.

"Get them off!"

"I thought you didn't need my help."

From the powder room, we heard the sound of angry voices and the clash of steel on steel. "You may need mine," I pointed out.

She sighed. "Some days I really hate my job."

I managed to get to my feet, but having my hands bound threw my balance off. I fell onto the steps, bounced off and ended up on my abused butt. "I hate mine all the time," I said bitterly.

"Okay, you're a Pythia."

"We go through all that, and you believe me because I have a bad attitude?"

She started working on the cuffs. "That and the fact that the Guild can't do spatial shifts."

"So why did you attack me?"

"Because you aren't supposed to be here! This isn't even supposed to be possible!"

"Maybe the power thinks I need training, too," I pointed out.

"The power doesn't *think*. It isn't sentient. It follows a strict group of rules, such as those built into any spell. One of which is that you can't interfere in a mission that has nothing to do with you!"

"I'm not interfering," I said crossly. "I just wanted to talk! You're the one who—"

"And in case you didn't get the memo, we're the good guys!" she added furiously, cutting me off. "We don't go around changing time!"

"Never?" I asked skeptically. Because if Agnes hadn't broken that rule, I wouldn't be alive.

"Oh, God." She threw up her hands. "Here we go again. Every initiate starts out thinking she can save the world."

"Can't you? You're Pythia. You can do anything you want."

She laughed. "Oh, you *are* new." She tugged on the cuffs. "Damn."

"What?"

"They're stuck."

"What do you mean stuck?"

"I mean, they won't open," she said patiently.

I pulled on them until it felt like my wrists might pop off. "Why not?"

"I don't know. I don't design these things. I just use them."

"What kind of dumb-ass philosophy is that?!"

"You drive a car, don't you? Do you know how that works?"

"The general principle, yes!"

"Well, I understand the general principle here, but for some reason they aren't releasing." She worked on them for another minute until things suddenly went silent in the next room.

"What's going on?" I whispered.

"Do I need to explain the difference between clairvoyant and mind reader?" She gave up on the cuffs and dragged me to my feet, almost dislocating a shoulder in the process. "I still don't trust you," she said flatly. "But if you help me with those two, I'll give you a hint."

"A hint about what?"

"What did you come here to ask?"

"I need a little more than that!"

"Tough."

We glared at each other for a few seconds, until I sighed and gave in. A hint wasn't what I was after, but it was better than I had now. And it didn't look like I was going to get anything else. "Fine."

We stared into the doorway together but didn't see much. The lamp appeared to have gone out, and the sounds of fighting had stopped. That probably wasn't a good thing.

Without warning, Agnes took off across the darkened room. I followed the best I could, but running through pitch blackness with bound arms and a sore butt is even harder than it sounds, and there were obstacles everywhere. Agnes somehow managed to avoid them, but I tripped over some firewood and plowed into a support column, scraping my cheek and stubbing my toe in the process.

I lost sight of her while trying to right myself and then almost ran right past her. A hand reached out from behind another column and dragged me over. "I think I lost a toe," I gasped, waves of pain radiating up my leg.

"Shut up! They're in a small room over there!" She gestured in the direction of the slightly-less-dark pouring out of an open doorway. "The mage doesn't have a gun, but Fawkes might, so no heroics." She paused for a minute. "Sorry. I forgot who I was talking to."

I glared, but she didn't see it, having already started moving. I caught up with her and we burst into the small room together. The mage was sitting on a barrel holding an old-fashioned matchlock gun. *His* cuffs had come off nicely, I noticed jealously. They were on the floor, along with a sword and the lantern. Fawkes was standing alongside the wall and showed no surprise at seeing us; in fact, he didn't appear to notice that we were there. Spelled.

I saw all that in the split second before Agnes shot the mage. The bullets would have taken him right between the eyes if he hadn't been using shields. As it was, they just seemed to piss him off.

"I'd prefer you didn't do that," he said testily when she stopped.

"You can't remain shielded forever," she shot back. "And that gun only has one bullet."

"But which of you gets it?" he sneered.

Agnes changed tactics. "What's the plan, genius? Because you can blow this place up, but it won't do any good. Parliament doesn't meet until tomorrow morning. And at midnight, a party of the king's men are going to show up and spoil your fun. That's why Fawkes failed, remember?"

"But when they show up this time, they'll be met with a few surprises." He nodded at a line of little vials laid out on another barrel. They were the kind mages used in combat, and most of the spells they contained were lethal.

"I thought you people were against war," I said, mainly to give Agnes time to figure something out. I had nothing.

"There's going to be a civil war in about fifty years in any case. We're merely speeding up the timetable—and building a better world in the process."

"A better world that may not have you in it! If you start a war now, it could kill off your ancestors or alter the world in ways that guarantee they never meet. You could be committing suicide!"

"Not if I stay in this time."

"You'd stay here?" I asked incredulously.

"Unlike you, I risked my life to get here!" he snapped, suddenly angry. "Of course I'm staying!"

Agnes glanced at me. "Stop trying to reason with this joker. Go ahead and do it."

"Do what?"

"Stop time. I'd take care of it, but I can't pull that trick twice in a row. It takes too much energy."

I fidgeted. "Uh, Agnes?"

"Your bad luck to get the mission with *two* Pythias!" she said with a smirk. The mage began to look a little worried.

I felt the muscles knot around my spine again. Of course, that may have been from the cuffs. "Um, there's . . . sort of a problem."

"What problem? You've done it before, right?" she demanded.

"Well, yeah. But it all happened sort of fast, and I'm not sure exactly—"

"Don't tell me you don't know how!"

She was glaring at me, so I glared right back. "Hello! No training, remember? That's why I'm here!"

"That's why you're useless!" she yelled, poking me in the shoulder with the gun. Her expression was pretty fierce, but her head was doing some weird wobbly thing, like her neck was broken. I stared at her for a heartbeat before realizing that she was nodding at the mage's little vial collection. Oh, great.

She poked me again, this time in the stomach, and it hurt. I stumbled away from her, moving a few steps farther into the room. "Oh, so what? I can't perform on cue so you're going to shoot me? Is that how this works?"

"Maybe I will," she said furiously. "A Pythia who can't do anything is no help to anyone. The people in your time would probably *thank* me."

She had no idea. I retreated a few more steps, almost within arm's reach of the vials. "You can't kill a Pythia or her designated heir, or the power won't go to you," I reminded her. "Even I know that much!"

"News flash, kiddo," she said, aiming for my head. "I already have it!"

Agnes let off a round and I screamed and ducked, only half acting the terror thing. I lurched into the barrel, tipping it over and scattering vials everywhere. The mage cursed and leveled his gun at me, but Agnes picked up Fawkes' fallen sword and chucked it at him. He instinctively ducked and fell backward off his seat.

I dropped to the floor, trying to feel around behind me with tightly bound hands. My fingers touched two small vials and I grabbed them. I couldn't see them, but it didn't matter; I wouldn't have known what they were anyway. I stared over my shoulder and, as soon as the mage popped his head up, I flipped them at him.

The first burst against his shields in a scattering of dry orange powder and didn't appear to have any effect. But the second, a blue liquid, bit a chunk out of his shields. I started looking for more of those while Agnes kept alternating gunfire with throwing things: a wooden footstool, a burnt-out torch and a dead rat all sailed past my face to go splat against the mage's shields.

I flinched back from the rat, and then I saw it—another blue vial, nestled up against the bottom of a barrel. I crouched awkwardly, scrabbling around on the grimy floor, and at last my fingers closed over it. I didn't wait for the mage to pop back up this time, just chucked it over the pile of casks.

For once, my aim must have been pretty good. He screamed and shot out of the hedge of barrels like he was on fire. He sprinted past me, shedding sparks in his wake and— Oh, crap. "He's on fire!" I screamed.

Agnes tripped him up and he went sprawling just outside the door. She sat on his butt and clocked him upside the head with her gun. He collapsed like a sack of sand.

"You wanted a hint," she panted, batting out the flames on his back. "Here it is. You're clairvoyant. Use your gift."

I waited a few seconds, but she didn't say anything else. "That's it? *That's* your big hint?"

"What did you expect?"

"Something else! Something more! There has to be . . . I don't know, some kind of trick to it!"

"*You're* the trick," she told me, retrieving his cuffs. "Why do you think clairvoyants are chosen as Pythias? If anyone could do it, these morons wouldn't screw things up every time they try to 'improve' things. They can't see what effect their actions will have; they have to guess. We can *know*."

A headache started to pound behind my eyes. I hadn't realized how much I'd been counting on Agnes to help me until this minute, when she refused. "Maybe you can know," I told her. "My gift doesn't work like that. Some days, it doesn't work at all!"

"Maybe you need to exercise it a little more. And to answer your earlier question, fiddling with the time stream usually causes more problems than it solves. Trust me on that one."

"So that's it?" I asked furiously. "That's what you have for me? Don't mess with time and trust my gift?"

"That's all you really need." Agnes dragged the mage's hands behind his back and clicked the cuffs on. Once he was secure, she looked up at me, and for the first time, her gaze held a flicker of compassion. "Your power will work with your natural ability, training it—and you—over time. Eventually, you *will* learn what you need to know."

"If it was that easy, you wouldn't spend decades training a successor!" I said quickly before she could shift out on me.

"I never said it was easy. Nothing about this job is. I said you will learn."

"And what if I don't last that long?!" I screamed, but Agnes was already gone.

Chapter Three

I arrived back at Dante's, Vegas' hell-themed casino and my current hideout, exhausted, filthy and steaming. The worst part was, I'd gotten exactly zip out of it. I might be the world's chief clairvoyant, but my power didn't seem to know that. It came and went, ebbing and flowing like the tide, but never on such a precise schedule. And that meant I couldn't do visions on demand. I couldn't choose what I saw and what I didn't. I wasn't that strong and I never had been.

Despite the lurid theme of the casino, the penthouse was sleek, Scandinavian and contemporary, with a soft blue and gray color scheme that I usually found soothing. It wasn't working so well today. That was doubly true when I walked into the living room and was immediately accosted by a couple of half-crazed thugs. I'd have been worried, except that they were mine. Sort of.

Marco, the one weaving a quarter through his fingers as he surveyed me, was six foot six with a twenty-inch neck. The guy made dump trucks look petite. The fact that he was a vampire was almost irrelevant.

I didn't know the other guy, but that wasn't unusual. Marco's partners constantly changed, but they were always vamps armed to the teeth. This one was no exception and looked enough like Marco—slicked-back dark hair, barrel chest and tree trunk legs—that they might have been related. Of course, they just as easily might not. That description fit almost every babysitter I'd had in the last three days.

"What's the deal here?" Marco asked, his voice thick with muscle. "You *said* you was going for a fitting. That you had to get naked for this designer guy, so we might as well stay here since you wasn't letting us in the room anyway. You *said* you was just going downstairs. That you'd be *right back*."

"I don't have time for this," I told him. I ached pretty much everywhere, except for my shoulders, which had stopped screaming and started going numb. It was making me think about lack of blood flow and gangrene. "Can you get me out of these cuffs?"

"Yeah, I'll get right on that." He made a savage gesture, and the quarter sailed through the open balcony doors and took out a window on the next building. It made me jump, since Marco had so far shown no emotion whatsoever. "As soon as you tell me what's going on. Because I'm thinking we got a communication problem, you and me."

"You took advantage of our trust," his partner added in a high-pitched squeak.

"What's going on is that I need to get out of these cuffs and into a bath!" I snapped, my temper hanging by a thread. "Mircea is coming—"

"Yeah. I know," Marco said tightly. "The front desk called to say he's on his way up."

"He's on his way *now*? Why?"

"You have a date."

"Appointment. And that's not until two a.m.!" I whirled, looking for a clock, but of course I didn't find one. Clocks made you think about bedtime and bath time and dinner-time instead of gambling the night away in blissful igno-rance. The casino didn't like clocks.

"It's five to two," Marco informed me, shoving his hairy wrist in my face. "You've been gone *all night*."

Shit.

"You want to get me killed, is that it?" he demanded. "I piss you off somehow I don't remember? You working out some kinda grudge?"

"No! I ... just lost track of time. I was busy." In fact, I wasn't all that great at timing my shifts yet. I'd planned to come back a few minutes after I left, in which case I wouldn't have had to worry about explaining things to the deadly duo. Not that I should have had to do so in the first place.

Marco scraped something gray and hairy that was absolutely not smashed rat off my shoulder. "Doing what? Dumpster diving?"

I counted to ten and reminded myself not to overreact. The muscle twins were only doing what they'd been told. Getting rid of them was going to require talking with the one who'd sent them, and even that wasn't likely to work. Because their master also considered himself mine, and he liked to keep an eye on his property.

Mircea Basarab had been born a nobleman in fifteenth-century Romania, when one's woman was almost as prized a possession as one's horse. They were also treated about the same: dressed up and shown off on important occasions, and petted and pampered and kept under careful watch the rest of the time. And although he had since modernized his wardrobe, his vocabulary and his job description, his attitude toward women was remarkably constant.

Not that I *was* his woman, as I'd mentioned several times. By coincidence, it was the same number he hadn't been listening. I somehow had the feeling that something similar would happen if I brought up getting rid of Marco and friend. For someone who could hear a pin drop three rooms away, Mircea could be amazingly deaf.

It wasn't that I objected to the idea of protection—quite the opposite, in fact. Far too many people had my name on their to-do-nasty-things-to list. But while vampires are formidable opponents—especially the masters, which judging by the power he was leaking all over the place, Marco definitely was—they tend not to perform so well against certain kinds of opponents. Like revenge-minded ancient deities. For what I was facing, I needed something a little more subtle with a lot more punch. Not that I had any idea what that was yet.

I heard the elevator outside the penthouse ding and went into panic mode. I fled to the bedroom, followed closely by Marco. His buddy must've remained in the living room to greet the master—and hopefully to stall him.

"Tell him I'm not up yet," I said, trying to wriggle under the bedclothes.

Marco shook his head. "That ain't gonna work. You knew he was coming. He's gonna expect you to talk. He's gonna expect some quality time. And if there's cuffs involved, he's gonna expect them to be his."

I shut my eyes, trying hard not to think about Mircea and handcuffs. And got an inspiration. "The bathroom. Hurry!"

We ran into the gray and white opulence of the adjoining bath and I slammed the door. "Quick! Fill the tub. And get me out of these cuffs!"

Marco didn't ask questions, just started hot water flowing into the huge soaking tub and threw in half a container of bath salts. Bubbles foamed up everywhere as he bent to examine the restraints. After a few seconds, he said a bad word. "These are magical cuffs," he told me so softly I could hardly understand him over the rushing water. I guess he was worried about vampire hearing. "They ain't gonna come off easy. We're gonna need a mage."

Pritkin would have normally been my first choice, but he already considered my intelligence to be sadly underutilized. If he saw me like this, I'd never hear the end of it. Not to mention that he'd demand to know where I'd been, and I hadn't had time to come up with a good lie yet.

"Find Francoise," I whispered. She was a witch and a good friend. There was an outside chance she wouldn't laugh at me. "And get my bra off, fast!"

Marco shied back, and for the first time an expression broke through that tough demeanor. It was terror. "You're cute, but you're the master's woman. And ain't no woman alive worth that kind of—"

"I'm not propositioning you!" I hissed. "I need to be in that tub with my cuffs hidden under the bubbles until you get back, in case Mircea pokes his head around the door. And I can't wear a bra and pull that off!"

"Then add more bubbles or something, because ain't no way in hell—"

"Help me out here, Marco. Unless you *want* him to know you lost track of me for most of the night?" Truth be told, I wasn't thrilled with that idea myself. Mircea was already of the opinion that I should be hidden away somewhere for my own protection, and I didn't need anything adding fuel to the fire. The Pythia's power wasn't absolute, and he was damn tricky.

"I'm still not ripping your bra off," Marco said stubbornly.

"I am pleased to hear it," a voice said from the doorway.

Marco spun in a move too fast to see and went dead white. I looked past him and found myself staring into a familiar face. One with a full-lipped mouth curved enough to be almost feminine that contrasted starkly with strong, masculine features. Mircea.

"It's not Marco's fault," I said quickly, because a vampire who disobeyed his master usually met a very serious fate.

"Not entirely," Mircea agreed. His voice was calm, but his cheeks were flushed and a pulse throbbed at his temple. He looked to be in the middle of a slow-burning, very tightly controlled freak-out. And that really wasn't good. Mircea's iron control was legendary, although a few incidents in the recent past had shaken it somewhat.

Come to think of it, most of them had involved me.

"Out," Mircea said, and Marco didn't need to be told twice.

I was on his heels until a heavy hand descended on my shoulder, right over the suspicious stain. I caught sight of myself in the rapidly fogging mirror, and suddenly it was all too much. "I have fish guts in my hair," I said.

"I can see that."

"And I think there may be r-rat," I admitted tearfully.

Mircea studied me for a long moment and then relief softened his grim expression and he let out a sigh. "I am more concerned about the gunpowder," he said, pulling me in.

"Most of it didn't blow up," I told him, trying to pull back so that the God-knew-what clinging to my sweat-streaked upper body didn't stain his silk shirt or drop onto his Italian loafers.

"Good to know," he said calmly before drawing me into a fierce embrace. Mircea kissed like he wanted to live in my skin, slow and thorough, with teeth and tongue, like he never ever wanted to stop. Like he was afraid.

He took a second longer than me to open his lids. When

he did, I was confronted with eyes that had gone bright amber. They're usually a rich brown, changing colors only when his power is surging. From a distance, it's impressive; this close, it was dazzling.

The rest of the package wasn't too shabby, either. His hair was mahogany and below shoulder length, although it was hard to tell because it was always pulled back into a slim gold clip at his neck. Well, almost always. The few times I'd seen it in disarray flashed across my mind unexpectedly and heated my cheeks.

Despite close contact with me, his clothes were dirt free and as usual were showcasing the sheer expense of restraint. Today's outfit consisted of a long-sleeved shirt striped in black on black and black slacks. The clothes were so casually elegant that I immediately wanted to pull them out of shape. Of course, the body underneath might have had something to do with that.

Mircea's fingers unerringly found the gash in the back of my jeans. They slid carefully over the small wound below and his lips tightened, but I didn't get a demand for information. I hadn't really expected one; Mircea was subtler than that. "We've been searching for you for hours" was his only comment.

"But Marco said he didn't tell you—"

"An oversight that will never reoccur."

Uh-oh.

Master vampires protected their families, and in return they received unquestioning obedience. Most of their servants were physically unable to disobey, with the only exceptions being those who reached master status themselves. But even in their case, going against a direct command was extremely difficult, especially when they served one of the few first-level masters in the world. Marco must have been really strong to be able to flout Mircea's orders.

And now he was in trouble because he'd covered for me.

"What are you going to do?" I asked, worried.

"Discipline my servant." His usually mellow voice was suddenly flat and hard.

"Mircea . . ."

"Do you know what some of our enemies could have

done to you in five hours, Cassie?" His fingers tightened fractionally on my skin. "I do. I've spent all night with the possible scenarios running through my mind."

"He didn't know I'd left the hotel. I told him that I was—"

"He knew."

"How? And if Marco didn't tell you I was missing, how did you know?"

He didn't answer, just leaned over and turned off the tap. A mountain of feathery white bubbles had foamed over the side of the bath and spilled onto the marble tiles, making the floor even slipperier than usual. They didn't seem to bother Mircea, who sat on the side of the tub to examine the cuffs.

"Ah, yes. An older version, but I think I recall—" He did something and, at last, they snapped open.

I sagged against him in relief and didn't even notice that he'd gotten my bra off until a thumb swept over a nipple. "Mircea . . ." I started to make some kind of protest but forgot halfway through.

He dropped to one knee and undid my shoes, while I held on to his shoulders and bit my lip. "Most men would have taken advantage of your previous position," he told me. His face was still stern, but eyes were laughing.

"You're not most men."

"Kind of you to notice." He tossed my filthy shoes, socks and bra into a corner. "And I prefer you to have the full use of your hands." I swallowed and he finally smiled for real, his hands lingering on my waist.

"I don't like the idea of someone suffering because of me," I told him.

"He won't be suffering because of you." His fingers found the button on my jeans, and I stepped back, grateful for the steam that might help explain my furious blush. It was stupid—it wasn't like Mircea hadn't seen me in less—but the idea of standing there in a thong with him still fully clothed was doing bad things to my blood pressure.

He moved with me, arching an eyebrow. He trailed a finger along my waistband. "Is there something in there that will surprise me?"

"I hope not," I said fervently. "About Marco—"

"He disobeyed my direct command to be immediately informed of any danger to you. I could not ignore such a challenge to my authority, even were you not involved."

"That doesn't make me feel any better."

"I will not permanently injure him, Cassie," he told me, sounding as if it was a major concession—which was probably the case.

He unzipped my jeans and pushed them down my hips before I could protest. I stepped out of the puddle of filthy denim, caught between desire and serious embarrassment. He tossed the jeans aside, hooked a finger under the little bow on the front of my thong and pulled me to him.

He was still smiling, but it had changed. Something about it made sweat start to prickle at the base of my hair and my arms to curve around his neck. His lips fit against mine like a missing puzzle piece.

Dark and sweet, Mircea's taste was intoxicating, like the crisp midnight scent of him. It sent liquid shivers to the pit of my stomach and made my toes curl. I heard myself groan into his mouth, my entire body leaping at his touch, and suddenly a kiss wasn't enough. I wanted to taste all of him, to learn the texture and sensitivity of every inch of flesh.

But that was exactly what I couldn't do. If I wanted any chance of making up with the Circle, I had to avoid things that might increase their distaste for me. Like rumors connecting me to a Senate member.

The North American Vampire Senate was one of six sovereign bodies that ruled the world's vampire population the way the Circle did the mages. It and the Circle were currently allies, but it was a new association that had done little to erase centuries of dislike and mistrust. The Circle viewed a Pythia who was out of their control as bad enough; one under the thumb, or so they believed, of the vampires was a worst-case scenario.

Unless it was a Pythia dating a senator, that is.

Not that Mircea and I *were* dating. In fact, I'd been studiously avoiding him lately. Add lingering traces of a childhood infatuation, a powerful devotion spell that had only recently been lifted and a guy who even non-bespelled women went stupid over, and what did you get? A mess.

I knew what I felt for Mircea, but I wasn't sure why; even

worse, I didn't have any idea what he felt for me. While under the spell, he'd been genuinely infatuated. But with it no longer in the picture, I had to wonder what attraction I would hold for a five-hundred-year-old master vampire if I wasn't the reigning Pythia and we weren't in the middle of a war.

Until I found out, I didn't want my heartbeat to pick up speed every time I thought of him. I didn't want to feel that smile, lazy and suggestive and full of promise, when he kissed me; didn't want to smell the intoxicating scent of his neck under his shirt collar, to taste his sweat and hear his voice break. I didn't want to want.

"Dulceață," Mircea said quietly, using the pet name he'd given me as a child, meaning "dear one." And despite everything, that word in that voice made my heart give a little start behind my ribs.

It didn't matter what my heart said, I reminded myself. My heart told me stupid stuff all the time. My heart should just shut the hell up.

"Come back to MAGIC with me," Mircea murmured, his hands finding the muscles of my neck and beginning to expertly knead away the tension. I told my body not to respond and it obeyed as well as it ever did when it came to Mircea—not at all. "My personal apartment is extensive. You can have your own room"—he nipped me lightly on the neck—"if you want it."

"I don't like MAGIC," I told him unsteadily, turning away. I lost the thong and submerged myself in the tub.

"It's the safest place for you," he said lightly.

MAGIC, short for the Metaphysical Alliance for Greater Interspecies Cooperation, was the supernatural community's version of the United Nations, allowing mages, vampires, Weres and even the Fey—when they bothered to show up—to talk out their difficulties. It had some of the strongest wards anywhere, powered by a potent energy source known as a ley line sink. Mircea was right—it was the safest place around.

For anyone not fighting a god, that is.

"There is no safe place for me," I told him shortly, searching around under the bubbles for my loofah.

"Not if you continue to evade the protections placed around you." Mircea pushed his sleeve up and plunged his arm into the almost scalding water, finding the loofah easily. He turned me around and began to wash my back in long, soothing strokes. I tried not to relax—I knew damn well what he was up to—but my body had other ideas. When he zeroed in on the knot at the small of my back, I couldn't bite back a groan.

He finished my back and pulled me against him. He abandoned the loofah, lathered his hands with soap and began to wash my shoulders and arms. "You'll ruin your clothes," I protested weakly.

"I have others."

I sighed and closed my eyes, letting my body go on autopilot for a few minutes. The warmth of his hands slowly worked the tension out of my muscles, making me feel almost human again. Soon I was holding out an arm or leg when instructed, so he could wash my elbows and the underside of my breasts, my calves and the back of my knees. . . .

I could feel his breath on my cheek as I relaxed back against the tub. My hand unconsciously went to his hair, feeling its softness as he massaged me with slow deliberate strokes, pulling a deep sigh from my aching body. God, it was unfair how easily he could make me melt, every good intention lost in pleasure after only a few touches. "I love how responsive you are," he whispered, his fingers trailing a path of goose bumps down my stomach. When they brushed between my legs a moment later, I felt like I might climb out of my skin.

I sat up abruptly, grabbed a washcloth and took over before I ended up agreeing to whatever he wanted. "What are you doing, Mircea?" I asked unsteadily.

He sighed and sat back on his heels, but he didn't pretend to misunderstand me. "Trying to keep you alive."

"That won't happen by hiding me away somewhere. And cowering in a corner until Apollo finds me isn't—"

"Apollo." Mircea's voice held disdain. "You honor him by continuing to use that name."

I shrugged. "It's what he calls himself."

"Because he enjoys pretending to godhood."

"Whereas he's really only an immensely powerful, ancient magical creature from another world," I said sarcastically.

"Whatever he is, the Circle is better equipped—"

"No. They're not. They're in even more danger than I am."

As the ancient legends said, Apollo had once lorded it over the Earth along with others of his kind. Among other things, their rule had involved a lot of smiting of worshippers who didn't grovel sufficiently or, worse, failed to grovel at all, being too busy attempting to eject some godly butts from the planet. But the mages of the day hadn't had much success with that: the "gods" had their own form of magic, one that was so different from the human variety that all attempts to dislodge them had failed.

That had continued to be true until Apollo's sister, Artemis, realized that humankind was heading for extinction and gave some mages the spell to banish her kind and block the way back to Earth. The only ones not affected were of the demigod variety who had enough human blood to anchor them to this world, and most of them were soon rounded up and imprisoned by the magical community. Human rule over Earth was reestablished, and the Silver Circle formed to guard it.

That might have been the end of the story, except that Apollo had been able to keep in contact with his servants, the Pythias, through the power he'd bestowed on them. The Circle knew that, but the fact that the power migrated to a new host as soon as the old one died had made dealing with them a problem. They couldn't kill every clairvoyant on the planet, so they compromised by ensuring that the Pythias stayed firmly under their magical thumb. That had remained true for thousands of years.

Until me.

The Circle's fear of what Apollo might do through me was the main reason for their dogged attempts to put me in a grave situation. That was highly ironic, since almost the only thing I'd done with the power so far had been to use it against their old enemy. That had stuck me between the proverbial rock and a hard place, with both the Circle and Apollo wanting me dead.

It was nice that they could agree on something.

To add to the irony, the Circle and I were currently allies—at least technically. They had joined with the Senate, with whom I had an understanding, against Apollo and everyone he'd been able to con into supporting him—some rogue vampires and a powerful group of dark mages calling themselves the Black Circle. And so far things weren't looking that great for our side, mainly because Apollo didn't have to win in order for us to lose.

Artemis' spell had a weakness—it took too much power for any one person to maintain. That was one reason the Circle had been set up in the first place: to parcel the load out onto thousands of mages. The Circle also had the advantage of being eternal, which dodged the inconvenient fact that spells don't usually outlast the demise of the caster. With new mages being recruited as fast as the old ones died or retired, the Circle hadn't had to worry about the deaths of individual members threatening the spell—unless it was the deaths of thousands of members.

All Apollo had to do was to keep chipping away at the Circle's numbers and, sooner or later, there wouldn't be enough people left to maintain the spell. The doorway would reopen and he and his kind would be back for an encore. And I doubted the magical community would enjoy, or survive, the experience. The other side was united, and if we didn't manage the same soon, they'd wipe the floor with us.

"We have done some research," Mircea told me, pouring shampoo into his palm and starting on my filthy hair. He paused to pick something out of it, which I deliberately didn't look at, and then continued. "Based on the size of the Circle when the spell was first cast versus what it is today, we estimate that our enemies would have to destroy more than ninety percent of the current mages for the spell to fail. Not a likely scenario."

It was a little hard to think with his fingers kneading my scalp, but I tried anyway. "But not an impossible one. And where apocalypse is concerned, I'd prefer a sure thing."

"And I would prefer you to stay out of it." He pulled me to my feet, and a warm drizzle from a rainforest shower head set into the ceiling began sluicing the suds away. I frowned at him through silvery beads of water, too annoyed to be embarrassed.

"Apollo won't let me stay out of it," I pointed out. "Other than the Circle, I'm at the top of his hit list. It's going to be a little hard to draw him out without using me as bait."

"There is a vast difference between being bait and being a target," Mircea noted, wrapping a huge Turkish bath towel around me. The black silk of his shirt had gotten wet and was clinging to the muscles in his stomach and arms. I tried really hard not to stare.

"Funny; they feel about the same from where I'm standing."

I gingerly got out of the tub and sat at the dressing table to check the extent of the damage. The furrow carved by the bullet in my hip was gone, courtesy of Mircea, I assumed. He had a limited ability to heal injuries and had helped me once before. A puncture mark I didn't remember getting stung my calf and there were a few burn marks on my hands. They matched the still-tender scars on my stomach and wrist from a recent adventure I was trying hard to forget.

Mircea's eyes lingered on the scars, too. "Magical healers can work miracles compared to their non-magical counterparts, but there are things even they cannot heal," he said softly.

"I guess I've been lucky."

Mircea didn't say anything, but his expression was eloquent. Luck didn't last forever. How long would it be before mine ran out?

A finger brushed aside my hair and trailed lightly over two little bumps on my neck. They weren't noticeable, being tiny and the same color as the rest of my skin, but Mircea found them easily. Not surprising, since he'd put them there. They were his mark, the one that identified me as his in the vampire world.

We might as well be married as far as vamps were concerned, despite the fact that I hadn't actually been asked. Hadn't, in fact, realized what was happening until the marking was long over. It wouldn't have mattered to another vampire, who would have considered herself lucky to belong to a Senate member. But although I might have grown up with them, I wasn't a vamp. And I wasn't thrilled with the idea of being owned, no matter how nice the fringe benefits.

"You aren't going to distract me," I told Mircea severely, because he was doing a damn good job of it. "I need to come to terms with the Circle, and they aren't going to understand my living with you."

"You're already living with me. I own this hotel."

"It's open to the public and you aren't here on a regular basis. Moving into your personal quarters, even if they are the size of a house, isn't the same thing. The Circle won't like it."

Mircea bent down and trailed his lips over the twin marks, making me shiver. "Do you know, *dulceaţă,* I am getting very tired of hearing about what the Circle does and does not like."

"So am I. But we have to face—"

He stopped me with a kiss that turned my spine to Jell-O. This wasn't the way this argument was supposed to go, I thought vaguely as my fingers curled into the wet fabric of his shirt. I was right; I should be winning. And nobody should be sticking a tongue in anybody else's mouth.

"You're too precious to lose," he told me, when I broke for air.

"If anything happens, I'm sure the Senate will—"

"I wasn't talking about the Senate," he said, a strange smile ghosting his lips.

Our eyes met and it was suddenly hard to breathe. "Oh." I felt oddly small and strangely powerful at the same time.

"And I am not proposing to take you to MAGIC, at least not immediately. I have been called away on family business."

"Again? You just got back."

"And because I cannot trust you not to undermine my servants in my absence—"

"I didn't—"

"—or to stay out of trouble for even a few days, you are coming with me."

Chapter Four

The family's customized Boeing Business Jet wasn't so much a plane as a flying hotel suite. It had glove leather seats the size of recliners in the dining area that were clustered around a shiny maple table. There was more maple on the walls and a luxurious coffee-and-cream-patterned carpet on the floor, and the bathroom boasted almost as much granite as the one at Dante's.

Mircea was sitting on a cream leather sofa in the lounge area, looking perfectly at home in a silver-gray shirt and tie and a sleek black suit. I felt a little too informal in a pair of jean shorts and a blue and white striped tank top, but I hadn't had a chance to ask where we were going before getting dressed. At least I was clean.

Mircea had been staring out the window instead of at the forty-seven-inch plasma TV on the wall, but he looked up when I returned from my exploration. "There's an actual bed in the next room," I informed him, before realizing how that sounded.

His lips did a slow curve. "We aren't going that far."

"Where *are* we going, exactly?"

"To Radu's home, near Napa."

I knew Mircea had a brother named Radu. I'd even met him on one very memorable occasion. But this seemed an odd time for a social call.

"It has been my experience that family business never waits for a convenient time," he commented when I said as much. "Although this will be a quick visit. The Consul is expecting to receive her African and European counterparts in two days, and I must be there."

"They're coming *here*?"

"With their entourages."

"But . . . I didn't think consuls traveled much." A consul was the head of a senate and as such was seen as too valuable to risk. Not that the ones I'd met had seemed in need of much protection. They were pretty scary all on their own.

"These are difficult times. The danger in not combining our strength is far greater than any risks required to do so. If we don't align our interests for the war, we may soon find ourselves without any."

Mircea sounded like maybe he'd made that argument more than a few times lately. "Is that a prepared speech?"

He ran a hand over his face, and for the first time, he looked tired. "Yes, but it's not supposed to sound like one."

A steward came in and set a silver tray with some covered chafing dishes on the coffee table. They turned out to be hiding eggs, bacon and thick-sliced French toast. Orange juice in a cut crystal carafe sat on the side, along with a small bowl of fresh peaches. The sun wouldn't rise for another hour or so, but my stomach grumbled anyway. I'd missed dinner by about four hundred years.

I ate some of everything, even the eggs, despite the pearl-gray caviar the steward had insisted on piling on top. Mircea had coffee. But as stimulants don't work too well on vampires, I doubted it was doing much for him.

He resumed staring out the window while I ate, which alone would have told me that something was wrong. He was the reigning champion of idle chitchat. And that was with someone he didn't know.

Everyone on the Senate had a job, what in a president's cabinet would be called a portfolio. Mircea was the Consul's chief negotiator, the go-to guy when people were being stubborn about giving her what she wanted. Normally, he was able to engineer miracles, bringing even the most obstinate types around to her way of thinking. But this time, she might have asked too much.

"Do you really think the other senates are going to get on board?" I asked.

"What do your cards say?" he countered, obviously not wanting to give odds.

The only tarot deck I had on me had been a present from an old friend who'd had them spelled as a joke. I didn't know who had done the charm, but it was a damn good one. Doing a spread with them was a real pain, but they were eerily good at predicting the overall magical climate of a situation.

"It won't be a normal reading," I warned him, fishing them out. "They don't shut up long enough."

I'd barely gotten the words out when two cards popped up all on their own from the deck.

"The Emperor," a light tenor proclaimed, while a deeper voice majestically intoned, "Death!" After that, it was a little hard to tell what they said, as they kept trying to talk over one another. They got progressively louder in the process until I finally managed to shove them back in the pack and snap it shut.

"The Emperor stands for strength, assertiveness, sometimes aggression," I told Mircea, who was looking amused. "If referring to a person, it usually signifies a father or father figure, a leader or employer, or a king or despot. If to a situation, it indicates a time when bold moves are needed for success."

"Should I worry that the Death card came up as well?" he asked lightly.

"Not really. It almost never means actual death. Normally it foretells the end of something—a dream, an ambition, a relationship . . ."

"For some reason I do not feel particularly reassured" was the dry response.

"In this case, it modifies the Emperor," I explained. "The two cards are often associated with each other. An emperor only secures power through the death of his predecessor, he stays in power partially by the fear of death he inspires and his power ends with his own death."

Mircea frowned. "We will shortly have three consuls together for the first time in centuries. Do not take this the wrong way, but I sincerely hope that your interpretation is not the correct one."

So did I.

"What do you plan to do with the alliance, if you get it?" I asked.

"Defeat this god of yours. We cannot reach him—he isn't in this world; a situation we hope continues—but his followers are. To eradicate the threat, we must remove them. All of them. But such an operation will require a combined effort."

A combined effort. Why did I see a problem there? "If the other senates agree, who will lead them?" I asked slowly. "The Consul?"

Mircea sighed and rubbed his eyes again. "That is one of many sticking points. None of the consuls are accustomed to taking anyone else's direction, nor have they been for hundreds of years."

"So it's your job to convince the world's five most powerful vampires to take orders from her?"

"Essentially."

"And I thought my job sucked."

He smiled slightly. "In fact, I do not expect to persuade them all. The Consul has a reasonably good relationship with the European and African consuls, which is how we were able to convince them to visit. And I have some influence at the Chinese court. But we have little leverage with the Indian durbar and none at all in Latin America. If we bring even one of those around, it will surprise me."

"But still, even three or four senates united has to be some kind of record, right?"

"If we can pull it off, yes. But half the senators hate the other half, in many cases because of slights hundreds of years old. Not to mention jealousies, rivalries and too-sensitive egos. Without any real proof of our allegations to offer them, I am not sanguine about our chances."

"We're at war. That seems pretty tangible to me!"

"But against whom? Apollo is not here. All they see are the same old enemies—the Black Circle and a few rogue vampires—with whom our senate has successfully dealt on previous occasions. As a result, they are extremely suspicious of the necessity for an alliance. I believe they suspect us of inventing the divine connection in an attempt to bring them under the Consul's subjugation."

I blinked, absorbing all that. I hadn't seen much of Mircea in the last few days, but I'd assumed that I was just really good at avoiding him. Or, more likely, that he'd noticed the distinct lack of Cassie in his vicinity right away and hadn't cared. But that had made me feel pathetically like a kicked puppy, so I'd focused on the fact that he had a perfectly good reason to be absent.

Mircea and I had both been affected by the love spell gone haywire, but he'd been hit by it far harder and, because of some time complications, had had to deal with it far longer than I had. I'd assumed he was taking some time to recover and had been glad of it, considering how he'd looked when I last saw him. But it didn't sound like he'd been getting any rest at all. And now this family thing had cropped up, whatever it was.

"You should try to take it easy for a while," I said, frowning. "You aren't exactly at your best right now."

One of those expressive eyebrows went up. "I beg your pardon?"

I sighed. That hadn't come out right. "I mean, everybody thinks master vampires are pretty much invincible. Only that's not true, is it? You can get tired and . . . and things." I'd seen him hurt and vulnerable recently, and the image had stuck with me. It was yet another reason for keeping my distance.

I'd learned the lesson years ago—never let people get too close. Care, but not too much, because sooner or later, I was going to lose them. My mother's attempt at a new life had ended in a car bomb arranged by a vampire who'd wanted a Seer at his court. She was too smart to take the job, but he thought her daughter would be perfect—if only I didn't have pesky parents around to tell me what a jerk he was.

Tony, the vamp in question, had also tortured my childhood governess to death in a fit of pique, after I'd grown up enough to figure things out and flee from him. Others I'd left behind, either at Tony's or while moving about from place to place, trying to stay one step ahead of the servants he had searching for me. But however it happened, sooner or later, I'd look around and the people who meant something were gone. I'd learned the hard way that keeping my distance made it easier for everyone in the end.

Keep it superficial, stay far enough away, and no one even noticed when you left.

"Is something wrong, *dulceață*?"

"No." I swallowed. "Nothing. I just wish . . ."

"Yes?"

"I wish you could take some time off," I told him.

Mircea's face still looked grave, but his eyes were smiling. "I'm afraid a vacation is out of the question at the moment."

"Well, maybe you could think of something else that relaxes you."

Amber sparked somewhere deep in his eyes. "A few things do come to mind."

I gave him a look. "I mean, maybe you could work on something different for a while? They say a change is as good as a rest."

The growing amber flecks seemed to hold the light and warm it. "I am always happy to experiment." He tucked a stray curl behind my ear. "Did you have anything particular in mind?"

I licked suddenly dry lips, trying not to think about what five hundred years of experience could dream up. "N-not really."

"Then I suppose we'll have to wing it." He pressed me back against the sinfully soft couch cushions and kissed me. When his tongue touched mine, my brain suddenly started suggesting all sorts of interesting possibilities.

And then the captain came on the intercom to announce our successful landing. I looked around in surprise. I hadn't even noticed the descent.

"We could stay here for a while," someone who sounded a lot like me said breathlessly.

Mircea kissed me again, quickly this time, before getting up. "Tempting. But I have to go."

"You mean, *we* have to go."

"I brought you with me to keep you safe—not to put you in more danger." He started to walk away, but I grabbed his sleeve, managing to put a few wrinkles in its perfect drape.

"Danger? I thought we were visiting your brother."

"I am. You are staying here. Radu is having a few problems and I don't wish you involved in them."

"Maybe I can help," I said, starting to get up. Only to find that I couldn't.

I looked down to see a familiar silver bracelet tight around my wrist. I pulled on it, but it was securely fastened through the arm of the couch, caught on something inside the plush leather—the frame, by the feel of it. Damn it, I'd forgotten to ask for the cuffs back!

"Mircea!"

"This shouldn't take long, and you will be well cared for until I return," he said. And then he just walked out.

I yelled and rattled the cuffs loud enough to wake the dead, but nobody came to help me. I tried shifting and ended up on the tarmac outside the plane—still attached to the couch—in time to watch Mircea drive away. I didn't know where Radu lived, so I couldn't follow him. Not to mention that it was kind of hard to envision being of much use chained to a huge piece of furniture.

I shifted back onto the plane, fuming, and a ghost popped in. That wouldn't normally require comment, as it happens to me all the time—one of the annoyances of being clairvoyant. But this was a little different since this ghost I knew.

Billy Joe was wearing the jaunty Stetson and the ruffled shirt he'd died in a century and a half ago. Normally, the shirt is a brilliant crimson that easily catches the eye. At the moment, it was a pale, faded color, like it had been left out on a wash line too long. It got that way only when his energy levels were close to bottoming out.

"Don't start," I told him before he could open his mouth. "I tried to find you before we left. I knew you needed a draw." Billy and I had a long-standing arrangement in which I fed him extra energy and he fed me information. Neither of us ever got as much as we wanted out of the deal, but it was better than nothing.

"Damn right I need a draw, but that isn't why I'm here." He noticed my wrist and his frown changed to a smirk. "You and the vampire getting kinky?"

"He didn't want me following him."

"So he tied you up?" Billy laughed. "Did you even get any first?"

I glared at him. The skin of my wrist burned where Mircea had touched me, a fluid heat that spread through me and brought an answering flush to my cheeks. "Just because you have a habit of popping in on me at all times of the day and night doesn't give you the right to—"

"Guess not," he said, hiking an insubstantial butt cheek onto the sofa. "So get out of those and let's go. You got an important meeting to make."

"If I knew how to get out of them, I'd have already done it," I said testily. "And what meeting?"

"Oh, I don't know. Which one have you been trying to set up for the past three days?"

It took me a second to get it. Pritkin had been pestering the Circle to meet with me ever since Apollo entered the equation. But I hadn't actually expected him to get anywhere. Once a member of the Circle himself, Pritkin had broken with them over his support of me. I'd assumed they wanted his head on the platter right beside mine.

"The Circle wants to meet? Since when?"

Billy rolled his eyes. "Since yesterday. Word came in shortly after you left to chase Agnes. Don't you read your messages?"

"What messages? I didn't get any messages!"

"Pritkin went by your place about a dozen times, but you were never there. So he started leaving notes with that huge guy."

"Marco."

"Yeah. That's the one."

"Marco didn't give them to me." Or even mention them—or Pritkin or the meeting. I was beginning to think that he was right. We had a communication problem.

Billy shrugged. "Mircea must have ordered him not to."

I opened my mouth to say that Mircea wouldn't do that but shut it again before the words got out. Who was I kidding? Mircea totally *would*.

"The Senate likes the idea of a Pythia under their control," I said, working it out. "And if the Circle and I make up—"

"You might get a little too cozy," Billy finished.

"So Mircea was delegated to get me out of the way before the meeting." I felt my face flush, remembering that scene in front of the mirror. So I was too precious to lose, huh? Too important to him?

"Uh, Cass?" Billy was looking at me a little funny. "The meeting is at Dante's—Pritkin insisted. Something about neutral ground. Anyway, we got less than an hour before the mages show up."

I started to stand, only to be jerked back down again. "I'm kind of chained to a sofa," I pointed out.

Billy grinned. "Bet Pritkin could get you loose."

I sighed. Yeah, but I'd never live it down. "He's in his room?" I asked resignedly.

"I think you'll fit," Billy said gleefully. "If we push."

I sighed. *Never.* And shifted.

Like me, Pritkin had recently gotten an upgrade in accommodations. They were roomier than the old version, but to be on the safe side, I landed in the corridor outside. And my large leather accessory landed on top of Marco's friend. He was a vampire and the sofa was built to be lightweight for air travel, so it didn't hurt him. It didn't make him too happy, though.

"Marco said you might show up," he said, lifting it off and dumping it to the side. "He also said you wasn't to be allowed to talk to the mage."

My eyes narrowed. "I'll talk to whomever I damn well please," I told him, trying to drag the sofa around so I could knock on the door.

He put a foot on the nearest couch cushion and took out a cell phone. "She's back," he told it while I pulled and tugged and got nowhere. "Marco says I'm to take you upstairs," I was informed.

"You and what army?" I grunted. "And get your foot off my sofa."

The vamp regarded my leather appendage for a second and then looked toward the elevator. The thought process didn't appear to be swift, but he did eventually arrive at the right conclusion—it wasn't going to fit. "I'll have to break it in two," he said, grabbing the other end. "Sorry, but I'm sure the master will buy you another one."

"It's Mircea's," I said quickly. "It's his sofa. And he's really, really attached to it."

The vamp looked suspicious. "To a sofa?"

"It's a designer original, hand-dyed to coordinate with the rest of the furniture on his BBJ. You mess it up, and they'll never get another one to match. It'll stand out like a sore thumb. It'll be embarrassing."

We stood staring at each other for a long minute, and the vamp blinked first. "I don't want to embarrass the master," he said slowly, reaching for his cell phone. But he'd forgotten to put his foot back on the couch, so I gave a mighty heave and slid over within arm's length of the door.

"Hey!" He was there in a heartbeat, with his hand on my arm. So I kicked the door instead of knocking. "You gotta go back upstairs. Marco said so!"

"Tell Marco to go to hell!"

"Trust me, I'm already there," Marco informed me from the stairwell.

Damn it! I tried to kick the door again, but Marco grabbed the end of the sofa and dragged me back out of reach. "You're coming with us. Deal with it," he told me.

An elderly couple came out of the next room while we were standing there glaring at each other. The man was wearing a blue polo shirt and a pair of plaid shorts that started around his armpits and just brushed his knobby knees. The woman had on a Chippendales souvenir tee, a pair of bright red jogging shorts and matching Keds. They both looked about ninety.

"You're gonna have to move your couch," the old man said. "The missus and I gotta get to the elevator."

"If you don't get to the buffet early, the eggs get all dried up," the woman agreed. "They should cook more eggs."

"You heard the man," I told Marco. "Move the sofa."

Marco rolled his eyes. "It's your fucking sofa. Why don't you move it?"

"That's no way to talk to a lady," the old man told him. "And how's a little thing like her going to move a big sofa like that anyway?"

"You look like strong boys," the woman chimed in. "Why don't you move it for me?" She batted her eyes at Marco's buddy, who started looking slightly panicked.

"Take the stairs," Marco told her. "It's better for you."

She frowned. "I had hip replacement surgery. I can't do stairs."

"Don't tell my girlfriend what to do!" the old man said, looking pissed. "This is a public hallway. You can't block the way like this! I'm going to report you to the management if you don't move this thing right now!"

The old woman beamed at him. "Isn't he something?" she asked me.

"Chivalry isn't dead," I agreed.

"You want this sofa moved?" Marco asked. "You got it."

He picked me up, dumped me on the couch, and yanked up one end. His buddy got the other, and the two vamps started carrying it down the hall. Either of them could have managed it alone, probably with one hand, but we had an audience.

The man and woman followed us to the elevators and pressed the button, and then we all waited until an empty car arrived. The door pinged and the two lovebirds got on. The woman held the door, but I shook my head at her. "It won't fit."

Marco glanced from the couch to the elevator and reached the same conclusion. Scowling, he put down his end of the sofa, shifted me to one side, and stomped a size thirteen foot down through the middle. There was a loud crack and the sofa broke clean in two.

"Oh, my," the woman said, her foot firmly planted in the elevator door. It looked like the eggs could wait.

"Oh, jeez." Marco's buddy was looking from him to the sofa, back and forth, like he couldn't quite believe his eyes. "Oh, man, you shouldn't have done that. That was a special couch. That was Lord Mircea's favorite couch!"

"Lord Mircea doesn't have a favorite couch!" Marco told him, trying to shove me onto the elevator. But the piece I was attached to was still too big, especially with two people already on board.

Marco grabbed the sofa arm that my cuffs were stuck through as if he meant to wrench it off, but his buddy stopped him. "I can't let you do that," he said seriously.

Marco stared at him for a moment. "Can't let me do what?" he finally asked.

"I can't let you do any more damage to Lord Mircea's property. This is a special couch. See that leather? It was *custom dyed*. You can't just go out and buy another one, not and have it match." He surveyed the pieces with a worried frown. "The leather split along the seam. Maybe it can be repaired. Maybe we can—"

I never heard his suggestion, because Marco planted a fist to his jaw with enough force to send him sailing back against the wall. It shuddered when he hit, and a wall sconce tumbled to the carpet, shattering into pieces. The vampire didn't look so good himself, sliding slowly down onto his haunches.

Marco glowered at him. "Don't ever challenge my authority again. I'm in charge of this detail. You do what I tell you." He turned back to the sofa and got a grip.

"Don't do it," his friend warned, slowly getting back to his feet.

"What did you say?" Marco asked softly, turning toward him again.

"I said. Put. It. Down."

"Okay." Marco let go of the sofa and carefully pushed the old woman's foot out of the door. "Show's over. Nothing to see here," he told her, and hit the button for the lobby. As soon as the elevator car was away, he launched himself at the other vamp.

I'd known what was coming and was ready. Half a sofa weighed a lot less than the whole thing and was more maneuverable, too. I got to my feet as they staggered into a stairwell, cursing and clawing, and started dragging myself back down the hall.

Normally, I'd have shifted, but I'd already had a hard night—a trip of four centuries isn't fun—and then had had to shift back from the airplane. Plus the small detour to the tarmac. I was pooped. And I didn't think meeting the head of the Circle completely out of juice was a good idea.

I knocked sharply on Pritkin's door. This time it opened to reveal a half-shaved war mage with a razor in his hand. He was wearing nicely pressed dress slacks and a sleeveless undershirt that fit him like a second skin. But for once it wasn't the well-defined arms and muscular shoulders that caught my attention. It was the hair.

His short blond mane fell in waves over his forehead and just brushed his collar. It looked soft. It looked under control. It looked *normal*.

"Your hair." I gaped at it.

He ran a hand through it. "I haven't had a chance to deal with it yet."

"Do you have to?"

Green eyes narrowed. "Where have you been?" he demanded. "And why aren't you dressed?"

I didn't reply because suddenly Marco was there with a scowl on his face and a rip in his suit. "All right," he said, panting slightly. "Let's go."

"How do you think Mircea would like you manhandling me like this?" I asked, looking down at the hand gripping my bicep.

"The master wants you to wait for him upstairs."

"You called him?"

"No. He left a message in case you showed up. I guess he knows you."

I ignored that. "Since when do you deliver messages?" I looked at Pritkin. "He didn't give me any of yours. I wouldn't have even known about the meeting if it weren't for Billy."

"Why didn't you give her my messages?" Pritkin demanded.

"Billy and I have this theory," I told him, "that maybe the Senate isn't too happy about—" I stopped because Marco clapped a hand over my mouth. Pritkin knocked it away, and the two sized each other up.

"I haven't had dinner yet," Marco told him. "Bring it."

Pritkin glanced at me and finally noticed that I was attached to something. "Why are you handcuffed to a chair?"

"It's part of a couch," I told him.

The elevator dinged and the old man and woman got out. They skirted the damaged furniture in front of the elevators and walked down the hall toward us, her limping slightly because of her hip. They finally reached us and the old man scowled. "I thought I told you to move that thing," he said querulously. "I forgot my medication. I have to take it with breakfast or I'm messed up the whole day. And your sofa is blocking my door."

Marco closed his eyes for a minute and then picked up the sofa. He broke off the arm that I was chained to and handed it to me. Then he proceeded to rip the rest into tiny pieces while the old couple watched him with big eyes.

He'd almost finished when his buddy, looking pretty beat up, came running out of the stairwell leading a detail of security. Since the hotel is owned by one vamp and managed by another, it isn't too surprising that most of the security force is also among the life challenged.

"I'm her bodyguard!" Marco yelled at them as six vampires piled onto him. "You don't understand—she's in danger!"

"Uh-huh," the leader of the patrol said, eyeing the old couple. "It looks like we arrived just in the nick of time."

"Tell him!" Marco ordered me.

I opened my mouth and then closed it again. Marco was a new arrival on the scene in Vegas, having been brought in from Mircea's court in Washington State. As a result, most of the casino employees didn't know him yet. With luck, the guards wouldn't get confirmation on his identity until after my meeting with the Circle was over. I stood there silently as they dragged him away while he stared at me with little narrowed eyes.

"Sorry about that," the security chief was telling the old couple.

"You could comp us a buffet," the old woman said hopefully.

"Damn straight," the old man agreed. "There's something wrong when a fella can't even get to his meds."

"What the hell is going on?" Pritkin demanded.

I held out the arm with the cuff. "Get this thing off and I'll fill you in."

Chapter Five

Half an hour later, I was standing in Dante's lobby getting smacked around by a blond. For once, it wasn't Pritkin. "Stop that!" The willowy creature at my side slapped my hands. I'd been trying to surreptitiously wipe my sweaty palms on the full skirts of my dress, but I guess I hadn't been subtle enough.

"I'm not hurting anything," I said as someone started sniffling nearby. I looked around, but all I saw was the gimlet-eyed group across the hotel lobby. They were filing in by twos and threes, attempting to blend in with the crowd. But despite the fact that Dante's employees dressed in everything from sequined devil suits to dominatrix garb, they weren't doing so great.

It might have been the heavy coats they wore despite the fact that the temperature outside was threatening to shatter thermometers. It might have been the ominous bulges under said coats. Or maybe it had something to do with the fact that they all looked like they dearly wanted to kill someone. Since that someone would be me, I thought a few sweat stains might be forgivable. Too bad Augustine didn't agree.

"After the way you brought back my last creation?" he sniffed. "Don't even talk to me."

I shifted my feet guiltily. Augustine was a dress designer who thought pretty highly of his work. That was why I'd stuffed the remains of the last dress he'd made for me, which had suffered a few unavoidable indignities, into a trash bag and hid it in a Dumpster. Somehow, he'd located it anyway. And when I showed up at his shop in the casino promenade half an hour ago, out of breath and desperate for something to wear to this meeting, he'd pointed to the poor, tattered remains.

Augustine had made it clear that off the rack was too good for me and flounced out. But half a minute later he'd had to flounce back in when Sal, my new, self-appointed assistant, had backed him into the workroom with a fang-filled smile. Apparently, Mircea hadn't had time to alert the entire family to the fact that he'd prefer I miss this meeting. And Sal wasn't about to let me embarrass us all in front of the Circle.

I'd gotten my dress—a rich green velvet that made me look vaguely like I was wearing Scarlett O'Hara's curtains—barely in time to drag it on and sprint over here. Since it was an Augustine creation, I kept expecting it to morph into something or try to bite me, but so far it hadn't done anything interesting. Except do its damnedest to make me look more sophisticated.

It had its work cut out for it.

Nothing was going to turn my five-foot-four frame statuesque, I hadn't had a chance to redo my makeup, and an attempt to tame my flyaway curls with hairspray had given me helmet head. Not that it mattered: the Circle already knew what I looked like. They should, considering how many wanted posters they'd sent out.

Casanova, the hotel manager, sidled up, frowning. He was looking stylish as usual in a wheat-colored suit that set off his Spanish good looks and fit like it had been made for him, which it probably had. He gave me a glass and a glare. "What's the matter? Is your corset too tight?"

"I'm not wearing a corset." For once, Augustine had refrained from trying to asphyxiate me.

"Then would you mind attempting to look a little less like you're about to fall over? You are supposed to be projecting an aura of strength."

I took the champagne, but my hand was shaking enough to spill a few drops onto my bodice. "I'm trying!" I hissed as someone began weeping softly. "And what the hell is that?"

"Us, going up in flames," Casanova said, leaving as abruptly as he'd come.

Augustine was looking a little smug. "Okay, what did you do?" I demanded.

"Call it insurance," he said cryptically as more leather-trench-coat-wearing "tourists" filtered in through the door. They were war mages, the Circle's version of a police force, FBI and CIA all rolled up into one maniacal package. I'd expected to see at least a few of them around as a precautionary measure. This was more than a few.

I did a quick visual survey and decided we might have a problem. Because the agreement Pritkin had worked out explicitly stated that each side could have no more than a dozen members present at the meeting. Ours were scattered around the room, mostly vampires on loan from Casanova. The mages had also fanned out, and while it was a little difficult to be sure with all the real tourists around, I was fairly certain I counted more than a dozen. Make that absolutely certain, I decided as another trio nonchalantly wandered in.

One day I was going to find allies who didn't try to kill me on a regular basis. One fine, fine day.

Francoise, the pretty brunette witch flanking me on the other side from Augustine, shifted uncomfortably. "Pritkin, 'e ees 'ere, no?" she asked, her French accent more pronounced than usual. That meant she was nervous. Probably because, while she still had a little trouble with English, she could count as well as I could.

"Yeah."

"I do not see 'im."

"That's kind of the point."

I'd have preferred to have Pritkin glued to my side, in case this went the way of every other encounter with the Circle I'd ever had. But he'd argued that he could keep a better eye on the overall scenario if he had more freedom of movement. Francoise was there to run temporary interference if things got out of hand.

I wouldn't have told her for anything, but that didn't make me feel a lot better. I didn't doubt her ability, but the fact was that the Circle didn't play by the rules. Sometimes, I didn't think they even *had* any rules. And they were supposedly the good guys. No wonder I was always in trouble.

"Zere are too many mages," Francoise muttered, casting a glance at the entrance, where two more were sauntering over the bridge that separated the land of the living from the underworld. Below them, a couple of Charons were poling boats laden with clueless tourists across the Styx, or what passed for it. The vacationers were laughing and tossing coins into the water, making the usual jokes about paying the ferryman.

"They won't try anything surrounded by norms," I said, more to convince myself than her.

"Zey are already trying somezeeg!" she pointed out, frowning like someone who badly needed to be cheered up by some decent leadership. I kind of felt that way myself; unfortunately the one in charge was me.

"Are you planning to wait for them to attack?" Pritkin's voice was loud in my ear. He'd done some sort of spell to allow us to communicate, or so he'd said. I should have known he'd use it to eavesdrop.

"If I leave, what then?" I asked reasonably. "We need the Circle."

"And we need you alive!"

"They haven't done anything yet."

"Other than deceive us," Pritkin said in his let-me-explain-this-to-you-in-little-words voice. "We said a dozen; I've counted more than twice that many. And if they will break one promise, why not another? We'll have to try again."

"And what if they refuse to meet again?" They didn't like me already; a deliberate snub might be the last straw. If we were ever going to reconcile, someone had to take a risk and show a little trust. And it didn't look like it was going to be them.

"Miss Palmer . . ."

"I thought we'd agreed that you were going to call me Cassie."

"There are a few things I'd like to call you. Now get out of there!"

"I'll shift out if there's trouble," I promised.

"If they explode a null bomb, you won't be able to shift!"

"We discussed this," I reminded him. "If they use a null bomb, it will cancel out all magic in the area—including theirs—and Casanova's boys will wipe the floor with them. I only want to talk to Saunders for a few minutes."

"He isn't here! He sent one of his lieutenants instead. Richardson. He just came in."

And sure enough, three mages had broken off the pack and started toward me. I didn't have to ask which one was in charge. The man in the center was middle-aged and distinguished looking, with startlingly blue eyes and graying auburn hair that was swept back from a high forehead. He was wearing a business suit in a neat gray pinstripe with a bright blue tie. He looked more like a diplomat than a warrior. Maybe they actually did intend to talk.

"Get out now!" Pritkin repeated, sounding furious.

"If I leave, what then?" I whispered. "We don't have a Plan B."

"And if you die, we'll never have a chance to form one!"

"Damn it, Pritkin. We need the Circle!" He didn't reply. Maybe because Richardson and his cold-eyed buddies had arrived.

"I thought we'd agreed no more than twelve per side," I said, and immediately wished I could take it back. I hadn't planned to start off sounding so suspicious. If this meeting had taken place a month ago, I'd have handled it differently. But weeks of constant running, almost dying and frequent betrayal had sharpened my usual defensiveness to something approaching hostile paranoia.

Richardson didn't look ruffled, however. "Had we met at a neutral site, we would have kept the bargain. But this"— he swept out a hand to indicate the gothic gloom of Dante's lobby—"is not neutral."

"It's a public place! And if you had an objection, you might have mentioned it before now!"

"A public place owned by your master and run by his servants."

"I don't have a master."

He smiled condescendingly. "That is what the vampires said. They speak highly of you." It didn't sound like a compliment.

"But you don't believe them."

"Tell me about Nicholas," he said instead of answering.

It took me a second to respond, because I'd known Nick only by the abbreviated version of his name. He'd been a war mage acquaintance of Pritkin's, one who had turned against the Circle but hadn't joined my side. He had preferred his own.

I paused, wondering how to explain the complex series of events that had left the only book with a translation of Artemis' spell in Nick's hands, forcing Pritkin to kill him to keep it safe. I really hoped Nick and Richardson hadn't been friends. "He was going to use the Codex for his own ends," I finally said.

"Yes, so we were told. Unfortunately, there isn't a shred of evidence to that effect. Unless you perhaps still have it? Even a page—"

"It was burnt."

Richardson pursed his lips. "How unfortunate."

"Pritkin did what was necessary—"

"On your orders."

I started to argue the point but shut my mouth without saying anything. I hadn't ordered Nick's death, but I'd known how Pritkin worked and what his solution was likely to be. And I'd made no attempt to stop him. It was one of many decisions weighing on my conscience these days, although I still couldn't see another alternative. If Nick had succeeded, we'd all be dead now—probably even him.

"We did what we had to do, whether you choose to believe that or not," I told him.

"We all do," Richardson commented mildly, offering his hand.

This conversation wasn't going as well as I'd hoped, but at least we were talking. It was a start.

His hand was warm and slightly damp and his grip was firm—a little too firm. His fingers tightened as he drew me close, bending his head as if to say something privately. But all I heard was a low-voiced incantation that sent a sharp frisson running over my skin.

"Nick was my son," he said gently.

I stared up at him, seeing the resemblance that should have registered before—the auburn hair, darker than Nick's carrottop but with the same natural wave, and the eyes, surprisingly translucent when the light was right and dark as sapphire at the rim. And the expression, which told me as clearly as if he'd screamed it that talk wasn't what he'd come to do.

Francoise muttered a spell, but before she could finish, Richardson flung out a hand and she went flying. Two of Casanova's security team started forward, but the mages flanking us threw up a shield that they couldn't penetrate. That wouldn't last, but then, it didn't have to. Richardson reached out and, with a savage motion, ripped open the air.

The darkness of the casino's lobby was suddenly brilliant with icy blue light that highlighted the patched areas in the carpet and the hidden speakers in the corners. It made Richardson's eyes brighter and colder even than they were while washing all human color from his face. I tried to shift but nothing happened. I pulled back, but his grip had turned to steel.

"We need each other," I reminded him. "You don't want to do this!"

His face took on an expression that was nothing like a smile. "Oh, but I really think I do."

A movement caught my eye and I looked up in time to see Pritkin jumping down from the second-floor balcony. But it was too late. Richardson jerked me to him, an arm encircled my waist and we were gone.

I knew what had happened as soon as I saw the familiar tunnel of leaping energy all around us, although the sensation in my stomach—rising, sinking, a bit like flying, only far more terrifying—would have been enough. We were skimming the surface of a ley line, a term the mages used for the rivers of power generated when worlds collide: ours, the demon realms, Faerie or any of a hundred others.

For the width of a couple of football fields on either side was a sea of glimmering blue, a thousand shades from robin's egg to sapphire running together like an electric ocean. In front and behind, energy sparkled and danced along gleaming bands of pure power, telescoping out to an infinite vanishing point. It wasn't a calm picture: everywhere knots and snarls of blue-tinged lightning were tossed up like flotsam or, as someone had once explained it to me, magma in a tectonic drift.

The mages had long ago learned how to skim along the surface of these metaphysical hot spots, surfing their currents to rapidly travel from one point to another. The lines didn't go everywhere, which was one reason trains, planes and automobiles were still in use by the magical set. Another was the fact that most people didn't have shields strong enough to navigate this otherworldy highway system. Without them, the energy of a ley line would turn a human into dust in seconds.

"Shift, damn it!" Pritkin's voice echoed in my ear, the connection staticky and weak.

Yeah. Like that never would have occurred to me. I glared at the passing stream of vivid color and wished I could yell back. But if Richardson learned we could communicate, he'd probably figure out some way to block it. The only way to retain my tenuous connection with Pritkin was to keep my mouth shut.

"Cassie! Can you hear me?"

I realized that I had to say something. He couldn't help me if he didn't know what was wrong. "Why can't I shift?" I asked Richardson.

"You can't shift?" Pritkin repeated. His voice was wavering in and out, like a badly tuned radio, and I wasn't sure he'd heard me.

"Because it doesn't make sense that *I can't shift*," I repeated as loudly as I dared. "And don't tell me you used a null bomb, because then your shields wouldn't work. We'd both be dead by now."

"I used a null net," Richardson said, strangely matter-of-fact. He sounded like we were having the conversation over lunch instead of hurtling down a magical river that was trying its best to consume us. "The power you've usurped won't help you."

"A null net?" I prompted, hoping someone would take the hint. It was a little hard to fight something I'd never even heard of.

To my surprise, Richardson filled me in. "A bomb is designed to project the null effect outward—to stop a battle, for instance. A net does the opposite, projecting the power inward, over a more limited surface—in this case, your body." He sounded pretty pleased with himself; I assumed the net had been his idea. "It blocks your ability to access your magic but does not interfere with that of anyone around you."

Pritkin used one of his favorite swear words, so I knew Richardson wasn't lying. "Are you still on the Chaco Canyon Line?" Pritkin demanded, like I'd know. I'd experienced the part thrill, part terror of ley line travel only recently, since most vampires don't find rivers of fire a fun way to get around. Tony had never used them, and as a result I wasn't up on all the ins and outs. I knew that different worlds intersecting created different colors, due to variations in the atmospheres, but I hadn't even begun to know which color went where.

I wouldn't have had a chance to answer anyway, because a burst of power exploded right in front of us like a solar flare. The arm around my waist tightened convulsively, almost cutting off my air, as we spun out of control. The centrifugal forces were greater at the borders of the lines, where thick bands of power helped to push mages out of their version of a subway. Only we weren't leaving. My captor merely used the opportunity to regain control before we were back in the midst of the stream.

"All this blue is blinding," I said breathlessly. "I don't know how you can see to navigate."

"He's taking you to MAGIC," Pritkin confirmed.

"Yes, we're on the Chaco Canyon Line, on our way to MAGIC, where she will stand trial for her crimes. Is there anything else you'd like to know, John?" Richardson asked politely.

"He can't hear us," Pritkin informed me quickly. "He's guessing based on your comments. They weren't exactly subtle."

Well, excuse the hell out of me, I didn't say.

"You can't let him get you to MAGIC," Pritkin continued. "Once you're in the Circle's cells, it will be almost impossible to get you out. I'll create a diversion. Use the opportunity to force him out of the line, and I'll follow you down."

Right. Because I'd navigated a ley line on my own all of once, and that had been using an artificial shield because no way were mine up to this kind of stress. I'd almost gotten myself killed, and that had been without a war mage to incapacitate—one who I couldn't knock out, even were that physically possible, because then his shields would go and we'd both die. The same was true if Pritkin's "distraction" made him lose his concentration.

"Tell me, in your head, do these plans actually sound like they're going to work?" I asked.

Richardson made a huffing sound that might have been a laugh. "Just do it!" Pritkin snapped.

I ignored him. I wasn't going to risk getting fried if we were going to MAGIC. Because, yes, it was the mages' stronghold, but it also happened to be the vampires'. And while the Consul didn't like me much, she saw me as a potentially useful tool—and in vamp terms, that was better than affection. By now, Casanova would have informed the Senate that I'd been taken, and none of them was exactly slow on the uptake. Richardson might get more than he bargained for when we arrived at MAGIC.

Since I couldn't very well tell Pritkin that without also alerting Richardson, I used the time to begin calculating what the Consul was going to demand for saving my life. No way was I getting this for free, even if it benefited her, too. That wasn't how the game was played.

A few moments later, Richardson started maneuvering us toward the side of the line again. I braced myself for what was usually the bumpiest part of the ride, which turned out to be a good thing. Because we hadn't even started to exit when something smashed into his shields, shuddering them all around us.

For a split second I thought it was another flare until a weirdly distorted face appeared in front of me. It was bathed in jumping blue light, like a photograph taken underwater, and was squashed into the mage's shields as if pressed against a glass bubble. But the wild blond hair and furious green eyes were the same as ever.

Shit.

The mage stared at Pritkin for a startled second, apparently as shocked as I was, and then he scowled and jerked us hard to the left. We bounced off a thick band of power running along the side of the line and ricocheted back the other way. As we passed Pritkin, who was trying to pull up from a dive toward where we had just been, Richardson threw a spell that exploded against my partner's shields like a bomb blast.

I screamed, knowing what it meant if Pritkin's shields failed. But before the blast even cleared, he plowed into us again, hard enough to almost force us out of the line. Unfortunately, Richardson recovered quickly and hit back, bouncing Pritkin's bubble of protection so far into the distance that it was lost from sight among the jumping blue maelstrom.

"Pritkin! Get out of here!" I yelled, the need for subtlety over. I received no reply. I really hoped that, for once, he'd been sensible and retreated. He was at a serious disadvantage otherwise. He couldn't hit Richardson hard enough to risk rupturing his shields and killing us both, but the mage could attack him with impunity.

Make that mages. A flicker of movement caught my eye and I glanced behind us to see a dozen or more ripples in the energy stream, like sharks slicing through water. And off to the left, something dark appeared against all that jumping color. I deliberately didn't look directly at it in case I tipped Richardson off. He didn't see it, but apparently one of the mages following us did. A bolt of energy—red instead of blue—flashed past to explode against Pritkin's shields.

"No!" Richardson yelled. "Not inside the line!"

Nobody paid him any attention. Two more bursts screamed by us moments later, barely missing Pritkin, who dodged out of the way at the last second. Leaving the spells to burst against the river of power below.

I didn't see what they did—we were moving too fast and were almost immediately beyond them—but I felt it. The line trembled and wavered all around us, and energy bands that a moment before had been straight and more or less steady were suddenly arcing across our path. The already dangerous flow of the ley line became a raging torrent, tossing us around like a speck of dust in a cyclone. Lightning or something equally energetic sparked off the mage's shields as we spun, rolled and bobbed uncontrollably, swimming on wild currents of power.

I caught a glimpse of Pritkin barely avoiding being speared by a tower of blue flame. But he ducked under a fiery arch the size of a house and it surged past him. We weren't so lucky. Richardson swerved to avoid a stuttering mass that had erupted right in front of us and ran straight into another one hard enough that the impact reverberated through my bones.

Glowing streaks and odd swirls of light curled all around us. For a moment, all I could see were bursts of power exploding everywhere, burning through our bubble of protection like acid, before the mage made a sudden, violent motion and tore us free. The current tossed us to the side of the line, where a thick band of power threw us back once more, straight into the path of the granddaddy of all fissures.

It covered half the line's width in a towering column of angry blue fire. A tidal wave of prickling energy rushed over me as we breached the outer skin, and then it flared into a blinding brightness. I couldn't see anything, blue-white light filling my vision and my brain, overwhelming and unbearable.

My eyes slowly adjusted to show me the inside of the flare. Power pulsed everywhere in glowing blue-white streams that sheared chunks off Richardson's remaining shields every couple of seconds. They couldn't last at this rate—and as soon as they were gone, so were we.

Richardson must have had the same thought, because he started prying my arms off his waist. "I regret that there will not be a trial," he said as I struggled and fought. "I looked forward to hearing you beg for your life."

My fists bunched in his suit coat, trying to hold on, but he tore them loose and got his hands around my wrists. "Please! You can't do this!" I screamed, my eyes on the leaping wall of fire outside.

"I suppose that will have to do," he said regretfully. And with a brutal shove, he sent me flying backward, straight into the heart of the flame.

Chapter Six

My scream lodged in my throat as reality whited out and I was consumed by a pain so pure that it took over everything: my body, my thoughts, even my name. I tried to breathe through the panic that was threatening to choke me, but I couldn't even tell if I had lungs anymore. I tried to reach out, desperate to feel, see, do *something*, but if I still had a hand it didn't connect with anything. For a long moment, I really thought I was dead.

And then it was over.

The pain was gone between one breath and the next, leaving me shaken and very, very confused. I gasped in air and it tasted wrong, sharp and bitter, but I could breathe. My head was spinning, my nerves were stuttering like a junkie's and I could feel my heart in my fingertips. But it didn't feel like my muscles were ripping themselves loose from my bones any longer, which I counted as a plus.

I risked opening my eyes and looked down in disbelief at my unmarked hands, at my body that for some reason was not being incinerated. But once my eyes adjusted to the intense light inside the flare, I didn't have to wonder why. A familiar golden haze surrounded me on all sides, pushing against the jumping blue field, keeping it back.

The field was in the shape of Agnes' stolen ward, the one passed onto me by my mother before she died. It was given only to the Pythias or their heirs, and it was designed to be powered by the collective energy of the Circle. That wasn't true anymore—they'd cut me off as soon as they realized that it might interfere with their plans for my early retirement—but a friend had managed to fix it. He'd set it to draw from the only other power source of that magnitude available: that of my office.

It was the same pool of power that should let me shift out of here, if the null net had stopped working. I tried to access it again but went nowhere. Yet the ward burned brighter than I'd ever seen it, with an almost blinding golden light. I decided I didn't much care about the reason right now—I was just grateful for it.

Especially considering what the fissure was doing to Richardson's shields.

The column of pure energy tore through his remaining protection like it wasn't even there. For an instant the light haloed him, with every eyelash, every seam on the tailored suit, every ghostly freckle on the bridge of his nose clearly visible. He screamed, eyes opened blind and dilated, mouth wide and soundless, as light spilled through him, bright enough to give me a glimpse of dark bone inside incandescent flesh.

Then he was gone, with nothing to show that he'd been there but a few ashes that the current snatched away.

Even when I squeezed my eyes shut, the image was there, burnt in white-hot light behind my eyelids. My stomach rebelled and bile burned my throat. I pressed my arms over my stomach and waited for the same thing to happen to me, for my ward to fail, for the end. Then something hit me, sending me spinning off into the main current of the stream, jolting me back into myself, to the reality of *get out, get out now*!

Only I wasn't sure how.

I had a little experience with ley lines, but this no longer looked much like one. The thick bands of power that usually stayed along the outer edges were fraying, shooting electric tendrils from one side of the line to the other. Twisting surges of deadly blue fire—some as thick as a large tree trunk, others no wider than my finger—crisscrossed the corridor, forcing me to throw myself first to one side and then the other in a deadly game of dodgeball that I was sure to lose.

It was the smaller surges that were the most deadly, jittering here and there so quickly that they were almost impossible to avoid. They turned the previously stable corridor into a leaping, burning mass of flame, spotted by dark specks where the war mages' bodies blocked out the light. One shimmering band hit a mage who had almost caught up with me, exploding his protective shell and sending the blazing body straight at me.

He struck my ward like a bird hitting the windshield of a speeding car and exploded—there was no other word for it. The smell of burnt meat reached me, drowning out the harsh tang of the ley line's air as flaming pieces of his body tumbled past. I screamed as the force of the movement pushed me once more toward the edge of the line. But unlike before, I didn't bounce back. The outer bands of power had unraveled too much, and this time nothing caught me.

Electric blue dissolved into darkness as my body was thrown clear. I had a brief glimpse of a sky like a bruise: blue/black, septic yellow and festering, angry green. And then I was falling toward the ground hundreds of feet below.

I dropped like a stone and landed with a jolt. Despite the ward, my head hit brutally hard, thumping against dirt as rigid as concrete, causing my ribs to howl in protest. For a second, everything went white and ringing. I lay there, gasping, trying to get air back in my lungs but they didn't seem in the mood to cooperate. I finally managed to suck in some oxygen and used it to groan.

Shudders ran through me at odd intervals, mimicking the electric pulses of the line, while my stomach informed me that, yes, it was possible to be motion sick even while lying totally still on the ground. Opening my eyes sounded like a bad idea, as I wasn't particularly interested in seeing what the mages had planned for an encore. But not seeing was even worse.

I looked up and lay there transfixed, unable to do anything but stare at the sight of a blue gash spanning half the length of the sky. It spewed bursts of power like sun flares in every direction, shedding embers like transient stars. Some hit the ground, scorching the sand and setting the nearby scrub brush on fire.

It looked like we'd left Vegas behind and were somewhere in the desert. But that was the only good thing. You weren't supposed to be able to see ley lines—they didn't exist in our world, or any other. They were the metaphysical borderlines, the buffer zones between realms. It suddenly occurred to me to wonder what would happen if one of them ruptured and two worlds came into direct contact.

Why didn't I think it would be good?

A raw wind pushed at me, tossing my hair around, while my stomach kept doing slow rolls. I got to my knees, gagging on the electric air, trying to scan the area for any sign that Pritkin had made it out. But my vision kept blurring. Or maybe that was the ripples, like waves, that were flowing over the sand, flooding the desert like underwater light. Everything seemed to move, but nothing was him.

"Pritkin!"

I didn't need to yell—the communication spell could pick up even a whisper—but I did it anyway. It was hard to hear anything with the wind screaming around me as the sky writhed and shredded. I stared upward until my eyes watered from the strain, and I yelled again at intervals, but there was no response.

Maybe the spell had failed, I thought desperately. Maybe that's all it was, some minor glitch. Or possibly whatever was happening to the line was throwing up interference that he couldn't break through. That had to be it, because Pritkin was virtually indestructible. And because I didn't think I could take it if it was something worse.

My tried-and-true philosophy of keeping people at a distance was taking a beating lately. It wasn't working so well with Mircea, and Pritkin had somehow bulldozed past every defense I had before I'd even noticed. I still wasn't sure how he'd done it.

He wasn't that good-looking, he had the social skills of a wet cat and the patience of a caffeinated hummingbird. In between crazy stunts and, okay, saving my life, he was just really annoying. When we'd started working together, I'd assumed it would be a question of *putting up* with Pritkin; then suddenly the stupid hair was making me smile, and the sporadic heroics were making my heart jump and the constant bitching had me wanting to kiss him quiet. And now I cared more than was good for me.

So, of course, he was gone.

"Pritkin!" I screamed it again, my eyes searching the widening gap above me, but there were no little dark specks that might be my partner bailing out. Had he seen me leave? Or was he still searching? No, that couldn't be it. That would be crazy and reckless and stupid.

And very Pritkin.

"—is ruptur ... now!" The garbled phrase was loud enough to make me jump and to practically crack my eardrum—and I'd never been so happy to hear anything in my life.

"I'm already out! Stop looking for me!" I yelled, but the wind blew half my words away.

"Are you ... right? Can you ... before—"

"Stop talking! Why are you still talking? Bail out, damn it!"

"—the ground. Stay—"

"Shut up! Stop giving me orders and *get the hell out of there*!"

I didn't hear his answer, if he gave one, because the sky exploded. Blue lightning had been threading through the seething clouds, and now a huge branch arced downward, hitting a nearby hill with enough force to blow sand half a mile high. I hunched down with my arms over my head, trying to protect myself from the resulting hail of rocks and debris. And a hand descended on my shoulder.

I turned, grateful and furious, a few appropriate comments trembling on my lips—and looked into the face of a stranger. He was tall with spiky black hair and startled hazel eyes. It looked like someone bailed out early, I thought. And then my ward flared, throwing him back a dozen yards.

I watched his body arch pale and limp against the night, and then I turned and ran in the other direction. A flash of lightning hit nearby, with a thunderclap that threw me blind and rolling across the ground. I stumbled and almost fell down the side of the hill, stunned and furious. I was sick of having to dodge the people who should have been my allies while I fought my enemies and theirs. And where the hell was Pritkin?

The residual static in the air had the hair on my arms standing up as I scrambled back to my feet. I glanced back at the mage, but he didn't look too dangerous at the moment. His body lay in the weird, contorted position he'd landed in, sprawled across the dirt like a broken doll. I paused, my heart pounding wildly, flight reflex kicking in, sweat springing to the surface of my skin.

Normally, I wouldn't have wasted any sympathy—my ward doesn't flare unless there is a serious threat. That and the fact that he was with the guys who'd just tried to kill me was all the incentive I needed to get out of there. Except I couldn't. Because he'd landed facedown in a pile of loose sand deep enough to suffocate him.

The wind wrestled with my hair while I struggled with the life-or-death decision that had been dumped on me. I didn't have Pritkin's knowledge of magic. My only real defenses were my ward and my ability to shift, and neither was inexhaustible. Letting him suffocate might be the only sure way to stop him from dragging me off to a swift trial and a certain death.

But that level of ruthlessness wasn't in me.

More important, I didn't want it to become me.

I felt the chill in my chest that always came before I did something really stupid. I ran over, intending to kick him faceup and get out of there. But his damn coat weighed a ton and he wasn't exactly a lightweight. By the time I finally managed to flip him, I was panting from the effort and he still hadn't moved. "Hey." I shook him. That didn't seem to do a lot of good. "Hey, you!" I slapped his face. "Come on, don't die on me."

He didn't answer. He also didn't try to grab me again. He just lay there like a broken doll.

"I'm serious. You don't want me to have to try CPR. I killed the dummy fourteen times."

I don't know if that did it or if he'd had time to come around. He coughed up some sand and gasped in a breath, blinking grit out of his eyes. He got a clear look at me and an arm snaked out and latched onto my shoulder, jerking me down to the dirt.

My ward flared but only dimly this time. And although I could hear it sizzle against his palm, he didn't let go. So

I kneed him in the groin and, when he collapsed, hit him in the back of the neck like Pritkin had taught me. He fell back against the sand with a thud.

I stared at him, awed and slightly freaked out. The workouts that Pritkin called "a decent warm-up" and I called "evidence that you've gone *crazy*, oh my God, I'm having a coronary" had actually paid off. Despite the fact that that had been the point, it was a shock.

As was the fact that he'd landed facedown again.

Son of a bitch!

I finally managed to turn him over, decided I'd done my good deed for the year, picked up my skirts and ran. Psycho war mage aside, it had been almost a relief to have something to distract me from the unwelcome awareness that Pritkin was still inside the line. And that the fissure was widening and pretty soon no one was going to be able to survive in there no matter how good their shields and, oh, look, I was thinking about it after all.

There wasn't much natural cover, but some of the dunes had long shadows that, with the wind and the debris and the dim, rippling light, should have been enough to hide me. Except for the dress. I called Augustine every name in the book and invented a few new ones while my dress sobbed and cried and whined about a tear in its hem and a smear of dirt on my backside. The damn man had apparently spelled it to protest—loudly—whenever it got dirty.

It had probably seemed like a cute joke back at Dante's; here, it wasn't so funny. I might as well have a neon sign over my head glaring, HERE SHE IS. I stayed huddled where I was for a moment, watching the wind pull cayenne-colored veils off the ground and spread them across the electric blue of the sky. And every time a wave of airborne dust hit us, the dress moaned that much louder.

I dragged myself to my feet, hoping to get far enough away that the damn thing wouldn't matter. But the wind had picked up even more to the point that it felt like it would actually lift me off my feet any minute, and visibility was going south fast, with lightning sputtering overhead like a bad fluorescent bulb. And then someone tripped me.

I went down in a tangle of sobbing velvet right before a hand reached out from the dark and wrapped around my throat. My ward didn't flare at all this time, so it was down to old-fashioned, dirty fighting. I wasn't nearly as strong as the mage, and no matter what Pritkin said, strength does matter. Not to mention that war mages train in human as well as magical techniques, and I still couldn't shift.

Weird strobelike flashes started exploding across my vision. But it wasn't from the choke hold, at least not entirely, because something really not good was happening to the sky overhead. The mage's head whipped around, a hand still on my throat, and we watched in silent awe as one lightning bolt was followed by another. Within seconds the sky was filled with them, the line shedding thousands of crackling fingers of energy as its massive bands of power unraveled.

In the middle of all that tumult, my eyes somehow managed to focus on a tiny dark smudge. Someone was bailing out a dozen stories above us. "Hold on; I'm coming," Pritkin told me, sounding calm despite the pyrotechnics going on all around him. I didn't answer, but the mage saw him, too. He dragged me to my feet and put a gun to my temple.

Pritkin landed hard, letting his shields absorb the crash instead of taking the time to form them into a parachute as I'd seen him do once before. He was coming for us at a dead run, but above him, off to the east, the sky tore open like a dozen blue stars had been born all at once. And each one contained the dark form of a war mage. Either they'd seen him leave and figured out that I wasn't up there anymore, or else it was getting too hot in there even for them.

I watched their shields flow up into a dozen little chutes to carry them gently toward us on the night breeze. The maneuver would preserve whatever was left of their shields, while Pritkin's had probably been severely weakened by the ley line battle and the fall, and mine were nonexistent. We were so screwed.

"Don't be a fool, John," the mage shouted. "You can't fight these odds! You'll have to find someone else to help your ambition!"

Pritkin paused and glanced upward at the pulsing wound in the sky. "I don't know what you've been told, Liam, but my sole ambition at the moment is to survive the night."

"Then go! I'll tell them you overpowered me. Leave the pretender and I will stall them long enough for you to get away!"

I blinked at him, but Priktin didn't look surprised. "You owe me more than that," he chided. "She goes with me."

"I'm afraid not," Liam said, although he looked torn. Not torn enough to let me go, though.

"Release her and I will stay and face what passes for justice in the Circle these days."

"You would die for this one?" Liam asked incredulously.

"I have been trying to avoid it" was the dry-as-sandpaper response.

"Then go, while you still can!"

"Not without her."

"A life debt is not transferable," Liam said furiously. "I might owe you my life, but I don't owe it to her!"

Pritkin lunged forward and Liam struck out with an elbow, catching him on the chin. It snapped his head back hard enough to break his neck, had he been fully human. Thankfully, he wasn't. He rolled back to a crouched position and flung out a hand. I didn't hear an incantation, but he'd done something. Because Liam jerked like he'd been shot and hit the ground hard enough to carve a furrow in the dirt.

I scurried back out of the way as Liam looked up. Stray light played over his face, distorting the features with odd ripples and shadows. If I hadn't known better, I'd have guessed him for the one with the demon father. He threw a spell that caught Pritkin in the upper body, knocking him off his feet and using up what remained of my patience.

I hadn't wanted to carry a gun to a supposedly friendly meeting, so the only weapons I had were a couple of ghostly knives that resided in a bracelet around my wrist. Despite their appearance, they were deadly, which was why I hadn't already used them—I was supposed to be trying to keep the Circle intact, not to help destroy it. But if I had to choose between Liam and Pritkin, Liam was toast.

Pritkin had staggered back up, looking the worse for the wear. But when he saw what I was doing, he shook his head. "Don't kill him!"

Liam was also back on his feet, but he didn't attack. "She

wields a dark weapon—what a surprise." The mist in his eyes grew thicker, coalescing into something unpleasant as he stared at me. "Like father, like daughter!"

"My father worked for a member of the vampire mafia," I admitted, "but that doesn't make him—"

But Liam wasn't listening. "Be grateful I don't put a bullet in your head right now," he spat. "I can guarantee that no one would question it!"

The hate in his face killed any impulse to try to win him over. I stopped extending myself, my defenses slamming firmly into place. I didn't reply, just sent him an expression that was the facial equivalent of the finger.

I was sick of the Circle treating me like roadkill because I hadn't come out of their precious initiate pool. Okay, my track record wasn't perfect, but considering the amount of training I'd received for this job, it could have been a lot worse. And maybe I'd have done a little better if they had ever made the slightest attempt to work with me.

"It would be the last thing you did," Pritkin promised.

Liam sucked in a breath. "How can you defend her?" he demanded. "Consider what she came from! A dark mage for a father, a ruined initiate for a mother, a vampire for a surrogate and, if the rumors are to be believed, another for a lover! Can't you see what's coming? Hell, man, open your eyes! She's already divided the Circle and helped to start a war, and she hasn't been on the throne a month yet! What's next?"

"She hasn't been on the throne at all," Pritkin replied as the two men circled each other. "Thanks to you and the rest of the Circle, she's never even seen it."

"And she never will," Liam said flatly. He launched himself at Pritkin and the two men lurched around the sand together.

Meanwhile, the clouds above us had formed themselves into what looked an awful lot like a tornado. A big, blue tornado spitting lightning at everything in its path. It whirled and writhed as if possessed, twisting bluish black clouds into a violent surge of pure force. Heat was coming off it—dizzying, sear-your-skin heat—while the inner column glowed with a light that permeated even the clouds. It painted the landscape with madly leaping shapes and cast light shadows on the other war mages, who had landed and were now running for us at top speed.

I ignored them, far more worried about the way the clouds were funneling down into a sharp point maybe a mile away. "Is it supposed to do that?" I asked hysterically.

Both men paused to look at me, but then the rest of the mages were on us and the fight began in earnest. Half a dozen jumped Pritkin, while I stood there and watched as the awesome power of the ley line pulsed, crested—and drained into the breach it had made into our world. Someone grabbed my arms, pulling them back brutally, but I hardly noticed. The tornado or whatever it was finished spiraling down to some goal just out of sight. And then the sky burned white.

I had time to see Pritkin turn his face away, the bones beneath his skin etched in the instant of brilliant glare. The surrounding brush and boulders and the worn leather of his beaten-up coat were all suddenly, vividly clear as the flash seared away their color. The flare was followed by a sound louder than a thunderclap, only worse; it knifed through my eardrums, filling my whole head with the vibration of it.

My eyelids squeezed shut, but a soundless white light burned through my lids as the ground rumbled beneath my feet. A hot rush of wind tangled my hair and the mage holding my arm abruptly let go. I raised my hands to help shield my eyes, but the light was already gone. After a moment, I cautiously peeked out from between my fingers, trying to get my vision to work again. But for a long moment, I couldn't see anything but a leaping field of red.

The haze eventually lifted to show me a black sky littered with stars instead of searing white or dancing blue flames. As incredible as it seemed, it was over. Except for the fierce hail of debris. The mages combined their shields to protect the area while I crouched down, hands over my head, as rubble smashed against the shield in blooms of red-orange fire.

The barrage finally stopped and the mages dropped the shield with a wave of relieved sighs. Something brushed my hand, and I looked down to see a few gray flakes trembling on the breeze before blowing away. Ash.

All around us, a soft rain of ash was falling, filling the air, covering the sand. Something over the hill was burning. Great boiling clouds hung on the horizon, eating the stars, dark at the tops but red-lit from below where flames fingered the sky.

"My God," someone said, "it hit MAGIC."

Chapter Seven

There was a small quiet as we all stared at the hill. I could hear hollow echoes of the blast reverberating in my head and feel sweat trickling down my cheek, stinging a cut on my lip. Then someone started walking toward the ridge, a black silhouette against the dim glow, and we all followed.

I made it to the crest of the dune and froze. The canyon looked like a giant meteor had hit it. Where a cluster of adobe buildings had once stood, there was nothing but a yawning crater, black and still smoking. The initial heat must have been incredible. In places the sand had taken on a runny, glasslike sheen, melted in an instant.

Nothing moved.

No, I thought, but it was distant and blank. We all stared at the place MAGIC should have been for a long moment. Finally, somebody started moving and the rest of us followed. We picked our way down an old path until it was lost under a drift of dirt and rock thrown up by the explosion. Judging by the colors, some of it had come from far underground. The once pale tan landscape was now raw umber, old gold, blackened bronze and ash gray. It was also slippery in places, where cooling glass hid under the softer sand that was still raining down. I kept my footing because Pritkin had me by the arm, his grip mirroring the tight clench of his jaw.

The mages seemed to have forgotten I was there. We sidestepped over broken stones together, across drifts of white-speckled ash, under clouds of fine black particles that billowed up with every movement and settled over our clothes, our faces, our hair. I could taste them at the back of my throat. Nothing could have survived.

My legs suddenly gave out, dumping me in the dirt. I rested my head on my knees and took slow, deep breaths, forcing the hollow, aching fear pushing at my ribs to still. More ash floated up, threatening to choke me, and I didn't care. I saw a succession of faces across my vision, all friends who lived and worked at MAGIC—or had. One in particular caught my breath. Rafe, my childhood friend, was the closest thing I ever had to a father. And he was buried under there along with the rest, assuming he hadn't been incinerated by the explosion.

Part of my brain was busy running the odds, looking for an angle that would provide a way out—even when I knew damn well there wasn't one. I wrapped my arms around my torso and shook but not with grief. Not yet. It was rage that stopped my throat and made it almost impossible to speak. It felt like being flayed, being hollowed out and filled with boiling acid. I'd never experienced so much anger, such a bitter desire to strike back. Because this wasn't something that our enemies had done to us.

I'd said we were going to tear ourselves apart; I just hadn't thought it would start so soon.

The mages were shuffling around like zombies, blank faced and disbelieving. Their feet stirred up black and gray clouds, disturbing the embers. Something was burning underground. There were glowing orange-red spots beneath the ashes, dotted here and there like a huge funeral pyre. I watched them with eyes that stung and watered from more than the particles in the air.

The Senate was gone. Beyond the personal tragedy, it was a military disaster—*the* disaster—that would almost certainly hand Apollo a win. Not today, maybe, but soon. Whether their arrogance allowed them to see it or not, the Circle couldn't hold out alone against the forces he had amassed. It would be lucky to last the month.

"Shift us inside," Pritkin said, his voice a harsh rasp. Several nearby mages heard him and turned to look at me, expressionless and tense as drawn wire.

I slowly lifted my head, gazing at Pritkin through a haze of grief and rage. His eyes were dark and wild, the pupils devouring the green, leaving a corona of feverish jade. He looked wounded; he looked the way I felt, as if he'd done the calculations, too. As if he already knew we'd lost.

"I thought we'd at least get to fight the war first," I said.

"The lower levels. Cassie—with MAGIC's wards, some may still be intact!" He gripped my arms like there was some kind of urgency. Like any wards could have held against that. "Take us there!"

"Null net," I said, unable to get anything else out.

"Remove it!" I heard Pritkin order someone, but I didn't bother to see who. Sweat was running down my back, soaking the seam of the dress, and I must have touched something hot because my palms were burned. "She is innocent of the charges. Let her prove it—remove the net and she'll help us!"

"Help us?" Liam stepped forward, almost unrecognizable with his grubby face, blossoming black eye and hate-filled snarl. "She killed a dozen mages tonight!"

"The fissure killed them," Pritkin retorted. "And she had nothing to do with that."

It was like Liam didn't hear him. "They were good men! Richardson most of all, killed while still in mourning for his son—another of her victims!"

The unfairness of the accusation should have bothered me. It would have, ten minutes ago. Now I didn't even blink. For some reason, I wasn't angry anymore; instead, I felt empty, like someone had hollowed out my body and replaced my bones with dry wood, like I'd break if I moved too fast.

"She didn't kill Nick," Pritkin said, maintaining his temper although his glare could have powdered diamond. "She wasn't even there when it happened. And Richardson died in the fissure."

"So you say," Liam sneered. "Yet she survived."

"Barely."

"I don't understand why you threw everything away in support of her, but it may not be too late," Liam told him, suddenly earnest. "Help me bring her in and I'll vouch for you. We all will. You can say anything—that you were bewitched, that she and those vampires did something to you—and as long as she's out of the way, the Council will believe it. We need people like you now more than ever!"

"And the girl?" Pritkin demanded.

"She'll get a trial," Liam said, his face closing down.

"A trial she'll lose."

"It's one life! One life against the thousands who will die if we can't bring cohesion back to the Circle. You or I would gladly give our own lives in such a cause. If she's any kind of Pythia, can she do less?"

"You can't have it both ways," Pritkin said harshly. "By your reasoning, she's evil and must be destroyed before she can help our enemies, or she's innocent and must be destroyed to preserve the Circle. Either way, she dies."

"For the common good!"

"For the Circle's good. I'm not so sure that has much to do with what's good for everybody else. Not anymore."

"What did she do to you?" Liam asked, his voice soft with amazement. "You almost died defending the Circle on more than one occasion!"

"It was a different organization then."

"Nothing has changed! I know Marsden has been stirring up trouble, but—"

A spell came out of the night and dropped Liam to his knees. I looked around, confused, because Pritkin hadn't cast it. A tall African-American mage stepped forward as Liam toppled over. He had a buzz cut and enough muscles to give Marco a run for his money. "We don't have time for this," he said harshly, and waved a hand at me.

My power suddenly came rushing back, a steady hum running under my skin, through my bones, singing in my cells, *ready, ready, ready*. I pulled it around me like a familiar coat as the mage glowered at me. "Caleb, meet Cassie," Pritkin said dryly.

The mage didn't look to be in the mood for pleasantries. "We have no way to get them out, assuming there is anyone alive down there. But you do," he told me.

It had the flavor of a command more than a request, especially in his deep baritone. But at the moment, I wasn't feeling picky. I didn't really believe anyone had survived that, wards or no. But I had to know for sure. "I can take only two people with me," I said.

"Me and Pritkin," Caleb said, extending his hand. I eyed it unhappily. I'd already taken one mage's hand tonight, and look where that had got me.

Pritkin didn't say anything, letting me make the decision for once. Only there wasn't much of one to make. Whatever my feelings toward the Circle, right now, I needed the help. I took his hand. "Where to?" I asked Pritkin.

"How strong is your ward?"

"I think the ley line blew it out. Why?"

"That creates a problem," he said, glancing at the other mage.

"Don't look at me," Caleb said grimly. "The line all but fried me before I could get out of there, and what was left I expended shielding us from the debris. I'm done." There was a general round of agreement from the watchers. It looked like nobody had shields worth a damn.

"What difference does it make?" I demanded. The idea that there might actually be survivors had lodged in my head and was beating a frantic tattoo against my skull. I felt almost dizzy at the rapid shift of emotions—from disbelief to rage to numb horror to barely acknowledged hope—all in the space of maybe half an hour.

"We can't risk shifting in there without a ward," Pritkin said flatly. "MAGIC's shields may have held, but if not, we could find ourselves inside a landslide—"

"Then I'll shift us back out!"

"—or solid rock."

"We have to risk it!" Pritkin was usually the one pulling the crazy stunts. This was no time for him to learn caution.

"We can't." It sounded final.

"Watch me," I told him seriously.

"There is a difference between courage and foolhardiness! Dying yourself will not help—"

"And neither will standing here! Rafe deserves better than that from me. He'd give *me* better than that!"

Caleb looked confused. "Rafe?"

"Vampire," Pritkin said shortly.

"You'd risk your life for one of those things?" Caleb asked me, incredulous.

"Yeah. Too bad you don't have friends like that. But if they're all war mages, I can't say I'm surprised," I snapped.

"Miss Palmer." That was Pritkin, and since he was back to formal mode, I assumed he wasn't happy. Unfortunately for him, neither was I.

"I'm going with or without you. So which is it?"

He looked like he wanted to argue, but he couldn't stop me from going alone and he knew it. "Take us to the Senate chamber," he finally said. "It's on the lowest level and well-warded. If anything survived, it should have."

"Hold your breath," I told them. "If we shift into the middle of a mess, I'll get us out. Don't panic."

Caleb looked at Pritkin. "Did she just tell me not to panic?"

"She doesn't know you."

"Guess not."

I didn't bother to comment. I took a deep breath and shifted.

It was second nature now to fling myself outward, everything blurring around me as I streaked through insubstantial layers of stone, thought translating instantly to motion. It was less familiar to land in a vast mud pit. But that's where we ended up, in a suffocating ocean of muddy water, over my head deep and impossible to see or breathe through.

I was about to shift us back out before we could die an unfortunate and very moist death when the guys started swimming, taking me with them. A moment later, we surfaced with a splash and a gasp. The air was warm and full of dust and already going stale. Whatever method this place used for air circulation seemed to be off-line.

I floundered around, trying to free my hands from Pritkin's and Caleb's iron grips so I could wipe the mud out of my eyes. Even when I managed, it didn't help. There was absolutely no light, with the enormous iron chandeliers that usually light the Senate chamber either dark or missing. But at least I could breathe.

Until someone forced my head back underwater.

It was so unexpected that I sucked in a lungful of mud and choked while I was towed what felt like half the length of the chamber. My head finally broke the surface again, but I couldn't seem to get any air. Pritkin hit me on the back—hard—half a dozen times until I probably had bruises but, mercifully, also clear lungs. I clutched the edge of something solid and pondered the wonder of oxygen for a minute.

Light spun up and expanded from a sphere in Caleb's hand, allowing me to see a few yards into the gloom. Not that there was much *to* see. The Senate's main meeting hall was normally mostly bare, with a high ceiling that disappeared into shadow, leaving plenty of space below for the massive mahogany table that formed its only major piece of furniture. Except for today, when little was visible besides the undulating black ocean. And what I could finally identify as the Senate table, floating despite its weight and currently serving as our life raft.

A loud clanking noise suddenly came from overhead. It sounded like rusty machinery and reverberated harshly off the walls. Caleb held up the sphere and light glinted off the jagged metal tips of the chamber's chandeliers.

They were enormous, easily twelve feet across, with rows of barb-filled rings sitting one inside the other. I couldn't tell how many darts there were on each ring, but it looked like a lot. And every time a ring emptied, it dropped back to a lower tier, allowing a new one to cycle up into place. The sound had been the closest chandelier rotating a new set of lethal darts to bear on us.

I'd forgotten the tendency of the fixtures in the Senate chamber for launching iron spikes at intruders, mainly because they had never before viewed me as one. "Why are they shooting at us?" I demanded. As if they'd heard me, a barrage of foot-long projectiles tore loose from their moorings and came hurtling our way.

Our combined weight had pushed half of the table underwater, leaving the other half raised like a partial shield. But even the rock-hard mahogany didn't stop them all. My eyes crossed, taking in a particularly vicious-looking dart that had partially penetrated the wood, stopping barely an inch from my face. It had hit with enough force to push out finger-length shards ahead of the razor-sharp point, one of which brushed my cheek. Somebody let out a small, hiccupping scream.

"Be silent!" Pritkin hissed in my ear. "The wards are attracted to motion and sound."

Now he told me.

"The ley line breach confused them," Caleb whispered. "They're targeting anything that moves. Shift us into the corridor outside!"

I started to answer when there was a reverberating crack overhead. One of the darts that had missed us was sticking out of the wall, where its force had widened a fissure that had already been leaking water. What had been a spout was now a waterfall, and from the sound of things, it wasn't the only one. It looked like an underground stream had ruptured. Trust me to find a way to drown in the desert, I thought as a flood of icy water poured onto my head.

It was heavy enough to knock my grip free and send me falling back into the void. I reached out, desperate to find a handhold, and something brushed my wrist. Something living, but not human-warm.

I jerked back, the small hairs on my arm prickling at the ghostly touch. I got a vague glimpse of it—motion, something like eyes that glittered in the almost darkness, *teeth*.

Oh, shit.

Hands grabbed me roughly under the armpits and hauled me back to the surface. Where I quickly discovered that I'd drifted beyond the protective shadow of the table. Pritkin jerked me out of the way right before two darts plowed into the water, and we ducked back into place with a slither of legs and flailing arms.

I gripped his shoulder hard, scanning the area where I'd just been. But the only thing in sight was the light from Caleb's sphere reflecting off the ripples. "I think there's something in the water," I gasped.

"I'm more concerned about what's in the air!" Caleb snapped. "Get us the hell out of here!"

"And go where?" I demanded. "In case you've forgotten, there are wards in the corridors, too!" Dagger-edged sconces studded MAGIC's hallways every five feet. We wouldn't even make it to the stairs.

"Yes, but those don't work! We hadn't finished repairs from the last attack yet!" He meant the storming of the complex a month ago by a group of suicidal dark mages. For once, I was grateful to them.

I nodded in relief and grabbed his hand, but Pritkin pulled back when I reached for him. "It's your call," he told me seriously. "But we don't know what we'll find once we get out of here. It would be wise to conserve your energy if you plan to rescue anyone."

Caleb stared at him incredulously. "You actually think they made it out of here without being turned into shish kebabs? And even if they did, this place is more than half flooded—putting the corridors outside completely underwater!"

"Something that would not overly concern a vampire," Priktin said, meeting my eyes in understanding. Caleb was thinking about the disaster from a human perspective, but the people in this section of MAGIC hadn't been human in a long time. If they had survived the initial blast, they might actually be okay. Rafe might be okay. I felt a little light-headed suddenly.

"It looks like no easy way out, then," I said reluctantly.

"You can't be serious!" Caleb was looking at me like I'd lost my mind.

I bristled, because I wasn't any happier about this than he was. "I can only shift so many times in a day, and taking two people with me drains my strength pretty fast," I told him flatly. "Pritkin's right. If I exhaust myself now, I won't be able to help any survivors. Even assuming we find some."

"Then how do you suggest we get out of here?" he demanded, glaring at me. Like I'd come up with this idea instead of his buddy.

"You're war mages," I told him irritably. "You figure it out. Preferably before we drown."

"Yeah, you're a Pythia all right," he muttered.

"I'll check out the corridor," Pritkin offered, stripping off his heavy coat. "It might not be as bad as it looks." He took a deep breath and dove—leaving me alone with a war mage who, until a few minutes ago, had been doing his best to hunt me down. From his expression, I could tell that Caleb was thinking the same thing.

"I guess it's a compliment for one of us," I said a little nervously.

"Not really. If I kill you, how do I get out?" I stared at him, and he was expressionless for a drawn-taut moment. Then he sent me a brief flick of a smile. "John knows me."

Yeah, I thought darkly. He'd known Nick, too.

"What was that?" Caleb suddenly demanded, whipping his head around.

"What was what?"

He ducked the sphere underwater, but there was nothing to see but our legs churning up the mud. After a minute, he brought it back up, where it highlighted a scowling face. "I thought I felt some—" he began, and then his head disappeared.

I stared blankly at the spot where it should have been for a second before looking around frantically for a dart with a scalp. But there was nothing. Nothing except tiny ripples in the water.

I scanned the surface, but the only clue to his whereabouts was the ghostly glow of his sphere, sinking fast. Somehow I didn't think he'd suddenly decided to take a swim. And then a trio of darts thumped into the wall behind me, giving me something new to worry about. They almost hit a dark shape that had been crouched on a jut of rock, making it leap outward to avoid them. Of course, it jumped straight at me.

My arm jerked up and my knives met the creature halfway through its arc, slamming into it right before it slammed into me. I had a brief impression of hot, stinking breath and bloodstained jaws, and then it was on me. A body thick with fur and muscle knocked me out of the water and back onto the scored and pitted tabletop.

A guttural growl vibrated through my skull as a clawed foot slashed at the wood. It caught the bell of my sleeve, ripping it completely off. I rolled to the side just as a heavy head came crashing down, burying powerful jaws in the thick planks beside me.

My instinct was to run, but there was nowhere to go. Instead, I ended up with handfuls of wet, stinking fur as I fought to keep the slippery head against the table, where it could chew on wood instead of on me. But even partly trapped, it was strong and ferocious.

Claws raked my dress, and for once I was grateful for Augustine's exuberant use of fabric. The heavy, waterlogged folds kept my skin from getting shredded as badly as the material. Powerful legs scrabbled on the slick tabletop, trying to find purchase, while my knives stabbed it over and over, the little blades punching holes that splattered hot blood over my chest, arms and face.

Despite my efforts, the creature finally tore free of the wood by ripping out a large chunk of it. It turned with serpentine quickness, reared up on hind legs directly over me—and was stabbed in the back by a dart. The iron wedge exploded out of its midsection and over my head, soaking me in gore as it passed.

I slid back into the water, trying to stifle a scream. It was easier than usual, thanks to the bubble of panic that had lodged somewhere between my stomach and throat. My fingers tightened convulsively on the slab of wood while I gasped and choked and tried not to move. I really didn't want to end up like whatever had just tried to eat me.

A moment later, Caleb's head broke the surface. He still had the sphere clutched in his fist as he heaved and coughed and brought up what looked like a quart of muddy water. "You all right?" I asked when I could speak.

The light glinted off the drops beading his buzz cut, silver on black, and the dark trickle of blood sliding down his temple. "Better than it is."

"You killed it."

"Hope so." His smoker's growl was a little more prominent.

"Good," I said shakily. "What was it?"

"Don't know." His eyes focused on something just behind me. "You kill that?"

I looked at him blankly before following his gaze to where my knives had impaled something furry and scaly and really, really wrong to the tabletop not three feet away. I shrieked and jerked back, and the knives followed the motion, letting go of their prey to be reabsorbed by my bracelet. And untethered by anything, the gory body slid slowly off the tilted side of the table.

Caleb pushed it aside, giving the darts a target other than us. We crouched in the dark, hearing the steady thud of metal into meat, until Pritkin surfaced at my elbow a few moments later.

Pritkin popped up at my elbow a moment later. He gasped in a lungful of air before catching sight of the dark hulk of the creature floating a few yards off. "What is that?"

"The welcoming committee," Caleb said straight-faced. "What did you find?"

"The corridors are flooded, but the nearest staircase is clear from about halfway up. It's doable."

"If we make it that far," Caleb growled, glancing upward.

As if it had heard him, the chandelier finally stopped rotating. Without the scrape of metal on metal, the chamber was almost silent. The only noise came from the water lapping against the walls and splashing into the flood. And the even softer sounds of wretched sobbing.

Both men tensed and Caleb waved the light around, but of course he didn't see anything. "What is making that noise?" Pritkin demanded.

"Augustine's idea of a joke. He spelled my dress," I told him.

Pritkin sized me up for a moment. "Take it off."

"What?"

"I can use the charm on it to confuse the wards."

The arm that wasn't holding on to the table crossed protectively over my chest. "But . . . I'm not wearing anything underneath."

"Nothing?"

"Maybe panties." At least I thought I was. After the day I'd had, I wasn't really sure.

Pritkin pinched the bridge of his nose. "Would it help at all to remind you that I've seen it?"

"Once! A long time ago! And it was really, really dark!"

He started to say something and then seemed to catch himself. "Give me what your maidenly modesty can spare, then."

"Why do you need it again?"

"Oh, for— Give me the damn dress and I'll show you!" Before I could reply, he pulled out a knife, reached underwater and sliced off what felt like half the skirt.

"Why do these plans of yours always involve me getting

naked?!" I whispered viciously—to no one because he'd already gone.

In a minute, another row of darts tore loose with the earsplitting sound of shredding metal. They ignored us in favor of targeting Pritkin and the row of sobbing fabric he was sticking in cracks and crevasses along the wall. The material was fast turning into tatters as dart after dart hit it, fracturing the stone behind and letting in what could now literally be called a flood. Between the crying dress and the rushing water, the wards suddenly had plenty to shoot at besides us.

"Come on!" Caleb tugged me out of the protective shade of the table. "That charm won't last forever!"

We swam full out for the far wall, staying underwater as much as possible. The wards had rotated away from us to fire volley after volley in Pritkin's direction, their rusty clanging a cacophony in the enclosed space. I peered into the gloom every time we surfaced, desperately trying to see him, but the light was just too low. The most my eyes could pick out were brief flashes off multiple knifelike edges, as dozens of darts were flung through the air.

I was still looking when I swam into the wall. Caleb steadied me and then ducked underwater for a minute. "The door is just below us," he told me after surfacing. "John was right: the corridor is completely flooded. But the stairs are only about fifteen feet to the left." He started to dive again, but I caught his arm.

"John will be all right."

I stared at the hail of darts that were still being unleashed behind us. Chunks the size of boulders had been carved out of the wall where they hit, with a spiderweb of cracks radiating out from the larger ones. "How could anyone be all right in that?"

"Trust me—I know him."

"So do I," I said savagely. "That's what's worrying me!"

A crack echoed through the room, loud enough to momentarily drown out the wards. And the next second, a huge piece of the wall gave way, dropping almost whole into the flood like the calving of a glacier. It hit the water with the granddaddy of all belly flops. The resulting wave reached even us, slamming me back into Caleb.

"Don't move," he whispered as the nearest chandelier rotated our way, drawn by the disturbance of the water. It swiveled this way and that, sending darts slicing through the waves crashing all around us.

"We're going now," Caleb said in my ear. "Okay?"

I searched the dark one more time for any sign of Pritkin, but there was nothing. Damn it! I should never have left him!

"Cassie!"

"Okay." It came out more like a croak. I'd never felt so helpless.

That was the longest fifteen feet of my life. I ducked underwater, following the dim light of Caleb's sphere through the black rectangle of the doorway. And almost immediately I realized I had a problem. I'd planned just to follow Caleb, but although I knew Caleb was somewhere right up ahead, I couldn't see him. There was too much dirt and debris in the water, choking off what little light his sphere gave out and leaving the flooded corridor almost pitch-black.

I quickly lost all sense of direction, unable to find up or down in the dark, freezing water. Everything looked the same, and the burn in my lungs was making it hard to concentrate. My pulse pounded sickeningly at my temples, and a flood of cold ran through my limbs, turning them sluggish and slow to respond to my brain's frantic commands.

My grasping fingers finally found something that felt like a doorway and my foot scraped against a jagged surface that might have been stairs. I kicked against it instinctively but didn't go very far. The remains of my waterlogged outfit dragged me down as I tried to fight my way toward the dim undulation that I really hoped was the surface.

Then a hand wrapped in the front of my dress, threatening to strangle me, and with a kick and a heave, I broke into air. I grabbed the sleeves of a wet white shirt and stared at the man wearing it. For a second, everything went gray except his face. His eyes looked too green, too clear, with a diamond-sharp, surreal edge. It took me a moment to notice that his face was flushed and his eyes were bright as lightning. The lunatic had enjoyed himself.

"How the hell did you get here before me?" I demanded, gasping as much from relief as lack of air.

Pritkin shrugged. "I took the back door and came around."

"Pritkin. There *is* no back door."

"There is now. The projector punched a hole in the south corridor."

"Bit of a design flaw," Caleb rumbled.

"I don't think the wards were ever tested over a sustained period," Pritkin told him. "Something to keep in mind when we rebuild." He finally noticed my expression and frowned. "Are you all right?"

"Fine."

"You don't look fine."

"I'm trying to remember all the reasons you are indispensable and can't be killed slowly and painfully."

He ignored that and hauled me to my feet. I gathered up my tattered skirts, along with whatever dignity I'd managed to salvage. Then the three of us squelched up the stairs.

Chapter Eight

Caleb's sphere made little headway against the gloom and was soon covered in a thick layer of dust. It was like the one I felt clinging to my skin, gritty and all-encompassing, as if the place resented not being able to drown us and was trying to slowly bury us alive. It didn't have far to go.

The swath of destruction carved by the ley line hadn't reached down this far, but it looked like some of the tremors it caused had. There were cracks in the walls as big as my thumb and chunks missing from most of the steps. We picked a zigzag path up the solid parts to the top, only to find yet another dark-as-night corridor.

Pritkin took point while Caleb brought up the rear. The rooms in this section were mostly residential, including the palatial suite used by Mircea when he was in residence. We stepped through the doorway into his rooms, and it was suddenly difficult to tell that we were in an underground fortress in the middle of a crisis.

The walls were covered in drywall painted in tasteful, muted colors of wine and deep gold. They complemented the Italian marble floors, the gilt moldings and the hand-painted ceilings. Mircea was the Senate's chief diplomat, so his quarters took on the role of embassy. It was here, among the priceless antiques, Swarovski chandeliers and unknown paintings by the world's great masters, that he welcomed dignitaries, soothed ruffled feathers and struck deals.

Away from the main entrance, signs of the disaster were

more apparent. In places, the elegant Venetian plaster had erupted with raw red stone, the bones of the place peeking through the veneer. And everything was covered in a layer of fine red dust. I could taste the tang of it in the back of my mouth and feel it coating the inside of my nostrils. Even an overlooked spiderweb high in one corner was caked with it.

Pritkin found a couple of candelabras and some matches, giving us each a light source, and we split up to make the search go faster. The two mages concentrated on the common areas, while I went down the main hallway, opening bedrooms. Most were pristine except for the dust, their elegant furnishings untouched. But Mircea's private rooms were in more disarray.

The bed linens hung half off the large pedestal bed, and one pillow clung to the mattress in a silent battle of wills with gravity. The ornate wardrobe was open, but most of the clothes, like the priceless paintings on the walls, had been left behind. Yet there were only blank niches in the walls where Romanian folk art had recently stood.

Mircea's home away from home was beautiful, elegant and designed to impress. As a result, it said little about the man who lived here. Like the BBJ and the Armani wardrobe, it was what people expected to see. But I found it telling that his servants, when fleeing for their lives, had left the Sèvres and the Swarovski and had grabbed a collection of painted tin crucifixes and worthless wooden spoons.

It bothered me that, in their position, I wouldn't have known what to take. I stared around at the things they'd left, like an intricately carved set of jade figurines on a shelf, and realized that I'd have probably made all the wrong choices. I didn't know what were treasured memories and what were just decorations. Like I didn't know his hopes, his dreams or his fears, if he had any . . .

My heel caught in a puddle of silk by the bed. As I freed it, I found one personal item that had been overlooked in the rush: an old, beat-up book. The black leather cover was worn at the edges and the gilt lettering on the front had mostly faded, with only a few small specks left to gleam in the candlelight. But it was undoubtedly a photo album.

I glanced around, but the guys were nowhere in sight. I

knelt on the floor and opened the cover with slightly shaking hands. Mircea had the diplomat's ability to talk for hours without actually saying much, and what he did say was often suspect. I'd heard two versions—so far—about how he became a vampire, and still had no idea if either was true.

But photos didn't lie. At least, not as often as master vampires. And suddenly I was confronted with a whole album containing hundreds of photos of Mircea.

Only it didn't.

The photos had a theme, all right, but it wasn't him. On every page the same face stared out at me—that of a beautiful, dark-haired woman of approximately my age. She combined sloe-eyed sultriness with petite delicacy and would have stopped traffic in no makeup and wearing a muumuu. Only she preferred form-fitting clothes that showed off a trim, athletic figure.

One picture showed her eating at a café. She was wearing old-fashioned clothes—forties era, at a guess—consisting of a white short-sleeved suit and a striped scarf. She was waving a fork around and laughing at someone off camera. Her hair was glossy and sleek in a sassy bob that made a mockery of bad hair days. Her nose didn't turn up at the end, her cheekbones were sculpted, and if she had any freckles they didn't show. She could have been a model for an early issue of *Vogue*.

I stared at her, the album open on my knees, feeling strangely dizzy. I felt something else, too, something I couldn't quite define, but it heated my cheeks and burned in my stomach like acid. There were no photos of me in this room. Not one. But there was an entire album devoted to this mystery woman. Whoever she was, obviously she was important to Mircea.

More so than me.

Something hit the clear plastic protecting the image, rolled to the edge of the book and was absorbed by the cracked leather binding. I blinked away more somethings, vaguely appalled. This is stupid and petty, I told myself. With everything I had to worry about, here I was, preoccupied with who Mircea might be— God, I couldn't even think it. And that was even more stupid.

What had I believed, that he'd been some kind of monk for five hundred years? After seeing the way women regularly threw themselves at him? And I couldn't very well be jealous of events that had happened long before I was born, even if they did involve beautiful, sophisticated brunettes.

I looked down at a crinkling sound to see that my fist had balled around the page with the photograph, crushing the plastic and threatening to put permanent creases in the paper. Okay, maybe I could. All right, I very definitely could.

Mircea's sexual history was something I'd been able to put out of my mind, at least most of the time, because I hadn't known any of the people involved. At least, I hadn't thought so. Now I wondered.

He was closer than I'd like to the Chinese Consul, who had become fond of him while he was on a diplomatic mission to her court and who still sent him expensive presents every year. He'd also been pretty friendly with an icy blonde senator and a passionate raven-haired countess—and those were just the ones I knew about. The women had been pretty diverse in status, personality and background, but they had one thing in common: they were all heart-stoppingly beautiful. Like this woman.

I flipped to the back of the book and got another shock. The brunette turned up again, but this time, she was jogging through a park. And the earbud to an iPod trailed down across her left shoulder. I went back through the album and realized that the photos were in chronological order—old sepia images from maybe the nineteenth century giving way to early black and white, then to bold sixties-era color and finally to the modern day. And, except for superficial details, she looked the same in every photo. She was a vampire, ageless and eternally beautiful.

Just like Mircea.

I put the album down with shaking hands and told myself to get a grip. I was just really emotional right now, that was all. That's why I was feeling this way, like I wanted to gouge those pretty dark eyes out with my thumbs.

That was so very not me it was scary. I didn't get possessive about people, any people. I never had. And Mircea and I didn't have an exclusivity agreement, didn't have any agreement at all, in fact. He could see anyone he wanted.

Only for some reason it hadn't occurred to me that he might actually *be* seeing—might, in fact, be doing a hell of a lot more than just *seeing*—someone who made me look like one of Cinderella's ugly stepsisters.

With my thumbs.

"Find anything?" I turned to see Pritkin coming in the door. He glanced around without interest. Maybe he didn't realize whose room this was, or maybe he just didn't care. Mircea was only another vampire to him, and Pritkin had never been fond of those.

"No. Nothing." I didn't make any attempt to hide the book, and his eyes passed over it uninterestedly.

"Same here."

"Feels like a ghost town," Caleb murmured, joining us. I disagreed. Ghosts were livelier than this.

"They must have gotten out," Pritkin said. "Trust the vampires to have an escape route even in a supposedly impregnable fortress."

"But I doubt they stuck around to help anyone else," Caleb added, glancing at me. I didn't deny it; I doubted they had, either. "There may be people farther up. Let's go."

We were in the foyer, heading for the main entrance, when the crystals in the chandelier overhead started to chime. A blue and white vase that I really hoped wasn't Ming danced across the central table and crashed to the floor before I could grab it. The ground beneath my feet groaned and shuddered for a long moment, and I had to brace one hand against the wall to keep my balance.

"An *earthquake*?" I said in disbelief. "What's next? A tsunami?"

"It's probably the upper levels settling," Pritkin said, but he didn't look convinced. "We should hurry."

We exited into the corridor and Caleb started for a door near a set of steps cut into the rock and going up. "I wouldn't do that," I advised.

He paused, his hand on the doorknob. "Why not?" He gave me a suspicious look from under lowered brows, like he suspected me of assisting the vamps to hide some nefarious secret.

As if they needed my help.

"Those are Marlowe's rooms." Kit Marlowe, onetime

playwright, was now the Consul's chief spy. And in the paranoid Olympics, he took the gold. I was betting that even in a magical fortress surrounded by guards, he'd warded his rooms. And, knowing him, probably with something lethal.

Caleb took his hand away under the pretense of straightening his lapels. And didn't put it back. I guess he agreed with me.

The emergency lights were still working on the next level, casting a red stain over the old rocks. The passage at the top of the stairs turned a couple of times, passing shadowy rooms filled with strange equipment. Cables snaked underfoot, walls were lined with a lot of slimy things in jars, upended cages were everywhere and the overhead fluorescents flickered like horror movie lighting.

"Sigourney Weaver shows up and I'm out of here," I muttered, surprising a laugh out of Caleb.

"We already killed the alien," he reminded me.

"You sure about that?" Pritkin asked.

He was a little ahead of us, around a bend in the passage. We caught up with him to find that this level was also empty—of people. But there were plenty of other things prowling, flying and oozing around to make up for it. It looked like someone had been running a menagerie that the disaster had set loose. A very creepy menagerie, I decided after getting a close-up look at something pale pink and orange that was sliming its way out of a hole in a crate. A mass of jellylike similar creatures could be seen inside, waiting their turn. The pretty colors didn't help obscure the fact that it was frighteningly like a huge slug.

Only it had small, angry, coal-black eyes. Intelligent ones.

I scrambled back, fighting an urge to lose my dinner, while Caleb swore and pulled a gun. I caught his arm. "What are you doing?"

"What does it look like?" His brief good humor was completely gone.

"You can't just kill it."

"You didn't have that problem in the chamber!"

"We were being attacked in the chamber!"

"And now we know by what. Some perverted experiments your vampires were running!"

He took aim again, but I guess his powder must have been wet, because the gun didn't fire. He scowled, muttered a spell and tried again. This time, the gun worked fine, but I knocked his arm and the shot went wild.

The sound was enough to send a small stampede down the corridor, away from us. "I said, no killing!"

Caleb glared at me. "She's Pythia," Pritkin reminded him quickly.

"Not mine," Caleb said grimly.

"Then who is? Or do you intend to fight this war without one?"

The two stared at each other for a moment, and then Caleb swore. "We can't do this with those things jumping us at every turn!"

"They don't look too interested in attacking to me," I pointed out.

"And what about the ones that are?"

"We'll take care of them if and when we find them."

"And if these creatures find a way out of here? You want to let something as potentially lethal as the things we killed loose into the general population?"

"We're nine levels down! And these don't look too dangerous to me."

"Looks can be deceiving. We know nothing about their abilities, about why the vampires were breeding them," he argued stubbornly.

I watched as the slug thing started to ooze away from us. The underground streams would probably survive the pending implosion. What if the creature got into the water system? What if several did, and they started to multiply? There could be thousands within weeks.

"Most will die anyway," Pritkin pointed out quietly, "of starvation or drowning or by being crushed under a mountain of rock." He nodded to where a couple of sort-of birds were already feasting on something's remains, tearing off strips of flesh with their long black beaks. "Or at the claws of the larger predators. It's kinder this way."

I stared at the impromptu feast and felt my stomach roil. "Do what you have to," I finally said. "I'll be at the top of the stairs."

The sound of gunfire and the smell of smoke followed me

up. It was dark and silent at the top except for a faint blush of light from below. I sat down, wrapped my arms around my knees, leaned my head against the wall and tried not to think at all. Which was when a hand reached out from the dark and covered my mouth.

I was dragged kicking and fighting into a blacked-out room. A light flared—only a single candle—but in the dense dark it shone like a searchlight. It highlighted a small table cluttered with papers and the man sitting behind it. His curls were in disarray and his cashmere sweater was dirty and torn. But the bright brown eyes and quick smile were the same as ever. "Rafe!"

He stood and moved around the desk and I all but threw myself in his arms. I'd known he was probably okay, but some part of me hadn't believed it until now. My heart expanded in my chest at the sight of him, whole and unhurt, exhilaration flooding my veins like bright water.

"Look what I found prowling the corridors," Marlowe's voice said cheerfully from behind me. "She has two mages with her, Pritkin and one I don't know."

"I assume they are the cause of the gunshots?" Rafe asked, smoothing my tangled hair.

"They're doing mercy killings of the experiments," Marlowe said, sounding amused.

"Now?"

"Why not now?" I asked.

"Because the wards will fail in fifty-three minutes," Marlowe answered, "rather taking care of the problem." The ground rumbled under our feet again as if to underscore his words.

"Then why are you two still here? We haven't found any bodies, so I'm guessing there's a way out."

"There are several," Rafe agreed, glancing at Marlowe.

I turned to find the Senate's spymaster regarding me thoughtfully. The candlelight gleamed off the small hoop in his left ear and leapt in his dark eyes. I knew that look; I'd been getting it a lot lately. It usually meant, *I wonder if she's actually stupid enough to fall for this?* And usually, the answer was yes.

"I'm going to hate this, aren't I?" I asked, resigned.

"Perhaps not." Marlowe tapped the roll of papers on the

desk, which I now realized was a schematic, presumably of MAGIC. "You are here on a rescue attempt?"

"Yeah. Only, so far, we haven't found anyone to rescue."

"Most of those who survived the blast have already been evacuated. However, one area remains populated—the mages' holding cells."

"The prisoners are still here? Why?"

"A cave-in," Rafe said. "For security reasons, there is only one way into the cells, and the wards failed in that section." One long finger traced a line on the map two levels up from our position. "It cut them off from any hope of rescue."

"We went over the schematics and questioned the mages, but there's no convenient back door," Marlowe added. "And the cave-in is too extensive for us to clear in the time we have. Almost the entire length of the passageway was affected."

I blinked at him. "I must have heard wrong. You remained behind to rescue *humans*?"

He grinned behind his goatee. "Well, one, anyway."

"What about the others?"

He shrugged. "You can rescue them, too, if you like."

"Oh, thank you! Now tell me what this is really about."

"The answer to a prayer," he said piously.

"You pray?"

"Naturally," he said innocently. "Of course, I didn't say to what."

"Stop teasing her, Kit," Rafe reproached. He looked at me. "If we are to rescue anyone, we must hurry."

I decided I could get the story out of Rafe later. "It's not that simple," I told them. "Spatial shifting doesn't work the same as time travel; my power doesn't give me a preview. Without knowing where I'm going, I could end up inside a wall or, in this case, a bunch of rock."

"It is thirty meters to the area we believe to be clear," Marlowe told me.

"You *believe*?"

"The wards are reporting that area as safe. However . . ."

"However, what?"

"They may not be completely reliable. Not with this level of damage."

I stared at him. "*Not completely reliable* means I could

shift into the middle of a rockfall, Marlowe! No guesses—this is going to be hard enough as it is. I have to know!"

He just looked at me, but Rafe's eyes slid to the right to an area still swathed in utter darkness. A hissing sigh came out of the gloom, and a moment later, the Consul appeared so suddenly that it was almost as if she'd shifted in. I knew better—she'd probably been there all the time, but she'd been so still I hadn't noticed her. And considering that she was dressed in her everyday outfit of live, writhing snakes, it was a good trick.

Ancient, kohl-rimmed eyes sized me up, and as usual, they didn't look as if they liked what they saw. "I will tell you *exactly*, Pythia," she informed me. "And then you will do as we have bid."

It wasn't a request. She swept regally out the door and Rafe, Marlowe and I followed. Rafe went downstairs to round up Pritkin and Caleb, while Marlowe and I ran up two flights after the Consul.

The dust became thicker as we ascended, and small siftings of sand were starting to trickle down the walls every time there was a mini-quake. "What happens when the wards go?" I asked as we reached a tumbled mass of stone and dirt at the top of the second flight of steps.

"The levels above this one have solidified into a solid mass," Marlowe told me. "Without the support of the wards, their weight will crush anything below it."

"So, no pressure, then." I stared at the passageway to the left, which, as Marlowe had said, was totally blocked. Red sandstone from the lower levels had mixed with deep yellow from the upper, forming a jumbled mass that didn't appear to have even a small gap at the top. It was like the corridor had been reabsorbed by the rocks around it.

"We believe that it is blocked almost to the cells themselves, which have an independent ward system for added security," Marlowe told me quickly.

"I need more than a good guess," I reminded him.

"You shall have it," he said, steering me back down a few steps.

We both looked up at the Consul, who remained at the top. "You never saw this," she ordered.

"Saw what?" I asked, bewildered. She was just standing

there, a slim figure who, I suddenly realized, was only about my height. Funny; she'd always seemed taller.

Marlowe's arm curved around my waist, moving me back even farther right as there was an abrupt burst of motion. Suddenly there were snakes everywhere—a thick mass of black, squirming shapes that boiled up around the Consul's feet and legs. They swarmed up her body, twined around her neck, flowed over her face and twisted into her hair. A particularly fat one forced its way past her lips and started down her throat, distending the flesh on either side of her neck as it undulated.

"Marlowe! Do something!" I cried, horrified.

He didn't say anything, but his grip tightened as more snakes appeared and began to cleave her flesh, their black bodies sheathed in red as they forced their way inside her. I could see them moving in writhing patterns under her skin, the small ones pulsing like overfilled veins, larger ones distending her form in ghastly ways as they tunneled inside, seeming determined to consume her. There was a sound like a ripe fruit bursting, and suddenly there was no woman at all. Only a corridor filled with slick, gleaming creatures writhing in a puddle of bloody goo.

"Oh, God!" I stumbled backward and would have fallen without Marlowe's arm around my waist. I stood transfixed by shock and revulsion as the truth slowly dawned. The Consul was still there; she'd just changed form.

The snakes found holes in the rockfall through which a human could never have fit. We watched them wriggle away, slipping into the earth as easily as water, until they had all disappeared. Then Marlowe slowly lowered me into a seated position.

"Are you going to be sick?"

I shook my head. I was too freaked out to be sick. "I'd heard stories. . . ."

He sat on the step next to me, facing the darkness below, and stretched his legs comfortably out in front of him. "About us turning into mist or wolves or bats?"

"Yes. But I didn't believe. . . . I thought they were myths."

"For the most part, they are. There are very few of us who live long enough to acquire the sort of power needed for bodily transformation." His voice was admiring, as if the Consul had done a particularly nifty parlor trick. "I've heard stories that Parendra—the Consul's Indian counterpart—can do it, too. They say he becomes a cobra."

I didn't say anything. I was too busy trying to swallow the lump that had risen in my throat. It felt like I might be sick after all, and then I wondered how the Consul would take that, if she'd be offended when she got back, all hundred pieces of her. . . .

I swallowed the lump back down.

"It can be a little . . . disturbing . . . the first time you witness it," Marlowe said, glancing at me. "I recall being somewhat taken aback myself."

Taken aback. Yeah. That covered it.

We sat there for a few moments while precious seconds ticked away. And then she was back. Dozens of dusty, scaly bodies wriggled their way out of gaps in the rockfall and fell onto the sticky floor. I blinked, and the Consul was the Consul again. She staggered over to the far wall and stood there, trembling slightly, looking more shaken than I'd ever seen her. Marlowe started toward her side, but she waved him back.

"It is blocked for thirty-two and one-half meters," she told me, sounding perfectly composed. "All the way to the mages' holding cells. Their wards are all that is keeping this level intact, and they will not last much longer." She looked at Marlowe. "You will accompany the Pythia on her errand."

I shook my head. "The more people I take with me, the faster my power is drained." And it was pretty low already.

"And the more desperate men become, the less clearly they think," Marlowe responded. "These cells are among the most secure in the Circle's control. As a result, they house the most dangerous criminals. You cannot go alone."

I wasn't sure I could go anyway. The idea of shifting into a place I'd never seen was making me feel a little faint, not to mention that I wasn't entirely clear on exactly how far a meter was. "So, it's about thirty yards, right?" I said nervously.

Marlowe sighed. "A little over thirty-five. But perhaps you should add one to be safe."

Right. Like anything about this was safe. But it was either try or accept defeat and go home now. And we were running out of time.

The ground shook again, longer and more violently than before, throwing me to my knees. The vibrations ran through my skin into my bones, doing weird things to my balance even this close to the ground. And then a crack opened up right in front of us, exposing jagged, striated rock, with sand pouring over the edge like water.

Marlowe snatched me back as the floor beneath us completely disintegrated. Vamps don't fly, but he moved fast enough that it almost felt that way. The next thing I knew, we were down to the curve in the stairs, choking on a billowing cloud of dust.

"Go now!" the Consul ordered. I hadn't seen her move, but she was somehow beside us. I didn't wait to see how much more ground we were about to lose, just tightened my grip on Marlowe's shoulders and shifted.

We landed in another world—cold, sterile and dust-free, with sputtering lights and gray concrete walls. "This way," Marlowe said, pulling me down a corridor.

We passed a long row of cells, most of which had an occupant. I quickly realized that, unlike in human jails, the people incarcerated here weren't conscious. They were frozen in some form of stasis, leaning against the walls of their three-foot-deep cells like department store mannequins, staring outward with expressions ranging from startled to angry to defiant.

I stared back at them in mounting concern. Ten, fifteen, twenty—and this was only one half of one corridor. There was likely at least this many in the other direction, and probably more than one passageway. . . .

It was simply impossible. I could feel it in my bones, like the jerking pulse of my own heart. There was simply no way could I shift so many. Even if I'd been well-rested, I could have made only four or five trips, taking out two at a time. As things stood, I'd be lucky to rescue the man the vamps seemed so interested in and still get the rest of my own party out.

We stopped in front of a cell containing a middle-aged man with frizzy brown hair. Marlowe worked to get the ward on his door to release while I glanced at the cells on either side of him. One contained a red-haired woman with a sly, calculating look on her face. The other held another middle-aged man who was losing the fight with male-pattern baldness, despite there being charms for that sort of thing. Maybe he'd been too proud to use them—his expression was certainly haughty enough—or possibly the Circle didn't allow such vanities in its cells.

Neither of them looked particularly sympathetic, but the thought of what was about to happen to them sent cold chills across my skin nonetheless. This was my doing. Not my fault—I hadn't told Richardson to betray us, hadn't thrown the spell that caused this. But if I'd left that meeting when Pritkin had warned me, none of this would have happened. His voice came back to me suddenly: *"They'll die of starvation or drowning or by being crushed under a mountain of rock."* I looked into the man's face and shuddered.

A ward snapped, the buzz ringing in my bones like a struck tuning fork, and the frizzy-haired man tumbled bonelessly into Marlowe's arms. "How many can you take?" Marlowe asked me.

"I . . . not this many," I said, admitting the obvious.

"Tell me which ones."

"Which ones?" I stared at him. "You're asking me to choose who lives and who dies."

"Someone has to do it," he said with a shrug, hoisting the man onto his shoulder. "And the Senate has no stake here. We have the one we want."

I looked at the red-haired woman again. She had gray eyes that, in the flickering light, seemed almost conscious, almost aware. We stared at each other, her stiff and lifeless as a doll, me as wooden as a carved statue. In a few more minutes, she'd be dead. Or I'd take her and the rest would die. Like the human servants the vampires had housed upstairs, like anyone who had happened to be on the upper levels. It seemed so horribly random.

"There has to be a way," I said desperately.

"A way to do what?" Marlowe asked, his brow knitting.

"To rescue them. All of them. We can't just leave them here!"

Marlowe stared at me blankly. "Yes. We can. In approximately forty minutes this entire level will collapse and in the process take out those below it. Your compassion is admirable, but if we don't leave soon, none of us will get out of here. And I, for one, would miss me."

"And I'm sure a lot of these people would be missed, Marlowe!"

The light directly above us took that moment to blow out, raining plastic and glass onto the corridor floor and throwing Marlowe's face into shadow. The darker atmosphere accentuated the harsh planes of his face, making them visible behind the jovial mask. For a moment, he looked as dangerous as everyone always said he was.

"If there was a way to save them, we would do it. But there isn't," he said flatly. "And keep in mind where we are. For all you know, these people deserve their fate."

My gut clenched, my usual deny-repress-ignore method for dealing with uncomfortable facts suddenly not working so great. I looked up and down the corridor at the faces, young and old, hard and soft. They had won the Circle's enmity, but so had I. If Richardson had had his way, I'd be in one of these cells, too. They were no different from me, except that they were about to die. Condemned because I'd made a stupid mistake.

Chapter Nine

Green light from inside one of the cells dyed my hands an eerie, ill color. I pressed them tight until they ached, staring around at dozens of faces. The temptation to finally use my power was almost overwhelming. I'd been thinking about it, had it in the back of my mind ever since I saw that burnt, dead landscape, the milling group of shell-shocked mages, the empty space where MAGIC should have been. Because Marlowe was wrong—I *could* do this.

I just didn't know if I should.

"Cassie, the mouth of the nearest escape tunnel is ten minutes from here, and it is a further ten beyond that to safety," Marlowe said. "Time is not our ally."

I felt a hysterical laugh building in my throat but tamped it back down. "Yeah, well, that's the question of the day, isn't it?"

A small frown creased his forehead. "Cassie—"

"I need a minute, Marlowe."

"To do what?"

"I don't know yet!"

This was one of those times when I really lusted after that nonexistent training. In the last month, I'd sort of come to terms with the fact that I was time's janitor, there to clean up the messes left by other people's attempts to play god. That wasn't what had been keeping me up nights. This was. The idea that, sooner or later, I was going to run across a situation where the person wanting to change time would be me.

I could go back, make sure I missed that meeting, prevent all of this so easily. There would be no destruction of MAGIC, no loss of life. . . . It seemed almost too easy. And that was what scared me. I'd changed one small thing before and almost killed Mircea. What would changing something this big do? I didn't know, and that terrified me.

Agnes had said not to mess about with time, that it almost always caused more problems than it solved. But she'd also said that the reason the Pythia was a clairvoyant was because we could look into the future and see the outcome of our actions. She'd said to trust my gift. But that was just it—I'd never trusted it.

My whole life, it had shown me nothing but bad news, had been a source of nightmares instead of daydreams. One of the few things I'd liked about becoming Pythia was the fact that my visions had tapered off. Instead of one every two or three days, weeks had passed with nothing. And now I suddenly found myself in a situation in which lives depended on that despised gift.

I really hoped Agnes had been right.

"I'm going to try something," I told Marlowe. "It'll only take a minute."

"You've already had a minute."

"And now I'm taking another one!"

I closed my eyes and tried to concentrate. I could practically feel the disapproval coming off him in waves, but he didn't say anything. And after a few seconds, I calmed down enough to make the attempt. Only I wasn't sure how.

I'd struggled with my talent all my life, but mostly to repress it. Only rarely had I deliberately tried to see things, and most of those efforts had been failures. And now I was asking the impossible, to see a potential future in place of the real one. I didn't really expect it to work.

But it did.

I picked my way over blackened rubble to the entrance of Dante's—or what was left of it. The buildings had been bisected by a line of destruction, cracked open like a broken tooth. A wash of dirt had collected in the carved letters over the main doors, which now opened onto nothing.

Only part of one tower remained, ruined rooms cut open and exposed to the elements. Water-stained, faded furniture leaked over the sides and a few tattered curtains still shifted in the breeze. The rest was a blackened shell, with only a faux stalagmite sticking up here and there, like burnt and wrinkled fingers pointing at the sky.

I crawled through a door half obscured by rubble to a floor knee-deep in windblown debris. It had been part of the lobby, although it was only possible to tell by the location and overall shape. The bridge was gone, as was the Styx, the reservation desk and the employees' dressing rooms. The lobby bar was still there, a jumble of overturned tables, broken bottles and a slanting drift of sand from two missing windows. It was also home to a chattering colony of rats. I quickly backed out again.

I sat down abruptly in the shadow of the remaining tower, sending up a little cloud of dust. The sun was glaringly hot through the missing roof, and it was the only shade available. But it came at a price.

Every time I looked up, I saw some new horror: a human rib cage, yellowed with age, housing a family of foxes; random bones, several with teeth marks on them where some long-dead animal had feasted; and a crumpled Dante's uniform behind the desiccated remains of a potted palm. Where once there had been constant life and bustling activity, there was suddenly only dust and decay, everything brown and withered and so very still.

The vision shattered, the dead world spinning backward at a dizzying pace. I looked up to see Marlowe kneeling beside me. I was on the floor, although I couldn't remember how I got there. "What is it?" he asked urgently. "What did you see?"

"I'm not sure."

Agnes had been partially right—my power was trying to tell me something. I just didn't know what. MAGIC had been destroyed, not Dante's. And even if the breach had taken place in Vegas, a major casino wouldn't just have been left there like that, with no signs of attempted repair or even demolition. None of this made any sense.

But one thing was clear: I'd asked my power to show me what would happen if I changed time. I didn't understand the message, but the general gist hadn't seemed positive. And without some major confirmation, I didn't dare meddle with anything.

"Can you describe it?" Marlowe asked, helping me to my feet. When I looked into his face, I saw only concern. The frightening glimpse behind the mask was gone, and the kind, genial man I'd always known was back.

Not that that meant anything.

"It . . . was a jumble. It happens like that sometimes." I couldn't change time, but I could use the time I had. I could do a lot with forty minutes, if I had help. But I wouldn't get it from Marlowe. The Senate wasn't likely to risk a useful tool to help a bunch of convicts.

"I think you were right," I said. "We need to get out of here."

Marlowe hoisted his prisoner like a sack of potatoes and took my hand. I shifted us back only to find Rafe, Pritkin and Caleb crowding the small stairwell. "What *is* this?" Caleb demanded, catching sight of Marlowe's burden. His hand dropped to his weapon belt.

"A rescue," I said, grabbing Pritkin's shoulder. "The cells are full and the passage is blocked. Any ideas?"

"Yes."

"I was hoping you'd say that," I said, and shifted.

We landed in the middle of a tremor and fell to our knees. The corridor shook, setting the industrial pendants overhead swinging and popping a block out of the wall like a shotgun shell. It exploded against one of the cells on the opposite side of the corridor. It didn't faze the ward, but it peppered us with shards like minuscule hailstones and scattered gray dust over the floor. I closed my eyes and resisted the urge to curl into a ball and put my hands over my head.

When I looked again, Pritkin was regarding the exploded block with a scowl. "We don't have much time," I told him, getting back to my feet. "Marlowe said it's a twenty-minute hike to the surface from here."

"I know. Raphael showed us the schematics. Caleb is working on a faster alternative." But he continued to kneel there, scowling fiercely.

"Pritkin! Come on! What are you waiting for?"

"Inspiration," he said, gesturing at the cells. "It's worse than I thought. If the outer wards had held, the walls would be stable. But they're buckling under the weight from above. That means that the only thing keeping this place intact are the inner wards."

"The inner wards?"

"The ones on the cells."

I looked at the row of prisoners and my jaw dropped. "But . . . how are we going to get everyone out? If we disable the wards—"

"Then the weight from above will crush us all," he finished grimly. "And once they go down, they aren't going back up again. Not with this kind of damage."

"Crap."

"Exactly." He stared at a cell for a few seconds. "If we can preserve the wards on at least half the cells, it should buy us enough time to get away."

"Get away how? Because I can't shift out this many!"

He glanced at me as if surprised that I'd be worried by a little thing like that. "I can get them out as long as enough wards remain to keep the roof up."

His tone made it sound like getting through thirty-five yards of rockfall in roughly that many minutes was no big deal. I opened my mouth to ask for specifics and then realized we didn't have time. Besides, if Pritkin said he had a plan, then he did, and it would probably work. But that didn't mean I had to like it. "You're talking about leaving half these people to die."

"Not necessarily." His gaze turned considering. "You could shift in."

It took me a second to get it. "I could bypass the wards, and bring the people out with me!"

"If you can shift that precisely. There's not much room for error."

I glanced at the nearest cell, which held a large, hairy, tattooed man in a tank top. There was very little extra space that I could see around him. But in the next cell was a slim woman, and between her and the ward there was maybe two feet. "I can try," I agreed.

I shifted past the ward and inside the woman's cell. It was a tight fit, and there was some sort of energy field that wrapped around my limbs like a blanket, trying to paralyze me. I didn't give it time, just grabbed her wrist and shifted out again.

"How much energy did that cost you?" Pritkin asked, catching her before she could collapse.

"Not much. But I won't fit in all the cells."

"Do the best you can," he told me, glancing up at the swaying light fixtures. The place was becoming rapidly more unstable. Every moment we stayed upped the chances of our getting killed by falling debris before the place could crush us to death. "And make sure you keep back enough energy to get yourself out of here, if this goes wrong."

"Sure, because it's not like any of this was my fault," I said sarcastically.

He grabbed my arm hard enough to hurt. "I mean it."

I blinked at him, taking in the tense set of his jaw, the tight press of his mouth and the more-than-slightly-maniacal gleam in his eyes. I'd never tell Pritkin this, but there were times when he really reminded me of a vamp. He had the same way of flipping into the scariest person in history, and then flipping right back out and never noticing the difference.

"Okay," I said meekly.

He nodded curtly and moved to the cell with the tattooed man. He started on the wards and I went to work avoiding them. The tiny hops, only a few feet at a time, didn't take much energy, but there were a lot of cells. And no matter what I'd promised Pritkin, I couldn't look into people's faces and tell them, *Hey, sorry you have to die, but I'm getting really tired.*

By the time I reached the end of the row, I was soaked in perspiration, my skin was a sickly white and my hands were shaking violently. I leaned against the wall and watched Pritkin release another person the old-fashioned way. Together, we'd freed about thirty people, most of whom were lolling drunkenly against walls or sprawled unconscious on the floor.

Pritkin glanced at me and frowned. "Take a break," he said curtly.

"How? We aren't even halfway yet." And I hadn't seen what was on the next corridor.

Pritkin's eyes moved from me to the cells to the half-unconscious young man who had just fallen into his arms. He had wavy black hair pulled into a short ponytail, pale skin and an athlete's body. He looked to be around thirty. Pritkin propped him against the wall and shook him. The young man stirred, blinked his eyes open and looked up groggily. Just in time to get slapped hard across the face.

"What are you doing?!"

"Bringing him around. Some of the prisoners are war mages—or used to be. They can help open the cells."

"What are war mages doing in here?"

"The current administration has a habit of locking away those who get too vocal against its policies," he said shortly.

Two more blocks burst from the wall before I could comment. The once orderly pattern was starting to look like a toddler with missing teeth. "There's another cell block beyond this one," Pritkin said. "Although with any luck, it isn't fully occupied. Can you finish here?"

I nodded and he slipped around the corner. I stumbled down the corridor and knelt beside the mage. "Wake up! We need your help!"

He looked up at me with bleary eyes. They were a weird color, almost no-color, like rocks viewed through river water. I took another look at the number of cells remaining and then pulled my arm back and slapped him as hard as I could.

"I'm awake!" he said heatedly, his eyes sharpening up fast. "What's happening?"

"A ley line ruptured, destroying most of MAGIC. We're trying to get everyone out, but a cave-in cut off the passageway from the prison wing. We need you to help release the rest of the prisoners while we look for a way out!"

"There isn't one," he said, sitting up with his hands on his head, like a hangover victim. "It's a prison. It's supposed to keep people in."

"If you want to live, you'll help us think of one," I said grimly.

"The Circle will rescue us."

"The Circle evacuated an hour ago!"

"I don't think so," he told me nastily. "We're war mages. We don't simply abandon our colleagues."

"Then what are you doing in here?'

He glared at me. "That's none of your concern! The point is that you're wrong."

"You'll figure out otherwise in about twenty-five minutes," I said. "But it'll be a little late."

"Fuck that." The red-haired woman I'd noticed earlier had come around. She crossed to the other side of the corridor and started working on the ward imprisoning a tall Asian woman. "I'm not dying today."

The corridor shook again, and the war mage gave a start. He noticed the missing blocks, and for some reason, they seemed to shake him. "The external wards are down. Why?"

"Because they're being crushed from above by a few thousand tons of rock!"

The older balding man had slipped to one side and was trying to pull himself up on shaky arms, but they kept collapsing. "Are you okay?" I asked.

"I'll be all righ'," he slurred. "'N a minute."

"The longer you're in stasis, the worse it gets," the redhead told me as her friend collapsed into her arms. "What's the date?"

I told her and she nodded with no visible reaction, but the war mage gripped my arm. "You're lying!"

"Yeah, because that's what I feel like doing when a mountain is about to drop on my head!" I told him, exasperated. "Lie about trivialities!"

"It isn't trivial. If you're telling the truth, I've been in here for over six months!"

"And you're going to die in here if you don't move your war mage ass," the redhead told him. The corridor was shaking pretty much continually now, the situation deteriorating every second. It seemed to do more than her words to convince him, and he staggered to his feet.

The balding man was also up, although he looked like death—gray faced and slack-jawed. But he stumbled over to a cell and started working on it. And the Asian woman was already on her feet and working furiously beside the redhead.

"If the way is blocked, how did you get in?" the war mage demanded, starting on a nearby cell.

"I'm Pythia."

He blinked, taking in my damp, ragged outfit—now liberally smeared with dust—and my frazzled hair. "What happened to Lady Phemonoe?"

"The same thing that's about to happen to us! Minus the crushing thing. Does it matter?"

"No, no." He looked confused. "I apologize, Lady. I didn't realize who you were. Peter Tremaine, at your service." And he actually bowed.

I stared at him. A courteous war mage. The world really was coming to an end.

And then Pritkin ran back around the corner followed by half a dozen groggy people. He glanced at the cells that still had to be emptied. "You aren't done yet?" he demanded.

The world righted itself.

"Commander!" Tremaine came to a pretty good approximation of attention, considering that he was still swaying on his feet. "We are proceeding apace with the extrication, sir!"

I blinked at him and then looked at Pritkin. "Commander?"

"Later. Get the rest of them out!"

"We'll be done in a minute," I told him. Half of the freed prisoners were now lucid and working on the cells.

"We don't have a minute!"

"Find a way to get us out of here and leave the prisoners to me!" I said, exasperated.

"The prisoners *are* the way out." He gazed up at the ceiling for a moment, where half of the wildly swinging lights had now gone dark, and then his gaze shifted to the floor. "The upper levels are gone; we'll have to go lower. And to do that, I'm going to need magic users—strong ones."

"And then what?"

"And then we blast a hole through the floor. With the outer wards down, the only thing standing between us and the next level is a ton or so of rock."

"And you can move that much in the next few minutes?"

"I can move that much in the next few seconds, with the right people."

"Point them out to me." We went down the corridor, pausing at each cell, Pritkin muttering under his breath about this one or that one. I got the impression from a few of his comments that most of the people I was releasing weren't in Tremaine's category. Pritkin was looking for power, not politics or moral persuasion. I only hoped he could control them.

"That should do it," he finally said as I shifted out with the last one. Which was good, because I was about to have to tell him that no way could I do even one more jump. I was having trouble just focusing my eyes. Fortunately, Pritkin had something else to worry about. "We can't do this and shield all of you as well," he said.

"Clear this hallway and get everyone around the corner," I told Tremaine, who jumped to obey. Damn, I could get used to this.

A couple minutes later, we were ready to make the attempt. I was crouched around the corner with most of the prisoners, while Pritkin's crew positioned themselves at the end of the first passage. I'd assumed he was going to do a countdown or give some kind of warning, but I'd barely gotten into place when a massive explosion rocked the floor beneath our feet and brought half the ceiling tiles down on our heads. Somebody screamed and someone else cursed and I knew this was the end.

Only it wasn't.

The rocks behind the ceiling tiles remained in place, the walls continued to bow but not break and there wasn't even that much dust in the air. I peered cautiously around the corner, leaving sweat-smudged fingerprints on the concrete, expecting the worst. What I saw instead was a huge hole in the once solid floor.

Pritkin hopped up out of the hole, covered in red dust like an Indian in war paint. "Again," he ordered. I drew my head back just as another huge explosion rent the air.

The reverberations from it hadn't even worn away when a mass yell came from his group. "We're through!" I heard someone say, and then I was hugging the wall to keep from being trampled as the crowd surged forward.

"Cassie!" Pritkin's arm found my wrist and jerked me around the corner. "Hurry up! Even if Caleb succeeded, we're running out of time!"

"Exactly what is he trying to do?" I asked, but didn't get an answer.

Everyone was shoving and jostling, and those getting stepped on were screaming. Some of the tougher crowd were literally running over the older and weaker prisoners in their way. And that was a problem for more than one reason. Because the hole the mages had cut was big enough for only two, maybe three people at a time. And a logjam caused by line jumpers could block the whole thing.

Pritkin pulled a gun and fired a couple of shots at the remaining ceiling. "In order," he barked.

Most people stopped and looked up, the terror fading from their eyes slightly at the sight of someone taking charge. But a big guy in the middle of the line wasn't so docile. He had a red ponytail and beard stubble that almost matched his florid face.

"I helped cut that thing!" he told Pritkin. "I'm not waiting in line to see if I live long enough to use it!"

"Don't," Pritkin warned him. The man's response was to throw a slighter man out of his way and start pushing forward, sending the crowd back into panic mode. And Pritkin shot him.

I didn't even realize what had happened for a few seconds. Until the man stumbled and fell to one knee, a bright spot of color appearing on the tail of the white T-shirt he was wearing. Then he slowly toppled over onto his side.

"I said, in order," Pritkin repeated calmly. The crowd quickly rearranged itself into a nice, straight line.

I stared at the fallen man, stunned. No one tried to help him, and a few people even stepped over him so as to not lose their place in line. I started to move forward, but a heavy hand fell on the nape of my neck.

"Shift out of here," Pritkin told me. "Now."

"I—I don't know that I can make it quite that far," I admitted. Unless the surface was a couple feet away.

Pritkin swore and jerked his head at Tremaine, who was already on his way toward us through the crowd. "Take her to the front of the line," Pritkin told him, handing him a weapon. "Get her out of here. Shoot anyone who tries to stop you."

"What?" I pushed a matted clump of hair out of my eyes. "Don't be ridiculous. I'm not going without—"

"I could stay," Tremaine offered quietly.

"Did you not hear me, mage?" Pritkin's voice didn't get any higher, but Tremaine snapped back to attention.

"Yes, sir!" His hand clapped onto my shoulder and Pritkin let go.

I caught my crazy partner's arm. "What do you think you're doing?"

Pritkin hadn't met my gaze since he'd hauled me out from around the corner, but he did now. His eyes looked strange, but maybe it was the lighting. "You're one of the most adaptable people I've ever met. You'll find your balance," he told me apropos of absolutely nothing. I was starting to think he'd been hit in the head by a rock.

"Pritkin! What the hell?"

He didn't answer, or if he did, I didn't hear him. Because Tremaine was already pulling me through the crowd, gun in hand. No one tried to stop us.

"I'm not going!" I said as we reached the gaping pit in the floor. With its red, jagged rocks next to the pale concrete, it looked like a hungry mouth.

"The commander said—"

"I don't care what the commander said!" I told him furiously. "I'm Pythia. Are you sworn to my service or not?"

Tremaine looked torn. War mages were required to swear an oath to obey the reigning Pythia. Of course, since the Circle didn't recognize me as legitimate, that didn't actually apply in my case. But he was in no position to know that. He pulled me aside and motioned for the people behind us to go ahead. Another three prisoners were swallowed up as he showed me his wrist.

"The time," Tremaine hissed in my ear. I blinked at the dial of his watch. We had fourteen minutes before the wards on this level failed entirely.

I looked back at the line of remaining prisoners and did a few swift calculations. "We can do it. There should be enough time."

"To get off this level, yes. But to get away?" His face remained impassive; I suppose to avoid panicking the crowd. But his eyes were anything but calm. "Everyone isn't going to make it."

"But ... Pritkin—"

"The commander is staying behind to control the crowd. Otherwise, no one would get out."

I looked up and met Pritkin's eyes. He was watching me

narrowly, and I knew that expression. It meant he was about two seconds from coming over, grabbing me and dropping me down the hole headfirst.

"Okay. Let's go." I didn't give Tremaine time to say anything. I turned and, as soon as the people who had just entered dropped out of sight, I followed.

The hastily constructed tunnel dropped straight down for about eight feet but was navigable because of all the sharp, shattered rock lining the sides, providing both handholds and opportunities for sliced palms. I managed to make it to the small ledge at the bottom of the first tunnel with a minimum of blood loss, only to see another sloping downward at a steep forty-five-degree angle. I assumed that was where the second spell had hit.

I had to wait until the previous spelunkers cleared the way, and then took their place. A few seconds after I entered the second tunnel, I saw Caleb's face peering up at me out of the dark. "About time," he rumbled. I scrambled forward and took his hand.

He helped me out, but a rock slid under my foot, sending me stumbling into a bulbous green fender. Caleb set me on my feet, and I quickly moved out of the way so he could help the next person to exit. That turned out to be Tremaine, who joined me along the wall. For a moment, we stared at the very odd sight of a corridor filled as far as the eye could see with cars.

And not any old cars. I didn't know the names of most of them, but a couple Bentleys and a silver Rolls-Royce sparkled under the emergency lights not too far away. Buttery leather, gleaming chrome and a rainbow of custom colors marched away from us in a long line.

"What is this?" Tremaine asked softly.

"Our way out," Caleb threw over his shoulder. "The Consul generously donated her antique car collection when I pointed out that having convicts drive it out of here was the only way to save it."

"But I thought MAGIC's garage was on the surface," I said. I clearly remembered stealing a car from there once.

"Yeah, for your common Porsches, Jaguars or Ferraris," Caleb said sardonically. "The junk they keep around for the servants. Apparently, it isn't good enough for Her Highness."

"Lucky for us," Tremaine murmured. He looked at me. "We need to get you a place in one of the cars."

"The vampire Raphael is holding one for her in the black Bentley," Caleb told him. "Better hurry. They're starting to move out now." And sure enough, I could hear the growl of powerful engines starting up from the front of the line and smell the exhaust of unfiltered emissions permeating the air.

"Which car are you taking?" I asked Caleb.

"Whatever one leaves last."

"Then I'll go with you," I said, folding my arms and leaning against the wall.

"You said you were leaving!" Tremaine reminded me, putting a hand under my elbow.

"I never said anything of the kind. And get your hand off me."

Tremaine looked at me helplessly and then at Caleb. "Take over for me here," the older war mage instructed him. Tremaine moved to the tunnel in time to help out a middle-aged woman who sent him a luminous smile through the tears running down her face. Caleb led me down the line of cars and into the shadow of a doorway. "What the fuck?" he demanded.

"I'll leave with you and Pritkin," I repeated, deliberately keeping my voice even. It wasn't easy. I felt like I wanted to jump up and down and scream at everyone to *move*, damn it! To stop creeping and start flying out of here. I knew that wouldn't help, that they were already moving as fast as they could, and that starting a panic would only slow things down even more. But it still wasn't easy to simply stand there.

"You're the Pythia," Caleb told me. "You can't die in here."

"I'm Pythia?" I did a slow blink. "Since when? The last time I checked, I was a rogue initiate you were trying to hunt down."

"You know what I mean."

"No," I told him honestly. "I don't."

Caleb put a meaty hand behind his neck and rubbed it as if he had a headache. "There might have been some kind of . . . miscommunication . . . about you."

The panic of a dozen near misses in the last twenty-four hours crowded the back of my throat, jostling for room with more current fears. Like Pritkin not making it out of the death trap I'd dragged him into. Like the fact that that little speech of his was suddenly sounding a lot like good-bye. And the fact that there wasn't a hell of a lot I could do about it as drained as I was.

I really needed somebody to yell at, and Caleb was handy.

"A miscommunication?" I asked him furiously. "Which one would that be? When the warrant was issued for my arrest? Or when the shoot to kill order was given? Or, hey, maybe it was when the huge freaking *bounty* was put on my head!"

It was Caleb's turn to do the slow blink thing. "If a mistake was made, you have a legitimate grievance," he said. "But dying to prove a point won't help anybody. Pritkin was right: there's a war on and we need a Pythia. If you're it, you have a responsibility."

"My responsibility is the people I brought down here!"

"Pritkin and I will get out!" Caleb said, looking exasperated. "And when you do, I'll be with you."

"Cassie!"

"I can shift away if need be," I reminded him. "Shouldn't you send someone in the car who doesn't have a life preserver?"

He regarded me narrowly. "You can still shift?"

"Absolutely."

Caleb didn't look happy, but he nodded. "All right, then. Stay here. I'll come get you in a few minutes."

"I'd rather be doing something."

"All right. You could help by getting people sorted into a vehicle with a competent driver. They don't have to navigate—there's only one way out. But they have to be able to drive a stick."

"Got it."

Caleb took over at the tunnel's mouth again, while Tremaine and I grabbed the dust-covered prisoners and stuffed them into cars. The line was moving swifter now, a blur of color and noise as cars made their way along a tunnel that was scarcely wider than some of them. I assumed the Consul's chauffeurs were vampires, and with their reflexes, a tight squeeze didn't matter. But some of these drivers weren't as skilled. I saw more than one fender get crushed as the car behind it got a little overly enthusiastic, and a number of polished side panels were going to need repainting from scraping against unforgiving rock.

And then the end of the line rolled into place, the last car for the last group out the door. I slipped toward the tunnel's mouth in time to see a familiar blond head and pair of broad shoulders emerge. For some reason, Pritkin was facing backward.

"Pritkin!" I ran toward him, almost dizzy with relief, only to hear a thundering thud overhead and to have him obscured by a billowing cloud of thick red dust.

"In the car! Everybody in the car!"

I distantly heard Caleb's voice, but I couldn't find him. The exhaust fumes and the dust were a choking, blinding mist, the floor shook violently under my feet and rocks and gravel rained down on my head. Then something hit me in the temple, driving me to my knees, and the world went red.

And then nothing.

Chapter Ten

I woke up to find myself lying in a backseat, draped over a couple of smelly red men. Tremaine and Caleb looked like the Blue Man Group would if they'd suddenly changed their color scheme—completely coated in a thick red paste from head to foot. Dust and sweat, I realized as my eyes managed to fully focus. And I was in no better shape myself.

My lungs felt caked with about an inch of desert and I was having trouble breathing. I managed to cough, and that was both good and bad, because it opened my airway a little more, but then I couldn't stop. I coughed and hacked and gagged and coughed some more until I was sure I was going to bring my lungs up.

It would have helped to have had some water, but there wasn't any. Because we weren't out of the woods yet. I slid into the modest gap between the two mages and peered over the seat. A red man who I vaguely recognized as Rafe was at the wheel. The speedometer said eighty-six despite the fact that the narrow red tunnel we were hurtling down couldn't have been more than half an inch away from the car on either side.

Pritkin was riding shotgun, but he didn't turn around to look at me. I sat back and tried not to stare at the almost hypnotic tunnel arrowing out in front of us. I heard a distant thud and the walls shook. No one said anything, but Tremaine's hand gripped the door handle tight enough to crack his coating of mud.

"What was that?" I asked when the shaking finally stopped.

"Another level collapsing on top of us," Tremaine answered, sounding a little choked.

"We had to go down a freight elevator to a lower level to avoid being crushed," Caleb added. His voice was expressionless, but his hands kept clenching and unclenching on his thighs.

"Only the Senate level is below us now," Rafe chimed in. He sounded the same as always, although I noticed he had a pretty good grip on the wheel. "And it is completely flooded. I am afraid this is as far down as we can go."

Pritkin still didn't say anything.

We were in some kind of bulbous mid-century car, huge and gray and probably made of solid steel. Too bad that wouldn't hold against a few thousand tons of rock. "How many levels are still on top of us?" I asked, not sure I wanted to know.

"That was the last before ours," Tremaine said, and a small giggle escaped his lips before he clamped them shut.

"Can you shift?" Pritkin suddenly asked me, his voice harsh in the stillness.

"Why?"

"You told Caleb you can shift. Was it true?" I licked my lips and saw him watching me in the driver's mirror. "You lied."

Tremaine looked slightly shocked, as if surprised that a Pythia would do such a thing. He obviously hadn't known Agnes. Caleb put a hand to his head. "I should have knocked you out and shoved you in a car."

"Yes! You should have!" Pritkin snapped.

Rafe merely sighed. "You shouldn't tell lies, *mia stella*," he reproached, and floored it.

The car leapt ahead, its gas-guzzling engine tearing through the tunnels at what the speedometer now reported was in excess of one hundred miles an hour. I decided not to look at it anymore. I only hoped it was going to be enough.

At that speed, even vampire reflexes aren't perfect, not to mention that I'm not entirely certain that the tunnel was actually wide enough in places for the car. Dirt and rocks went flying, along with the two side mirrors and part of the back bumper. The rest of it trailed along behind us, hitting enough sparks off the stone floor to have started a fire if there had been anything to burn.

Then something hit the panel behind my seat hard enough to bruise my lower back. I sat up and twisted around to find a man's fist poking through the upholstery. "Who is that?" I demanded, sliding lower to get a look.

"The man the commander was forced to shoot," Tremaine told me as the mysterious hand wrapped around my throat.

Caleb took out a gun and smashed the butt down on the man's wrist. I heard a howl, and the hand was withdrawn. I sat up, careful to stay well away from the back of the seat. "I thought he was dead," I said.

"Not yet," Caleb replied.

"So you put him in the *trunk*?"

He shrugged. "This was the last car."

We hit a particularly narrow patch, and everyone slid to the center of the seats as the doors on either side buckled like a soda can in a giant's fist. "Who designed this tunnel anyway?!" I screamed, as the side windows shattered.

"It hasn't been in use in years," Rafe said. He burned rubber and we shot out into a slightly broader area in a burst of rubble and glass.

"Why not?"

"It was shut down in the thirties after Lake Mead was created. The lake bisected the old route."

"What do you mean, *bisected*?" I didn't get an answer, because there was a rumbling and a groaning behind us and another billowing wave of dust. And suddenly we were flying out into dazzling sunlight.

The ride immediately became incredibly smooth, with no traction at all other than the wind whistling through the missing windows. I realized why when I wrenched my neck around to look behind us and saw a small cloud poofing out of the pale side of a cliff. The cliff we'd just fallen out of.

"Oh, shit."

We fell more than fifteen feet before nose-diving into a boulder the size of a VW Bug, cartwheeling over and finally hitting a shining expanse of water. The car was built circa 1955, which meant that it had no air bags, and I wasn't even wearing a seat belt. We should have been dead. But Tremaine somehow managed to get a rudimentary shield around us, which popped shortly after encountering the boulder, but spared us the worst.

We survived; the car wasn't so lucky. But at least it sank slowly enough for us to slither through the windows and for Caleb to drag Red out of the trunk. He accomplished that by kicking out the partition between it and the backseat, and I think he might have kicked Red a few times, too. Either that or the guy couldn't swim, because he didn't give us too much trouble on the way to shore.

Cell phones don't work all that great after being drowned, leaving us with little choice but to hike around the side of Lake Mead. In one direction, heat shimmered off miles of dusty earth, scrub brush and distant purple hills. In the other were towering clay-red cliffs with a stark white mineral line striping them near the water's edge. There was little vegetation to soften the austere canyon, giving the place an oddly alien vibe: a big body of water in an almost bare landscape, like a lake on the moon. But with the cobalt sky and the deep azure of the river, it was undeniably striking.

I trudged through the shallower water near the shore, the high heels that were miraculously still strapped to my feet catching on underwater rocks and threatening to trip me. I didn't care. I just kept gazing around in something like awe. Everything was blisteringly hot and breathtakingly beautiful.

It took me a few moments to notice that everyone was looking at me oddly. I just laughed, almost giddy. We'd made it—dust-covered, red-faced and dripping wet, but *alive*. Rafe grinned with me, and a second later, even Caleb had cracked a smile.

We eventually came to a small trailer park. Most of the plots marked off by white stripes of paint were empty except for some windblown gravel. It was summer, and few people thought that 120-degree heat equaled a fun vacation.

I watched dust devils blow across the sand like miniature cyclones while the guys broke into one of the trailers that stayed there all year round. It looked like it came from

the same era as the car, miniscule and vaguely round, with
white aluminum sides and a small covered patio. A bedrag-
gled honeysuckle vine was trying its best to decorate the
latter, along with a wind chime made out of old forks.

They rattled in the strong breeze coming off the lake
as the door opened and Rafe came out. "No phone," he
told me. I shrugged. I hadn't really expected one. He had
a large yellow and white bottle in his hand that turned out
to be sunscreen. "I left some money on the counter," he
told me, as if worried that I might think less of him for
stealing.

"Blocks eighty percent of UV rays," I read. I looked at
him skeptically. "Think this is going to help?"

"At this point, I am willing to try anything," he said,
slathering the milky stuff all over his face and hands. Despite the fact that most of the dust had washed off on the
way here, Rafe was still bright red. Noonday sun is hell on
vampires.

"Here." Pritkin poked his head out of the trailer and
handed me a bottle of warm water. Since I'd already swallowed half a gallon on the swim to shore, I passed it to Red,
who was looking a little shaky. Pritkin's shot might not have
been fatal, but the guy had lost a lot of blood. He needed
medical help and we all needed to get out of the heat.

Tremaine emerged a minute later, carrying some plastic
deck chairs. "I'm going to hike up the road to the ticket office, see if they have a working phone," he announced.

"You going with him?" Caleb asked Pritkin as Rafe and
I got Red off the concrete and into a chair.

"Hadn't planned on it. Why?"

"He's a convict. None of this changes that."

"Cassie and I also have warrants out for our arrest," Pritkin pointed out. "Are you planning to turn us in as well?"

"I'm planning to do my job," Caleb retorted. "Or do you
think I should let this one go, too?" He nudged Red with
his knee. Red spit out a mouthful of water and started looking slightly hopeful. "Where do we draw the line, John?"

"You know what he did."

"And I know what they say *you* did."

"And I thought you knew me better than to believe it."
The two men stared at each other for a long minute while

Red and I watched and Rafe smeared himself with more SPF 80.

Caleb swore. "You have to go in. You have to *end this*. If there's been a mistake and she really is legit, people need to know."

"Then tell them," Pritkin snapped. "Not vague rumors or memos from higher-ups, but what you *heard*, what you *saw*, what you *experienced*. But don't be surprised if you end up in a prison cell for your trouble."

He and Tremaine took off without another word, and Caleb settled against the trailer, arms crossed and a dark frown on his face, watching his prisoner. I don't know why. It's not like any of us were going anywhere.

Rafe went back inside and emerged a few minutes later with a couple of white sheets that he proceeded to wrap around himself. With his riotous brown curls and easy smile, he looked like a particularly charming bedouin. A bedouin with a face full of sunscreen and a pair of designer sunglasses.

"Where'd you get the shades?" I asked.

"Rome. They're Gucci."

"Very nice." I glanced at Red. "Vampires have coagulants in their saliva that aid in healing. If you're still bleeding, Rafe could stop it."

Red gave Caleb a panicked look. "You keep that thing away from me! I know my rights! You can't let him feed!"

"He's offering to help you," Caleb said mildly.

"Yeah, help me out of a few pints! I know how they are!"

"I believe the bleeding has stopped, *mia stella*," Rafe said wryly. "And I do not normally feed from, ah, that particular region."

"What region?"

"Pritkin shot him in the ass," Caleb said bluntly.

I looked at Red with more sympathy. I could relate.

A small gust of wind blew some sand in our faces, making me cough and settling onto everyone's hair, turning it vaguely pink. I lifted my sweaty hair off my neck and wished for a headband. God, it was hot.

Fortunately, it wasn't long before Pritkin was back, along with an older man in a golf cart. He seemed to be under the impression that we'd been in a boating accident and needed transport back to Vegas. He had already called us a cab.

"Where's Tremaine?" Caleb demanded.

"Waiting for the cab," Pritkin said blandly.

Caleb scowled, but he kept his comments to himself in front of the norm. He and Red got into the back of the golf cart, and Pritkin got in front. Leaving me and Rafe to follow on foot.

"That wasn't very gentlemanly," Rafe noted, watching them drive off.

I didn't say anything.

It took us five minutes to make it out of the campground, up a small hill and down the road to the ticket booth. We found Pritkin outside, leaning against the booth. Caleb and Red were in the golf cart, taking a short nap. The ticket taker was inside, apparently fascinated by his shoelaces, which he'd knotted into some pretty intricate shapes. Tremaine was nowhere in sight.

"Do I want to know?" I asked.

"We have perhaps half an hour before they wake up," Pritkin informed me. "Peter has gone to the highway to arrange transportation."

"I thought a cab was coming."

"We can't afford to wait that long. McCullough is wearing a tracker; all prisoners do as a precaution. The Corps is preoccupied at the moment, which doubtless explains why a team has yet to arrive to pick him up. But with our luck, they will be here any moment."

The Corps was the military arm of the Circle; i.e., war mage central. I was definitely in favor of moving on before any more of Pritkin's old buddies showed up. But something else he'd said caught my attention.

"A tracker?" I blinked dust out of my eyes. "You mean, if he goes anywhere, they know it?"

"Essentially."

"I don't see it on him."

"It's a spell, not a physical device," Pritkin said impatiently. "Is there a reason for your interest?"

"Yes. Can you check to see if I have one?"

He handed me a bottle of water from the ticket taker's

fridge and splashed his face with another. "You have three." He started down the road at a fast enough clip that Rafe and I had to hurry to keep up.

"Wait a minute. How do you know?"

"One of them is mine."

"You *bugged* me?"

"It isn't a listening device, Miss Palmer. It merely records your location. Which, considering how many people wish to kidnap and/or murder you, is a reasonable precaution."

"If it's so reasonable, why didn't you mention it?"

Water and perspiration had turned his usually pale eyelashes dark and clumpy, emphasizing the color of his eyes as he rolled them. "Because I wanted it to work! Something it would not have done had you persuaded the witch to remove it."

"Her name is Francoise and you're damn right she'd have removed it!"

"Which is why I didn't mention it."

If I'd been less exhausted, I'd have been livid. As it was, the best I could manage was disgusted. "When I was growing up at Tony's, I was followed everywhere," I told him. "By bodyguards, by my governess, by someone all the time. I had zero privacy. But even Tony didn't go so far as to put a spell on me!"

"He doubtless didn't have anyone competent enough to cast it," Pritkin said, striding ahead.

I shouted after him. "You said *one* was yours. It doesn't worry you that two other groups are tracking me?"

Rafe cleared his throat. "Ah, Cassie . . ."

"Mircea bugged me?" I guessed.

"And Marlowe, I believe."

"Why? Was he afraid Mircea might not tell him everything?"

Rafe looked shocked. "We all have the same desire, *mia stella*: to keep you safe. And a new version of the spell was recently perfected. It is much harder to detect, even by mages."

"Then why not remove the old one?"

"We were not aware that the mage was also planning to cast one on you. And if someone did abduct you, they would expect to find such a spell."

"So the original was left to give them something to re-move, in the hopes that they wouldn't look any further."

"Exactly!" Rafe seemed pleased that I'd grasped his point so easily. Yet he managed to totally miss mine. Sometimes I forgot that Rafe, who had taken to modern clothes and cars, music and art, almost better than any vamp I knew, had been born in the same century as Mircea. No wonder he didn't understand why I'd object to having my every movement followed. The women back then had probably enjoyed it.

Pritkin met my eyes. He got it; he just didn't care.

"You could have asked me," I pointed out, keeping my temper because I was too tired for anything else.

"You admitted that you would have had it removed."

"If you had explained that you'd done it for my safety—"

"Yes, because safety is so important to you!" He rounded on me. "So important, in fact, that you deliberately lied in order to stay in a situation you knew was perilous. For no reason!"

"No reason?" I felt my face flush with more than sun-burn. "I had the impression that you needed my help!"

"Until the prisoners were freed, yes. Afterward, there was nothing more you could do and no reason for you to remain. You should have left when I instructed you to do so!"

"Partners don't abandon each other to die."

"If the alternative is to stay and die with them? Yes! They do!" His words were angry, but his face was oddly still, strained and pale.

I tried again. "I *am* concerned with safety. But I can't al-ways do my job and—"

"That was *not* your job. Rescuing those prisoners had nothing to do with the time line! Had I guessed that you were foolish enough to almost get killed over them, I would never have agreed to help you!"

"It might not have been my job, but it *was* my doing. If I hadn't gone to that meeting—"

"Then we wouldn't know that there is a problem with the lines."

I frowned. "What are you talking about? The battle—"

"Should have had no effect. If the lines were that unstable, they would be useless to us. Someone or something must have weakened the structural integrity of that line before the battle."

"Some*one*? You think this was deliberate?"

"I don't know. But I've never heard of anything of the kind occurring naturally, and the fact that the breach targeted MAGIC is highly suspect."

I thought about the incredible power of a ley line, all those acres and acres of jumping, brilliant energy, and didn't believe it. "But *how*?"

"I can't explain it. No one has that kind of power. Not the dark, not even us."

"Apollo does." And if anyone had reason to want MAGIC destroyed, it was him.

But Pritkin didn't seem to think much of that idea. "If he could send that amount of energy to his supporters, he would have done so long ago and destroyed the Circle at the outset. Thankfully, you possess the only remnants of his power on Earth."

The conversation had to pause at that point because we'd reached Tremaine and, just beyond him, his idea of a ride. He shot us an apologetic glance. "It seems that any food that doesn't make it into tourists' stomachs is made into high-quality pig feed," he explained. "And Mr. Ellis here hauls leftovers from several casinos to a recycler. He's kindly agreed to drop us at Dante's on his way back for another load."

"It's on my way," the old man repeated cheerfully. "Now settle yourselves any old where. The drums are empty; you won't hurt anything."

Empty, as it turns out, is a relative term. The buffet sludge leaking over the sides of a half dozen black plastic drums was joined by several weeks' worth of dried flotsam rattling around the truck bed. It was also about one hundred degrees with no shade, causing Rafe to hunker down with the sheets pulled up over his head.

"Are you all right?" I asked him, worried. Rafe was a master, but only fourth level. The sun didn't merely drain someone like him of power; it could hurt or even kill him in sufficient quantities.

"Well enough," he told me, but he didn't sound good. Thankfully, it was only about twenty-five miles into town.

"I don't get it," I told Pritkin, who shook his head before I could even frame a question.

"Not here."

"I don't think he's listening," I said, nodding at the driver. The radio was blaring Johnny Cash at ear-ringing decibels, and that was from where we were sitting. The sound in the cab had to be deafening.

Pritkin just looked at me, so I turned to the nice war mage. "I don't understand what stopped that thing. Once there was a tear in the fabric between worlds, why didn't it continue all the way to the end of the line? Like ripping a seam when the thread's cut?"

Tremaine looked nervously at Pritkin, who muttered something but answered the question. "My best guess would be that the ley line sink at MAGIC had enough energy to seal the breach. In your analogy, it would be like encountering a knot in the thread."

"But what if that hadn't been enough? What would have happened?"

"The tear would have continued until reaching a vortex big enough to counter it."

"And that would be where?" I asked, getting a very bad feeling.

"The line where the eruption occurred runs from MAGIC straight to Chaco Canyon, where there is a great vortex—a crossing of more than two dozen lines. It is one of the most powerful in this hemisphere."

"Chaco Canyon?"

Pritkin grimaced. "New Mexico."

I stared at him for a moment, sure I'd heard wrong. "*New Mexico*? You're saying that thing could have continued for hundreds of miles?"

"Leveling every magical edifice across three states," he agreed tightly.

"And a lot of nonmagical ones," Tremaine added, looking horrified. "Even some norms can pick up on the kind of energy a powerful ley line throws off. Traditionally, a lot of human structures have been built around the lines, even when the builders didn't know why."

Pritkin nodded. "If someone has found a way to disrupt the lines, it could be disastrous. Both for us and for the human population."

I thought about the seared plain, the death and the destruction we'd left behind. "I think it already has been," I said quietly.

At least I didn't have to worry about any war mages who might still be prowling around the casino. By the time we made it back, our closest friends wouldn't have recognized us. Or wanted to get within ten feet of us.

I picked a desiccated wonton wrapper out of my hair, thanked the driver and skirted a long line of cabs to the front entrance. Despite the fact that we were covered in garbage and leaving a trail of dust that would have done Pig-Pen proud, no one gave us a second glance. The place was a madhouse.

Hundreds of tourists had crowded around the reception desk, yelling and waving papers at the usually suave Dante's employees, who were looking a little stressed. Luggage was piled in heaps on the floor and on overflowing carts as harried bellhops ran back and forth, trying to keep up with the demand. Children were crying and threatening to fall in the Styx. An overtaxed air-conditioning system was straining to lower the temperature to maybe ninety degrees. And a bevy of new, life-challenged guests were clogging the lobby bar.

For a minute, I saw a double scene, the ruined bar from my vision transposed over the real thing. Then I shook my head and it cleared, leaving me looking at a muscle-bound type who had one of the fetish-clad waitresses by the waist. She was kicking and screaming and not with pleasure, but the senator didn't seem to care. He'd been born in ancient Rome, where the manners relating to bar wenches had been a little different. Fortunately, the southern belle by his side wasn't in a good mood. She cut her eyes up at him, frowned and nailed his hand to the table with a swizzle stick. He eyed her unfavorably as he pried it loose, but he did let go of the waitress.

"What is the Senate doing here?" I asked Rafe, only to discover that he'd disappeared. I glanced around but didn't see him in the uproar. "Where did Rafe go?" I asked Pritkin.

"He left as soon as we arrived," he told me, eyeing the dozen vamps, luggage in hand, who were waiting by an elevator.

None were Rafe. "Did he say where he was going?"

"No. But he probably went to check in. It appears that the Senate and its servants were instructed to rendezvous here."

"It looks more like they're moving in."

"They are," Casanova said, hurrying over. "And ruining me in the process. I have three conventions booked for this week and two more for next, and I've been ordered to cancel them all! Oh, and you're being moved out of the penthouse. The Consul outranks you."

"Since when?" I demanded.

"Since this is a vampire-run property and she's head of the Senate."

"There are other hotels! Why does she have to stay here?"

"Other hotels aren't a well-warded property with a portal to Faerie. Welcome to MAGIC Two," he said in disgust.

"Sorry," I told him, because he seemed to expect me to say something.

"I need a little more than that, like the key card to the penthouse. Our machine's busted." He caught my expression. "You aren't going to make a scene about this, right?"

"I'm kind of in the mood for a scene," I admitted. Casanova said something in Italian that I won't repeat. "And that's not going to help you any."

He gave me a speculative look. "Then how about this? I was planning to evict those deadbeat kids you foisted off on me—"

"They're orphans!" I said, outraged.

"Not all of them."

"They don't have anywhere else to go!"

"I'm weeping on the inside."

I sighed. "What do you want?"

"I told you. Move out of the penthouse nice and quiet, and I'll find somewhere to put the kids."

"I'll move out of the penthouse nice and quiet, and you'll leave them where they are," I countered. I was too tired for this, but if I didn't didn't spell things out, Casanova would have them sleeping in the Dumpsters out back. And it wasn't like I could get them rooms somewhere else.

The kids in question called themselves the Misfits because their magic had chosen to manifest abnormally, ensuring that they would never fit into the mainstream supernatural community. The ones with more dangerous powers had been confined to a series of "schools" the Circle had set up, where they were supposed to be taught to control their often dangerous powers. But most would never evidence enough control to suit the Circle's standards, meaning that they would never graduate. Or leave.

Tamika Hodges, a friend of mine and one of the Misfits' mothers, had tried to get her son released by legal means. When that failed, she'd taken a more direct approach and broken him out. She'd released some of his friends at the same time, thereby landing her at the top of the Circle's most wanted list right alongside me. With the help of the Senate, I'd recently cut a deal that got her out of trouble for her various crimes. But the deal hadn't included the kids, which was why they'd been hiding at Dante's until I made nice with the Circle. At the rate things were going, they were going to be here awhile. Assuming Casanova didn't throw them into the street.

"They're occupying two very nice suites!" he protested.

"There are eight of them—nine if you count the baby! What were you planning to do, stuff them in a broom closet?" He looked shifty. "They stay where they are or no deal," I said flatly.

"All right! But you owe me."

Before I could give the reply that comment deserved, my eyes locked with those of a tall, exquisite creature across the lobby. And the poor, shredded, dirt-and-garbage-covered remains of my dress suddenly began screeching like an air horn. It was loud enough to draw every eye in the place.

"Shut it off!" Pritkin yelled.

"How?!"

He tried some kind of spell, but it had no noticeable effect. "The Corps is probably still here!" he informed me, as if I could do anything about that.

And then it got worse. "Murderer!" Augustine shrieked, raising an arm to point at me. And thereby drawing whatever eyes hadn't already been turned my way. "Murderer!"

"Take it off!" Pritkin told me, grabbing the hem.

"Corps or no, I'm not streaking through the damn lobby!"

"Here." Tremaine shucked the standard-issue war mage topcoat he was wearing and passed it over. It was midcalf length on him, which meant it dragged the floor on me, but I didn't feel like complaining. I pulled it on, trying not to think about the audience I'd suddenly acquired.

"Two teams just came in the front door," Tremaine warned.

"Give it to me," Pritkin ordered. I unbuttoned the shrieking dress with shaking fingers and dropped it around my feet, feeling like a flasher. Pritkin grabbed it, and he and Tremaine took off, waving it above the heads of the crowd and drawing the war mages' attention—for the moment.

I clutched the coat around me and ran in the other direction, toward the employee dressing room. Luckily, I'd worked at the casino for almost a month now, so I had a locker all of my own. Unluckily, its sole contents were a sequined bustier and a pair of three-inch heels.

I slammed it shut, one eye on the doorway, and chewed a nail. Several employees stopped to stare at me, taking in my sunburned face, tangled hair, and filthy, topcoat-clad body. I really needed a shower, but taking one here was out of the question. The only thing worse than getting caught by the Circle was getting caught by the Circle naked. I needed somewhere to recharge, somewhere I could get a change of clothes and a bath, somewhere safe. And only one place came to mind.

Sometimes, it really helps to have a witch for a friend.

Chapter Eleven

A string of furious French was the response to my knock. "I 'ave until four!" I was informed through the door. "Go away!"

I tapped on the door again—carefully—because a powerful witch in a mood is not someone to take lightly. Especially when she knows as many archaic spells as this one. "Francoise—it's me."

The door flung open to reveal a really unhappy brunette. Her long hair was everywhere, her chic green and white sundress was streaked with dust and she had a bulging garbage bag in one hand. From the look of things, it contained most of her clothes.

"Cassie!" Her eyes widened and a second later I found myself enveloped in a bone-crushing hug. "I was so worried! I was afraid the Circle 'ad taken you to MAGIC!"

"They did."

"But . . . 'ow did you escape? Zey say it was destroyed!"

"It's a long story." I glanced at the garbage bag. "I take it you've been evicted?"

The scowl returned. "Casanova, 'e say zat ze Senate needs my room for one of zere servants. So I must go! Today!"

"There's a lot of that going around."

"I 'ad thought to ask if I might stay with you," she admitted.

"What a coincidence."

"*Mais c'est impossible!* You are ze Pythia!"

"And the Consul likes a view."

Francoise said some uncharitable things about the Consul. Since they were in French—which I'm not supposed to speak—I didn't contradict her. It was also a fact that they were all true.

I flopped onto the bed. I'd only meant to sit down, but I swear the mattress was spelled. It just pulled me in. I tried to kick my shoes off, but mud had welded them to my feet. I decided I didn't care.

I lay there for a few minutes, listening to Francoise tear the room apart. "Any ideas?" I finally asked.

Francoise grimaced. "Randolph 'as an apartment."

"Randy?" I opened an eye to watch her flush slightly. "Tall, corn-fed, crew-cut blond with biceps like boulders? That Randy?"

"When 'e 'eard that ze employees 'ave to move, 'e called me."

I rolled over onto my stomach and propped my chin in my hand. "Did he?"

The flush became a blush. "'E 'as an extra room."

"Uh-huh." And I'm sure he meant for her to stay in it, too.

She sighed. "'E ees very 'andsome, *non*?"

"Yeah." If you liked the laid-back surfer boy type, Randy was the man. He was also a genuinely nice guy, for someone possessed by an incubus. "So what's the problem?"

Francoise shot me a look. "You know what ees ze problem!"

"He wouldn't feed off you," I assured her. For one thing, she'd curse him into next week.

"I know zat!" She filled another Hefty bag with the extra pillow and blanket from the closet, the bedside lamp and the hotel's iron. When she picked up the last, the cord fell out the back.

"Then what is it? And you need that long skinny black thing." She looked blank. "It makes it go," I added, and she nodded and went hunting under the bed.

Francoise had issues with modern equipment. "Modern" meaning anything invented after the seventeenth century. That's when she'd been born, and when she'd met a bunch of dark mages with an entrepreneurial streak.

The Fey would pay top dollar for attractive, fertile young witches who could help them with their population problem, but most of the likely candidates were either too well-guarded or too powerful to be taken easily. But the mages had caught Francoise at a vulnerable moment and quickly bundled her off to a slave auction in Faerie. She'd lived with the Fey for what had seemed like a few years, until seizing the chance to escape—only to discover on her return that four hundred years had passed in our world. The whole thing just left Rip van Winkle standing.

"Zees?" She held up the cord.

"That would be the one."

It went into the bag, along with a painting that she climbed up onto the bed to rip off the wall. "It ees zese ozzair women," she told me, tugging on the painting. "I tell him, I weel not be—what ees ze word? Many women with one man?"

"Harem."

"*Oui.* I weel not be a harem!" she said, and tugged really hard. The painting came off the wall, flew across the room and put a dent in the door. Francoise hopped down and checked out the damage. The frame looked a little wonky, but apparently it passed muster because it went into the bag.

"I can see where that could pose a problem. He has an incubus to feed."

"I tell heem, geet rid of it," she said, making one of those wild French gestures that mean anything and nothing. "But *non. 'It changed my life,'*" she mimicked.

"Maybe it did," I said carefully. "Casanova recruits a lot of his boys from small towns who don't think they have much of a future."

"'E ees 'ere now," she said fiercely. "'E does not need it anymore. I theenk it ees the ozzair women 'e does not wish to give up!"

I tried to find something to say, but everything was too jumbled, too out of control in my head. Thoughts and feelings I didn't want to examine kept pushing their way to the front. I wondered if Mircea felt the same way now that a spell no longer bound us together. Would he want other women? Or did he already have one?

He came from an era when it was common to have a wife to play hostess and a mistress or two with whom to play at other things. I'd never heard anyone speak of a long-term lover in connection with Mircea, but then, I hadn't asked, either. And I'd never been to his main court in Washington State. That was despite the fact that he'd discovered my existence when I was eleven, after a call from Raphael, his resident stooge at Tony's court.

Mircea was Tony's master, which by vampire law allowed him to put a claim on me. At best, he'd hoped that I might inherit the Pythia's position and give the vampires their first shot at controlling that kind of power. At worst, I was a genuine clairvoyant, and those aren't a dime a dozen. But he'd nonetheless chosen to let me grow up at Tony's rather than take me back to court with him.

I'd always assumed that had been to ensure that the Circle didn't find out about me. They had a proprietary interest in magic users in general and clairvoyants in particular, and they might have given him trouble. Tony's court was a lot lower profile than Mircea's, and therefore safer. But now I wondered if maybe there had been another reason as well.

A beautiful dark-eyed reason.

I groaned and threw an arm over my eyes. Damn it! There were only ever questions when it came to Mircea, never answers. It was starting to get really old.

My head hurt, my body ached and I wanted to just stop thinking for a while. But something about those photos was nagging at me. I suddenly realized that Mircea hadn't appeared in a single one, which seemed a little strange considering how many there had been. I'd have assumed that he was the one taking the pictures, but the woman hadn't been looking at the camera in any of them, at least not that I could remember. It was like she hadn't even been aware of it.

So what the hell was he doing? Paying someone to take photos for him, to keep track of her? And if so, why? Why not just take her if he was that smitten? Who could a master vampire possibly need to stalk?

I could only think of a few options, none of which seemed all that likely. Did she belong to another master, maybe even another Senate member? In that case, yes, he could refuse to give her up. But masters traded their servants all the time, and Mircea was perfectly capable of talking the moon down from the heavens when he wanted. If he was that motivated, he would have found something or someone the woman's master would have taken in trade.

So was she a senator herself who'd rejected him? That seemed even less plausible. Most vampires viewed sexuality as merely another marketable commodity. I couldn't imagine any senator turning down Mircea's advances when they would likely bring her an important political alliance. Vampires almost always thought in terms of profit and loss, even about intimate relations. And there would be no profit in refusal.

That left me with one idea, and not one I liked. The Senate had recently suffered some losses in the war. Was it possible that the woman in the photos was one of the senators who had died? Could that album have been some kind of memorial Mircea had compiled of his lost love?

The thought that he might have been pretending interest in me even while mourning someone he'd loved for decades, maybe centuries, made me almost physically ill. And what hurt the most was that he hadn't needed seduction to get me on his side. I'd already been there. He just hadn't noticed.

"What ees it?" Francoise asked, sounding concerned.

I realized that I'd totally missed whatever she'd been saying, too busy pondering my train wreck of a love life. I sat up and blanked my face, but she just raised an eyebrow. Damn it. It had been too long since I'd had to regularly control my features. I was out of practice.

"Nothing. It's just . . . I sort of know how you feel."

She looked surprised. "Lord Mircea, 'e 'as a woman?"

"I don't know." I got up and started to pace, but the damn high heels hurt my feet. I sat back down again. "I don't know anything. We never talk."

"*Pourqoui pas*?"

"He's been gone most of the time lately, on Senate business. And when I do see him, he has so much else on his mind that it's hard to bring up relationship stuff." Next to war, politics and the supernatural world threatening to implode, it seemed a little trivial. But the result was that

I'd somehow ended up married—at least from the vamps' perspective—to someone I knew next to nothing about.

"You should talk to 'im," Francoise said, eyeing the overhead light fixture. Luckily for Dante's, it was bolted into the ceiling.

"Yeah." Only every time I tried, talking wasn't what we ended up doing. Not to mention that I had absolutely no idea how to broach the subject of a possibly recently deceased ex-lover. Or whatever she was.

Francoise arched an eyebrow and started to say something, but a rap on the door saved me. She threw up her hands, turned around and snatched it open. Randy stood there looking sheepish, as much as is possible for a guy wearing skintight black jeans and a matching muscle shirt. At least I think it was a shirt. It might have been paint.

"What are you doing 'ere?"

He shrugged, setting a lot of muscles rippling. "I thought I could help you move. To wherever you're going," he added quickly as Francoise's expression darkened.

"We 'aven't decided zat yet," she said with a good attempt at nonchalance.

"I think I might know a place," I told her, prying my weary body off the bed.

A few minutes later, me, Randy, Francoise and her bags of loot arrived at what had once been a tiki bar on the hotel's fourth floor. It had recently suffered an unfortunate fire and renovations were still ongoing. The rebuilt stage smelled of varnish and the bare drywall on the walls still awaited paint. It was probably the only quiet place in the whole hotel.

Unfortunately, quiet was about the only thing the bar's back room had to recommend it. The place was tiny and had no bathroom, and we had to move boxes of plastic leis and condiment packets out to make room for a second bed. But it was livable. I should know; not so long ago, it had been my room.

"Okay. This is . . . cozy," Randy said, looking around.

"It used to be a storage closet."

"I'd have never guessed." I shot him a look and he shrugged. "At least you won't get evicted." No, I didn't suppose so. No self-respecting vampire would be caught dead in it.

"I like eet," Francoise said, trying to navigate the maybe one-inch-wide aisle between her bed and the wall.

"It's just temporary," I promised.

"Yes. Lord Mircea will arrange something for you." I could already see her mentally removing my bed.

I'd been thinking more of the room next door. It was smaller but a lot more colorful than this one, with a floor-to-ceiling stained glass window depicting a battle scene. The window had met an unfortunate accident—they seemed to be pretty common around here since I showed up—and hadn't yet been replaced. A plastic sheet printed to look like it had been stapled over the gap but it let in the heat. I needed to ask Casanova when he thought a replacement might be expected.

But that could wait. There were more pressing issues at the moment. I left Francoise to arrange things to her liking and borrowed the key to her old room. If I was lucky, I'd have time for a shower before I was evicted again.

I woke hours later to a thump and a scream. The latter started in a falsetto and ended up in a baritone, which was enough to tell me that it wasn't Francoise even before the profanity started. I tensed, my lids flew open and I saw a hulking eight-foot shadow looming over me. I screamed.

"Honey, I know it's last year's wig," someone snapped. "But it's Liza. It's timeless."

I reached up and flicked on the overhead light, and the shadow resolved itself into an eight-foot-tall woman rubbing her shin. Part of the height was due to the aforementioned towering black wig and part to seven-inch platforms. The rest of the package was swathed in a skintight sheath short enough to be considered a shirt and constructed entirely of black sequined bow ties. It strained over shoulders wider than most men's and showed off heavily muscled legs. The total effect was linebacker in drag.

It took me a minute to realize that was because she was, in fact, a linebacker in drag.

"Who are you?" I demanded shrilly.

She looked insulted. "Darling, have you been living under a rock? I'm *Dee Sire*."

I just looked at her.

"Of the Three D's?"

I shook my head.

"We used to be the Double D's, but then we picked up a third . . ."

I had no idea what she was talking about, but a quick survey showed that whoever she was, she didn't appear to be carrying a weapon. Unless she had one stuffed in that enormous wig. She could have stuck an AK-47 in there and no one would know.

"What are you doing in my room?" I asked a little more calmly.

"I know how it is: you have one too many drinks, you're looking for the ladies' and you stumble in here. Fair enough, but, sweetie, this ain't your room."

"It is at the moment," I said testily, looking around.

Francoise was nowhere to be seen, probably still out with Randy. He'd talked her into dinner and she'd invited me along, but Randy had been giving me pleading eyes behind her back and anyway, I'd been too exhausted to eat. Not to mention that the only clean clothes I had were the Dante's T-shirt and sweatpants I'd bought at the gift shop to sleep in. No one had seemed to know where my luggage was and everything Francoise owned was six inches too long on me.

"What do you want?" I asked, finger combing my hair.

"No need to get snippy. And if you don't want to wake up in the stockroom with no idea how you got there, I'd lay off the sauce."

"I don't drink! And I know exactly how I got here. I was— Wait a minute!" I stopped, staring from her to the still-locked door. "How did *you* get in?"

Dee wasn't listening. She'd pulled a silver bejeweled phone out of her enormous bosom and was stabbing at it with a crimson talon. "Get me Dee Vine," she told it, and paused for a beat. "Don't give me that! Tell her to stop primping and answer the damn phone!" There was another pause and she rolled her eyes. "Dee Vine, my ass!" she told me. "She ought to call herself Dee Crepit; the bitch has to be going on sixty. No amount of makeup is going to hel—lo Dee, you gorgeous thing . . ."

My stomach grumbled plaintively, a counterpoint to the throbbing in my skull. My last meal had been breakfast with Mircea and that had to be . . . I wasn't even sure. A long time ago. I started looking for my shoes.

"Well, I don't know, do I?" Dee asked. "The only other person here is some wino in wrinkled sweats . . ."

I looked down at myself and then glared up at her. She made a kissy face at me but didn't apologize. I found one shoe under Francoise's bed, but the other was nowhere to be seen. It had vanished like a sock in a dryer.

Dee grumbled into the phone some more and then clicked it shut. "They moved the rehearsal and didn't bother to tell me." She watched me crawling around the floor. "What are you doing?"

"Trying to find my other shoe." I held up the one I'd located and she snatched it with a little cry.

"Oh, my God. That's a Jimmy Choo Atlas gladiator sandal!"

"Uh-huh." Sal had picked them out. They were a little flashy, but at least all the straps had kept them on my feet. Otherwise, my bruises would have been joined by some seriously lacerated soles.

Dee lifted the sandal delicately, holding it up to her face. The patent surface was looking a little battered after its recent adventures and mud caked the heel, which had lost its end cap. She stroked its side softly. "Oh, my poor, poor baby."

Once upon a time, I'd also taken an interest in fashion, as much as my limited budget allowed. But lately, I was more interested in whether I could run in a pair of shoes than in whose name was on the box. And I'd never cooed to my footwear.

"It's just a shoe," I said impatiently.

She hugged it to her huge chest, glaring at me. "People like you shouldn't be allowed to own fashion." She stuck a massive calf up on the bed, a long nail pointing at her shiny red platform. "See these? Four years old and not a scratch. And they're off the rack!"

"It's been a rough day."

She shook her head hard enough to almost dislodge the wig. "That's no excuse. We've all been there, but you take the designer shoes off and *then* you puke."

"I'm not drunk!"

She was too busy petting the shoe to listen. "I could so work a pair of these."

I eyed her maybe size fourteen foot. "I don't think they come in your size."

"Oh, please. What's a little blood? I'd bind my feet up like a geisha if I could afford—"

"Well, I'd trade them for a pair of Keds and a good meal," I muttered, and looked up to find huge fake eyelashes fluttering in my face like a pair of angry moths.

"You would?" Dee asked, a little breathless.

"Yeah. If I don't get something to eat soon, I'm going to—"

She gave me a shove and I stumbled back into the wall— and kept going. I fell down what felt like a water slide except with no water. In its place was a blur of color and a roar of sound—and then I was tumbling head over heels into an alcove. It had rough wood floors, stucco walls and a pay phone with an out of order sign.

Something taupe and muddy lay right in front of my nose. I grabbed it. "My shoe!"

"*My* shoe," Dee said, stumbling out of the wall behind me. She plucked it out of my hands. "Keds and a meal— that was the deal, right?"

"Yes, but . . ." I stared at the wall we'd just fallen out of. "There was a portal in my room!"

"No kidding." Dee peered out of a set of red velvet drapes in front of the alcove.

"Why?!"

"Because it used to be a nightclub with undead performers," she threw over her massive shoulder. "How do you think they got them in and out? Walked them through the main casino floor, so they could munch on a few tourists in passing?"

I scowled. "You can't go around telling people this kind of stuff. You just met me. I might be a norm for all you—"

"Scrim."

"What?"

"The whole group, Dee Vine, Dee Licious and me. We're all Scrims."

"What difference does that make?" Scrims were just mages who didn't produce much magical energy. They varied in ability, from those who weren't very good at magic to those who couldn't even cast a simple spell. Like the Misfits, they weren't popular in the magical community, but they weren't locked up because nobody viewed them as a threat.

"Scrims can detect magic," she said impatiently. "We're like bloodhounds on a scent, drawn to it like queens to fashion. Speaking of which, those bitches I work with would kill for these shoes. Literally—I'm talking a stiletto to the neck. We have to be careful."

"Look, I just want a sandwich—"

"It's all about you, isn't it?" she hissed. "This is an act of mercy. I have a friend who can restore these babies to their proper glory but I have to smuggle them past the hags. Oh, shit! There's one now!"

Dee snapped the curtains shut and started stuffing the shoes down her already overpadded front. She'd just finished when the curtain was snatched back to reveal a tall, gaunt person in a black see-through body stocking, sequined pasties and black satin hot pants. "She" had purple lipstick, purple feathers on her long, fake eyelashes and the pale, expressionless face of the overly Botoxed.

"That look went out with the eighties," she drawled, staring suspiciously at Dee's now ultrapointy breasts.

Dee draped an arm around my shoulders. "Darling, meet Dee Ceased—"

"Dee Vine!" the woman snapped.

"Careful with the emotion, love. Your forehead might fall off."

Someone laughed and edged in around the ample space left by Dee Vine's scrawny form. The newcomer was a seven-foot-tall African-American in a blond wig, her ample curves spilling over the top of a full-length red-sequined dress. "That's what I was telling her. Then we can call her Dee Composed."

That won her a glare from her costar. "Like you've never had work. You're over forty without a line!"

The newcomer ran hands in opera-length, red satin gloves down her curves. "And it's all natural, baby. Ain't you heard? Black don't crack."

"Are we gonna get this rehearsal on or not?" Dee Vine demanded. "This dump opens in two days!"

"I'm going to grab a bite first," Dee Sire told her, pushing me through the miniscule opening between the two queens.

"Another few pounds and what'll be cracking around here is your ass out of that dress!" floated after us as we emerged into a dark club.

The theme seemed to be Wild West saloon, with a long bar, clusters of round wood tables, sawdust on the floor and a couple of old-fashioned swinging doors. We stepped through them into the middle of a ghost town. Or at least Dante's idea of one.

Most of the casinos in town were trending away from Vegas' overly kitschy roots, but not here. Dante's had a vested interest in maintaining its reputation as the home of the wild, the wacky and the tacky. The more the scarier; that was Dante's motto.

The overall theme of the casino had begun as various versions of hell, as evidenced by the lobby. But over time, that had pretty much devolved into a hodgepodge of all things supernatural. The more there was to distract the eye, the less likely that anyone would notice that not all of the "acts" were fake.

Nowhere was that better realized than on the casino's main drag. Wooden sidewalks creaked and groaned mysteriously, even when no one was on them. There were hitching posts every so often for ghostly horses that only showed up in the darkened windows of the stores they faced. There was a water tower at one end with a hanged man dangling from it, turning gently in a nonexistent breeze. And the sky overhead was constantly dark, except for a few fake bolts of lightning flashing occasionally.

Of course, this was Vegas, which meant the old wooden shops had been slutted up with neon signs featuring glowing cacti, dancing martini glasses and tap dancing skeletons. There was one advertising "Drag on the drag" outside the saloon we'd just exited. And there were tourists everywhere.

"Look at this!" Dee was indignant. "I wouldn't wait in those lines for seventy-five percent off at Saks, much less a Tombstone Taco."

"I don't care. Right now, anything I can put in my mouth is fine."

"Oh, honey, if only you were a boy," she sighed, and pulled me into the madhouse of Main Street.

It was not only busier than usual, it was creepier, too. Along with the tourists in bright colored tees and the Dante's employees in costumes and face paint were a large number of pale, elegant observers watching the melee through jaded eyes. The senators' servants had arrived in force and midnight was lunchtime. And the street was a walking buffet.

"This is ridiculous," Dee said as people kept trying to pose with her. I guess they thought she was one of the costumed performers who appeared here and there for photo ops. Only they were dressed in a gothic version of Old West attire, not Dee's glittery bow ties.

"You know, I could just call room service—"

"No way. A deal's a deal." She spied an opening in the throng and towed me through.

We ended up at the Last Stop train station. It was a steakhouse filled with conductors wearing white face paint, with deep black circles under their eyes and wild Beetlejuice hair. Among others, the menu featured Punched Ticket Porterhouses, Terminated T-bones and No Return Rib Eyes. The smell was enough to make my stomach complain loudly, but the place was hip deep in people and the line snaked around the corner.

Dee parked me by the menu sign. "I know a guy in the kitchen. Stay here. I'll be right back." She waded through the throng like a bulldozer in heels, scattering tourists left and right.

I leaned against the sign, trying not to get stepped on, and watched the people go by. A costumed brunette in black lace and burgundy satin sashayed down the street a few minutes later, flirting and laughing and posing for photos. And getting steadily closer to a group of three too-pale loiterers.

The performer stopped near the trio to straighten a garter, smiling at them flirtatiously. She obviously liked admiration, and they were giving it to her in spades. Her smile grew as they surrounded her and didn't falter even when their hands brushed down her arms. She was still smiling when they started to feed.

It was the PC way to do it, drawing her blood up through the skin in molecules so small, even she didn't notice, but three on one was a definite no-no. Three hungry vampires could drain a human in less than a minute, and she was already looking unsteady on her feet. I glanced around, but there was no security in sight. Wonderful.

I darted across the street before I could talk myself out of it just as a master vamp approached from the other direction. He grabbed the girl and sent her spinning into a party of Japanese tourists. They happily started posing for photos while she blinked at them dazedly, her cheeks pale under a liberal amount of blush.

I breathed a sigh of relief. It looked like the Senate had their own security in place, and he looked pretty pissed off. The master hoisted one of the three delinquents into the air by his expensive lapels, looked him over with a slight curl to his lip and tossed him casually into the water tower. That would have been great, except the tower was a prop with no actual water in it. It hadn't been designed to withstand the force of a 180-pound vampire hitting it at about ninety miles an hour, which it demonstrated by groaning and toppling slowly into the crowd.

People screamed and scattered as it hit down, including the two remaining miscreants who'd started the whole thing. The master cursed and went after them, leaving me standing in the street in front of the downed tower. Everyone who wasn't running for the sidewalks was looking right at me—including two war mages.

For an instant, we locked eyes, and I saw theirs widen in recognition. Shit! I ran for the nearest sidewalk, intending to get out of sight and shift—assuming I could. But the crowd was six deep on either side, and nobody felt like letting me through. I looked back to find the mages almost on top of me. I changed course and scurried for the fallen tower. Maybe, if I could get underneath—

An arm reached out of the aluminum side of the tower

and pulled me in. Only I didn't end up there. There was a moment of disorientation and then I popped out on a balcony hanging off the facade of a fake feed store. "I thought I told you to stay put!" Dee said, pushing a fallen curl out of her face.

"What did you— How many portals *are* there?"

"Never counted. A bunch were put in for a magic act a couple years ago and nobody ever shut them down. They don't use magic unless they're activated, so . . ." She shrugged. "Anyway, I got you an End of the Line burger and fries. Will that do?"

I took a greasy sack that smelled like heaven. "Absolutely," I said fervently.

"Okay, then. We're making progress. Now *stay here* while I go look for some shoes."

"Gotcha." The balcony was more for show than anything else and only a few feet wide. I'd have to eat standing up, but at the moment, I didn't care.

Dee nodded and stepped back through the side of the building, heedless of any watching eyes, not that there appeared to be any. The crowd was fixated on the mages, who were studying the fallen tower suspiciously. One cautiously stuck an arm in the side, which disappeared up to the shoulder—and reappeared on my side of the portal.

It flailed around for a second, almost brushing against me twice, while he craned his neck and looked around to see where it came out. He didn't see me, but someone in the crowd did and pointed. The waving arm snatched at me, I jerked back and it grabbed my sandwich bag instead. And disappeared.

"Damn it!"

The mage pulled my lunch out on his side of the portal, dropped it on the ground like he was afraid it was contagious and threw a fireball at it. The crowd roared in delight, apparently deciding that this was some unscheduled entertainment. I almost cried.

"That was my lunch, you idiot!" I yelled right before he stepped through the portal.

He appeared in my face, startling me, and I instinctively pushed him away. He fell back through the portal, stumbled out of the tower and landed on his ass. He glared, scrambled up and pulled a gun.

For a moment, I didn't believe he'd do it. There were a couple hundred people around; no way would he risk killing one of them while trying to take me out. The Circle hadn't impressed me with their sanity, but they weren't that crazy.

Then he pointed the gun, not at me, but at the fallen tower.

I threw myself out of the way just as he shot at point-blank range into the portal. The bullet came out my side, ruffling my hair on its way past, and shattered a lighted sign on the other side of the street. I was still staring at the sparks and broken glass when he launched himself back through—and this time he grabbed me.

I panicked and shifted—and since he was still holding on, he came along for the ride. We landed on the roof of the opposite building, or rather, he did. I was left dangling over the side, and in his surprise, he let go.

I shifted midair and ended up back where I'd started, woozy and nauseous. Shifting two people on no food and maybe five hours' sleep had wiped me out. I didn't think I could do it again. That proved to be a problem when the other mage popped out of the portal practically on top of me.

I did the only thing I could. I grabbed his coat, swung him around and fell back through the portal before he could curse me. I rolled out of the tower a second later, into the middle of the street, adding another layer of bruises. The crowd applauded as I struggled to my feet.

"They do it with doubles," I heard someone say. "The girl on the balcony was a lot more blond."

"You'd think they'd check for something like that," someone else said.

The mage stepped out of the portal and tripped over my body, kicking me painfully in the ribs. Down the street, his partner jumped from the roof and started for us through the crowd. I got my feet under me, kicked the still-burning remains of my lunch in the mage's face and ran.

"Over here!" I saw Dee waving at me, her wig towering over everyone else. A hand grabbed the back of my sweatshirt, but she jerked me over the heads of the last few people and it fell away. She swiveled on a heel, plunged into a ladies' restroom and shoved me into the janitor's closet. I didn't even have time to catch my breath before we fell through a wall.

We tumbled out into my room again a second later. I landed on the bed, but Dee hit her shin painfully on the side of the headboard. "Fuck it, that's twice today!"

I lay there, staring at the wall, wondering who was going to come through next. But nobody did. I guess the mages hadn't been able to pass the gauntlet of outraged women in line.

"Here!" Dee threw a package on the bed and pulled my shoes out of her bra. "God, what I do to look good," she said, clutching them to her heaving bosom. And disappeared.

Chapter Twelve

I tried room service, but after getting a busy signal for ten minutes straight, I put my new sneakers on and decided to go out.

There are things I am never going to like about Vegas: the relentless sun that reflects off sand and glass and concrete everywhere you look. The constantly changing skyline, where housing developments and gaudy tourist traps seem to pop up and fade away overnight, as if the whole city is set on fast-forward. And the crowds of tourists that are constantly underfoot. But you have to love a place just a little that serves up pizza and beer *to go* at midnight.

I reentered Dante's through a side entrance, intending to find a quiet place to picnic. But apparently someone else had other ideas. A meaty hand reached out of a stairwell and grabbed me around the wrist.

"If you want some pizza, you could just ask," I told Marco.

He glowered at me out of red-rimmed eyes but didn't say anything. Just breathed heavily and stuck a phone in my ear. "Cassie? Are you there?" a voice asked.

Damn. It was Mircea. And I hadn't even started to figure out what to say to him yet—about a lot of things. "What did you do to Marco?" I demanded, deciding to go with a good offense.

"Assigned him as your permanent bodyguard." Mircea's usually warm voice was cold steel.

"I meant as punishment."

"So did I."

I stared at the phone for a moment and then clicked it shut.

It almost immediately rang again.

I tossed it at Marco and continued walking. He followed. "You gotta take the boss's call."

"Or what?"

There was a slight pause. "He'll be mad."

"He's already mad."

"At me."

I looked up to find Marco practically shaking in his boots. His face was pale and his eyes were almost bugging out of his head. He looked terrified.

At that moment, I didn't like Mircea very much.

The phone rang.

Marco held it out to me and I took it. "*What?*"

"I thought you might wish to know that Raphael is in the infirmary."

I stopped walking. "Why?"

"The doctors tell me that he is dying." Mircea said something else, but I didn't hear him. I'd already dropped the phone and the pizza and was running for the stairs.

I don't remember how I got to the lobby and couldn't tell you the name of the person who gave me directions. I skidded into a table on the way and almost fell but managed to clutch it with both hands and hang on. Cursing, I started to take off again and ran into a solid wall of vampire.

Alphonse, Tony's onetime head henchman, set me back on my feet. As usual, his seven-foot-plus body was clad in a bespoke suit. This one was dark tan with a cranberry stripe, and he had a ruby the size of a quail's egg for a tie tack. More rubies glinted from a couple of finger rings and from the wrist of his longtime girlfriend, Sal. He had the suits cut loose to conceal the half ton of weaponry he carried but didn't need. Between him and Sal, they could have taken out a platoon.

Sal was all in red to match the rubies, from the skintight sheath designed to draw attention to her ample curves and away from her missing eye—lost long ago in a saloon brawl with another "hostess"—to her anger-darkened cheeks. "I

wish someone had done this to him, so I could gut them,"
she said by way of greeting.

"You've seen him?"

"Yeah." Sal wiped an arm across her face, smearing her
mascara. I stared; I'd never seen her look this rattled. She
noticed and smiled grimly. "You kinda get attached to
someone when you know him for a century and a half."

"He's not bad, for a pretty-boy painter," Alphonse
agreed. "You been in there?" He jerked a thumb at the set
of ornate doors down the hall.

"No. I just found out—"

"So did we. Fucking idiots didn't tell nobody he was here,
and he was too weak to do it himself. We're getting him
transferred to a private room."

"How . . . how is he? Mircea said something—"

"Bad," he said flatly.

"If you want to see him, you better do it now," Sal added
bleakly.

I ran.

Casanova had said that they'd had to cancel the conventions, but I'd assumed it was because they needed the space.
They did, but not only for rooms. The Murano glass chandeliers of the main ballroom, which usually looked down on
fashion shows and business luncheons, now lit up row after
row of cots. I could see them dimly through the glass insets
in the main doors but not reach them. Because the ballroom had another new feature—a pair of armed guards.

They were vampires, but they weren't part of Casanova's
security force. I knew all of them by now and they knew me,
whereas neither of these guys made any attempt to move
out of the way. "Human visitors are not allowed," one of
them said without bothering to look at me.

"I'll take my chances," I told him, but he didn't budge.
"My friend is in there." Not a word, not even a glance.
"He's dying!"

Nothing.

"She's with me," Marco said, coming out of nowhere.

"No humans," the guard repeated in the same abrupt
way, but at least Marco got eye contact. "Senate's orders."

"There have been problems?" Marco asked sharply.

The vamp shrugged. "Indiscriminate feeding. Some of

the injured were out of their heads. The nurses say they have it under control, but the Senate doesn't want any incidents. That means no human visitors."

"Well, this human is visiting whether the Senate likes it or not!" I said furiously.

"Keep it in line or I'll do it for you," the guard told Marco.

"Screw this," I said, and shifted inside—only to almost get run over by an orderly with a cart. More than a dozen of them were zipping here and there, patching up patients like pit crews servicing race cars. A nearby patient had his sheets changed, his pillow fluffed, his water jug refilled and his meds doled out in about the time it took for me to blink.

The guard was suddenly beside me. I hadn't seen him come in, but I saw him stop when Marco's hand latched onto his shoulder. Marco pulled back my hair to show off the two small marks on my neck. "She belongs to Lord Mircea."

The guard's eyes thawed slightly. "Don't let her run loose," he warned.

"Yeah. I get that a lot." Marco put a hand to my back and hustled me down the nearest aisle.

We stopped at a cot exactly the same as all the rest by one of the walls. The man-shaped patient who lay naked on top of the plain white sheets was covered head to toe in cracked and blistered flesh that glistened from ointment that didn't seem to be helping at all. His bare hairy ankles and long pink feet looked relatively untouched, but the rest of him . . . It was like he'd been parboiled.

His shoes, I thought blankly. Like his belt, which had left a pale stripe across his midsection, the heavy leather of his shoes had spared his feet the worst of it. But the light summer clothes and thin cotton sheets he'd wrapped around himself had been next to useless. They may have reduced the third-degree burns to second in a few places, but it was honestly hard to tell. A human wouldn't have survived that kind of trauma. And even Rafe was so disfigured that, without Marco's help, I would never have recognized him.

But he knew me.

"Cassie." It was a harsh whisper, like his lungs were on fire. My legs gave out and I collapsed to my knees.

"They say he was in the sun for hours." Marco sounded awed and appalled.

I didn't answer. A rush of adrenaline was making the room seem to pulse around me, but there was nowhere to run, nothing to do. I gulped in air, a little too much, a little too quickly, and choked, causing Marco's grip to tighten on my shoulder.

"Why did he do this?" I whispered. "He could have stayed behind—there was shelter."

"I heard you came back with some mages."

"They escaped with us."

"Yeah. People work together when their lives are on the line. But when they calm down, they revert to type."

I remembered Caleb's conversation with Pritkin. Had Rafe heard it and decided he couldn't trust them? My stomach rebelled as the implication hit—had he ended up this way because of me?

Rafe squinted up at us and tried to say something, but his lips had swollen so much that I couldn't understand him. "I think he wants his sunglasses," Marco translated. "Do you know what they look like?"

"They're Gucci," I whispered.

Marco found them on a nearby table and tried to put them on Rafe's face, but there was no way of resting them that wasn't going to hurt him. The moment they touched his raw flesh, he cringed and let out a hiss, and Marco snatched them back. I guess that explained the lack of hospital gown or top sheet. I couldn't imagine anything touching him and not being excruciating.

Marco was still trying to figure out the glasses dilemma when I heard a wet-sounding gasp and turned to see Sal staring at Rafe, her pale skin blotchy. Tears rolled and splashed down her face, though she didn't seem to care; she just raised her arm to swipe at her cheek without looking away from the bed. I'd never been so grateful for anyone in my entire life, because Sal was crying, *Sal* was, so I didn't have to.

"They said that he ... shouldn't be moved," Alphonse told me from behind her. The unspoken words, *wouldn't survive it*, hung in the air between us.

"This is bullshit!" Sal said, grabbing one of the passing

orderlies with a cobralike motion. "Why isn't anything being *done* for him?"

"Th-there's nothing to be done," the vamp said. He looked young, which didn't mean anything, but there was also very little power coming off him. And he wasn't very good at controlling his expressions. He glanced at Rafe and winced. "We had the healers look at him, but they said the damage was too extensive. That only his master had a chance of—"

"His master is hiding his cowardly ass in Faerie!" Sal snarled, her bloodred talons biting into the vamp's arm. "Think of something else!"

"There isn't anything else," the vamp said, starting to look a little panicked. "P-please ... I belong to Lady Halcyone. If I've offended—"

Sal released him with a disgusted snort, and he scurried away. From her expression, he was lucky that his lady and defender was a Senate member. But he was right. Vampires either healed themselves or they didn't, which was why it really worried me that Rafe hadn't dropped into a healing trance yet. Or maybe he had and he'd already come out of it unchanged. A sickening rush of dread pooled in my stomach.

I stared at him, remembering how quiet he'd been on the way back and how he'd disappeared in the lobby. I should have realized that there was a problem then, or if not, definitely when I took a shower later. The tip of my nose and the rise of my cheekbones had been sunburned enough to sting under the water. How had it not occurred to me that Rafe had to be much worse off? Nuclear-radiation-proof sunscreen or not, vampires under first level should never be out in direct sunlight. Everyone knew that; even people who hadn't grown up at a vampire's court. So how could I have missed it? How could I have gone to sleep and let this happen?

"Please, Rafe," I begged, my voice breaking. "*Please*—"

Sal had grabbed someone else, one of the Circle's healers as a guess, and dragged her forcibly over to the bed. She had black hair curling under her chin, an even tan and beautiful features. She managed to be unattractive anyway. "Release me immediately!" the woman demanded. "This is an outrage!"

"It seems we got a different idea of what constitutes an outrage," Sal told her. "Do something for my friend here or I'll demonstrate mine."

The woman flushed an ugly red. "We have already done what we could. Conventional medicine is of little use when the body it is being practiced on is already dead!"

"Then come up with something *un*conventional."

The argument continued but I stopped listening. Something unconventional. That was supposed to be my department. I was the one who'd inherited all this power, the one who was supposed to be able to fix things. But I didn't know how to fix this.

I tried to summon my power, but it wouldn't come. And attempting to force it resulted in the same thing it always did—giving me a headache and having it shy away like a skittish colt. So I tried to reason things out, but that didn't help, either.

I could go back in time and warn Rafe, tell him to leave with Marlowe and the others. But I didn't think he'd do it— I knew him better than that—and even if he did, it would only condemn everyone else in our car to death. We'd barely gotten out with Rafe at the wheel. No way would we have made it without vampire reflexes. And he was the only vamp who'd stayed.

There has to be something, I thought desperately. Something I'd missed, something I hadn't—

My power cut me off midthought. It had decided to come back, and with a vengeance. The makeshift clinic abruptly disappeared, overtaken by a vision so strong, I couldn't see anything else.

I was walking down a cracked highway half grown in with desert plants. I didn't encounter any people, but when I topped a hill and stared into the distance, I saw that I wasn't completely alone. The road was not just broken up and badly overgrown; it was a car graveyard.

Sunlight gleamed dully on the dust-caked surfaces of cars, trucks and SUVs. They were lined up in rows, like a rusted traffic jam, for as far as I could see. And although most of the vehicles were newer models, they didn't look like they'd moved for fifty years.

I started wading through the mass, but the cars were prac-

tically bumper to bumper and I decided it might be easier to walk on the sand. But when I stepped off the highway, the ground under my feet felt funny. It was dry and baked hard underneath, but on top was a layer of crumbling dust that crunched oddly under the soles of my sneakers.

I realized why a second too late, and jerked my foot back. But the bone I'd stepped on was dry and brittle enough that it crumbled to pieces anyway. More bones were everywhere, scattered like shells on a well-traveled beach. Staring ahead, I could see sand littered with white and brittle bits for what looked like miles.

After a minute, I continued through the maze, the glass from shattered windshields crunching under my feet. Some of the cars looked like they'd burned, but the pattern was random, not like that of an attack. Maybe the sun had reflected off of a shard of glass, igniting the fuel leaking from a decaying chassis. The blackened skeletons of twisted metal spotted the line, dark blotches against the field of yellow, like a leopard's spots.

Even the cars that hadn't burned were ruined, with drifts of sand and growing weeds obscuring any clues to what had happened. Every once in a while, I came across one with still-intact windows, but they were so caked with accumulated grime that it was hard to see inside. And layers of rust and dust had ruined the hinges.

I tried half a dozen of the best-preserved cars before finally finding one that I could force open. A billow of stale air rushed out, like the breath of a tomb, and something moved inside. I drew back with a little scream.

A desiccated body still sat in the driver's seat, held in place by a seat belt that had almost been bleached white by the sun. Forcing the door had jarred the remains, causing the head to detach from the rest of the corpse and fall into the floorboard. Its face stared up at me, turned to leather by the dry heat, a few tufts of brittle hair still sticking out from under a baseball cap and mouth caught in a frozen scream.

I stumbled away, but everywhere I turned, it was the same story—more tomblike cars baking in the sun. That's where the bones came from, I realized dully. From cars that hadn't remained sealed, from ones that animals could get into and—

I crouched down, my hand on a bumper, my head be-
tween my legs. For a long moment, I thought I was going
to be sick. But nothing happened except that the dizziness
finally passed and my eyes managed to focus again—on the
dust-caked remains of a license plate.

My breath quickened, my heart suddenly pounding in my
chest. I tried knocking the dirt away, but it was almost baked
on, so I clawed at it with my fingernails. I finally managed
to uncover the little plastic sticker with the year. And then
I just stared, the colors all blurring together in a smear of
primaries—red sticker, yellow dust, blue sky.

It was this year's date.

The vision shattered as abruptly as before, leaving me
trying to breathe through a white-hot spike of panic. Hands
gripped my shoulders and I couldn't break their hold. I
heard voices, but I was hysterical, close to hyperventilating,
and I couldn't make sense of them. Until a new voice spoke
my name, the simple word melting into a rich, golden tone
that washed over me like a benediction.

"It will be all right, Cassie." Mircea was murmuring the
same thing over and over while stroking my back, my hair.
And I kept trying to tell him that it wasn't, that it wouldn't
be. Because my power kept showing me nightmares instead
of the answers I desperately needed. Because I didn't understand what it was trying to tell me. Because Rafe was
dying and there was nothing I could do to stop it.

"But there is something I can do, *dulceață*," he said,
somehow understanding. "At least, there is something I can
try. I will be with you soon."

"Soon? What are you . . ." I opened my eyes to find myself lying half over Alphonse's lap, his hands gripping my
wrists, while Sal and Marco stared at me. Mircea was nowhere to be seen.

Before I could say anything, there was a commotion
outside. The doors opened and two big vamps in dark suits
came in. "Now, this is quite enough!" the nurse said. "The
rules governing visitors are clearly posted!"

The vamps ignored her and checked the area, even eyeing the patients on either side of Rafe with suspicion, before
dragging over a couple of large white screens. They hadn't
been in use at the time, not that I think they cared. "We

have limited space here and you're clogging the aisles," the nurse informed us. "All but two of you are going to have to leave."

Marco's "Sure" translated as "When hell freezes over." Sal and Alphonse didn't bother to answer her at all. Their attention had fixed on the main doors with the intensity of hunting dogs scenting prey.

The vamps finished arranging the screens around Rafe's bed, completely surrounding us except for the section facing the door. They took up positions on either side of the opening before one of them murmured, "All clear."

"You can't just barge in here," the nurse was spluttering. "I'm going to call for security—" She stopped and turned as the door opened again.

Mircea walked in.

He glanced around the room, one quick flick of the eyes that seemed to take in everything: the rows of cots, the rushing orderlies who were trying not to look like they were avidly watching, the bed with its ointment-stained sheets, and came to rest on Rafe.

Mircea studied him for a moment and then turned to the gaping nurse. "Thank you for providing such excellent care for my kinsman," he told her. "Your actions will be remembered."

Irony laced the words, but she didn't hear. "I—I—it was nothing. *Really*. We were *thrilled* to be able to do what we could," she said, still talking as Mircea walked behind the partition and calmly shut her out.

There was no more talk of throwing us out, and no interruptions. Not that I think Mircea would have noticed if there were. His attention was focused solely on Rafe, who appeared to have fallen into a light sleep.

"Raphael! Attend me!" His voice snapped like a whip, demanding obedience. And somewhere in the fog of pain that had fallen over him, Rafe heard. He opened his eyes a slit, a bare glittering against the raw flesh. "At this point, the process itself might kill you," Mircea informed him. "What do you wish to do?"

I didn't know what Mircea was talking about, but obviously Rafe did. He said something, but it was unintelligible. His voice was muffled, cracking, and I was suddenly grate-

ful that I couldn't understand. I didn't want to know what
went with the soft, broken sounds. One hand curled into a
painful-looking fist and he pressed it down with terrible,
leashed force against the soft surface of the bed.

"Then you must be willing to fight," Mircea responded.
"Life is not a gift, Raphael; it is a challenge. Rise to it!"

Mircea's eyes had lightened, brightened, mahogany fired
to gold-chased bronze. *Trust me,* they demanded, fierce
and proud and infinitely compelling. It was the look that
made me want to make really idiotic decisions that would
only end in heartbreak. Slowly, almost imperceptibly, Rafe
nodded.

And Sal pulled me up and out of the curtained area. I
looked around to find myself surrounded by the family. Sal
and Alphonse were there, along with Marco, the two security men and Casanova, who was managing to look suave
and frazzled at the same time.

"What are you doing?" I struggled as Sal pulled me toward the entrance. "Let me go! I want to stay with Rafe!"
My voice had risen three octaves in that short sentence,
which meant I was closer to losing it than I'd thought.

I tried to tear out of her grip, but of course that didn't
work, and her words caught me before I tried to shift. "It's
private," she said sharply.

"*What* is private? What is going on?"

"Mircea is going to try to break Tony's bond with Raphael," Sal said, biting her lip. "Normally, it wouldn't be a
big deal, but as weak as Rafe is . . ."

"What are you talking about? What difference does it
make who his master is if they can't save him?"

"You heard what that orderly said. The damage is too
great for them to do anything, not that I think they tried
too hard until we got after their asses. They took one look
at him and decided he was a goner."

She plopped down onto one of the seats that Alphonse
and Marco had dragged in through the main doors, and she
pulled me down into another one. We were flanking the
wall not far from the entrance in one of the few areas with
no cots. Instead, a jumbled bunch of medical equipment—
wheelchairs, gurneys, IV stands—had been pushed here
out of the way. Unneeded for the moment. Like us.

"I still don't see how changing masters is going to help!" I felt edgy and hot and weirdly tight in the chest, like I couldn't breathe. Like I had to do something or I might explode.

"Mircea made Tony, but Tony made Rafe," Sal said tersely. "And the blood is the life."

I'd heard that phrase all my life; it was a mantra among vampires. But I didn't see the relevance now. "But Rafe's blood isn't helping him!"

"Because it's *Tony's*," Sal said as if I was being especially slow. "It isn't powerful enough to let Rafe repair this kind of damage. But Mircea isn't Tony."

Alphonse snorted. "No shit."

"We get our strength partly from our own abilities and partly from our master," Sal explained, reaching for a cigarette. She noticed a couple of oxygen tanks nearby and stopped, looking frustrated. "The more powerful the master, the more powerful his servants. If Rafe has enough strength left to absorb Mircea's blood, to let it become his new source of life, he should heal."

"And if he doesn't?"

"What do you think?" she snapped, obviously tired of twenty questions. She glanced up at Alphonse. "I need a drink."

"Send Marco," he said, settling into a permanent-looking stance by the wall. "If the master pulls this off, he's gonna be weak. And by now everybody knows he's here. If someone was gonna hit him, this would be the time."

"He brought guards," Sal said.

"Two." Alphonse sounded disapproving. "I got ten more boys on the way, and I ain't budging till they get here."

"I *have* guards," Casanova said, looking insulted. "Not to mention those thugs the Senate imposed on me."

For once, Alphonse refrained from a snide comment on the quality of Casanova's stable. "And now you got more."

Sal looked at me and I looked defiantly back. I wasn't budging until I knew about Rafe. She sighed. "*I'll* go. This place is fucking depressing. What does everyone want?"

As soon as she left, I rounded on Alphonse. "How could turning someone weaken a first-level master? They do it all the time!"

Alphonse tilted his head back against the wall. For a moment, I didn't think he'd bother to answer. But then he cut his eyes my way and I must have looked pretty frantic, because he sighed. "For a master to turn a non-magical human, yeah—it's no problem," he told me. "Three bites from the same vampire in quick succession and that's pretty much it. But Rafe was already turned."

"So?"

"So to break the bond, Mircea has to drain Tony's blood from Rafe and replace it with his own. Normally, it's exhausting, but no big deal. A first-level master's blood is pretty damn potent, so it doesn't take a lot. But Rafe's so far gone, Mircea's gonna have to lend him extra power just so he can survive the Change."

"And that means draining himself dangerously low," I guessed, wishing I hadn't asked.

Alphonse scowled at a couple of orderlies who had been loitering around like starstruck teenagers ever since Mircea showed up. They quickly found somewhere else to be. "The master's gonna be hemorrhaging power whether this works or not," he rumbled. "I'm here to see that he doesn't pay for it."

There didn't seem to be much else to say, after that. The three of us sat there silent, unmoving and, in the case of the vampires, not even breathing. I couldn't tell how Casanova and Alphonse were feeling, because they'd lapsed into the non-expression vamps use when there's no reason to impress the humans. But I felt anxious, miserable and utterly useless.

For some reason, my brain kept going to the presents Rafe used to bring me whenever he went on a trip. They were always thoughtful, fitting whatever I needed at the time. As a rambunctious tomboy, I'd received a plastic gladiator helmet from Rome and a matching sword that I'd used to chase him through the halls of Tony's farmhouse. As an adolescent girl who wanted to appear more grown-up than she was, I'd been given small bottles of perfume from Paris, perfectly child-sized but filled with adult fragrances. And right before my escape from Tony's, Rafe had slipped me my very first fake ID.

He had never asked for anything in return, had never

seemed to expect or want anything. He was probably the only person in my life I could say that about. And now he was dying.

I usually wasn't a violent person. I'd seen so much of it growing up that it had lost its glamour for me, even before everybody and their dog started attacking me. So it took me a few minutes to put a name to the feeling flushing my cheeks and curdling my stomach. I didn't know who was behind the attack today, or even for certain that anyone was. But I knew one thing.

If I ever found out, I'd kill them.

Chapter Thirteen

I don't know when I fell asleep, but I woke up with my head against Marco's shoulder, which somebody appeared to have drooled on. My eyes were gummy and I felt like I'd been hit by a large truck. My shoulders and back were in knots and my head was pounding. But Mircea was outside the screen, leaning heavily on Alphonse's arm, and Rafe was—

"Rafe!" I bolted up the aisle, grabbed him and held on tight, whispering things that hurt against my throat. He still looked like death, but he was on his feet, and the skin that showed under the pale blue hospital gown he'd acquired was crisscrossed by scars but whole. The cracks were gone, the redness was gone, and he was standing. I was seeing it, and I could barely believe it.

"He broke your bond," Sal said, and the look she sent Rafe was half relief, half jealousy. She'd been after Mircea to do the same for her and Alphonse ever since they came to Vegas, but so far, he hadn't had the time or the energy to spare.

Rafe didn't notice the undercurrent. He just nodded, looking dazed and amazed and utterly exhausted. He glanced at me, but I wasn't sure he even knew who I was.

"My son requires a room," Mircea told Casanova.

"I have something ready. Your rooms are waiting as well, of course. And the Consul requests an audience at your earliest convenience."

"Tell her I will see her in an hour," Mircea said. Casanova blinked and started to say something but swallowed the words. Instead, he mutely led the way out of the infirmary.

Dante's had two penthouses, one in each of its twin towers, with the second reserved for the hotel's owner. The best thing about them from my standpoint was their sheer inaccessibility. Each suite took up a whole floor and the only way in was through a private elevator with key-code access. And just in case Spidey scaled the building or a bunch of ninjas rappelled out of a helicopter, we were joined by a dozen guards as we crossed the lobby.

Six took the elevator up ahead of us, and the rest waited to follow. Marco, Mircea's two guards, Casanova, Sal and Alphonse came up with us. And even in the plush elevator, which boasted its own padded bench seat and twinkly chandelier, that was a squeeze. I was all for security, but I didn't see how anyone was supposed to draw a weapon if we couldn't even move.

"Do we need a whole platoon?" I asked when we finally got the doors closed.

"The order went out after MAGIC fell: no one of senatorial rank is to go anywhere without an escort," Mircea informed me.

"But you're a master vampire."

"And you are Pythia," he said pointedly. "At the moment, our power merely makes us better targets."

"Not for long," Casanova said, his voice muffled because he'd ended up squashed behind two huge vampires. "The Senate has a staff working to strengthen the wards."

"Wards don't have eyes and ears," Marco argued. "They'll never replace a well-trained bodyguard."

Maybe not, I thought, but they were a lot less creepy. I didn't know the new guards, but I assumed they were part of Mircea's personal stable. Because they gave off enough energy in the confined space to send a current prickling over my skin. And it wasn't the usual light frisson, either. The energy in the air felt like an electrical storm, with power crawling over my arms, itching my scalp, making me want to scream.

Both masters, then.

I managed not to scrub at my arms, but when the nearest

turned flat gold eyes on me, I forgot my training and shrank back slightly. He smiled, a slow baring of fangs, while the other looked at me like I was something funky he'd found growing at the back of the refrigerator. Then the doors opened and we spilled out into a private hallway.

It contained a potted palm, a small strip of carpet and the six guards who had preceded us framing the only door. One of them hurried to open it and we passed into a large foyer. For a moment, I just stared. Unlike my old quarters, which could have belonged in any hotel on the strip, this one was themed. The motif being flogged to death appeared to be the Old West, or some designer's idea of it. The two-tiered chandelier was made of antlers, there were oil paintings of cowboys on the red flocked wallpaper, a cow skin rug made a black and white puddle on the floor, and a rough wood entry table supported a cowboy-and-rearing-horse sculpture in bronze.

Casanova noticed my expression. "The Consul preferred the blue suite," he said stiffly.

"Imagine that."

A wizened old vamp hobbled toward us, looking unhappy. "What's all this?" he demanded in a quavery voice.

Most humans would have taken one look at the liver-spotted hands and wild clumps of white hair and guessed him to be about a hundred. And they'd have been off by four centuries. He wore pince-nez on his long nose, despite the fact that they didn't help his blind-as-a-bat status, and he was almost deaf to boot. But Horatiu had been Mircea's childhood tutor and was the only person I'd ever heard tell off the boss.

"The master needs to rest!" Horatiu said, surveying the army of guards attempting to crowd in through the door. "Out, all of you!"

When the guards uniformly ignored him, he shuffled over to one of the larger vamps and began attempting to push him out the door. That had about as much effect as a fly trying to move a boulder, but Horatiu didn't appear to notice. The guard didn't fight back, just stood there with a long-suffering look on his face and let himself be pummeled.

"I'm sorry," Casanova told Mircea in a low tone. "I assigned a staff to these rooms, but Horatiu arrived with the refugees from MAGIC and—"

"Threw them out."

Casanova nodded. "He said they weren't trustworthy. I tried to reassure him, but—"

"It's all right," Mircea murmured.

"I said *out*. Are you deaf?" Horatiu demanded, now resorting to kicking. "How do they grow them so big?" I heard him mutter.

Sal sighed and lit another cigarette. "The guards are needed for the master's protection."

"And what do you think I'm here for, young lady?"

Alphonse opened his mouth and Mircea shot him a look. He shut up. "I'm sure Horatiu is perfectly capable of seeing to my well-being," Mircea said mildly.

"I'll sneak them in later," Casanova murmured, and Mircea nodded.

The huge vamp that Horatiu had been thumping reluctantly gave ground, getting pushed all the way back to the elevator before the old man was satisfied. Then the brushed nickel doors opened, spilling four more guards into the already packed hallway. Horatiu broke into infuriated Romanian while the rest of us followed Casanova into a large living room. Marco and the two guards Mircea had brought with him moved quickly through the apartment, checking for intruders. I wondered how they'd be able to tell. The obviously mad designer had only been warming up in the foyer; by the time he made it in here, he was working on all cylinders.

There were mounted heads on every wall, everything from deer and longhorn cattle to buffalo and reindeer, including two bare skulls flanking the flat-screen TV mounted above the oversized fireplace. A grizzly bear rug took pride of place under two cowhide-covered sofas facing each other across a lacquered horn coffee table, the whole lit by another horn chandelier. A neon cactus brightened a rustic bar in the corner, which had stools shaped like saddles. The whole managed to look pricey and outrageously tacky at the same time.

Mircea hesitated for a moment on the top step leading down into the sunken morass of kitsch, as if slightly stunned. "It was like this when I took over," Casanova said, sounding defensive. "I plan to remodel, of course."

"I dunno." Sal plopped down onto cow skin and stubbed out her cigarette in an ashtray shaped like a spittoon. "It's different."

"It's vulgar," Casanova snapped.

"And the rest of this place isn't?"

"It's fine," Mircea said, crossing the barn-wood floor to join her.

Casanova went to the wall and flicked a switch. There was the sound of a quiet motor, and what had seemed like a solid wall began to retract. It slowly opened to reveal a huge balcony with the long dark rectangle of a private infinity pool reflecting the glittering panorama of the Strip. Okay, maybe a person could forgive the decor for a view like that.

In addition to the master suite, the penthouse boasted three additional bedrooms, one of which had been earmarked for Rafe. Marco and one of Mircea's guards helped get him there, supporting him without making it obvious that that's what they were doing. I didn't think Rafe cared much about dignity at this point. When he raised his head to gaze numbly around, he looked wrecked, eyes heavy and mouth swollen.

"Do you need anything?" I asked, having followed them in. I didn't get an answer. Rafe was out as soon as his head hit the pillow.

"A rebirth is hard enough on its own," Marco said, noticing my expression. "And with the burns on top of it . . . he's gonna be out a while."

"He'll be okay, though, right?"

"He survived the process, so yeah. He should be fine."

I studied Rafe's face. He had deep hollows under his eyes and a few limp curls falling over his forehead. His bare wrists on top of the sheet looked fragile. He didn't look fine to me. "We need a nurse," I decided.

"We know how to take care of our own," the guard said dismissively. He was one of those who had given me the evil eye in the elevator. It didn't look like I was growing on him.

"I'm sure you do," I said, fighting to stay civil despite

nerves that had passed raw hours ago. "But considering the extent of his injuries, I would prefer to have a professional sit with him."

"Explain to her," the guard told Marco, ignoring me.

"They're not allowing unauthorized personnel in senators' quarters," Marco said. "That includes nurses."

"Then get an authorized one!" I could feel my pulse start to throb in my temple. "And I guess I should be happy you aren't referring to me as 'it,'" I told the guard, "but it's usually considered polite to *look* at someone when you're talking to them."

"Cassie—" Marco began.

"Rafe almost *died*, Marco! He needs proper care. Not some guy who's too busy blindly following orders to—"

I abruptly found myself jerked up to meet a pair of dazzlingly golden eyes glittering with a serpent's hypnotic stare. The guard was smiling, but there was nothing of warmth in the expression—the eyes too flat, the smile too amused, something a little too *hungry* about it to be kind. Like a cat that had some small animal cornered and was savoring the moment before snapping its neck.

"You wish me to look at you, human?" he asked silkily. "My pleasure." And the air in the room went electric.

I'd been through this kind of thing enough by now not to go into total shock and freeze up. Some of the vamps at Tony's had liked to play scare-the-human when there was nothing better to do, and I'd learned a few coping strategies through the years. But the strongest of Tony's goons had had only a fraction of this one's power.

Already, despite the tricks I'd learned for keeping my mind clear, I was starting to fog over. The room went dim as quickly as if someone had thrown a switch. A suffocating darkness shouldered in that crowded my lungs and wouldn't let me breathe. The only bright spots were two scarlet-tinged eyes with huge black pupils that had nearly devoured the gold. And all I could think was that Nietzsche had been right: sometimes when you look into the abyss, the abyss looks back.

Someone's hand was on my arm, but I could barely feel it, and I couldn't hear at all. The master's power filled my brain, stuttered along my nerves, blocked out everything else. I was starting to forget what I'd been saying and why it had seemed so important. In another few seconds, I'd forget a lot more—where I was, maybe even who I was—until there was nothing left but one simple idea: to obey.

Remember, I told myself savagely, digging my nails as hard as I could into my palm, and the pain dulled slightly the rushing voice in the back of my head. I stared into ancient, alien eyes and was too empty to play games. "Go ahead and show everyone how powerful you are," I said unsteadily. "But when you're finished, *I want a goddamned nurse in here!*"

The eyes held mine for another second, two—and then blinked and looked away. And just like that, the tension broke, the lights came on and the rushing sound was replaced by the soft breath of the air-conditioning and Marco's cursing. I could still taste bile at the back of my throat, acid and dark, but I knew who I was.

"You don't want to be doing that," Marco was telling someone while keeping a tight enough grip on me that I didn't fall. "This one's the boss's woman!"

The guard's eyes narrowed. "She's human." He looked confused and vaguely disgusted. "I haven't heard anything about—"

"Yeah. The master's been busy. I'm sure he'll get around to formal introductions eventually. In the meantime, be a little more careful, huh?" Marco dragged me away from the stunned-looking guard and back toward the main living space.

We reached the hallway and I stopped, needing a second to arrange my face before dealing with the others. Marco sighed and glared at me, arms crossed and brows knitted. And I decided that as long as he was already pissed off, we might as well get something straight.

"You need to stop introducing me like that," I said seriously. "Talking about me like I'm property—"

"Is the only thing some of them are gonna understand."

"Tell it to someone else. I grew up at a vampire's court; I know the protocol. And that's not it!"

"You grew up at the court of a two-bit hood with delusions of grandeur," Marco shot back. "You're gonna have to get used to the fact that Mircea's retainers are older and a lot more traditional than those you grew up with. And based on what I've seen so far, you don't know shit about protocol."

"All I did was ask for a nurse!"

"It's not what you say; it's how you say it. You don't talk to an old family master the same way as you would a brand-new vamp or a human."

"I've met plenty of older vamps!" I said, stung. "I've met the *Senate*—"

"And if you weren't connected to the master and also Pythia . . ." Marco shook his head. "I don't know."

"Other people's prejudices are not my problem," I told him furiously. I couldn't believe that I was getting this lecture from *Marco* of all people. A guy who acted like an extra from *The Godfather* was telling me I needed to improve *my* manners?

"If you don't learn some etiquette, they will be," he said flatly. "A lot of the older vamps are touchy. They've been around five, six hundred years; some even longer. They've been waiting to hit first-level status, to be emancipated, to become the master of their own fate. But it ain't happened yet. And most of 'em have figured out that it never will."

"What does that have to do with anything?" I asked, honestly bewildered.

"Some of our vamps didn't start with us," he hissed. "A few, like Nicu in there, have had three or four masters. For hundreds of years they've been shuffled around like cattle, with no control over who they served or what they did—no control over anything. All they've had—and all they're ever gonna have—is respect because of their age and abilities. And if they think you ain't showing 'em that respect, they're gonna react."

I swallowed, too drained for a lecture right now but sensing that this might be one I needed. No one at Tony's had been that old besides him and Rafe. And come to think of it, Tony had been pretty damn touchy about his dignity. I'd always thought it was because of his huge ego, and maybe it was. Or maybe there were still a few things I didn't understand about vamps.

"I'm sorry," I said quietly. "I didn't realize—"

"Yeah, I know. But these are things you have to think

about. Because you know what Nicu is thinking right now? He's wondering if this was a hint, if the boss's lady disrespecting him was Mircea's way of telling him that he's out of favor. He's wondering if maybe he's about to be disowned—again—and shuffled off to another court where he'll have to spend the next fifty years clawing his way into a position of respect. If he survives that long. He's wondering if the ax is about to fall."

I stared at Marco, sickened. "I'll talk to him. I'll explain—"

Marco rolled his eyes. "Yeah. 'Cause that'll go over great. Don't worry about it; I'll tell him you just don't know no better. But you gotta realize that things are different now. You're not a little hanger-on at a court nobody cares about. People pay attention to what you say, so you gotta do the same."

"Okay," I said, feeling about two inches tall. God, could today *get* any worse?

"I'm not the best person to be telling you this," Marco said, looking frustrated. "We gotta find you a teacher, and not one of those hicks you came up with—"

"You two may as well come in here," Sal called from the living room. "It's not like everybody can't hear you anyway. And we hicks would like a few words."

Great.

Casanova had gone when we reentered the living room, probably back to corral the chaos. But Alphonse, Sal and Mircea were sitting on cowhide. Mircea and Sal were on either end of the same sofa, with the middle seat occupied by lunch in the form of a young blond man. That left the other couch for me and the guys, although it was hardly a squeeze—the thing had to be nine feet long.

Sal and Alphonse topped up their drinks at the awful bar while Mircea finished his dessert. I recognized him as one of Casanova's stable who usually worked the front desk. We'd pulled a few shifts together and he gave me a slight smile as he got to his somewhat unsteady feet. One of the guards escorted him and the main course, a twentysomething brunet, toward the foyer.

Amazingly, Mircea looked tired even after a double feeding. He was sitting slightly slumped down, with his hands crossed over his stomach and his head tilted back. It would have been a normal enough pose for anyone else, especially after a hard day. But Mircea didn't do relaxed. He usually had a frisson of energy around him, and not just from the power he gave off. It was noticeably absent tonight.

I stared at him, trying to focus on his eyes and not on the tired lines around them. Mircea wasn't supposed to get tired. Or sick. Or hurt. It was one of the things that had made him so attractive to me, even as a child. In a world where alliances were constantly shifting and people were constantly dying, Mircea was stable, strong, eternal.

Except that he wasn't.

Which meant that he that, one day, I could lose him, too.

If I was honest, that was my biggest reason for not wanting to let him any closer than he already was. Having someone was the precursor to losing him. It had happened over and over. It was easier not to want anything—not from Mircea, not from anyone.

Wanting, needing—they were so close, and needing always hurt.

"Cassie?" Mircea was looking at me strangely. I suddenly realized that I'd just been standing there, staring at him.

"How much blood did Rafe take?" I blurted.

Mircea gave me a small smile, but Marco hung his head and Sal burst out laughing. "What?" I demanded.

"It's considered impolite to inquire about someone's Change," Horatiu informed me, tottering in with a folding table and a loaded tray. I jumped up to help him—and not just because the tray smelled divine—but good manners only won me a glower. "Sit down, sit down! Were you brought up by wolves, young woman?"

"By Tony," Sal said, reclaiming her seat.

"Ah. The same thing, then," Horatiu said, trying to balance the tray while wrestling with the folding table.

"Don't mind him," Alphonse said, rescuing my dinner before it hit the carpet. "That old goat lectures me all the time." That didn't reassure me much; Alphonse's idea of good manners consisted of remembering to bury all the bodies.

"That old goat can hear you," Horatiu said tartly.

"That's a first," Alphonse muttered, settling my dinner across my knees.

I hadn't realized how hungry I was until I smelled the roast beef sandwich Horatiu had rustled up. It had grilled onions and mushrooms and tangy little banana peppers and was pretty much my idea of heaven. The only thing that would have made it better was fries instead of the mountain of salad off to one side, but I didn't feel like complaining.

I dug in while Sal frowned at me. It didn't take me long to figure out why. She was hyperconscious of appearance, or so I'd always thought. But having met the family, her attitude was starting to make more sense. She might not have the age or the power of Mircea's masters, but she was damned if she wasn't going to outdress them.

"I look this way because the Consul threw me out of my room and somebody stole my luggage," I told her between bites.

"Your luggage is here, where it's supposed to be. What we couldn't figure out is where *you* were, as you didn't bother to inform anybody."

"You had me tagged—you knew exactly where I was!"

"We knew you were somewhere in the hotel," she agreed, as if monitoring my every move was no big deal. "But the wards around here interfere with the spell, so we couldn't narrow it down any more than that. Marco only managed to locate you when you went outside."

"For pizza. On her own," he grumbled under his breath.

Mircea didn't say anything, but his expression was deliberately blank. It made me very nervous.

"Coulda been worse," Alphonse said. "We spent half the day thinking it *was* worse. The tag said you was alive, but then they brought the car in—"

Damn. I'd forgotten about that. "Is the Consul really pissed?" I asked nervously.

"About what?"

"Her car. I know it was probably really rare—"

"It was a car." Alphonse shrugged. "It's no big deal. But everyone would like to know you survived."

"It's a long story."

"I bet. I saw that thing and I'd have given odds that nobody made it out. Burnt to a crisp."

I frowned. A lot of things had happened to that car, but

that hadn't been one of them. "It wasn't burnt. And if it had been, the water would have put it out."

Mircea lifted his head to look at me strangely. "What water?"

"The water in the lake. You know, that we nose-dived into?"

He was silent for a moment. "No, *dulceaţă*, I do not. The car exploded in the middle of the desert."

For a moment, I just chewed sandwich. I swallowed and drank some of my wine. "It exploded," I repeated.

"We believe it was a car bomb meant for the Consul. The Bentley was one of her favorites."

The gray whale we'd left at the bottom of Lake Mead had been a Packard. I'd seen the name written across its bulbous backside in big silver letters as it sank. None of this was making sense.

"She informed us that she asked Raphael to drive it out for her," he added.

And then I remembered. Rafe had been saving a seat for me in a black Bentley. I'd seen it in the lineup, a sleek, antique gem gleaming under the emergency lights. I'd almost forgotten until now because we hadn't taken that car. Somebody else had. Somebody who was now dead.

"I assume you shifted out before the explosion?" Mircea asked, watching me keenly. He knew something was wrong.

"We took another car," I said numbly. And if we hadn't, Rafe wouldn't have been in the infirmary today. He would have been dead. If I'd gone back in time to try to save him, I'd have killed him.

Chapter Fourteen

"Here." Sal shoved a glass into my hand. From the fumes, I was guessing it was straight whiskey.

I stared at the coffee table while I sipped it, but all I saw were hundreds of ruined cars baking under a cloudless sky. And all around them, an empty, dead landscape filled with bones. Had all that been the power's way of telling me that I was about to screw up big-time? Had it been trying to warn me about Rafe's death?

I really liked that idea, because in that case the images weren't something to worry about. The crisis was over, Rafe had survived, and for once, we'd dodged a bullet. But as much as I wanted to believe it, something about that idea bugged me.

The burnt-out cars I could understand, considering what had happened to the Bentley. But why not just show me that? The actual explosion would have been a lot easier to decipher than some eerie landscape filled with rotting vehicles. And for that matter, why show me a destroyed Dante's when I asked about preventing the attack on MAGIC?

I was sick of trying to figure out messages conveyed, not through language, but through nightmares! It was just one more reason I hated my gift. Once in a while, you got an image that was clear-cut and unmistakable. Like on my fourteenth birthday, when I'd been gifted with a vision of my parents' deaths in a car bomb, complete with sound and vivid Technicolor. Those types were bad enough, but at least they beat the more mystical variety, which could mean anything or nothing. Half the time you never understood them until the events had come to pass and it was too late.

"So this is what? The third attempt on the Consul's life in the last month?" Sal was asking.

"It is an ongoing problem," Mircea agreed. "Made more so now without MAGIC's extensive ward system."

"And by her refusal to go into hiding," Sal said, looking approving.

Mircea rubbed his eyes. I was beginning to know that gesture. "Yes, and while that has allowed us to identify several traitors, it is . . . nerve-wracking."

"She can't cower in the dark," Sal pointed out. "She's a symbol. People take their courage from her."

"That is also her opinion. Kit swears she is giving him ulcers."

Sal frowned and leaned forward, suddenly intense. "She understands that you can't just sit by and hope things work out! That you have to *make* things happen—"

"I thought he liked stubborn, powerful, complicated types," Alphonse interrupted.

"He likes them alive," Mircea said pointedly.

I pretended not to notice.

"How could one of the Consul's cars have a bomb?" I asked. "Aren't they cared for by her servants?"

"Yes." Mircea looked grim. "It would appear that we have another traitor."

"How many did that damn girl corrupt?" Alphonse asked angrily.

"That damn girl" was Myra, Agnes' former ward, who had joined Apollo's side. She'd figured out how to weaken the bonds between master vampires and their servants by using her abilities to go back in time and poison soon-to-be vampires. Vamps who were ill or dying when changed were never as strongly bound to their master's will. Horatiu, for example, had been on his deathbed when Mircea changed him, but the most he did with his greater freedom was to speak his mind.

Others had found more dangerous pastimes.

"There cannot be many more," Mircea said, looking like he really wanted to believe that. "Myra was targeting the leading servants of Senate members, weakening their bonds so that they could be persuaded to betray or kill their masters. That narrows the number of suspects to a relatively small group. And at the rate we're going, they will all have rebelled before long!"

"Wouldn't it be wise to isolate them or something?" I suggested. "At least until things calm down?" I didn't like the thought of one of those hard-eyed masters stabbing him in the back. Or anywhere else.

Mircea shook his head. "Unfortunately, the very ones under suspicion are also those of the most value to us. And at the moment, we need our strength."

"Yes, but if they're dangerous—"

"It would be more dangerous to deprive ourselves of their support," he said firmly. "And we may already know who the traitor is. An old adherent of my house tried to assassinate someone dear to me recently. He failed and was killed. But for months before that, he was on my staff at MAGIC. He would have had ample opportunity to set a trap for the Consul."

And so would a lot of other people, I thought but didn't say. If I knew Marlowe, he wasn't likely to leave any stone unturned in the investigation. Someone had almost assassinated his leader right under his nose. That had to sting.

"What would happen to the war if the Consul died?" I asked, pretty sure that I already knew the answer.

"Our participation would be severely curtailed while a replacement was determined. That could take months, as our laws allow anyone to contend for the position who has reached first-level status. That includes masters from other courts. And many of them are of the opinion that we need nothing from humans other than their blood."

"So there goes the alliance with the Circle," I said blankly. And possibly the war. I drained my glass, appreciating the warmth it sent coursing through me. My skin had suddenly gone cold.

At Mircea's request, I spent the next fifteen minutes bringing everyone up to speed about my day. He didn't interrupt, but he didn't look happy. And he actually drank the amber liquid in his glass instead of just swirling it around as usual.

"I will have someone examine your ward," he said when I'd finished. "I don't like the idea of your being without it."

"Yeah. Especially with the Circle still after me."

"Yes, about that," Mircea said, accepting a refill from Sal. "The Lord Protector called me this afternoon to ask about you."

"How kind of him." I stabbed a tomato with my fork.

Something that wasn't a smile lifted the corner of Mircea's mouth. "He assured me that Mage Richardson acted completely without his knowledge or consent, out of a spirit of revenge."

"So what's his excuse for the last month?"

"He asked me to convey his personal regrets to you ... and to arrange another meeting as soon as possible."

I smiled. I'd been waiting for a chance to use one of Pritkin's more colorful swear words. And if ever there was a moment ...

Mircea's lips quirked. "That is what I thought you'd say. Which is why I agreed to the meeting on your behalf."

"What?"

"Tradition states that the new Pythia's reign does not officially begin until she is confirmed at a ceremony by the Lord Protector of the Circle," he said mildly.

"I don't care about tradition!"

"But the magical community does. To be accepted as Pythia, you need the legitimacy such a ceremony would provide."

"That wasn't your view this morning!"

"It was, in fact. But that meeting was deemed inadvisable because of safety concerns. Kit had heard rumors that there might be trouble."

"Something you might have shared with me."

Mircea raised one of those expressive brows. "Would you really have chosen to miss such an opportunity?"

"I don't know. But it would have been nice to have the choice!"

"I will keep that in mind."

Sure he would. When he ran out of handcuffs. "I'm still not meeting with the Circle," I told him flatly. "And I don't need or want their blessing. Feel free to quote me."

"The Senate will guarantee your safety."

"You can't. You can't trust anything they tell you!"

"We don't. Which is why we have set the meeting to take place during the reception for the visiting consuls." Mircea paused, and for the first time that night his eyes glinted with the usual fire. "All six of them."

"Six?" Alphonse choked on his whiskey while the rest of us just stared.

"The first convocation of six consuls in history is meeting in two days' time," Mircea confirmed. His voice was steady, but there was definite color in his cheeks. It took a lot to make a first-level master lose control, even to that degree. But news like that would just about do it. The Consul might even have blinked.

"You work fast," I said. "This morning you could only get two."

"It seems that today's tragedy convinced the senates that this war is unlike any we have seen."

"And scared 'em shitless," Alphonse guessed. "Not that they'll admit it."

Mircea smiled slightly. "They have had a shock—something unusual for them. Their courts are also built on or near ley lines."

"They're afraid that what happened once can happen again," I reasoned.

He didn't look too concerned. "There is always a chance, of course. But the lines have been in use for millennia and there has never been a similar catastrophe. Our best guess at the moment is that it was a tragic accident."

"An accident that just happened to take place over MAGIC?"

"If the line was unstable, a rift could have occurred anywhere. But it appears that the battle was the trigger and it took place there. We will know more in a few days, when the turbulence within the line diminishes enough for an investigation."

"So, if there's no danger, why are the consuls meeting?"

"They may be under the impression that the threat is more serious than perhaps is the case," he said blandly.

"And you don't think they're going to be a little upset when they find out otherwise?"

"Early reports are often misleading. And by the time a

conclusive answer can be obtained, the meeting will have already taken place."

It sounded like Mircea was gambling that, given the opportunity to talk to them face-to-face, he could bring them around. And maybe he could. But I wouldn't have liked to look at that group and say, *Sorry, just joking*!

"Pritkin thinks someone sabotaged the line," I told him.

Mircea frowned. Since that was his usual response to any mention of John Pritkin, I ignored it. "To engineer such a breach would require a fantastic amount of energy. More than any known magical alliance possesses. Our experts are convinced that a naturally occurring phenomenon was to blame."

"Let's hope so," I said fervently.

"Where are the consuls meeting now that MAGIC is gone?" Sal asked.

"Here. Casanova is arranging lodging as we speak, and the wards are being reinforced." He looked at me. "That should not go beyond this room, by the way."

"I don't gossip!"

Mircea smiled. "That goes for everyone."

Yeah, but he'd looked at me.

Horatiu entered, leading a vampire in hospital scrubs. The nurse, I assumed. He looked at us nervously and gave a quick bow before ducking his head and scurrying past. And for the first time that night, I felt myself relax. A vamp medic should know how to care for Rafe.

Mircea was on his feet when I turned around again. That seemed to signal the breakup of the party because, within a moment, everyone had disappeared. For once, even Marco found somewhere else to be.

Leaving me alone with Mircea.

I started for the door, but a hand snagged the back of my shirt. "A moment," Mircea said quietly. I sighed but didn't fight it; we needed to talk.

I was ushered into the master suite, where I stopped dead at the sight of the designer's pièce de résistance. A full-sized cream leather Indian teepee, complete with brown, hand-painted buffalos and beaded fringe, was serving as a canopy for the bed. "Oh, my God."

"I'm beginning to sense a theme," Mircea said, tossing his suit coat over a buckskin-covered chair. A moose head with huge, outspread antlers loomed over it, its bright glass eyes looking oddly lifelike in the low light. Mircea took in the room, his expression slightly repulsed yet fascinated. "I believe there is only one thing to say at this point."

"What's that?"

"Yee haw," he said gravely, and took me down like a rodeo calf. Before I entirely figured out what was happening, I was on my back in the teepee with a vampire crawling on top of me.

It was completely unfair, I thought, that when I was tired and disheveled I looked a mess, and when it happened to Mircea he looked like a particularly elegant porn star. His hair was artfully mussed, his shirt was unbuttoned enough to show a glimpse of lean-muscled chest, and his dress slacks clung lovingly to muscular thighs. In contrast, I was wearing the rumpled sweats I'd slept in, which had also acquired a pizza sauce stain. And that was despite the fact that I had never actually had any pizza.

Not that it mattered much what my clothes looked like considering how fast I was losing them. My sweatpants went flying, ending up atop the leering moose head, while warm hands slid along my sides, pushing up my T-shirt. I sucked in a breath at the unexpected speed of it all and at the electric tingle that spread up my body.

"You're supposed to be tired!"

"I am. Which is why I am not berating you for almost giving me a heart attack." My T-shirt followed the sweatpants, and at least the eerie fake eyeballs on the moose were now covered up. Which was more than I could say for me.

"Vampires don't get heart attacks."

Mircea gave me a playful flick of his eyebrow and tugged my panties off. "Good thing."

I opened my mouth to reply when his palms bracketed my face, swiftly followed by his mouth hard and demanding on mine. And somehow my witty riposte turned into a pathetic whimpering noise in the back of my throat. Unlike his usual habit, there was no slow seduction this time; Mircea kissed me hot and wet and dirty.

"We knew you were at MAGIC," he told me a few moments later as I tried to remember how to breathe. "But with the interference from the breach, there was no way to know where you were or if you would get out in time."

"I wasn't in there very long," I said, trying to focus.

"*Dulceaţă*, you were in there for *two hours*." And for a moment, the mask slipped. For an instant he looked . . . hungry, in some way I couldn't quite define. Not the predatory desire I'd seen on a few occasions, but more like need. Like some huge, gaping hole had opened up inside him since this morning.

His hair was mussed from having my hands all over it. I reached out and smoothed the worst of the snarls. I wondered if he'd lost friends today, if some of the people who didn't make it out of MAGIC were family. And then I remembered that Radu had been in trouble. And it had been bad enough to drag Mircea away in the middle of delicate negotiations.

"Mircea . . . is Radu—"

"He is well. He sends his regards." I felt a wash of relief. "He suffered some damage to the house, but it has given him the excuse to redecorate. I believe the term 'rococo' was used." He glanced at the moose head and his lips quirked. "Of course, he hasn't seen this place yet."

"You actually think he'd like it?"

"He has a fine-tuned appreciation for irony and the absurd," he told me, stripping off his shirt. "He would love it."

"You should tell Casanova not to bulldoze it, then."

"I'll do that," Mircea murmured. Fine cloth hissed, a zipper jangled and a leg slid between mine in a heady rush of skin on skin. Teeth grazed the soft skin of my neck and a tongue flickered over the vein. "*Dulceaţă*, are you familiar with the concept of a quickie?"

I laughed. There were about a hundred reasons why I shouldn't be here right now, but none of them seemed to matter next to the one overwhelming reason why I should. We were alive, we were *both* alive, along with the people we loved. It seemed like a miracle.

"Yes, but I didn't think you were." Mircea preferred long and slow and sensual, or so I'd assumed based on limited past experience.

"I am familiar with a great many things, as I will be happy to—" He suddenly went still.

His face had the distant look it got when he was communicating with other vampires long-distance. I didn't particularly understand how they did it; maybe it was merely better hearing, but I didn't think so. Like I didn't think I'd imagined his voice in my head in the clinic.

Mircea closed his eyes, his breath coming out in an irritated sigh. "This war is becoming very . . . *inconvenient*," he said, and rolled off the bed.

"What is it?"

"I am being summoned," he told me, shedding his last item of clothing on the way to the bathroom. His voice had been light, but his muscles looked tense as he walked away.

He stepped into the shower but it was glass sided and he didn't bother to shut the bathroom door. The water turned his hair to black silk and molded it to the shape of his skull. More moisture collected on his high arched brows and dark lashes, before cascading down his cheekbones to wet his lips. Other tiny streams poured over his shoulders and chest in fascinating rivulets, before running down the hard muscles of his stomach and thighs to splash around his feet.

The steam started to obscure the view after a minute, but by then I'd ended up beside the shower door with a sheet wrapped around me. I wiped a hand across the glass so I could see his eyes. "When was the last time you had a day off?"

"Today. I was away from my duties on family business—until the disaster caused me to return early."

"A day *off*, Mircea. Not a day doing another kind of work."

"There are too few senators and too much business for any of us to enjoy much leisure these days, *dulceață*."

He stepped out of the direct spray in order to lather up, turning to retrieve a washcloth from a bench in the corner. The motion caused a small cascade down his spine and over the taut muscle further down. My mouth went a little dry.

He paused to grin at me over his shoulder. "Wash my back?" he offered innocently.

I licked my lips and stayed where I was. "Tell the Consul she'll keep and maybe I will."

A wet eyebrow quirked. "Would you like me to quote you?"

"Go ahead. She owes me a favor."

He didn't immediately respond, just added soap to the cloth and began to run it leisurely over his body. I knew what he was up to, but my eyes simply ignored my brain's order for them to look elsewhere. Instead, they followed that lucky washcloth as it roamed over the fine chest and arms, moved on to the satiny skin of his inner legs, and glided along the jointure of his hip to areas more interesting still.

I had the door open and a foot across the sill before I even realized it. "I do not believe she views your assistance in quite that way," he said, a slight smirk tugging at his lips.

I frowned at him and drew my foot back. "That's the problem. She needs to understand that I'm not her little errand girl."

"No one thinks of you in those terms," he said soothingly, pausing to rinse off all those fascinating bubbles.

"Don't patronize me, Mircea."

"I wouldn't dream of it." And, okay, there was just no doubt about it. That was a definite smirk. He apparently thought his little game was cute.

I'd show him cute.

I dropped the sheet and got in beside him, pushing him down onto the bench. I stood in front of him, taking my time checking out the bewildering array of available toiletries. "What are you doing?" he asked, eyes lazily slitting.

"You washed my hair. It's only fair I return the favor." I managed to just brush his cheek with one breast as I reached up to get the shampoo. I put one knee on the bench as I lathered him up, nudging his legs apart to make room. I might have nudged a few other things, too, but he merely watched, although something wicked lurked behind his eyes, feral and amused and hungry.

"The Consul acts like I'm one of her vampires," I said, massaging in the suds. "She orders me around and expects me to help with plans she doesn't even bother to explain. I broke a guy out of jail for her today and I don't even know his name!"

"You broke a great many people out of jail." His hands settled on my hips, his thumbs stroking me slowly.

"That's not the point! I'm her ally, not her servant. She needs to understand that." I picked the shower head off the wall and leaned against him as I rinsed. "So do a few other people."

"I do not consider you a servant, *dulceață.*"

"But you don't tell me anything." I nudged him again, a little more firmly, and the smirk faded. I smiled.

"In the last month, you have had experiences that would have broken a weaker person. You have enough on your plate."

"Don't you think that's for me to decide?"

"We obviously need to discuss this," he said, but his breath hitched slightly.

"I thought you were out of time."

"If you keep doing that, I soon will be."

"Doing what?" I asked, rubbing against him in a soft, sweet tease.

A sharply indrawn breath was followed by a movement so quick I couldn't track it with my eyes. But somehow I ended up against the wet shower wall, bubbles in the air and Mircea between my legs. His still soapy hands were slick and barely controlled as he slid them around my hips, pulling me against him. I had a moment to see amber eyes narrow, glittering and full of intent, before the weight of his body slid against me, *in* me, deep and hard and hot.

I made a little whimpering noise as my body expanded to accommodate him, and then my voice was busy giving orders as he pressed in each time—*harder* and *more* and *don't stop.* Every movement sent spikes of pleasure arcing up my spine, turning my muscles soft and helpless. Instinct sent my hands sliding down the long, lean muscles of his back, nails lightly running across his buttocks, caressing him. And the room suddenly went hazy, shimmering like heat on asphalt.

I kept my eyes stubbornly open; I didn't want to miss a single second of this. And for a few moments I even managed to keep that resolution. Until the sensation of the water pouring down his chest and over my skin combined with the feel of his movements inside me to drive me to the edge. Everything became a blur of heat and need, of words breathed over my skin like a caress, of hands and mouths etching the Braille of desire onto warm, wet skin. My eyes finally closed as I was savored, devoured, possessed.

Strong arms came around me as his rhythm began to falter, water-slick hands sliding over my face, my breasts, my hips before he sucked air between his teeth and tilted just so and that was it. The world went white before my eyes, my whole body condensing into a single point of pleasure. A toe-curling orgasm broke over me that left me shaking and laughing up at the ceiling as he finished in a staccato frenzy of motion.

And someone knocked on the door.

Mircea cursed in a string of low-voiced Romanian, his head against my neck, his wet hair trailing over my breast. After a moment, he snatched a big Turkish towel off a rack and wrapped it around me. I leaned against the wall, weak-kneed and breathless, as he wrenched open the door. *"Yes?"*

One of the blank-faced masters was there, radiating disapproval. "The Consul wanted to be sure you received her message," he rumbled.

"Tell her I will be with her momentarily," Mircea snapped, and slammed the door in his face.

"Marco says you can't do that to the older masters," I informed him as he dried off with abrupt, angry motions.

"You shouldn't take Marco's advice too much to heart. He is one of those he spoke to you about—one who has reached the farthest limit of his power. He is having, I think, some trouble accepting that."

"It still wouldn't hurt to be polite."

"It is obvious that you have yet to meet the family. I am terrorized by them, not the other way around, I assure you."

Mircea reentered the bedroom and started throwing on clothes without his usual grace. I followed, sitting in the teepee. "When will you be back?"

"Not for hours." He paused to kiss me quickly. "Get some sleep."

"I'll try." I was exhausted, but my brain didn't seem to know how to cut off anymore. When the endorphins wore off, I'd probably be wide awake, staring at the ceiling, thumbing through my ever-growing catalogue of horrors. It wasn't a pleasant thought. "Do you want some help?" he asked, sitting beside me.

I nodded. Anything to avoid replaying today's events or seeing Rafe like that again ... Mircea's arms slipped around me and a wave of peace flowed over me better than any drug. I hadn't expected it to take hold so fast. I had a dozen things to talk to him about, to ask ... and suddenly I couldn't think of even one. Sleep was dragging at my consciousness, my body going thick and heavy, and I couldn't make myself open my eyes again.

"It's over; everyone's safe," I heard him murmur. The arms tightened abruptly. "Even you."

I had no idea what that meant, but I was drifting. Mircea's hand was running slowly up and down my spine, the other heavy on the back of my neck. I breathed out and let the weight pull me under.

Chapter Fifteen

I woke up chained to the bed. "Goddamnit!"

Mircea was standing by the vanity, pulling on another sinfully expensive shirt. This one was crisp and white with French cuffs and unobtrusive links. The tie he looped carelessly around his neck was the perfect shade of gold to bring out the flecks in his eyes. I glared at him.

"I have finally found a way to ensure that you will be here when I return," he murmured.

"This isn't funny," I told him, tugging uselessly on the cuff. It was a little hard to look serious when I was naked and my hair was plastered to my face and I was in a freaking *teepee*, but I was damned if I wasn't going to try. "I mean it, Mircea! Let me go!"

He gave me a slow smile in the mirror. I hated when he did that. "I will make you a deal," he said, coming over to the bed.

"I don't want a deal! I want out of these!"

He ignored me. "I have to fly to Washington briefly on Senate business. I will be back late tomorrow night or the next morning. I would like to know that you are safe in my absence."

I sighed in frustration. "What do you think I'm going to do? My power is still bottomed out from yesterday, I'm worried about Rafe and, in case you haven't noticed, I don't have any clothes!"

"Your clothes are there." He indicated a matched set of

Louis Vuitton luggage sitting by the bathroom. I'd assumed they were his, although they weren't his style. Probably something Sal had picked up in an attempt to mold me into less of an embarrassment. "And I think a day or so of rest before you meet the Circle would be wise."

"I agree! So let me go!"

"I have your word that you will stay here until I return, resting and visiting with Raphael?"

"I was thinking about going shopping."

"As long as you take Marco." He extracted a credit card from his wallet and handed it to me. It was a platinum AmEx with my name on it. I could probably charge a house, and he wouldn't care. Of course, I didn't need a house; I already had a very nice gilded cage.

"I don't want your money, Mircea. I want to talk about this." I rattled the cuff. It made an ominous clanking sound, which perfectly fit my mood. "We need to come to some kind of understanding."

"I agree," he said smoothly. "You must understand that you are a target."

"I've been a target all my life!"

"Not like this," he said emphatically.

"What about the Consul? I don't see you locking her up!"

"I think Kit would like to try."

"So did he bug her, too?"

"Bug?" He looked momentarily confused.

"The trace charm. Pritkin says I have one from Marlowe *and* one from you!"

"How kind of him to mention it."

"I want it removed."

"Kit is concerned for your safety."

"I don't trust him."

"But you do trust the mage?" he asked with a smile. It wasn't a particularly pleasant one.

"More than Marlowe, yes!"

"You know nothing about him," Mircea said, and there was a definite bite to his tone. "No one knows anything about him. The Circle's records state that he was born in Manchester in 1920, yet the proof was supposedly destroyed in an air raid—"

"You've been checking up on him?"

"—and there is the little matter of our meeting him one hundred and forty years before that in Paris."

Damn. I'd been hoping that Mircea hadn't recognized Pritkin on our last journey back into time. It had been a pretty crazy trip and the much younger Pritkin had looked a little different. But vampire eyes—especially Mircea's—didn't miss much.

"The Circle's records must be wrong."

"The Circle's records are rarely wrong. And even if that were the case, no two-hundred-year-old mage looks the way he does—"

"A glamourie could—"

"—or is that vigorous! I am beginning to doubt that John Pritkin is even his real name!"

I didn't say anything. Pritkin and I had finally gotten to a first-name basis recently, or at least, he'd started calling me Cassie. I hadn't returned the favor because Mircea was right: "John" wasn't his name. It was an alias he happened to be using this century to hide the fact that he hadn't been a run-of-the-mill war mage even before he'd broken with the Circle. Of course, Pritkin was an alias, too, but it felt more fitting somehow, maybe because that was what he'd been called when I first met him. And it wasn't like I could use his real name.

Even today, "Merlin" tends to turn heads, especially in the supernatural community.

All societies have their heroes, and it was Pritkin's misfortune to be one of ours. It didn't matter that the old stories were almost entirely fiction, or that the truth had been darker and a whole lot grimmer. It didn't matter that a medieval writer had even changed his name—from the coarser-sounding Myrdden. It only mattered that he was a legend and they are hard to come by.

If Pritkin's real identity became known, it would rock the magical world and make him a target for ... well, pretty much everyone. Every dark mage out there would want to drain him and every white mage would want a photo op. For the intensely private man I knew, it would be hell.

Mircea was regarding me narrowly. His expression said

that he suspected me of knowing more than I was telling and was pissed that I wouldn't come clean. Yeah, like he didn't have secrets.

"He can't be trusted," he said flatly when it became obvious that I wasn't going to get hit with a sudden attack of memory.

"Pritkin didn't chain me to a bed, Mircea!" I reminded him. "So at the moment, he's a little ahead on trust points."

He looked like he was going to say something and then sighed and glanced at his watch. "The cuffs were to get your attention, nothing more. They are easy enough for someone with your power to defeat, once you know the trick. But you must promise me to take more care. Remain here where you are well guarded. Take at least two bodyguards with you whenever you must leave. And do not fight Kit on the trace."

"He's a spy! You don't really think this is a simple trace, do you?"

He quirked an eyebrow. "And what are you afraid he will discover, *dulceață?*"

"You know damn well that's not the point! I grew up being followed around by Tony's thugs."

"And you resented it."

"Of course!"

"And therein lies the difference between us," he told me seriously. "I was also accustomed to such attentions from a young age. I never went anywhere alone; it was too dangerous. From the time I was born, I was a target for rival factions of the family, for jealous nobles, for invaders. A pawn in a political game that threatened constantly to engulf me and everyone I valued. I learned early on: safety was far more important than privacy."

I stared up at him. I rarely saw Mircea look completely serious; he would joke on his deathbed, if he ever had one. But there was no humor in his face now.

"I still want it off."

"I will make inquiries." He leaned over and kissed me lingeringly. "Now, do I have your word?"

I sighed. "Yes! Now will you *please* . . ."

He ran his eyes over me, and some heat sparked in

their depths. But he undid the cuffs. "Pity," he murmured, grabbed his jacket and was gone.

I spent the rest of the morning in the pool, swimming laps and avoiding the growing number of masters inside. A steady stream of gold-eyed vampires from Mircea's Washington estate filtered in all day, replacing Alphonse's crew. A few curious types stared at me through the living room windows, but none were willing to brave direct daylight to come out and say hello.

I came back into the apartment itself only when Sal returned from a shopping trip. I helped her carry a few dozen packages to her room, and I couldn't help but notice that some had Augustine's distinctive blue and silver seal. He was becoming as famous for the boxes as for the contents. Sal sat a large one on the bed and we watched it do its thing. It unwrapped itself and then refolded into an origami dragon complete with tiny, useless wings and little silver flames coming out of its mouth.

It slowly waddled to the edge of the bed and toppled off while Sal held up what I originally thought was a burlap sack. "This is for you. It's going to solve these wardrobe slips you keep having."

I regarded it warily. "Does Augustine know you bought it for me?"

She grinned. "Worried?"

"A little." I had enough problems without my skin turning blue or whatever he'd dreamed up this time.

"Relax. He thought it was for me."

"And you think it'll fit?" Sal was three inches taller than me and built like Mae West.

"Just try it," she prompted. "It's the new thing."

It didn't look like a new thing. It looked like an old thing: a plain slip dress and jacket made out of coarse brown fabric. But it had been a nice thought. I pulled it on over the bathing suit and turned to look in the mirror.

I blinked a couple of times, because what I was seeing didn't make sense. I was suddenly wearing an elegant little cover-up in a deep blue that complemented one of the bands in my suit. It had a drawstring neckline, a mesh body and flippy little skirt. It was actually cute.

"It's called a wardrobe-in-one," Sal told me, opening more packages. An origami lion prowled to the edge of the bed before leaping off. It was soon followed by a paper eagle, which unfolded foot-long wings and soared to the top of the dresser.

"I don't get it," I told her, watching the dragon emerge from under the bed, a large dust bunny in its claws.

"The idea is an outfit that can morph along with the wearer's needs, allowing you to go from work to shopping to evening with no need to change clothes." She ran the hem of the cover-up through her fingers, her eyes narrowing. "I thought he was using some kind of glamourie, but this actually feels like different fabric."

"It's really cool," I told her, and then bit my lip. "It must have been a lot, though." She'd already bought me several outfits, none of which had been cheap. And it wasn't like I could return the favor. I assumed that the Pythia usually received some sort of salary, but—surprise—I hadn't been getting a check. And Mircea's shiny new credit card was staying on his dresser where it belonged.

"We hicks have to stick together. Especially around here." She shot a glance out the door. At first, I didn't see anyone there, but then I noticed the edge of a finely pressed pant leg peeping past the door frame. One of Mircea's masters was loitering in the hall.

He wasn't there to eavesdrop—he could have done that from across the apartment—and besides, he'd stuck a leg out so we'd know he was there. Why he wanted us to know, I had no idea. But I could feel my cheeks reddening as my blood pressure soared. Maybe Mircea didn't mind tripping over people all day, but I hadn't had five hundred years to get used to it. And it was getting old fast.

I stomped over to the door and poked my head out. And immediately wished I hadn't. It was Nicu, the one master I'd already had a run-in with. Of course.

"Yes? Can I help you with something?" I asked.

Those flat gold eyes met mine and held, but there was no attempt to overwhelm me this time. "You are the master's woman," he said. And stopped.

I didn't intend to discuss my personal life with a guy I barely knew. Besides, there was no point. From Nicu's perspective, I was Mircea's woman because Mircea said so. My feelings were irrelevant.

I sighed. "And?"

"Your bodyguard is not here." He sounded disapproving.

"Marco's shift starts at sundown," I said, not getting his point. Assuming he had one. Maybe this was the ancient master version of small talk. "I'm not planning to go out until then."

"I will guard you until he arrives."

I tried to remember Marco's lecture and be diplomatic. "That's great. Really. But, um, there's only Mircea's people here, so I don't think—"

"There are others," he said, cutting me off. Apparently, this manners thing worked only one way.

"What?"

"You are in a room alone with the traitor's child."

I still didn't get it, but then Sal was there, smiling coldly. "He means me, Cassie. Because the toad who made me betrayed his master and joined the bad guys. Leaving me and Alphonse—and the rest of Tony's old stable—under suspicion."

"Mircea's going to change her as soon as he gets the time!" I told Nicu heatedly. "Just like he did for Rafe!"

I may as well have saved my breath. Nicu just crossed his arms and settled back against the wall, those coinlike eyes fixed on Sal. He'd obviously said his piece and he was done.

"Come on." Sal tugged on my arm, getting me away from Nicu before I said something stupid. "Don't you want to see what I bought for me?"

Half an hour later, we had a paper menagerie stalking, slinking and crawling its way around the floor and Sal was in a good mood once again. She spun in front of a floor-length mirror, the deep coral charmeuse of her skirt hugging every curve. And I decided this was the best chance I was going to get.

"Um, so. Do you know anything about the Senate members who were hurt in the war?" I asked casually.

"Four were killed, two were injured," Sal replied promptly, adjusting the fit of the top, which already fit like a second skin. "Although Marlowe's pretty well recovered, or so he lets on. I hear he got hit in the head one too many times and keeps it bandaged up when he isn't around people. But that could just be a rumor. Why do you ask?"

I shrugged. "Mircea said the Senate's been overworked lately because of the casualties, and I was just wondering about them. Were any women injured?"

"Only Ismitta." Sal held up a triple strand of pearls and admired the effect with the dress. "She put up a hell of a fight, even after they got her head off. I heard she killed two guys with it tucked under her arm."

"But she's dead now?"

"Oh, no. Other than Marlowe, she's the only one to have survived. But with an injury like that, well, even a first-level master is going to be out for a while. I heard she's gone back to Africa to recover. There's some shaman over there supposed to have had experience with this sort of thing."

"Africa?"

"Yeah. Don't know what part, though. She looks kind of Ethiopian."

Ismitta wasn't the girl in the photos, then. So the pretty brunette probably wasn't on her deathbed. Which meant that there was no reason why I couldn't just ask Mircea about her. For some reason, that didn't make me feel any better.

The fun ended with the arrival of a fussy little man in a rumpled suit, with a big bag and a bigger scowl. The wardsmith Mircea had promised. Apparently he'd just finished a shift with the detail trying to bring the casino's wards up to the Senate's exacting standards. By the shadows under his eyes and the snap in his voice, it seemed like maybe he was feeling a little overworked. But that changed when he got a glimpse of my ward above the back of my swimsuit.

"Oh, yes, yes." He traced it reverently with a fingertip. "I've heard of this, of course, but never thought to see it. They said it was lost years ago."

I didn't feel like going through that whole story. "Can you fix it?"

"I'll need to remove it. If I may?"

I paused and then nodded reluctantly. It had never left

my skin since my mother had placed it on me as a child. But it wasn't much good to me in its current form.

The mage said an incantation and I felt a trace of heat running along the familiar pattern on my back. Magical wards dissolve into the skin when on the body, mimicking the look of a tattoo. Off the body, they look like small gold charms, such as the one now filling his palm.

"Hmm. Let's see." He poked at it with a few odd-looking instruments. "When did you begin to have difficulties?"

"After leaving the ley line."

"No, it was after that mage attacked you," Sal reminded me, joining us on the sofa.

"Oh, yeah. I forgot."

The mage's brow wrinkled. "You suffered a magical attack?"

"Two. Well, sort of. They were both by the same guy."

"And then you got shot at by MAGIC's wards," Sal said. "And almost eaten. Or did I get that backward?"

"It sort of happened at the same time."

"Did you say *eaten*?" the man demanded.

"And then there was the cave-in and the car crash," Sal added.

"You were in a car crash?" The wardsmith was starting to look like he thought his leg was being pulled.

"Yes, but it doesn't matter," I told him. "The ward felt like it was fritzing out even on the first attack."

"Which attack?"

"The one by the war mage," I said patiently.

He closed his eyes and breathed deeply for a minute. "Let me see if I understand. You were in a ley line. When you left, you were attacked. Your ward held, but it felt weak, and then . . ."

"I was attacked again and it collapsed. That's why I think the ley line did it."

"Unlikely. Out of everything that you say happened to you, the line would be the least likely to cause damage. This is far stronger than the average war mage's shields, and even they—"

"You don't understand. I wasn't in *a* ley line. I was in *the* line, the one that ruptured yesterday. I was thrown directly into a fissure."

"And the ward held?" he demanded incredulously.

"Yeah. Well, long enough for me to get out, anyway."

He tinkered some more, muttering to himself. "You are a very lucky young woman," he told me after a while. "I cannot think of another ward that could have withstood a threat of that magnitude. If you had not been able to channel the combined power of the Circle—"

"I didn't."

"I can assure you, you did."

I was beginning to wonder where Mircea had got this guy. "No, I didn't!" I said, exasperated. "My ward was designed to take its power from the Circle, but it doesn't anymore. They cut me off. A friend of mine set it to draw from the power of my office instead."

The mage packed up his big leather satchel. "Well, your friend obviously didn't know what he was doing, because I can assure you—"

"My friend was an excellent wardsmith!" I said heatedly.

"And I am a master wardsmith with almost sixty years of experience!" he snapped. "I am telling you that your ward is set to draw its power from the Silver Circle. It isn't doing so now, of course, because it needs repair. But it *was* doing so yesterday or you would be dead." He closed his case with an angry little snick.

"Can you fix it?" Sal asked.

"In time. However, this isn't something I can patch up here. I'll have to take it with me—"

He stopped because her long nails, gold today, had wrapped around his wrist. "Drop it."

He bristled. "I assure you, young woman—"

"Sweetheart, I haven't been young in a century," she said, baring bright white fangs.

He paled but recovered fairly fast. "Be that as it may, the fact remains that I can do nothing here."

Sal looked at me. "You really want this bozo handling the repairs?"

"Not really," I said, torn. I didn't like the guy, and I sure as hell didn't want him taking my ward off somewhere. My back already felt naked and wrong. But I really didn't like the idea of facing the Silver Circle again without it.

"I'll take care of it," Sal said, relieving him of the ward.

She stuck it in her bra as a couple of the creepy guards escorted the indignant man out. "But it may take a little while. Can you stay out of trouble for a couple days?"

"Ironically, that's how long I have until the meeting with Saunders," I reminded her. "I'd really like my ward back before then."

"I'll see what I can do."

I spent the rest of the day in the penthouse eating, sleeping and checking on Rafe every twenty minutes, until the human nurse they had doing the day shift started to get a little snippy. I knew how he felt. By nightfall, I'd swum until I was pruney, done my nails, eaten all the ice cream in the fridge and played twenty games of poker with Sal, all of which I'd lost.

That was despite Billy Joe stopping by for a draw and giving me some free advice. I should have known better than to listen to him. He was stuck looking twenty-nine for the rest of his ghostly life because that's what he'd been when a couple of cowboys who he'd cheated at cards shoved him in a sack and dropped it in the Mississippi.

By the time the sun started toying with the horizon, I was bored out of my mind and it was getting harder and harder not to focus on the upcoming meeting with the Circle. I'd gone to the last one in good faith, unarmed except for a bracelet they hopefully didn't know about. But the idea of showing up like that again wasn't appealing, especially now that my ward was on the fritz. I needed a few surprises of my own, and I wasn't going to get them here. Besides, the guards were really starting to freak me out.

Marco swaggered in a little before sunset. I assumed he was making a point about his power or something, because a couple of the guards sneered at him. They'd been up all day.

"I need to go shopping," I told him.

"I ain't hanging around no lingerie section while you try stuff on," he said bluntly.

"We're shopping for weapons," I said, grabbing my purse.

"What kind of weapons?"

"Nasty ones."

And for the first time ever, I saw Marco smile.

Chapter Sixteen

"That's not something you see every day."

I had my head inside a large trunk and didn't bother looking up. The observation could have applied to almost any of the items in the back room of the pawnshop. Unlike the front, which catered to the casual visitor with the requisite DVD players, camcorders and cases of mismatched jewelry, the back was stocked with items for the supernatural population of Vegas. But since the salesman had made the comment, I assumed he was referring to the two huge thugs who were lounging by the door, looking bored.

I shot them a narrow-eyed look, and Marco blew me a kiss.

Smart-ass.

Between one blink and the next, Marco was beside me, the old salesman dangling from his meaty paw. The guy looked terrified, his reading glasses sliding to a precarious position on his bulbous nose. "Hey!"

"He was reaching for you," Marco said, and forced the man's hand open. I don't know what he'd expected to find, but he looked slightly disappointed at the sight of a small tape measure. Not enough to release the guy, though, who was rapidly turning a worrying shade of puce.

"Yeah, because he planned to measure me to death." We were obviously going to have to have a talk about the difference between "maintaining security" and "being a dick." Marco just stood there. "Marco! Put him down!"

"Sure. Because I like the idea of returning to Lord Mircea with your mangled body draped over my arm. If I'm lucky, he'll just kill me."

"You're already dead."

"There's dead and then there's dead, princess," he said seriously, but he did set the old man back on his—rather shaky—feet.

"As I said, that's a rare find," the salesman said, adjusting his cloths. It took me a moment to realize that he was referring to the small brooch Francoise was holding. "The stones are blue when inert, but they turn orange if a malevolent spell is cast on the wearer."

I regarded it with a frown. It reinforced my belief that there was some law requiring magical jewelry to be extraordinarily ugly. But Francoise was nodding slightly, so despite appearances, the thing actually worked.

I'd asked her to come along to vet the merchandise and because I'd come armed with only my own paltry bank account. It was necessary for my pride and what was left of my independence, but it severely cramped my purchasing power. Still, if anyone knew how to get a deal, it was Francoise. She had a gift.

"Can it prevent a curse?" I asked. I could live with a little ugly for that kind of protection.

"Alas, no. But it will tell you what spell was used, which as you know is the trickiest step in removing it."

"It's not quite what I had in mind."

"Are you sure? Because I think I have the matching necklace as well; it glows when the person who cursed you comes within a dozen yards. I could give you a good price for the set."

I was almost tempted, just to get rid of him. He'd been hovering ever since we came in. Of course, that was mostly Augustine's fault.

The wardrobe-in-one seemed to know we were shopping and had morphed into a chic skirted suit. It had apparently convinced the salesman that I might be worth a decent commision. "Thanks," I told him, "but I'm looking for something a little more . . . proactive."

"Ah, well, in that case"—he hurried over to a metal cabinet standing by the back wall—"I have just the thing."

Marco bent to whisper in my ear. "Don't let him take you. This place has a rep for sharp dealing."

"Not much chance of that."

The cabinet door swung open to reveal shelves stacked with the same kind of jumbled, dusty mess that characterized the rest of the shop. None of the items appeared to be guns, grenades or other recognizable weaponry—or anything else of interest. But from the way the salesman was smiling, you'd have thought we were looking at Ali Baba's cave.

"Now, this is a real find!" He took out a tattered piece of black cloth about the size of a handkerchief and threw it into the air. Instead of falling, it drifted upward and began expanding. Within seconds, a bedsheet-sized undulating wall of darkness fluttered overhead—before suddenly dropping down on us, blocking out all light.

I heard Marco swear, a pissed-off sound that echoed faintly against the nothingness all around us. But his voice's timbre had changed; every sound seemed to undulate, fading in and out from screamingly loud to whisper quiet, sometimes within the same word. I could no longer tell if he was standing right beside me or had moved halfway across the room.

The salesman's cheerful tones drowned him out anyway and still sounded perfectly normal. "The Shroud of Darkness," he said dramatically. "Excellent offensive or defensive aid. Drop this onto an enemy and watch them stumble about whilst you attack with impunity or slip away unnoticed!"

The darkness wrapped around me like a wet blanket, moist and wool warm, almost smothering. The air I managed to draw in was musty and soup-thick on my tongue and strangely tacky, as if it was sticking to the sides of my throat going down. I don't suffer from claustrophobia, but in the Shroud's humid embrace, I felt it anyway.

Useful the thing might be, but it was dark, too, in more than just color. I scrubbed at my arms, trying to get the oddly solid blackness off and fighting panic when nothing I did helped. I bit my lip, but it wouldn't be long before I could no longer choke back a scream.

"Black magic," Francoise muttered, her voice echoing strangely.

"Get us out of here," Marco hissed. "Now!" His last word sounded loud enough with the Shroud's odd magnification to shatter eardrums. But a second later the dark lifted as abruptly as a sheet being pulled off my head. I stood gasping and blinking in the suddenly glaringly bright showroom, waiting for my eyes to adjust, while the salesman had the Shroud ripped from his hand by an angry vampire.

"Was that supposed to be funny?!" It looked like Marco wasn't a fan of sensory deprivation. Vampire eyes usually work even better in the dark than in daytime, so why was I getting the impression that he hadn't been able to see inside that thing any better than I had?

"I do apologize," the salesman said hurriedly. "But the Shroud is very old, very rare. Most people have never even heard of it. Spells are often used to fool the senses these days, but they are far simpler to throw off. With such an unusual item, it is easier to demonstrate what it does than to attempt to explain—"

"Explaining will do fine," I interrupted, and Francoise nodded emphatically.

"As you like." The salesman looked disappointed that his demonstration hadn't been well received.

"What kind of illegal crap are you selling?" Marco demanded.

"Everything we carry is completely legitimate," the salesman assured me, ignoring Marco. "No need to concern yourself about any trouble with the authorities."

"I generally don't," I muttered. The authority policing magical weapons was the Silver Circle, and I couldn't really get in more trouble with them if I tried.

The salesman gave me a sly look that contrasted oddly with his Santa Claus face. "However, we do have some antique pieces that don't, er, come under the more modern bans."

"Such as?" Maybe there was some esoteric antique that even the Circle wouldn't have heard about—something rare enough or weird enough to gain me an advantage.

"There's this lovely item. It comes from the estate of, how shall I put it, an adventurer?" The small off-white statue he handed me turned out to be of a Buddha-type figure with a jaunty grin. Miniature cracks zigzagged over the figure's fat little belly and were slightly darker than the rest of it, like old ivory. "Daikoku, one of the seven Japanese gods of fortune!"

"And?"

"It's a netsuke," Marco said, peering at the little thing. "I used to know a guy who collected them."

"A what?"

He shrugged. "Kimonos didn't have pockets. Traditional Japanese guys wore a sash around their waist with a purse tied on it. Only they didn't call it a purse, because they were guys, you know? Anyway, the netsuke held the two pieces—the bag and the belt—together."

"This isn't a netsuke," the salesman sniffed. "Admittedly, there were a number carved depicting Daikoku, but that's all they were—mere depictions."

"And this would be different how?" I asked.

"Because this *is* Daikoku."

I blinked. "That's a god."

The salesman didn't like my tone. "An ancient being," he correctly stiffly. "The medieval Japanese peasants didn't know how else to refer to him."

"And you keep him in a closet?"

"'Ow deed you obtain 'im?" Francoise broke in. She actually looked like she was buying this.

Then salesman must have thought so, too, because he brightened. "The soldier of fortune I mentioned acquired him some years ago in Fukushima," he explained. "I believe he stole him from another traveler. It was believed that if you took a statue of Daikoku from its previous owner, it would grant you good fortune in the form of a wish—as long as you weren't caught in the act. The old folk tradition probably arose from stories of the real statue's exploits."

"Like a *génie*." Francoise was regarding the little thing thoughtfully.

"Indeed. Except djinn are not known for benevolence. That is a dangerous old wives' tale. Should you ever come across a trapped djinn, I strongly advise you to leave it so."

"Shouldn't we leave Daikoku alone, too?" I asked skeptically.

"Oh, no," the salesman hurried to explain. "He isn't

trapped. Not at all. This is simply the form he uses to carry out his mission."

"And that would be?"

"To bring abundance, wealth and happiness into the world."

"Then why don't you make a wish and get wealthy?" Marco asked pointedly.

We all looked at the shopkeeper. "Er, well, because Daikoku doesn't always understand . . . That is, you have to be extremely cautious about how you phrase your request. There have been instances in which miscommunications have taken place."

"Like what?" I didn't know a lot about magic, but I was beginning to learn that everything *always* had a catch.

"Simply that he does grant the wish but perhaps not always in the way the wisher intended. The person from whom I acquired the item had such an experience. The former owner of the statue hired a group of mercenaries to retrieve his property, and they trailed the adventurer to a village in Tibet. They surrounded it and were closing in when, on the theory that it couldn't hurt, the man asked Daikoku to help him get out of there." The salesman broke off, looking vaguely uncomfortable.

"Did it work?" I prodded.

"Of course it worked. After a fashion. He was alive to sell it to me, wasn't he?"

"So what was the problem?"

"Well, you see, the mages knew what the man looked like. Daikoku therefore reasoned that changing his appearance would be an easy way of fulfilling his wish. But merely laying a glamourie or some such on him wouldn't work because the men chasing him were mages, with the knowledge needed to strip such a thing away."

"What deed 'e use?" Francoise asked, her forehead wrinkling prettily.

"Nothing. Or, rather, no mere disguise. He actually changed the man's form. And considering that the consequences would be death if the man was discovered, he made the change as . . . dramatic . . . as possible."

"Meaning what?" Marco demanded.

"He changed him into a woman," the salesman admitted in a rush. "An old Tibetan woman, to be precise. And of course, once the wish was granted, there was no way to change him back. There were no more wishes and the man, er, the former man, hadn't specified any conditions, so . . ."

"He was stuck?" Marco sounded horrified.

"I'm afraid so."

"And what ees so bad about being 'stuck' as a woman?" Francoise demanded. "Eet was preferable to dying, *non*?"

"Speak for yourself." Marco self-consciously adjusted himself. "I got things I would miss!"

"Just for the sake of argument, how much?" I asked the salesman. I needed to know what price range I was looking at here, or discussing any of the other objects was a waste of time.

He named a price that had my jaw dropping in shock. "*How* much?" I asked in disbelief.

"With the war on, prices have increased substantially," I was told. "Everyone wants to be properly armed."

I sighed, looking around at all the things I couldn't buy. "I don't suppose you have layaway."

He shrugged, catching sight of another customer. "My dear, I don't mean to offend, but unless you are unusually powerful, a magical tap would take decades to result in that kind of a return."

He bustled off before I could ask what he meant, but Marco caught my eye. "Don't even think about it!"

"Think about what?"

"You know damn well what. Once those leeches get their claws into you, there's no telling where it'll end. They may say they're only taking five percent or whatever the legal limit is, but how do you know? Unless you faint and fall over, most people aren't going to miss more, maybe even a lot more. Then you get in a fight where you need your magic, and, surprise, you got nothing. And you end up dead for what, a couple of bucks?"

"It's true!" The other bodyguard, another new guy, piped up. "I got in a fight with a mage once, and he said that was why I'd beaten him. Not that I wouldn't have anyway, but he said he was weak because some shysters had jacked him. And he was telling the truth—he tasted flat. No zip."

I stared at him.

"I mean, I think he would have, if I'd actually, you know, tried him. Which I absolutely *wouldn't*—"

Marco clapped a hand down on his shoulder and he shut up. "Just don't, all right?" he told me.

"I don't even know what you're talking about," I said impatiently. "You mean it's possible to tap into a person's magic?"

"That's the idea. You pawn part of your magic for a set time in return for a fee. You never heard of it? 'Cause people do it all the time. The mages do, I mean."

"I thought only dark mages steal magic."

"They do. They drain somebody every chance they get. But this doesn't take all of someone's magic. Just a small percentage. And since they gotta agree to it, it's legal. Just really stupid."

"Who buys it? And for what?"

Marco shrugged. "You want details, you gotta talk to a mage. All I know is, it's supposed to stay within the maximum agreed on and to end at a specified time. Only sometimes, that don't happen. Like I warned you, it's dangerous. The Circle usually keeps an eye on that kind of thing, but with the war on—"

"I get it." I knew for a fact that the Circle didn't have enough war mages to go around, not when most of them had been recruited for combat duty. A lot of little things were likely to slip through the cracks, including mundane police work like checking on pawnshop owners.

"And damn, girl, it's not like you need it!" Marco continued. "Lord Mircea could set you up with an allowance—"

"No, he couldn't," I said emphatically.

"He isn't known for being cheap, and you *are* his—"

"If you say property, I swear—"

Marco's cell phone went off, interrupting the conversation. "Sorry. Can't help you," he told it abruptly, and hung up.

"What was that?"

"Nothing."

"It sounded like Casanova."

The phone continued to ring, sounding shriller by the second. He finally got it back out and switched it off. "It wasn't," he said, meeting my eyes easily. Which meant absolutely nothing.

Vampires are great liars. They don't blush, fidget, perspire or have any of the other tells a human might when under pressure. But I knew how much could be concealed by a calm facade. Usually, the more expressionless they were, the more they were hiding. And Marco was looking pretty damn blank.

"Marco—" I didn't have time to call him on the lie, because Billy Joe streamed in.

"The Circle just grabbed a bunch of the kids," he told me without preamble. "I don't know how many. They were dragging them out when I left. Casanova tried to call you, but he couldn't get through."

I grabbed Marco's phone out of his pocket and hit redial. "Hey!"

"Don't start," I told him, glaring. I'd have said a few other things, but Casanova picked up on the first ring.

"What is going on?" I demanded.

"It's those damn kids again—" he began, before the phone was ripped out of his hand. I didn't have to wonder who was on the other end. Even if I hadn't heard the voice in the background, I didn't know too many people who would attack a vampire with so little compunction. The fact that she was all of five foot three and human made the fact that much more impressive.

"Jesse's gone," Tami informed me quickly. "The Circle grabbed him and a bunch of the other kids a couple minutes ago. Casanova says he's not allowed to attack the mages because of the treaty, but I didn't sign any damn treaty, and I swear if they hurt Jesse, I'll make them pay. They think they got a war now? They'll know they've been at war when I finish—"

"Where did they go?"

"I don't know!" She was crying, I could hear it in her voice, but she held it together. "They took off down the Strip in a couple limos."

The Strip was a block from here, and if it had its usual traffic snarl, we might be able to catch them. "It's okay, Tami. We're going to—"

"How is this okay?"

"Because we're going to get them back. You have my word."

There was a telling silence on the other end of the phone. I couldn't blame her. I'd given her my word before, when I promised that the kids would be safe at Dante's. And look how that had turned out.

What the Circle wanted with a handful of runaways in the middle of a war I didn't know, but I could figure it out later. Right now, we had to get them back. "I'll call you as soon as I know anything," I told her, and handed the phone back to Marco. "Let's go."

I started out the door only to have him grab me by the back of the collar. "Where are you going?"

"To get Jesse."

"And how do you expect to do that?"

"You drive," I told him, "and I navigate."

"I was told to keep you safe, not to go on some daredevil rescue. Those kids are not my problem. You are. And deliberately taking you into the path of the Circle is not in the game plan."

"It is now."

Dark eyes narrowed to slits. "I don't think so."

"Then let me put it another way. I'm going after the kids, whether you like it or not."

"You aren't going anywhere."

Francoise held up something behind Marco's head that caught the light. Car keys. I didn't pause to wonder how she'd managed to pick a vampire's pocket without him noticing. I lunged for the door.

Marco jerked me back, but Billy had figured out what was happening and decided to help. He knocked the cabinet of magical weapons over. It hit a nearby display case, listed to the left, and teetered there for a long moment. Then it crashed to the floor, its deadly contents spilling everywhere.

Some of the items remained inert, sliding or rolling to a stop after a short distance. But a set of shackles slithered across the floor like a metal snake, making tracks in the dust as it headed straight for Marco's buddy. He danced back, but it pursued him with ominous intent behind a counter. He gave a sudden yelp and disappeared from view.

Marco glared at me. "How did you do that?"

The salesman hurried up before I could answer and then suddenly turned white and started backing away, fast. I glanced behind Marco's head to see what looked like a swarm of black insects swirling up from a shattered vial. One of them flew into the overhead light, and one of the bulbs went out.

It took me a second to realize that it hadn't blown; it just wasn't there anymore. Another spot floated down onto a bottle on the counter, which winked out of existence like it had fallen down a well. Or a small black hole, which is what the things were starting to look like.

All around the shop, items were disappearing, or parts of them, in the case of those too large to fit down the holes. The little black menaces came in different sizes, but unlike the Shroud, they didn't appear to be expandable. The ceiling fan overhead lost a chunk from one blade, an old mirror was spotted with empty, black circles and the floor was missing half a dozen round chunks of concrete. I stared down at a teacup-sized one near my foot and didn't see anything on the other end—no foundation, no dirt, nothing.

Marco carted me back toward the door to the front of the shop, while his buddy reappeared, being dragged across the floor by the shackles, which had attached themselves to his ankles. One of the smaller holes floated down onto his wildly waving left hand, and just like the other items, it was suddenly gone. There was no blood, but there was no more hand, either. Just raw, red flesh and pale bone, sliced clean through like a demented cookie cutter had taken a bite out of him.

Marco let go of me to grab the salesman, who was trying to squeeze out the door ahead of us. "What the hell is happening?" he growled as several more holes appeared in his now hysterical friend.

"He'll be all right," the salesman babbled. "His hand isn't gone; it's simply misplaced."

"Misplaced?"

"Y-yes. It's rather like quarantine, in a way; it's being stored."

"Where?"

"That's a little complicated," the salesman muttered,

grabbing a magazine to use as a fan to push a couple of small holes away from us. The air current acted on them like they were made of tissue paper, sending them tumbling over each other back into the middle of the room—where they came to rest right on top of the other vamp.

He was cut off midshriek as one of them landed on his face, leaving a perfectly round space where his mouth had been. A few gleaming molars could still be seen, one with a gold cap, above the gaping wound. Another took out part of his chest, missing the heart but leaving a baseball-sized hole through his torso. I could see part of what might have been a rib and a rapidly fluttering thing that was probably a lung. There was no spurting blood, no seeping fluids. It was as if part of him was simply somewhere else and his body didn't realize it.

It didn't appear to be pleasant, though. He stared at us, his eyes huge, as the shackles succeeded in dragging him into the cabinet. The door shut behind him on its own with a final-sounding thump.

Marco released me, grabbed the magazine and the salesman, and started towing him back into the room. "Let me explain what's going to happen here," he said, batting at any holes that came near. "You are going to get him back. Right now. Or I am going to round these things up and force-feed them to you! Are we clear?"

"Of course. Naturally, there will be a small retrieval fee—" The door clicked shut on Marco's reply to that, which had included a few suggestions that I doubted were anatomically possible. I couldn't do much for Marco's partner except hope that the salesman could do what he said. But I could help the kids. Francoise pressed the keys into my hand and we ran.

Chapter Seventeen

Marco's car was actually a black SUV with windows tinted so dark they were probably illegal. But illegal was better than bursting into flames, I supposed. Not that there was much chance of that at the moment. The sun had been down more than an hour, with only the neon sign over the pawnshop left to light the dark street.

We took off in a squeal of tires, with me driving since cars were still a new experience for Francoise and not one she liked. She was riding shotgun. I'd hoped that she'd get distracted by the view up front and not freak out, but judging by her white-knuckled grip on the dashboard, that was working about as well as my plans usually did.

It also left me with a problem, since I now had to drive and keep a lookout at the same time. It was harder than it sounds, because limos are not exactly an unusual sight on the Strip and I'd neglected to ask Tami for a description. So I was left trying to find two limos together, only everyone seemed to be traveling solo tonight.

We pulled up behind a long black one a few minutes later that was stalled at a light. "Hey, green means go," I yelled, leaning on the horn.

The limo's doors opened, but no one got out. Arms covered in identical dark sleeves emerged from either side of the vehicle and closed them. The limo moved a few jerky yards forward, into the middle of an intersection, and the doors popped open again. Only this time, it wasn't just a couple of back ones. All five doors as well as the trunk started flapping open and shut all along its length, making it look like an elongated crow trying to take off.

"Ees zat normal?" Francoise looked confused.

"No." But it was something I'd seen more than once lately. One of the Misfits was a little girl whose parents had kept her, and her misfiring magic, locked away in a small room until she was old enough to leave for her special "school." As she grew, her power increased, along with her dislike for enclosed spaces. We'd had a tough time with her at the casino, because doors, windows and elevators all refused to stay closed when Alice was nearby.

"Can we go around?" Francoise asked, looking behind us at the increasingly long line of waiting cars, most of which were now honking angrily. A VW Bug edged around us and the limo and then hit the gas and rocketed through the intersection, winking its brake lights cheekily. A number of other cars followed, but I just sat there.

"I'm going to take a look," I told her.

"Why?"

The doors all flew open again and then slammed shut in unison. "That's why. I think Alice may be in there."

Francoise opened her door. "I weel go."

"No. Stay here. It's probably nothing."

"And if eet ees not notheeng?"

"I can get out faster than you. Besides, if something happens, I need you to go for help."

I left her staring at the steering wheel with a look of frozen terror on her face. Given the choice, I think she'd have rather faced the mages. I didn't share the sentiment, so I approached the limo with caution.

I'd have had to do that anyway since the doors were still opening and closing at random intervals, with one slamming shut in my face as I tried to enter. Instead of playing musical chairs, I waited beside one near the back until it opened again and then launched myself inside.

It was crazier inside than out, with crying children, yelling adults and someone screaming for the driver to hit the gas. But I was in the right place, because that was Jesse near the front of the limo, highlighted by a currently open door.

He was lying on a long, bench-type seat surrounded by no fewer than four mages.

I started for him, but a little girl grabbed me around the legs and I went down, and then somebody kicked me in the head. I don't think it was on purpose because it didn't hurt much, mostly managing to bruise my ear. But then someone's large boot came down on my wrist and that did hurt—a lot.

I screamed and a man jerked me to my knees. A young Asian-American with stylish black-rimmed glasses peered into my face. "Who the hell—" He stopped abruptly. I didn't recognize him, but it was kind of obvious that the opposite wasn't true. He had the expression of a man who knew he had half a million euros by the arm—the size of the bounty the Circle had put on my head.

The limo started up again before either of us could recover, causing me to fall heavily into the mage, who sat down hard on the backseat next to a sandy-haired boy with Coke-bottle glasses. As the car started weaving wildly through traffic, a pile of nylon rope slithered over the seat from a puddle around the boy's feet and began winding around me and the mage. I didn't have to ask how: the little boy was named Alfred, and he was telekinetic.

He looked calm enough, but he had a battered old backpack in a death grip. I would have suggested that he concentrate on getting the rope around the mage rather than both of us, but I didn't have the breath. It was all getting squeezed out of me by the nylon corset that was tightening by the second.

The mage started swearing and trying to reach inside his coat while I struggled to hinder him and simultaneously get a hand on my gun. But it was still in my purse, because I hadn't wanted to draw it in full view of traffic, and my purse was outside the ropes. All around us, a mini war was taking place, with yells and curses and the tinkle of breaking glass. Then there was an explosion and suddenly it was a lot lighter inside. It looked like something had taken out a couple of windows.

A particularly hard corner slung us onto the floor and I decided I'd had enough. I shifted about a foot to the left, which got me out of the trap but allowed the ropes to go slack where my body had been. Which in turn allowed the mage to get a hand inside that damn coat.

I didn't know what he might be carrying, but based on past experience, it probably wasn't anything that should be used inside a car filled with kids. I couldn't see my purse and I didn't have time to get to my gun anyway. I didn't have time to do anything but grab him, close my eyes and shift.

We landed hard in the middle of the road, rolling a couple of times in the direction of the vanishing limo, the SUV almost running us down until Francoise all but stood on the brakes. The SUV's front tire screeched to a halt about an inch away from my face. I stared at it, blinking, while the mage slammed an elbow into my ribs, trying to fight free of his encompassing cocoon.

Francoise leaned over the windshield and said something, and the ropes suddenly tightened, sending him back into mummy mode. "Gag heem!" she ordered, throwing me a handkerchief. I wadded it up and shoved it into the mage's mouth just as he got his chin free from the ropes. I'd forgotten; if they can speak, they're deadly. Thankfully, Francoise hadn't. I jumped on board, she revved the motor and we were off.

It quickly became obvious that Francoise had figured out the gas and the brake pedals—sort of—but was a little hazy on things like yielding, red lights and speed limits. Which meant she fit pretty well into Vegas' traffic. The limo was another story, lurching along in fits and starts a few blocks ahead.

We caught up with it as it turned onto Sands Avenue and started to pick up speed. Francoise took the corner too fast, tires squealing in protest, and slung me into the side door. But she stayed in control and floored the gas pedal.

"Get me close enough to shift inside," I told her.

"'Ow close?" She was white and shaking, and her eyes were a little wild.

"I don't know." I'd never tried shifting into a moving vehicle and I doubted it was all that smart. But if Francoise could get me with a foot or two, it might be feasible. "As close as you can get!"

She muttered something but slipped between two cars

and maneuvered the SUV alongside the limo, near enough that the driver hit the horn. I took a deep breath and shifted, landing in a heap in the narrow center aisle by the bench seat. I had half a second to verify that there were only three children in the limo: Alice, huddled in a ball on the floor, Alfred in the back and Jesse near the front being held by two mages.

Then four guns were in my face, one practically touching my nose. I grabbed Alice and shifted before they could fire, landing on the back bench again, alongside Alfred. "That was cool," he said, as I grabbed him by the front of his shirt.

"Get my purse!" I ordered, causing the mages' heads to swivel our way. Alfred grabbed my battered denim bag from the floor just as the mages threw a spell and we shifted out.

I landed in the backseat of the SUV, a child in each hand and exhaustion running through my veins. Francoise was watching me frantically in the mirror. She said something, but it was in French and I was too tired to even try to translate. "Your hair is on fire!" she screamed, doing it for me, as Alfred started whacking me in the head with his backpack.

I tore off my jacket, which was still in garden party shape, although the fabric was now an appropriate camouflage canvas. I used it to put out the flames as Alfred clambered over the seat into the front. "I can drive," he told her calmly. "She's going to need help to get Jesse."

"You're what? Twelve?" I demanded.

He gave me a look. "You're afraid of maybe getting a ticket?"

"You're *sure*—"

"Please. I've been driving since I was a little kid," he told me with a complete lack of sarcasm.

I decided that this would be another one of those things Tami didn't need to know about. I grabbed Francoise by the back of her camisole. "Are you okay with this?"

She nodded frantically, up for anything that involved getting out of the driver's seat. And then somebody must have recognized us, because an arm appeared out of one of the wildly flapping doors and tossed something in our direction. Francoise jerked the steering wheel hard to the right, slamming us into the side of the longer car and smashing the door back onto the thrower's arm. But it was too late to stop the small black sphere from bouncing on the hood, once, twice, and before it could hit a third time, I panicked and shifted—the car.

A wave of nausea and vertigo hit me that was so severe it took a few seconds for me to notice where we'd landed: catty-corner across the hood of the limo. A massive explosion rocked the road behind us, shattering the rest of the limo's windows and leaving a crater the size of a kiddie pool in the road. The back of the limo was also smoking, as if the bomb had taken out part of the trunk as well, although neither that nor the fact that the driver couldn't possibly see anything past the SUV had slowed him down.

I don't know if he was panicking or if he thought we were playing an elaborate game of chicken. But if it was the latter he was in for a surprise. Because I couldn't shift again, could barely tell which way up was, a fact not helped by the unmistakable feel of the SUV beginning to slide sideways off the hood.

"Francoise!" I hoped she had an idea, but all I got back was a stream of four-hundred-year-old French invective.

And then the bumping and the sliding and the earsplitting shriek of metal on metal suddenly stopped. As did the SUV, despite the fact that the limo continued on its crazy zigzag course through traffic. I realized with a lurch that we were somehow floating a dozen feet or so off the ground, wafting in the general direction of the curb like the giant leaf we weren't.

"Telekenetic, remember?" Alfred asked as we touched down.

Francoise scrambled out of the car so fast that she fell into the road. "I like ze horses!" she screamed, apparently addressing traffic. "Thees form of travel, it ees insane!"

I extricated myself from the backseat and stumbled out onto the pavement. Everything was a big, pale blur, and since I'd never shifted anything that large before—hadn't even known it was possible—I had no way of knowing how long it would be before the exhaustion would subside enough for me to get us out of here. But Jesse was in the limo that was fast disappearing into traffic, and if I didn't at least try to get him back, I didn't know how I'd ever face Tami again.

"Stop them!" I told Alfred.

"How?"

"The tires!" He nodded and sent a narrow-eyed look the limo's way. For a moment, nothing happened, and then both of the back tires blew simultaneously. The already smoking rear end of the car hit the ground, dragging a river of sparks behind it for a few seconds before veering off the road and slamming into a light pole. It bounced off, did a 180 and ended up back in the middle of traffic.

"Get back to Dante's," I told Francoise while digging around in my purse for the gun. "Help the kids."

"And who will 'elp you?"

"I can take care of myself." It might have sounded more convincing if I could have completely focused my eyes. She didn't say anything, just stood there with crossed arms. "Francoise! Please!"

"I can get us back," Alfred offered.

"'E probably drives bettair zan me," Francoise agreed.

I glanced from the limo, which was now rocking slightly side to side, to Alfred, who stared back placidly. The kid had to be on Prozac or something. "Stay on the main drag. Don't break any traffic laws or do anything to draw attention to yourselves." Other than the fact that the SUV's doors were all stubbornly open. "And, uh, tell Tami I'll explain when I get back."

Francoise and I darted into traffic and Alfred pulled out behind us. Neither was as dangerous as it sounds, because thanks to the big black barrier in the road, nobody was going anywhere. The horns were deafening, and even worse, a few people were starting to get out of their cars. The police couldn't be far behind.

Alfred did a highly illegal U-turn over the fake grass in the median and was out of there before Francoise and I even reached the limo. I wrenched open the nearest door, which in Alice's absence had stayed properly closed, and leapt inside. "Cassie!" I heard Jesse's voice but couldn't respond because I had a mage on top of me and another was trying to wrestle me for my gun. There was also a lot of kicking going on.

I kneed the mage somewhere painful and came up for air. "Jesse, grab my hand!" I had only one free, but one was all I needed. I waved it wildly in the air.

"What about the others?" he demanded.

"I have the others!"

"You found the other car?"

I stared down the length of the limo at him over the top of the mage's head. He'd given up on magic in favor of trying to choke me to death. "Other car?" I croaked. Oh, shit. I'd forgotten there were supposed to be two limos.

"They separated us so they'd outnumber us! Tell me you already found the other one!"

He looked eerily like his mother all of a sudden. I was distracted by a couple of guns zeroing in on my cranium, but Francoise said something that sent them flying. Then the driver somehow lurched the limo forward a foot or two, sending us all tumbling backward.

I slipped out from under the would-be choker, crawled behind a mage who had wrestled Francoise to the floor, and hit him on the head with the butt of my pistol. Unfortunately, that works better in the movies, because all it did was make him mad. But he did let Francoise go in favor of lunging at me, giving her a chance to clock him with a still-intact bottle of Pernod.

Shields were difficult to use in such a tight space, as there was little enough room to move as it was, but that didn't stop the mages from waving lethal weapons around. One of them leveled a gun on me at the same moment I turned mine on him. We froze, both of us looking at the other.

"Well. This is awkward," I said as Caleb glowered at me.

"I don't want to kill you," he said, and it actually sounded sincere.

"Ditto." I swallowed. "Only, see, you have someone I kind of want back."

He ignored that. "The warrants for you don't specify that you have to be brought in alive, but it would certainly be my preference."

"It wouldn't be mine," I told him truthfully. A quick death by spell or gunshot was probably a lot more pleasant than what the Circle would do if they got their hands on me with no witnesses.

He frowned. "You'd receive a fair trial. If the charges against you are in error—"

"The charges against me are a bunch of crap," I said with feeling.

"Cassie!" Jesse sidled up next to me. "We have to go!"

"What about the other mages?" It wasn't like I could turn around to see for myself.

"Francoise and I got 'em. Goddamn, she can fight!"

"Don't swear," I said automatically.

The frown on Caleb's face got a little bigger. "I'm not afraid to die," he told me, his weapon steady. "Can you say the same?"

I gripped Jesse's T-shirt a little tighter and grabbed Francoise's arm. "Hell, no," I told him, and shifted.

We ended up outside the car, which was better than I'd feared, but not anywhere near as good as I'd hoped. I'd been aiming for Dante's, but apparently I didn't have enough juice left for that. It was a problem, but not as big of one as the second limo that had pulled up and was spewing mages all over the asphalt. It looked like someone had found time to call for backup.

"I keep telling you I should be carrying," Jesse said accusingly.

"Shut up!"

I tried to shift again but this time got nowhere. Even worse, the mages had spotted us. It was like their heads were all on a string: suddenly, every eye was fixed on me. I needed a plan, but I didn't have time for one. I just knew that keeping Jesse with me was the best way to get him killed. I pushed the boy at Francoise. "Get him out of here!"

She didn't ask questions. She shoved something into my pocket and simultaneously muttered a word that caused a burst of light that blinded me. I felt her rip Jesse out of my grip and heard the sound of shoes crunching glass underfoot as they took off.

I decided that the best thing I could do to help her was to give the mages another target—one with a much higher bounty attached. Before the blinding light had faded, I turned on my heel and ran in the opposite direction. Right into Marco.

He caught me by the shoulders and shook me like a dog, obviously ready to rip me a new one. But then the light faded and he glimpsed the tide of dark shapes surging toward us. He snarled, baring a lot of fang, and shoved me behind him.

I bounced off his friend's chest, which was thankfully back in one piece, as Marco turned the Shroud of Night loose on the mages. It flew straight at them, its deep, inky nothingness making the surrounding night look like high noon by comparison. But rather than being the size of a sheet, it now covered half the road.

Marco started forward, gun drawn, but I grabbed his arm. "Let's get out of here!"

"Sure," he responded as the darkness cut through the mages' shields like they weren't even there. Marco's buddy tossed him an M16. "In a minute."

I grabbed the muzzle of the freakishly large gun. "What are you doing?"

"Like shooting fish in a bucket," he said with relish.

"You can't kill them!"

"Wanna bet?"

"Marco!"

He raised an eyebrow in a way that reminded me eerily of Mircea. "And what do you think they had in mind for you?"

It was a reasonable question, but it also wasn't the point. "I'm trying to keep the Circle intact," I told him as the Shroud boiled over the ground like a black mist. I assumed the mages were fighting to get out, but there was no sign of it from where we stood. No sound, no gunfire, no spells, no light. Nothing.

At least it hid us from the traffic, I thought, as Marco stared at me.

"Are you crazy?" He looked like he was seriously starting to worry about me.

"It's complicated," I said, marveling at the understatement. "But you can't go around shooting mages."

"Why not?"

It was obvious Marco wasn't going to give up on his proposed slaughter without a damn good reason. So I gave him one, although he didn't seem to understand my explanation about the vengeful god and the portal to another world and the ancient spell that the Circle supported that was the only thing keeping it closed. To give him credit, he did grasp the major point though.

"You're saying you got to keep alive the very people who want you dead?"

"That's what I'm saying."

"That sucks."

"Which will be the title of my autobiography, if I live long enough to write one. Now, can we get out of here?"

"My thought exactly." The voice came from behind me, and a gun was pressed to my rib cage.

I twisted my neck enough to get a glimpse of Caleb's face. He'd said he was willing to die to capture me. It looked like he hadn't been kidding.

Marco snarled, letting loose a barrage of bullets that ricocheted off the mage's shields, threatening everyone but him. "Marco! Cut it out before you kill someone!"

"I got every intention of killing someone," he said as Caleb pulled me back toward the limo. I couldn't imagine why—that car wasn't going anywhere—but we kept backing that way nonetheless.

Marco followed, but couldn't get past Caleb's shields. I felt around in my pockets, hoping that Francoise had shoved my gun in there, not that it was likely to help much against a war mage. She hadn't, but she'd left me something possibly more useful. My hand closed over something hard, and I looked down to see the grinning face of Daikoku staring up at me.

Francoise must have grabbed it when the cabinet fell over. And if it worked half as well as the Shroud, it might be able to get me out of this. But did I dare use it?

I clutched Daikoku tightly, feeling energy radiate outward from the cool surface under my fingers. Whatever this thing was, it was powerful—and therefore dangerous. But I'd seen enough war mages to know that the Shroud wouldn't hold them for long, and even if it did, Caleb hardly needed their help to take me in. I was seriously debating using it when the night tore open and Pritkin tumbled out of nothing.

Caleb threw a spell as soon as Pritkin left the ley line, but he had to lower his shields to do it. And Marco lunged for us the instant they dropped. Caleb had expected it and sent him flying with a muttered word, but the distraction gave Pritkin time to roll under a nearby car, out of view.

"Let it go, John!" Caleb called. "I'll guarantee her safety, but I'm taking her in."

A spiky blond head poked up over the car's roof. "You can't guarantee anything of the kind! Or have you forgotten what happened the last time the Council wanted a meeting!"

"Richardson was blinded by grief over his son. Nothing like that will happen again—you have my word."

"Your word isn't in question, Caleb. It's your judgment I doubt."

"There was a time when you trusted me with your life!"

"And there was a time when you used your brain instead of blindly following orders," Pritkin said, coming around the front of the car. There was a raw red spot in the dead center of his chest, like maybe his shields had given out a fraction before his buddy's spell did. "She goes with me."

Caleb's answer to that was to throw another spell. But Marco had been waiting on the sidelines, silent and dark, for exactly that. As soon as Caleb lowered his shields, Marco grabbed him and Pritkin grabbed me.

We started backing toward the ley line Pritkin had used to come in, but the mages had finished ripping the Shroud to pieces and were blocking the way. All eight of them. They didn't immediately attack—there was just enough doubt among them about whether Pritkin was a hero or a psychopath to be useful in a situation like this. But it wouldn't be long.

I needed to think, needed a plan, but they were coming for us and there was no more time. And even Pritkin couldn't fight those kinds of odds. I clenched my palm around Daikoku's cool shape, hard enough to hurt. "Give me the energy to shift us out of here!" I wished.

I hoped that was clear enough, and then just hoped it would work at all, as a long moment passed and nothing happened. I opened my fist and stared at the little thing, wondering if Francoise had stolen a dud. Then one tiny eye dropped in a tinier wink, and the world tore apart.

Chapter Eighteen

There was a sudden tumbling sense of vertigo and then a jolt that drove the air from my lungs. It felt almost like I'd shifted, but the pavement was firm under my feet and the smell of burnt asphalt and magic still hung in the air. I didn't wait for the dizziness to pass, just grabbed the warm body beside me and got us out of there.

I immediately knew something was wrong, because instead of a short free fall, as should have been the case with a shift no farther than Dante's, it seemed to take forever until I hit the ground again. I landed on my feet, but then someone crashed into me. I couldn't see who—it was pitch dark—but the impact drove me back a couple of steps. That would have been fine, except there was suddenly nothing under my foot but air.

I fell on my butt and went sliding at what felt like sixty miles an hour down a steep embankment. There were no trees or rocks to grab, only slick, sparse grass and a lot more mud. My flailing hand finally grabbed someone's arm, and I held on for dear life, tumbling and falling, until we finally slammed to a stop in—of course—a muddy puddle.

The impact tried to shove my tailbone up through my shoulder blades and made my teeth snap together. I stared up at the dim arch of the Milky Way while I tried to get my breath back, only to have a drop of water hit me right on the cornea. I wiped it away, dragging my muddy sleeve across my forehead in the process. Of course it would rain. Of *course* it would.

My usual post-almost-dying routine—and, God, there was an actual *routine*—mostly involved getting yelled at by Priktin and then going to get a sandwich. And a bath. And some aspirin. Since none of those was immediately available, I settled for rolling over to check on the source of the wheezing breaths coming from behind me.

I still couldn't see clearly, with only a sliver of moonlight for illumination, but he was swearing inventively enough to make sight irrelevant. Pritkin's grumblings are the soundtrack of my life these days, but my relief at knowing he was okay was immediately followed by the realization that there was something wrong with his voice. I fought to get free from the enveloping folds of the heavy leather coat I seemed to be wearing and the mud that had latched onto it with vicious suction.

I finally managed it and staggered over to the side of the puddle, dripping, filthy and exhausted, only to meet my own furious blue gaze. "What did you do?!"

I stared in complete shock. My voice wasn't that high, was it? I sounded like a little girl. A very pissed-off little girl. I was struggling to absorb the fact that my body was sitting there, yelling at me, when a chill wind tickled my neck and wrists and tried to seep under my clothes. I started to tug my sleeves down, but quit when I caught sight of the hands sticking out of them. I stopped moving entirely for a moment after that, except for my ass, which abruptly made contact with the ground.

The cold knife of recognition twisted in my stomach. The things at the end of my arms were a man's hands. To be more exact, they were Pritkin's hands, only for some reason I seemed to be wearing them. After a few frozen seconds, when even breathing became difficult, I realized what that bastard Daikoku had done.

I'd asked to be able to shift, but that hadn't been possible in my body. I'd also wanted to take Pritkin with me. Daikoku had granted both requests, but not by giving me some extra energy as I'd hoped. He'd switched our bodies. That had allowed me out of the body that was almost drained and into one that had enough fight left to get us gone. It had also ensured that I had no choice but to take Pritkin along.

Because I was stuck inside his skin.

"What happened?" Pritkin demanded, his clipped British tones sounding really odd coming out of my mouth. It occured to me that, with my eyesight, he probably couldn't yet see the truth for himself.

My mind groped wildly for something to say. "I can fix this," I finally got out, my voice unfamiliar in my ears. "I think."

"Fix what?" The question was spoken in a low, controlled voice, which wasn't good. Pritkin loud is in his normal state. It's when he gets quiet that you have to worry.

I would have answered, or tried to, but the realization hit me that this body was in a lot of pain. I looked down at my chest, more than a little freaked to see a half-burnt shirt, singed body hair and an irregular red patch underneath it all. Caleb's spell, I recalled. Pritkin's amazing healing abilities had already given it the slick, shiny texture of a half-healed burn. Except it didn't feel half-healed. It hurt like a bitch.

"You destroyed my fence." The accusation came from the man with the black-framed glasses and the floaty Einstein hair who was standing at the top of the hill, looking down disapprovingly.

I realized that the hard thing I was sitting on was a fence post half-buried in mud. I pulled it out from under my borrowed behind and looked up at the farmer. "Uh, sorry?"

"Well, there's nothing to be done about it now," the man said rather charitably, I thought. "Come up here and I'll make us something hot."

"Answer me," Pritkin ordered, and we were close enough that I could see past the naked horror in his eyes and spot the homicidal urge rising. I was trying to come up with a way of breaking it to him gently, but then the farmer pointed a flashlight at us, and I didn't need to explain. Because Pritkin was staring not at me but down at his chest. Which was currently a lot rounder than usual.

"What have you done?" His appalled whisper grated on my already ragged nerves.

"Got us out of there alive," I snapped. Okay, it wasn't an ideal situation, but neither was getting shot, strangled or spelled to death by the Circle. "And at least you're inside me. I've had to possess a vampire before," I reminded him.

Pritkin seemed at a loss for words—pretty much a first—but his steadily reddening face flushed even darker. He was going to give me a heart attack if he didn't cut it out.

"You need to calm down," I said more gently. I distinctly recalled my first out-of-body-and-into-someone-else's-experience, and it had been a little . . . traumatic.

"I am calm."

Sure. Which was why he looked like he was updating his hit list.

"Yeah, only that's my body you're using and I'm trying to make it to thirty before my first heart attack."

"Are you planning to sit there all night?" the farmer asked. "Get up here before you catch your death!"

"How?" Pritkin asked me, grasping my arms. It didn't feel anything like his usual iron grip. I swallowed.

"There's a path to the left. Less muddy than the way you came down," the farmer answered helpfully.

"It's a long story," I told Pritkin nervously.

"Give me the short version."

"A Japanese god with a lousy sense of humor?"

Pritkin just stared at me. Dark circles crowded his eyes and my hair was falling into his face. It looked like my body hadn't recovered from the fight yet. It had started to rain harder, and cold drops were running in rivulets down his cheeks and dripping off the end of his chin. He was obviously suffering and, to tell the truth, I wasn't thrilled about getting back a body that had a raging fever. We needed to get out of here.

"Let's get back to Dante's and I'll explain," I told him, gripping his shoulder. It felt strange, like the bones were too fragile under my new, larger hand, but I ignored it. I gathered my power around us and shifted—all of about four feet. We ended up sitting farther back in the mud puddle, almost up to our waists in smelly water. Pritkin sneezed.

"What happened?"

I shook my head. "I don't know." I was listening to the sounds of steps getting closer. The farmer had apparently given up trying to talk to the crazy people hanging out in his field and disappeared from view. But I could hear him as he traversed what I assumed was the path down.

"You're telling me you can't shift?" Pritkin demanded, apparently unaware that we were about to have company.

I tried again, just to make sure, and the same thing happened. Only this time, Pritkin lurched into me on landing and I slipped, taking an unexpected mud bath. I sat up, filthy and steaming, and spat out a mouthful of truly disgusting water. "That's what I'm telling you."

"But you got us here!"

"And it looks like we're stuck here."

I looked around for cover, but even with Pritkin's eyesight, there wasn't much to see. Other than an open-sided, tin-roofed shed, which appeared to be busy falling apart, there was only a flat plain filled with soggy grass and more mud. There were some indistinct black shapes silhouetted against the dark sky that might have been a tree line, but it was too far away to do us much good.

Then Pritkin's head jerked around and he threw up a hand. At almost the same second, something hit his shield and ricocheted back to explode against the shed's roof. The crash reverberated across the field and turned a third of the roof into a sizzling mess. I didn't have time to ask him how he'd managed to create a shield using my power, because it collapsed and he jerked me down beside him. Something else whizzed over our heads, more an impression of light and heat than a visual image, and then Pritkin pushed my face down into the muck.

"Over here! There's two of them!" I heard the yell as I surfaced.

A spell shot by and exploded just behind us, sending a wall of mud skyward before setting the row of heavy fence posts alight, like candles on a nonexistent cake. It occurred to me to wonder if it was the farmer I'd heard approaching, after all. Then I dodged one way and Pritkin went the other, barely in time to avoid a third spell.

Goddamnit, I didn't even know where we were! How had my enemies found me so fast? I didn't have time to figure it out, because someone grabbed me from behind.

I used one of the maneuvers Pritkin had been teaching me—which worked a lot better with his strength behind it—and broke the hold. A large, heavyset man wearing a dark Adidas sweatshirt stumbled back. He lost his footing on the slimy soil and went down, but the slew of magical weapons that had been hovering around his head flew straight at me.

I screamed and ducked with my hands over my head—like that was going to help. Only it seemed to, because nothing happened. I looked up to see the line of burning pickets hovering in front of me, getting impaled by knives and riddled by bullets, and Pritkin with a hand outstretched and a face pale with strain. Then I had to dance back to avoid another knife, this one in the hand of an angry mage.

Make that an angry war mage. Levitating weapons are one of their favorite tricks, allowing one man to act more like a squadron. In his little hoodie, Adidas didn't look much like a war mage, but he fought like one. Which meant I was in a lot of trouble.

"Switch us back!" Pritkin yelled as the knife ripped through the sleeve of my coat.

I glared at him. "Busy!"

The remaining pickets attacked Adidas while I sloshed backward, fighting to stay on my feet and to find a weapon, and then someone else came out of nowhere and tackled me around the legs. The new assailant was taller, whip-thin and wiry. We hit the ground, or what passed for it, with a splash and a squelch. I twisted and fought and somehow ended up on top, pressing his face into the mud with one hand while trying to locate Pritkin's holster with the other, which had ended up at the small of my back.

Adidas jumped both of us. I got hit in the ribs and cuffed upside the head, but I managed to gouge someone in the eye and got an elbow in someone else's neck. Then Adidas punched me hard enough to set my ears ringing, but the fight had taken us near the shed and I shoved him back under the dripping metal of the awning.

He screamed and somebody cursed. My head jerked up, expecting more trouble, only to see my own pissed-off form glaring at me. "Get out of the way!"

I dodged to one side just in time to avoid the spell that Pritkin hurled at the guy, which sent both him and the remains of the shed flying. But we were definitely dealing with a war mage, because he managed to concentrate enough even with a face full of liquid metal to get his shields up. The blow threw him into the air, but his shields cushioned the landing and saved him from the hail of flying shed fragments. I stared incredulously as he rolled to his feet and took off.

My fingers closed over the holster at last, and I struggled to my feet, gun in hand, only to be dumped back on my ass by Skinny. He also decided on retreat but took off in a different direction than his buddy. The dark swallowed him before I could get a shot off.

Pritkin jumped to his feet—or, more accurately, my feet—and ran full-out after Adidas. "Stay put!" he yelled over my shoulder.

"Pritkin!" He didn't even slow down. I gave up on Skinny and took off after my fast-disappearing body. Without his usual strength or his portable arsenal, he could end up getting me killed.

With the wind slapping me in the face and the rain in my eyes, it was tough going. Not to mention the waterlogged coat, a new, lower center of gravity and feet that felt too far from the ground. I stumbled twice and almost lost sight of them three or four times, but Pritkin's vision was better than good, and despite the heavier musculature, it was amazing how fast his body could move. By the time we crested a hill near the tree line, I'd almost caught them.

Pritkin and Adidas went plunging down the other side. I started to follow when something slammed into my left arm. The pain was so vivid that it blocked everything else out for a moment. Then a movement caught my eye and I turned in time to see that Skinny hadn't abandoned the fight after all—and to meet the force of his body as he leapt at me. We went down together, rolling and cursing and getting pummeled by the rocks hidden in the tall grass almost as much as by each other.

We crashed into a tree at the bottom of the hill, and luckily Skinny took the brunt of the collision, his head smacking against the trunk with a wet, thudding sound. It was hard enough to stun him or worse, but at the moment, I didn't care much. I'd taken a glancing blow myself, and a stab of agony ran through my temple before spreading over the rest of my skull, competing with the pain in my arm.

I looked down to find a second slash in Pritkin's sleeve and blood welling up to soak the leather. It took me a second to realize that I'd been shot. I took a steadying breath, yanked off his belt and tied it high on my arm, above the wound, using my teeth to draw it tight. If the mages didn't kill me, Pritkin was probably going to when I returned his body stuck full of holes.

"Are you going to let her tackle Jenkins alone?" someone demanded from behind me.

I spun to find that the farmer had caught up with me. His glasses caught the light, making him look like some otherworldly owl as he bent to relieve Skinny of his potion belt. He seemed awfully blasé for someone who had just witnessed a magical battle. But I didn't have time to figure out what his deal was. Down the hill, Adidas was being tackled by a small, determined figure.

I should have known Pritkin wouldn't give up on a pursuit just because he was weaponless, in unfamiliar territory and, oh yeah, using someone else's body. Damn it! I was going to end up shot in the ass again.

I left the farmer where he was and ran after them. The opalescent light leaking through the thick cloud cover was enough to show me the hellish fight going on. I winced as my body took a vicious kick to the stomach and wished Pritkin would do as he'd advised me and get out of the way. I was a lousy shot, but at this range, even I might be able to hit the target.

I never had a chance to find out. Pritkin took another hit, this one to the head, and stumbled back a few steps. But before I could fire, twin spells exploded in the night. One, from behind me, took out the mage's shields, and the other, from Pritkin's outstretched hand, sent him tumbling head over heels into the dirt.

For a moment, I thought I saw some odd flashes around him—in colors that didn't appear in nature. I blinked and they weren't there anymore, but I could still smell them, musky sharp and strange, and taste them on the back of my tongue, a jumble of sour and bitter and cloyingly sweet.

And then I reached Pritkin and was too busy checking him for injuries to worry about anything else.

"Are you crazy?" I shook him, but he appeared too dazed to care. There were no obvious holes, but it looked like the mage's elbow had come close to cracking my skull.

"I'm fine," Pritkin said, and took a nose-dive into the dirt.

I pulled him up and picked wet grass off his face. "You're still in one piece, right?" I asked, just to be sure.

"You tell me." His eyes focused on my reddened sleeve. "What's that?"

"A gift from Skinny."

"Who?"

"The other guy."

"Where is he?" Pritkin's gaze flashed around, although with my eyesight I doubted he could see much.

"He's out cold. At the moment, I'm more worried about this one." I toed the mage, but he didn't budge.

"You needn't be," Pritkin said shortly.

I gazed down at the utterly still form and realized what was odd about it. Even unconscious bodies breathe, but I hadn't seen this one's chest rise and fall once. "You killed him?"

"I certainly hope so."

"But he's a war mage."

"Ex–war mage. He has served other interests since leaving the corps."

"But . . . you're in my body!"

Pritkin wiped gunk out of his eyes. "You have magical ability. The fact that you haven't been trained doesn't negate that."

"I don't have that kind of power!"

"You have sufficient," he said tersely. "And knowledge is half the battle. That particular spell was esoteric enough that he didn't know it—or how to counter it."

I hunched Pritkin's shoulders against the chill night air and stared at the body at my feet. The guy had tried to gut me, something that tends to erode my sympathy. But it was still frightening to think that my magic could do something like that, could kill a man with a few muttered words. I shivered; my adrenaline was running low and the sweat under my clothes was drying cold against my skin.

"Come on." I got an arm around Pritkin and was surprised at how little he weighed. I really wanted my own body back, but I had to admit that I envied Pritkin his strength. "We need to get out of here."

"Switch us back first," he said. I hesitated, wondering how to phrase this. "You said you could do it!"

"I can! At least, I'm pretty sure, with some time to think about it—"

"Get us back where we belong!"

"It's not that easy!" I wasn't exactly an expert at out-of-body experiences, but I'd done it enough times by now to have the basics down, at least as far as getting my spirit back in its rightful place. The problem was Pritkin, or, more precisely, his spirit, which I didn't know how to stuff back inside his skin. And until I figured it out, I couldn't leave his body unattended. It couldn't live without a soul in residence, and mine was the only one currently available.

I explained this, but it didn't seem to improve his blood pressure. Neither did the fact that I couldn't shift. "Why not?" he demanded, glaring at me. The expression was eerily familiar despite being on my features, but it wasn't as intimidating as usual. Possibly because he currently looked like a very wet, very pissed-off Kewpie doll.

"I don't know." My head was throbbing in time with my elbow, and the wet, matted grass was starting to look really comfortable. "Maybe even your energy levels are too low." But that didn't feel right. It was more like something had blocked my attempts.

"Try again."

"If I end up with a brain aneurysm, it'll be in your head," I reminded him.

"I'll take the risk," he said immediately.

So much for the gentler sex. Pritkin as a woman was exactly like always—prickly, demanding and paranoid, looking at the world through narrowed eyes. "What does it matter if we rest for five minutes first?"

"It matters because these two weren't alone."

"And how do you know that?"

He jerked his head, and I followed his gaze to where a

group of dark shapes were running for us from the other side of the field. They weren't close enough to identify yet, but then a spell sizzled past, close enough that I could feel the tingle of its energy against my cheek, and identification became moot. Mages.

Pritkin grabbed my hand and we ran for the opposite tree line. An adrenaline rush hit my veins, opening up my lungs to the cool night air, wiping out the fatigue that had been dragging at me. But Pritkin wasn't doing so hot. Even with my help, he was taking gasping breaths and looking white and pinched by the time leaves slapped us in the face, and our lead was almost entirely gone. We ran on anyway, hearing our pursuers fanning out behind us, yelling to each other to make sure we couldn't double back.

So much for that plan.

It got quieter the deeper we went into the trees, the old dark branches closing ranks behind us, fallen leaves soft and silent underfoot. It also got rougher, with the cover overhead eventually so solid that the moonlight could hardly penetrate at all. I put Pritkin behind me because I could still see the dim, black outlines of the trees ahead, while I doubted that was true for him. But it didn't help much.

He was battered by the low-hanging limbs I shoved out of the way, which whipped back to hit him in the face. And he didn't have the advantage of protective clothing, as I hadn't dressed for a mad rush through the woods. But he pushed on anyway, trying not to slow me down, with blood trickling down his neck and his hands torn and bloody.

We'd been half running, half walking for maybe ten minutes when he hit a tree trunk and bounced off and then stumbled over another that had fallen partway across our path. I tried to tug him farther along, but he just shook his head at me rather desperately. His pulse was a fast flutter at his throat and his pupils were dilated.

I nodded and steadied myself against a tree, drawing air into my lungs so hard it hurt. Gray, flaky bark crackled under my palm, leaking resin that stuck my fingertips together. I propped my shoulders against the trunk and unclenched my hand from around my gun, which I'd clutched tightly enough to leave a dent in my palm. I spent a few minutes just breathing and trying to listen over the pounding of my heart. I really hoped we'd lost them, because Pritkin didn't look like he could walk, much less run, any farther.

"What do you hear?" he whispered after a few minutes.

I listened, and his ears picked up everything: the shush of wind in the treetops, the light patter of rain on the canopy above, the scurrying of some little animal—but nothing of the pursuit. I'd heard the mages stumbling around in the distance for a while, but even that was gone now. "I think we're alone."

But even as I said it, there were those strange flashes again, this time in the treetops. They were black against the indigo darkness of the sky but with glints of color I couldn't name. And now that I concentrated, I noticed other things, too: here and there were sighs not caused by the wind and brief scents that had nothing to do with nature.

"Wait—there's something here."

"Some*thing*?"

"Yeah."

And it was as if they'd heard. Suddenly the space around us was flooded with the cold, bitter taste of dead winter, the air thick with ragged shadows that darted before me like a tumble of snakes. One brushed past my arm, and I flinched away. Cold and hot and a thousand contradictions that my mind couldn't handle—and none of them good.

"Describe it."

"I can't! The colors are ... weird," I said, groping for words. And then several more flew past, and it was like viewing the world through a thousand glass wings, a cacophony of darting images. I ducked and my eyes crossed, trying to *see*, but that only seemed to make things worse. "Sharp edges, like a bird, only not," I said helplessly. "In the trees." God, what *were* those things?

"Rakshasas," Pritkin hissed, looking up.

"What?"

"Demons," he spat, rooting around in my coat, grabbing things out of the belt I was wearing draped low on my hips. It was weighed down with vials, each in a little leather sheath, that contained some pretty lethal potions. "They're shape-shifters."

I wet my lips. It would be really nice if he was wrong, but I doubted it. Because if there was one thing Pritkin knew, it was demons. Not only was he the Circle's best-known demon hunter, he'd once spent centuries in the demon realms courtesy of his father, Rosier, Lord of the Incubi.

Rosier had wanted to show off his half-human child, a hybrid experiment that other demons had said couldn't be done, and had dragged his proof into the next world without bothering to ask first. Pritkin hadn't enjoyed the experience, but then, neither had anybody else. Giving him the distinction of being the only human to be literally kicked out of hell.

I only hoped a return trip wasn't in the cards.

Chapter Nineteen

Another of the creatures brushed past me, and something ragged and fluttering, like a broken wing, trailed over my arm. It was icy cold and burning hot and utterly, utterly repulsive. A thick coil of nausea rolled in my gut as I stumbled back a few steps. I bit my lip to stay quiet, but a stray gasp trickled out between my clenched teeth anyway, prompted as much by the memory of the last demon I'd fought as by the current threat.

My heart thudded steadily faster, adrenaline ratcheting me into flight mode. I couldn't go through that again; I just couldn't. I turned blindly, preparing to run, not caring if the mages heard because I'd prefer to face the whole damn Corps than to ever feel those hands on me again.

Pritkin caught me. For a minute, I didn't see him but another face. I had a sudden flashback to the feel of Rosier's touch and the clammy, shudder-inducing sensation of his tongue on my flesh, lapping my blood as he slowly gutted me. A scream bubbled up in my throat.

A hand clasped hard over my mouth, but it was smaller than it should have been and softer, a woman's hand. My hand. The realization jolted me back to some semblance of control as I gazed down at my own furious blue eyes.

"Don't panic!" Pritkin whispered. "They're like vultures, drawn to fear as to approaching death. It will only bring them on faster!"

"Approaching *death*?!"

"Be silent!" He looked around and bit off a curse. "Where are they? In your body, I can't see them properly."

And didn't I wish I had that problem, I decided hysterically as another half-perceived thing stopped in front of my face. It hovered in the air, only I had the impression that "air" wasn't right. Whatever currents it was riding, they weren't in this world.

And then I realized why I couldn't see them too well either, even using Pritkin's eyes. They *weren't* in this world, at least not entirely. I watched, horrified and mesmerized, as the thing flickered in and out, like an image seen in running water. It didn't make logical sense; it didn't fit this world's rules about things like three dimensions and proper light spectrums. It was as small as a hummingbird and as big as a house, with no discernable face.

It reached for me, somehow giving the impression of a grin anyway, and I shrieked and stumbled back. Pritkin cursed and threw something, and whether by following my line of sight or pure luck, he hit it head-on. The thing's screech echoed inside my head, a deafening, unending roar that sent me stumbling to my knees, while it writhed and boiled and cursed.

And somehow I understood what it said, knew it was cursing me, cursing Pritkin in a dozen languages I shouldn't know, furious that this body still lived, still breathed, still protected me from it. "Not for long," a hundred voices purred, a low, hoarse sound that made my skin try to shudder off the bone.

And it winked out of existence.

I fell to all fours in shock, unable to breathe, and Pritkin knelt by my side. "Are there any more?" he demanded, but I couldn't answer with my brain gibbering hysterically. "Cassie!"

I finally sucked in a breath and choked, trying to tell him about the gathering flashes in the treetops and the rainbow of alien colors circling above our heads. *Like vultures*, he'd said, and, oh, God, that couldn't be good. But then there was a flash of light, and a stab of bright pain ripped into my injured arm.

I hurled myself sideways instinctively, my feet skidded out from under me and the forest erupted with crashes, curses and spells. A flock of birds hiding from the rain burst out of the treetops, Pritkin cursed, and things got ugly—fast. The mages had caught up with us.

They seemed to view me as the chief threat, because three of them concentrated on me while only one bothered with Pritkin. Which was probably one too many in his condition, but there wasn't much I could do about it. I'd returned fire even as I fell, crashing onto my right side and immediately rolling to one knee, trying to keep the gun up and aimed. A lot of my bullets connected—at point-blank range, even I'm a good shot—but they weren't doing any damage. The mages had shields up and the bullets trampolined off or were absorbed.

I gritted my teeth and kept firing, scurrying backward like a crab to present a moving target, until my back hit a tree and my bullets gave out. I managed to pop out the spent clip but reloading was a problem with my left arm now useless, like a dead limb attached to my body. The mages realized that and grinned, watching me fumble one-handed in the coat's many pockets, trying to find another clip.

It was obviously useless—even if I came up with one, they would kill me before I could slam it home—but I kept up the comedy routine anyway. I'd thought it might give Pritkin a chance to get away. Only that didn't seem to be what he was doing.

He'd already dealt with the guy who'd jumped him—at least that's who I assumed was sprawled on the forest floor, his head at a very unhealthy angle. Now he sprang forward and grabbed one of the mages in front of me, clamping a hand tight over his nose and mouth to prevent any sound escaping. One quick, hard twist and the mage jerked and went still. Pritkin went still, too, clutching the guy to his body. He waited until the mages dropped their shields in preparation for finishing me off. Then he reached around and lifted the man's gun.

He killed two of our attackers before the third had even whirled around. But the mage got a gun up and his shots bit into the dead guy Pritkin was holding with meaty-sounding thuds—right before he was taken out with a shot to the head. But that took Pritkin's last bullet, and a mage who had been smart enough to hold back, waiting in the shadow of the trees, stepped out and got him in a headlock he wasn't strong enough to break.

My gun was still empty and I wasn't likely to be much good in a fight one-handed. The only advantage I had was the fact that what I was doing was so stupid, no one would expect it. So I went with that, screaming and leaping onto the back of the mage trying to asphyxiate my partner.

"Don't kill him," Pritkin gasped as the mage backed me into a tree, slamming me against the trunk and sending a flare of agony up my injured arm. My gut twisted and I felt the edges of my vision go gray. It loosened my hold enough for him to get his hands around my arms and throw me over his head right into another tree.

"No problem," I croaked, sliding down the trunk.

I heard a commotion but was too busy getting my limbs sorted out, most of which were over my head, to follow it. I looked up to see Pritkin kneeling in the leaves, looking tiny next to the mage draped over him. The man's head rested against my chest, his body sprawled limp and warm over my thighs, his tangled hair wet with blood. His eyes were open.

There was an excited flutter in the treetops, and before I could move, a swarm of unearthly things dropped out of the sky. I realized what I'd seen from a distance earlier, when Pritkin had killed Adidas. Because this time, I had a front-row seat.

Wrong-colored things descended in a fluttering, clawing mass, dozens on each corpse. A creature on the body nearest me brushed a clawlike hand down its cheek softly, gently, almost like a lover's caress, and a ghostly mirror of the dead man's face emerged. The new ghost slowly sat up, dazed and blinking, detaching from its body in a shimmer of silver light.

My eyes focused on it thankfully, able to see it even in Pritkin's body because of my clairvoyant abilities. Soft and hazy, still indistinct as all ghosts were at first, it rose to its knees—or what it was still probably thinking of as its knees—and then to its feet. The creatures rustled and jostled each other as the spirit stood there before them, naked and defenseless without its body.

I'd seen thousands of ghosts before, but never at their birth, so to speak. The ones I stumbled across had had time to learn the ropes, to decide how they wished to appear to others. And to figure out that the confines of their new home—their graveyard or house or whatever they were haunting—served as their new body, in a way. It energized them, protected them, allowed them a small measure of freedom. Because without it, they were like these spirits, columns of pure energy exposed and vulnerable with their former protective shells crumpled at their feet.

But these ghosts never had time to find their way home. The pack edged closer, flickering in and out of sight. Slick with sweat, I froze in the darkness, muscles locked and singing with strain as icy panic gnawed at my spine. I knew what was coming. It was in the silent, mesmerizing smiles that lit the not-faces, in the half-starved hands that reached out to pluck at the spirit's form, at the naked want in alien eyes . . .

I watched, sickened, as the new ghosts managed to focus their senses on the approaching tide, as their faces changed and they opened their mouths to scream. And then the demons attacked. It *was* like a pack of vultures, I thought, horrified, as they tore into the ghosts with things my brain insisted on calling claws and beaks, although that wasn't right.

The demons ripped into the beautiful, shining souls, biting and slashing, tearing them to shreds in a matter of moments. Each demon crouched low over its bit of soul protectively, almost lovingly, as the rendered spirits shrieked and wept and sent hopeless cries into the deaf night. Even as the things finished their meal and started, one by one, to wink out of sight, the terrified, butchered souls cried on.

The forest rang with their silent cries, the darkness shone with their reflected light for a moment longer, and then all was silence. It was like a door had slammed shut. Leaving us alone with a bunch of rapidly cooling corpses.

I scrambled to my feet and half ran, half stumbled to where Pritkin sat in the wet grass. "Are you hurt?" My voice rasped in my throat because of course he was, he had to be.

He lifted a hand red with blood. It mingled with the rain,

dripping off his fingertips to the muddy ground. "It's not mine," he said, which would have been more reassuring if he hadn't slurred his words.

"Would someone please tell me what is going on here?" The farmer's voice came from over my shoulder.

"Some assholes jumped us; what does it look like?" I snapped, holding on to Pritkin with trembling hands. Damn it, now we had a norm to deal with, on top of everything else. My head was pounding and my eyes were still full of the carnage I had unwillingly witnessed. I didn't need this, too. I looked down at Pritkin, who appeared a little woozy. "Can you put him under a memory charm or something?"

"No," he said, struggling to stand up.

"They are a bit tricky with mages," the farmer added helpfully.

I rounded on the man—the mage—furious. "Would it have hurt you to sling a spell or two? Or have you forgotten how?"

"I think I remember a few," he said, looking amused. "But you seemed to be doing well enough on your own." I stared at him, shocked and amazed at his careless tone, until I realized that he hadn't seen that last part with the ghosts. His human eyes had been mercifully blind.

He switched that owl-eyed gaze from me to Pritkin. "Well, well. You do manage to get yourself into some interesting situations. Don't you, John?"

I looked back and forth between the two of them. "You know each other?"

Pritkin sighed, running a hand through my filthy curls. "Cassie, meet Jonas Marsden."

"Marsden? That sounds familiar."

"It should. Until about a year ago, he led the Silver Circle."

On closer inspection, the former head of the Silver Circle didn't look much like a farmer. Of course, he didn't look much like a renowned war mage, either. His clothes were normal, if boring—an old oatmeal sweater with suede patches at the elbows, a blue plaid shirt and brown slacks. But he'd have stood out in any crowd because of the hair.

It was even worse than Pritkin's, although in a totally new way. It would have been almost shoulder length if it hadn't insisted on floating away from his face as though trying to escape his head. He had static electricity hair when there was no static. But at least it was a nice shade—silver white instead of salt and pepper. And his eyes were very blue behind the thick glasses.

We followed him to a two-story farmhouse. It had walls of jumbled gray stone in all shapes and sizes and no discernable pattern all held together by a weathered slate roof. It sat on a hill overlooking the forest on one side and a river on the other. It looked pretty normal except that it listed faintly to the left, like it was trying to escape the garden that had gone wild and appeared to be trying to eat it. A third of it had already disappeared under massive old vines. It was charming, in a run-down, overgrown, slightly quirky way—except for the pentacle smoking on the front door, its thick lines bubbling dark and angry against the fresh green paint.

"You had visitors," Pritkin said, dripping onto the *Cave Canem* doormat.

"Will they be back?" I looked around nervously, unable to tell if anyone was sneaking up on us due to the aggressive flora.

"If they do, they won't get in," Marsden said cheerfully. "Renewed the wards myself last week. That's my blood under the last coat of paint."

I didn't find that statement as soothing as he apparently intended but was too tired and wet and freaked out to make an issue of it. I bumped the door frame walking in, adding another bruise to Pritkin's already impressive collection. His shoulders were broad and I hadn't yet adjusted to the way this body moved or took up space.

Even more annoying were the sensations caused by his body starting to mend itself. He usually healed almost as fast as a vamp, but he'd lost a lot of blood in the fight and it seemed to be slowing the process down. All along my left arm were weird crawling sensations—pins, needles, knives, *hot*—like something was moving under there. I'd loosened the makeshift tourniquet on the way back, but it hadn't seemed to help. I had my arms crossed to keep from clawing at his skin.

Marsden led us to the kitchen, which was huge, but its exposed wooden beams, bright saffron paint and log fireplace made it seem cozy. It also had a dog. It didn't help so much with the cozy.

It was large and shaggy and gray and it drooled a lot—a fact that was much less disturbing than its coal-red eyes. "What's wrong with it?" I asked Pritkin quietly while Marsden puttered around, brewing things.

Pritkin paused to regard the dog-shaped creature under the window for a moment. Then his eyes narrowed and he looked at Marsden accusingly. "Jonas! What did you do?"

Marsden turned, coffeepot in hand, and followed Pritkin's gaze. He looked a little guilty. "Well, I didn't have much choice, did I? They forced me to destroy his other form."

"You were supposed to release him!"

"After all the trouble I had trapping him in the first place?" Marsden snorted. "Not likely."

"Trapping what?" I eyed the dog warily.

"Nothing for you to worry about," Marsden said, placing a mug in front of me. "Have some coffee." I took a sip and had to work not to choke. Marsden's concoction could beat up espresso and take its lunch money. He noticed my reaction. "Is something wrong?"

I scrubbed at my chin, and beard stubble rasped under my fingers. I yanked my hand away. "I'd really prefer tea," I managed to say.

"Now I know you aren't John," he commented, but he bustled off to plug in a WWII-era kettle.

I watched the dog mangle a rawhide chew bone, half of which had already dissolved into soggy mush, and I could have sworn I saw something pass behind those eyes. Something that looked awfully familiar. I got up so fast, I turned over my chair.

"There's one of those things in there!" I told Pritkin, stumbling back against the fridge.

"What things?" Marsden looked intrigued.

"Rakshasas," Pritkin said, glancing at me. "And it isn't

one, although it would be less dangerous if it were. Rak-shasas can't hurt the living. They're scavengers, looking for an easy meal. They're drawn to murders, battlefields, places where violence is about to happen. They feast on the dead."

I sorted through that and picked out the relative bit. "You're saying there *is* a demon in there and it *can* hurt us?"

"Oh, no, no. He's perfectly harmless." Marsden patted my arm. "He was my golem for years. But when I 'retired,' the Council forced me to give him up. Said I wasn't a war mage any longer, and civilians aren't allowed to have them. Can you imagine? I led the Circle for almost sixty years, but I can't be trusted to keep one pesky demon in thrall!"

"So you put it in the *dog*?" Pritkin demanded.

"Temporarily, until I get a few things sorted. It seems to be working out all right. Orion has started piddling on the rug, but that could be his age."

"You have a devil dog?" I sat down again but moved my chair a little farther away. The dog chewed on, oblivious.

"Demon," Marsden corrected. "War mages are allowed to trap certain of the incorporeal demon races as our ser-vants. Very useful in combat, although ticklish to acquire in the first place. Poor Parsons," he added, and Pritkin winced.

"Who is Parsons?" I asked, deciding to just go with it.

"Who *was* Parsons. He wanted to trap a demon, you see, but he'd barely passed the trials. I told him he might want to give it a while, find his legs, so to speak, but he was hav-ing none of it. All the leading mages had golems—it was seen as a mark of prestige at the time—and he wouldn't rest until he'd acquired one, too."

"Did he?"

Marsden sighed. "Well... in essence... no. You see, when you summon a demon, there are several possible outcomes—"

"He didn't trap the demon," Pritkin said roughly. "It trapped him."

He and I looked at each other, hollow and blank and grave. I wasn't sure how much he'd been able to see of the demon attack through my eyes, but apparently, it had been enough. Or maybe he was just remembering similar scenes. And I'd thought I saw bad stuff. I couldn't imagine living with that kind of double vision all the time.

Marsden was looking thoughtful. "Do you know, I wonder if Parsons' disappearance had anything to do with the practice of golem-making falling out of fashion? You don't see that many with the younger sort, do you?"

I'd been around war mages enough by now to know that the crazy always came out, sooner or later. Nice to know Marsden was getting it on the table early. I glanced at the phone on the wall. "I need to make a call," I told him.

"You want to find out what happened to the children," Pritkin guessed.

"What happened is that I thought I could protect them, when proximity to me is probably what drew the Circle's attention to them in the first place! I wouldn't even put it past them to have kidnapped the kids in the hopes that I'd come after them."

"Possibly. But that doesn't mean they would have been ignored otherwise. They are dangerous—especially in a time of war, when they could possibly be recruited for the other side."

"They're not evil!"

"I never said they were. But they do have a grudge against the Circle, something that could be exploited."

"And the wards are online in any case," Marsden added. "I am afraid they interfere with telephone service."

"Your friend hid the children for years," Pritkin reminded me. "She can manage for a while on her own."

"She hid them before she was a target for the Circle," I reminded him right back.

"They'll be fine," he repeated, reaching for my mug. "If you aren't going to drink that—"

I snatched away my potentially lethal coffee. "You've had enough. You're going to make me sick!"

"I wouldn't have to work very hard. We're increasing the number of training sessions when we get back—you're in worse shape than I thought."

"At least I'm not an addict."

"Neither am I."

"Really." I held up a hand. It kept trembling unless I really concentrated. "How long has it been since your last caffeine fix?"

"Considering the day I've had? Far too long," he muttered, slowly resting his—my—head on his arms.

He did look bad. The wardrobe-in-one was having a rough day. Apparently, it didn't have a setting for demon fighting, or maybe it was just broken. It kept shifting to different shapes and patterns, all of which were muddy and wrinkled and torn in various places. The body underneath didn't look much better. A dark bruise was mapping its way across my left cheekbone, matching the ring of them that circled my right wrist like a bracelet.

"You look really pathetic," I told him.

One eye cracked, regarding me hopefully from behind a clump of lank curls.

"But you're still not getting my coffee."

"You owe me," he muttered, not bothering to lift his head.

"How do you figure that?"

"Look at me!"

"You wouldn't have gotten that way if you hadn't run off *toward* the guy who'd just tried to kill us."

Pritkin's head jerked up. "And we wouldn't be here in the first place if you hadn't gone after the Corps *on your own*!"

"Sugar?" Marsden set a tiny teapot and a cup and saucer in front of me. The saucer had cookies. Lemon cream. Yum.

I looked down to find my coffee missing.

I reached for it and Pritkin shrank away from me, huddled over the mug protectively. "Fine," I muttered, concentrating on my tea. I'd probably have to detox once we got switched back. Assuming we did. Now that I'd had a chance to think about it, I was feeling a little nervous on that point.

"You were going to explain how we ended up in the wrong bodies," Pritkin reminded me.

"I'd rather clear up a few things first, like why we're here. Wherever here is."

"You're in the country outside Stratford, my dear,"

Marsden said, and then paused. "Oh, that does sound odd, addressing John that way. May I call you Cassandra?"

"Cassie. And Stratford where?"

He blinked. "Upon Avon."

"We're in *Britain*?"

"Yes, the Circle has been based here for centuries. Shakespeare's old home has always drawn the tourists, you see. No one notices any rather odd types coming and going, as a result." He sipped his tea. "Everyone just assumes they're Americans."

I scowled at him. "I thought the Circle was based in Vegas."

"Oh, no." He looked slightly shocked at the idea. "That wouldn't do at all. I'd have never gotten any work out of the Corps then, now would I?"

"Our North American branch was based at MAGIC," Pritkin clarified. "And can we return to the point?"

I decided to man up to it—since I could actually currently do that—and fished the ivory menace out of Pritkin's pocket. "Meet Daikoku, one of the seven Japanese gods of luck." I left off the "good," since I hadn't seen much sign of that, and filled them in on the rest of the legend.

Marsden was biting his lip and Pritkin was staring at me incredulously by the time I finished. "You knowingly invoked an unknown, potent magical object without placing any boundaries on its power?" He sounded like he didn't quite believe it. "Have you gone completely mad?"

"It seemed better than the alternative."

"It wasn't," he said harshly.

Pritkin could piss a person off in record speed at the best of times, which these weren't. I felt my temper rising. "And why not?"

A muscle leapt in my cheek. I hadn't known it could do that. "Because djinn are demons! They lure the foolish into a pact by dangling wishes in front of them, and as soon as anyone takes the bait, they have him! They can do anything to him they want, any amount of harm, as long as they fulfill the technical requirements of the wish!"

"Just ask Parsons," Marsden agreed. "Only we can't, of course."

I glanced at devil dog, which had abandoned the puddle of mangled chew bone and was now lazily scratching. "The salesman promised that Daikoku isn't a djinn."

"And salesmen's promises are never exaggerated!" Pritkin's voice dripped sarcasm.

"We survived, didn't we?"

"We would have in any case. Caleb—"

"Was going to take me in!"

"I could have talked him 'round, had you given me—"

"Oh, don't even! We were surrounded. They'd pulled guns on us!"

"Guns no one chose to fire! They were attempting to capture you, not to kill you!"

"And you know this how?"

Pritkin slammed a hand down on the table hard enough to spill my tea. "Because you're still alive!"

The low-grade headache I'd had for what felt like a hundred years was back with a vengeance. "Being captured by the Circle might be a death sentence for me," I reminded him grimly.

"She might have a point, John," Marsden spoke up. He'd been looking back and forth between us, like a fan at a tennis match. "That's why I summoned you, actually."

"Summoned?" The word didn't make sense. "You summon ghosts or demons."

"And Pythias." He flopped a little chain out of his shirt. It had a small gold charm on it.

"Come again?"

"An old trick," he told me, pushing the plate of cookies at Pritkin, who ignored it. "The holders of your office have a habit of being elsewhere at crucial moments—or should I say, elsewhen? In any case, the Circle had this constructed some centuries ago as a way of recalling the Pythias in times of emergency. Once activated, it will bring you to us the next time you try to shift."

I stared at the wicked little thing in horror. "But if you could do that—why didn't the Circle recall me ages ago to stand trial?"

"Because I'm a foolish old man who misplaced it—along with a few other things—after I was forced out of office," he replied innocently.

"You kept me from shifting!"

"No. The charm merely brought you back when you tried it."

"You almost got us killed!"

"Nonsense. John was with you. And I didn't know I was going to be attacked the very moment you arrived, did I?"

I paused, having to rearrange my thoughts somewhat. I'd just assumed the mages had been after me. Everyone else was. "But they attacked us!"

"Doubtless thinking you were my allies."

"But . . . who were they?"

"I don't know most of them," Marsden said. "But their leader was an ex–war mage named Jenkins. He was disavowed for financial fiddling some years ago. He became an assassin-for-hire afterward—a very successful one, by all accounts. But we could never catch him."

"The man I pursued," Pritkin said shortly. So Adidas had had a name.

"Why did he want to kill you?" I asked Marsden.

"Because Saunders hired him, of course. Even now, he might find it difficult to persuade anyone in the Corps to murder me!"

"You have a number of enemies, Jonas," Pritkin protested. "Jenkins among them. We can't merely assume—"

"Don't be naive, John! If he could, Saunders would lock me up and throw away the key, but he's afraid the trial would give me a public platform and he doesn't want that. He prefers to dismiss my allegations as the ramblings of a bitter old man while he waits for his men to pick me off!"

"Saunders? Are you talking about the Lord Protector?" I asked, trying to make some sense out of this. Marsden nodded. "But why is the leader of the Circle sending assassins after you?"

"Because of you, my dear."

"I don't even know you!"

"But you do know Peter Tremaine. You released him from MAGIC's cells yesterday. And he came straight to me. It seems that he discovered the truth about the honorable lord's activities six months ago—"

"What activities?"

"—but was locked away on a trumped-up charge to keep

him quiet. Now that he's out, he is as determined as I am to have the truth known. And he is convinced that you can help our cause."

He beamed at me, all rosy cheeks and smiling eyes, and I felt my stomach fall. "What cause?" I asked fearfully.

He blinked, the thick glasses making his watery blue eyes look huge. "Oh, didn't I say? We're planning a coup!"

Chapter Twenty

I stared at the batty old man, speechless. It wasn't that I didn't believe him; he clearly wasn't joking. It's just that I couldn't imagine anyone suggesting suicide in such a bright and cheerful tone. No one sane, that is. I should have known that the Circle's old leader would have an extra dose of crazy.

I don't know what I would have said if Pritkin hadn't taken that moment to face plant onto the table. After some wrestling, he ended up with his head between his knees and me crouched beside him, running a hand slowly up and down his spine. "Are you going to be sick?"

"No," he said indignantly. And then promptly was.

"Oh, dear!" Marsden fussed as I held Pritkin's head. "I should have thought—you're both tired after all the excitement. We can talk about this tomorrow."

"Not if I have—" I began, and Pritkin kicked me. "I mean, yeah, tomorrow."

After some general clean-up, Marsden led us to a large bedroom at the top of the stairs.

"There are towels in the bathroom, and I'll fetch you something to wear." He sized Pritkin's current body up thoughtfully. "I picked up a few things in town today, but you're smaller than I expected. Still, we'll make do."

I bit back a comment. He didn't seem to find the idea of shopping for his intended kidnapping victim at all strange. But arguing with a crazy man was a waste of time. Not to mention that we were stuck with his hospitality until I could figure out how to get that damn charm away from him. Or get the phone working. Or get a partner with more energy than an anorexic mosquito.

"Where's mine?" I asked after Pritkin collapsed onto the bed. He looked like he was already asleep, despite the truckload of caffeine.

"I beg your pardon?" Marsden inquired politely.

"My room," I clarified.

He blinked at me. "Oh." He seemed a little nonplussed. "Oh, yes, yes, of course. Well, I suppose I could put you ... But we'll need fresh sheets."

He bustled off. I left him to it and went to find a bathroom. It confirmed my impression that Marsden wasn't married. There were no curtains over the frosted windows and no rugs on the floor, but there was a washcloth that had dried into an upside-down flower shape hanging off a faucet. Thankfully, there were also towels in a pile on the edge of the tub, and a little tower of the kind of soaps people keep for guests. There was also a modern-looking shower, a radiator and a wardrobe holding even more towels.

And nothing else.

I looked around, even peered behind the wardrobe, but no dice. I finally gave up and went to ask Pritkin. He was passed out on his back, leaking mud onto Marsden's nice cotton sheets. I shook him lightly, not happy about having to wake him, but his old boss was nowhere to be found and things were getting fairly urgent.

One eye slitted slightly. "What?"

"Sorry. It's just—there's a problem with the bathroom."

"What problem?"

"There's no toilet."

"This is an old house," Pritkin said, like that explained anything.

"And they didn't need to pee in the past?" I demanded.

He groaned and threw an arm over his face. "There's a WC down the hall."

"A what?" I asked, a little desperately.

"A water closet. It's in a separate room."

"Why? Why not put it in the—"

"Because a bathroom is where one goes to *bathe,* hence the name."

"That's bizarre."

"No, Miss Palmer," Pritkin said savagely. "It isn't. What is bizarre is that I currently have a *vagina.*"

I'd never heard quite that tone in his voice before, but it didn't sound good. I decided that I had enough information. I fled.

The WC turned out to be right beside the bathroom in a narrow little closet of a room. I was so relieved that the actual act of using it as a man wasn't nearly as traumatic as I'd expected. I dragged myself back to the bathroom and turned on the water in the shower to get it hot, too tired to risk the tub in case I drowned in it.

The filthy coat hit the floor, along with the thigh strap for the holster, the bandolier-style potion belt, the bloody keep-your-pants-up belt that I'd used as a tourniquet, the under-the-arm holster, the five knives and the heavy boots—complete with two more knives—that constituted Pritkin's idea of casual attire. It made a god-awful mess, but the floor was tiled and I promised myself I'd clean it up later. When maybe I didn't feel like I was about to fall over.

The idea of just passing out, dirt and all, was starting to look really attractive. But no. I couldn't sleep like this.

I had to tug the shirt off over my head one-handed, as the heat of Caleb's spell had turned the buttons into melted lumps and my left arm still didn't work. I glanced in the rapidly fogging mirror and, despite everything, had to smile. Pritkin was the only person I knew whose hair came out of a move like that completely unchanged.

But the fun part was still to come: trying to strip off the still-damp jeans with only one workable hand. It was harder than I'd expected, as sodden denim tends to cling. I stumbled into a towel rack and almost fell on my borrowed butt fighting them off. But as Pritkin had never adapted to the newfangled idea of underwear—apparently they hadn't had tightie whities in the sixth century—that was that. Except for a whole lot of dirt.

The shower was hot and I stood with my face directly in the spray, despite the fact that it woke up a thousand cuts

I hadn't noticed before. It didn't make the welt on my ass, where I'd landed on the fence post, or the raw, red patch on my chest too happy, either, but nothing's perfect. It did help with the mud, which had ended up smeared all in Pritkin's hair and down his neck.

Soap hurt, but I lathered up anyway, scrubbing away the worst of it and trying not to think about the fact that I had actual hair on my chest. And on my legs, I noticed, as I bent to wash between Pritkin's toes. They were long guy hairs that the water had turned from dark blond to light brown, acres and acres of them and not just on my calves. They climbed up my thighs too, I saw with mounting horror. And how freaking wrong was that?

I rested my forehead against the glass and just breathed for a while. Every muscle and nerve in my body felt tight and thrumming with tension, ready to part with a brutal snap if I so much as breathed wrong. Why was it always the little things that got to me? I could handle vast numbers of people wanting me dead—that wasn't new—or demon attacks or crazy ex–war mages or even the weight that definitely *should not be there* dangling between my legs. But for a moment I couldn't, simply couldn't, handle the hair.

I'd possessed people before, I reminded myself. I tried like hell to avoid it, but that hadn't always been possible. So why did this feel so different? Maybe it was because my previous trips into other bodies had been short, with the longest lasting a couple of hours. Maybe it was because I'd just almost died—again—and, hey, that never got old. Or maybe it was because it was Pritkin.

I'd possessed only one other person I'd known beforehand, and that had been by accident. It had lasted only a few very confused minutes, which had been more than long enough. This, on the other hand, was already promising to take my and Pritkin's relationship to a deeply weird level, and there was no end in sight.

The horrible itching under my skin suddenly stopped. I cautiously ran my fingers over the wounded arm, the movement sending a little more mud and some dried blood slushing down the drain. But underneath, I felt only whole, unbroken skin, without even a ridge to show where the injury had been. Pritkin's body had healed as if he'd never been hurt, all in the space of about an hour. It seemed that there were advantages to having a demon father.

Of course, there was a downside, too.

It was something I'd been doing a little reading on, lately. The old accounts were spotty and often contradictory, not to mention having been embroidered on shamelessly by every writer who heard the tale. But the earliest legends, before the romantic additions, all had one thing in common: they were pretty damn grim.

After Merlin's mother died in childbirth, her family disowned her half-demon child. He somehow survived anyway, becoming a local curiosity who lived alone in the woods. Some said he was a madman, others a prophet, still others whispered of an unusually powerful wizard, whose human magic was strengthened by demon blood. None had thought to speculate about what it had been like, growing up alone, shunned and regarded as a freak of nature.

And then there had been the sojourn in hell. Pritkin had once told me that, although hundreds of years had passed here on earth while he was gone, it had felt like he was away only a decade or so. But a decade in the demon realms didn't sound like fun to me. I didn't know for certain what it had been like, because he never talked about the things he'd seen. He was the most guarded person I'd ever met, with conversations about anything remotely personal quickly running into a wall of silence. But he never spoke of demons except with contempt or hatred, and he'd hunted the more dangerous ones mercilessly since his return.

I remembered his pale face and tried to ignore a prickle of worry. Pritkin had grown up with impossible events as a way of life and usually took them in stride, but this was different. Before he met me, possession was something he'd associated only with the more powerful demons. Being suddenly thrown into someone else's body probably reminded him a little too closely of the part of himself he preferred not to think about. I wondered what his reaction was going to be tomorrow with no assassins or exhaustion to blunt the effects. Why didn't I think it was going to be good?

After a while, the darkness behind my eyelids and the hot water pounding my skin leached away some of the tension from a day that, even by my standards, had sucked. I was almost calm again, or as close as I was going to get in this body, when a ghost stuck his head through the shower door. I yelped and jumped back, and my foot slipped on a sliver of soap. I ended up on Pritkin's butt, chest heaving, staring up at Billy Joe.

"What the hell?"

"My thoughts exactly."

I dragged myself up, wincing, using the spigot for a hand-hold, which twisted and sent a spray of boiling-hot water raining down on me. I leapt out of the shower, biting my lip on a scream, and grabbed a towel. "What are you doing here?"

"You first. Because I've been looking for you for hours and when I finally locate you, what do I find?"

"Sorry you've had such a bad day," I said viciously, patting at my red flesh. Damn, that had hurt.

"Not nearly as bad as you're going to have when you get back. People are freaking out. Francoise told everyone the Circle has you, so the Senate demanded your return and, of course, the Circle told them to get bent. When I left, that vampire of yours was threatening bodily assault on Saunders if he didn't give you up."

"Why? The Senate knows where I am. They have a trace on me!"

"Yeah, and it told them you're with the old head of the Circle."

I felt the blood leave my face. "Have they mentioned that to anyone? Saunders, for instance?"

"Is that a problem?"

"If the Circle finds out I'm talking to Marsden, I can forget about us reaching any kind of deal!"

"Yeah. 'Cause that looks so likely anyway."

"Can you find out if they've said anything? It's important."

"I can try."

"I really need this, Billy. There's some kind of internal power struggle going on and I don't want to get caught in the middle of it. I have enough problems."

"I can see that. Speaking of which, in case you weren't dying or stuck in one of the Circle's cells, Tami said to remind you that a bunch of kids are still missing. And that Alfred doesn't have a driver's license."

"I know. Tell her I'll be back as soon as I can."

"And that will be . . . ?"

"That depends. Among other things, Marsden has a charm on a cord around his neck. He used it to bring me here."

"And if you don't get it, he can use it to bring you back."

"Right. So can you—"

Billy shook his head, cutting me off before I even finished. "No way, Cass. I had to use a hell of a lot of energy to find you. I can't carry anything in this state. Now, if I had a draw . . ."

"You aren't the only one who's exhausted," I said, peering outside the door. Sure enough, there was a small pile of neatly folded clothes sitting there. "I'll get some sleep and eat a good breakfast and you can have a draw then."

Billy didn't answer. I turned from closing the door to see him eyeing the frothy mass in my hands. I ignored the slowly spreading grin on his face and sorted through the results of Marsden's shopping trip. I guess he hadn't expected me to bring a friend, because all the stuff was for the body I no longer had. None of the lacy, frilly things was going to fit my new form, even if I'd been willing to risk Pritkin's wrath and put them on.

I paused over the bottoms of a pair of pajamas. They were the plainest things there, light blue cotton with only a little lace around the ankles. But even they wouldn't work. Pritkin had too much leg muscle.

"If the mage sees you in those, he's gonna have your ass," Billy said gleefully. He waited a beat. "Of course, come to think of it, he already does."

A low throbbing ache had settled below my right eye. "Billy! Just go."

"Okay, okay," he laughed. "Don't get your panties in a bunch. No, wait—you can't."

"Billy!"

He faded away, still laughing. I was glad someone was having fun. I decided that I was too damn tired to even try to come up with a solution to the clothing problem, draped a towel around me and went to bed. It wasn't hard to find my assigned room—Marsden had left the door open and the bed turned down in the room next to Pritkin's.

I hit the cool sheets and stopped caring that I was in a strange room and a strange bed. The bathroom might be antiquated but the mattress was top-notch. I stretched, luxuriating in the way it took my weight, in how every muscle in my body was slowly going liquid—and fell asleep before my brain could remind me of all the things I had to worry about.

I saw myself standing alone in the middle of a field, with rolling hills spreading out to the horizon on all sides. I was wearing a simple white sheath and looked happy and unconcerned. It was bright and sunny, and a small breeze bent the grasses, toying with the hem of my dress.

With no warning, clouds rushed in from every direction, strangling the day. Their undersides were swollen and bruisered, flooding the land with a hellish light from one horizon to the next. Thunder groaned and rain began to fall, but the droplets had the same ruddy tinge as the clouds. And along with the taste of lightning in the air was an acid tang with a dark undercurrent of sweetness.

A drizzling cascade of thick, scarlet blood hissed down, like the leavings of a slaughterhouse, spattering my skin, my hair, my pale linen shift, before running in rivulets down my body. It drenched the gown and pooled under my feet, soaking the soil until it softened, until it opened up and I began to sink. And still the rain came, pouring into the earth, widening the fissure until I couldn't see myself anymore, until it swallowed me whole.

The red tide didn't stop there, but spread outward in all directions, like water rippling from a thrown stone. And where a moment before there had been abundant life, green and lush and full of health, there was only dust and decay, everything brown and withered and so very still.

I woke in a pool of sickly green light—moonlight filtered through the vines that draped the only window like curtains. I lay there, my heart hammering in my chest, and tried to tell myself that it had just been a nightmare. I was overdue for one, and my subconscious had never been subtle.

But that hadn't had the flavor of a dream, not even of a nightmare. I'd had enough visions to know one when it hit me between the eyes. Something was wrong.

I mentally rolled my eyes while trying to calm my rapid breathing. Of course something was wrong! The Circle was trying to kill me, I'd let Tami down, I'd just witnessed a wood full of monsters and, oh yeah, I was in the wrong body! It would be more surprising if something went right for a change!

But somehow, the litany of my problems didn't sound quite right. None of those matched the apocalyptic visions my power kept showing me. A dead Vegas, an abandoned highway turned cemetery, and now a scene of destruction with me at the center.

I shivered in the warmth of the suddenly claustrophobic little room, dizzy and half sick with too many swirling emotions. Ever since the destruction of MAGIC, it had felt like a storm was building. Something behind the scenes that I couldn't quite see, couldn't quite grasp, but something important nonetheless. Something vital.

I rolled onto my side and stared at the darkness. This last vision had been the most disturbing of all. Because it seemed to be saying that the destruction started with me. I hadn't summoned the bloody storm, but it had focused on me, almost as if it was using me to spread the wave of death.

Was my power trying to warn me that if the Circle succeeded in killing me, we'd lose the war? That would certainly explain the devastation. If we lost, I was under no illusion about what Apollo would do. The magical community had been the direct cause of his banishment; he wasn't likely to leave any of us alive to do it a second time. Even his dark mage allies might be surprised at the "reward" they received for helping him out.

I flopped onto my back, frustrated as hell. That interpretation seemed to fit, but I didn't see what I could do about it. I was already doing my best to come to some kind of deal with the damn Circle! I couldn't force them to accept me, any more than I could force them to get their heads out of their butts, look around and realize that we were in the middle of a war! We couldn't afford the infighting, as I'd been pointing out for some time.

Only nobody seemed to be listening.

I groaned and put my pillow over my head. I really

wished Mircea was there to knock me out again. I didn't
want to dream. Especially not when the only thing I got out
of it was a lousy night's sleep.

I woke a second time stiff with pain. There was a dull throb
in my right ankle from some injury not noticed yesterday,
soreness in my back and lingering tenderness in the injured
arm and the abused throat, all of it slowly forming a picture of a body again. A body with stubble scraping bright
against my cheeks and hair a lot *spikier* than normal.
   I frowned. The sleep haze started to lift as my hand
went exploring. It found a man's chest, hard with muscle, a
sweeping ladder of ribs, a ridged abdomen and a . . .
   I jerked awake with a sharp gasp of pure panic. It caught
in my throat, threatening to choke me, and for a moment, I
couldn't think at all. This whole experience was so alien it
shredded my brain. Because I'd had a lot of strange things
happen to me, but I'd never woken up as someone else.
   I stared out the window, gulping for air, waiting for my
pulse to edge out of heart attack territory. The vines didn't
do much to block the view beyond, where a bank of low-
hanging clouds were rolling restlessly over the sky. At least
they're black, I thought, as they began leaking.
   I spent a few minutes lying there, tracking the hypnotic
slide of drops down the windowpane. It was raining, but
it was daylight. What was the old saying? That meant the
devil was beating his wife.
   Or maybe he just wanted his dog back.
   If I didn't look at my body, I was okay. The bed was warm
and comfortable, with well-washed linens and fat feather
pillows. It was so tempting to go back to sleep, to forget
everything for a little while, to forget about Pritkin. Because he was going to expect me to fix our little problem,
and the truth was, I just had no idea.
   But if it was morning, Billy would be back soon. I had to
get a grip. I had to get up.
   I concentrated on the slow in and out of my breath, ribs
moving, lungs inflating, telling myself that most things were
the same, most things were familiar. A body was a body, after all: two arms, two legs, a head. Not much difference, really. I was doing pretty good until I looked down the length

of my new form to find a not-so-little something that wasn't
the same *at all*.

I scrambled back until I hit the headboard, but of course
my newest problem came, too. I stared at it in a sort of wondering horror, but it didn't go away. It just kept jauntily
tenting the sheet, obviously excited to welcome the new
day. *Now* what?

A quick poke to try to push it down only had it bobbing back up relentlessly. I tried again, starting to feel a
little frantic, and held it down this time. It was hot and hard
beneath my hand, like there was no sheet there at all. It
made me notice other things that were just plain wrong,
like breasts that were flat and no longer shifted with every
breath, like the heavy mat of hair arrowing down over my
abdomen, like the blond hairs on the patch of thigh that
had slipped outside the sheet.

Despite my little pep talk, this body did not feel more
or less normal. It had been easier to ignore that last night,
when I'd been so exhausted I'd been staggering. But now
I noticed things, like the current of electricity that ran beneath my new skin, rolling and hot and bothersome, making me sweat and shiver. Suddenly, everything was exciting,
from the soft kiss of the sheets to the vague tickle of air
filtering in around the old windowpane.

I'd never been so aware of myself, of the way I inhabited
muscle and bone and skin. I wondered if Pritkin felt the
same, sharp and fresh and vivid, with every sensation mad-
deningly familiar yet completely strange. I wondered if it
was driving him up the freaking wall.

I caught sight of my reflection in a mirror and it didn't
help. Long eyelashes drooped over flushed cheeks and the
usual tight lips were softened by surprise. The broad shoulders and nice arms were the same, the skin sleep-warm,
the signs of the fight almost healed. There were only a few
raised, red lines to contrast with the cream and gold.

My fingers slid over the beard coming in along his jaw
to the fine-skinned hollow just behind his earlobe, and
into his hair. He had nice hands, the fingers blunt and cal-
lused, the nails trimmed round and no-nonsense short.
He'd be *strong*, I thought, a shiver of awareness cutting
through me.

And the flesh under my palm leapt.

I snatched my hand back, swallowing hard, and the sheet slid off. And there it was, hot and huge, the stretch of it a biting, static ache. Maybe it'll go away on its own, I thought desperately. I held my breath, panic crowding my lungs, and it *actually got bigger*. Long and thick, it was darker peach than the rest of him, with an elegant bend to the left. I'll have to remember to tell Pritkin that he has a pretty dick, I thought hysterically, and shoved a pillow over it.

Someone knocked on the door.

I stared at it, horrified, and yanked up the sheet just before my own frowning face peered around the crack. "Do you mind?" I asked a little shrilly.

"Breakfast," Pritkin said shortly. He noticed my expression. "What's wrong?"

"Nothing! I'd just like a little privacy."

"You're in my body. Privacy is rather out the window, at this point." He came in, ignoring the glare I sent his perfectly pulled together form. Marsden's shopping trip must have included day wear, because Pritkin had on a nice pair of khaki capris and a yellow drawstring top.

"I need clothes, too," I reminded him, hoping he'd go hunt some up.

"Marsden sent you these. They're his but they should work well enough for the moment," he said, dropping a bundle onto a table beside a small armchair. And then he *sat down*.

"What are you doing?!"

"We need to talk."

"Now?"

"Why not now?"

"I . . . haven't had a shower yet," I said lamely, and then it hit me. Cold showers. That's what guys did about this sort of thing, right?

"You had a shower last night. Get dressed. We need to talk before you see Jonas." He crossed my legs, perfectly at ease, one strappy sandal dangling from one pale foot. I'd been ready for angry, bitter, miserable. I was having a hard time with the usual brusque impatience. What sucked the most was the sinking feeling that Pritkin was handling this better than I was.

"If I want another shower," I told him heatedly, "I'll damn well take another shower!"

"What's wrong with you?" he demanded. I managed not to shift under that piercing blue gaze. I hadn't known my eyes could look like that. But then, I doubted they did when I was in residence. And the fact that my own eyes were making me uncomfortable really pissed me off.

"What's wrong? *What's wrong?* I don't have *breasts*! I do have other things I *do not want*. What the hell do you think is wrong?!"

"I thought you were taking this too well yesterday."

"Running for my life tends to override other issues!" The pillow wasn't helping. If anything, it had made the situation worse, since Pritkin's body really seemed to like pressure and friction and heat. As well as just about anything else. I was starting to wonder why he ever got out of bed.

"I should think you would be accustomed to it by now."

There was something in his tone that had me looking up sharply. If he had a sense of humor I'd suspect him. "No. And it doesn't seem to be growing on me."

He waved it away. "We need to discuss our options. Jonas brought you here for a reason. He wants to deal."

"Yeah. And if the Circle finds out, I'm dead. They hate me already. How do you think they're going to feel if they believe I'm cozying up to their crazy ex-leader?"

"Not a great deal differently, in all likelihood," he said dryly.

"Are you seriously suggesting—"

"I am suggesting that you do not agree to anything but that you also do not summarily turn him down. If the Circle continues to be intransigent, he may prove useful."

"How? By starting a civil war? That would kill off mages at twice the rate and do Apollo's work for him!" I shifted, trying to get some relief, and accidentally pushed the problem into the pillow. And wasn't *that* the world's worst idea. My heart stuttered slightly, my breath hitched, and I thought, Oh, *God*.

"It may not come to that."

"And if it does?"

"I am simply advising that you do not turn Marsden down outright. Listen to what he has to say and tell him you'll think about it. Meanwhile, we'll try again to reach a compromise with the Circle. If they can be brought to accept you as Pythia, even for the duration of the war, it would be enough. Once Apollo's forces are defeated, we can deal with our internal troubles."

"Fine." God, this was actually becoming painful.

"We also need to determine how you are going to switch us back."

"I'm working on that." Please, please just *shut up* and *leave*.

"How? The salesman told you the effects are not reversible."

"Our bodies weren't changed, just swapped," I snapped. "And I've had a little experience with that. Assuming I don't get murdered by psychotic sadists masquerading as allies, I'll come up with something."

"Such as?"

"We'll discuss it later."

"I would prefer to discuss it now."

"I wouldn't!"

Something in my voice finally seemed to get through. "I suppose we won't be talking while you're in the shower," he said, getting up.

"We will not."

"Then I shall see you at breakfast. And remember, Marsden is not nearly as vague as he appears."

"Yes, okay, whatever."

He went to the door but paused with his hand on the knob, looking back at me with terribly amused eyes. "And lightly chilled is usually sufficient. I'd really rather you didn't scald me with cold."

I looked around for something to throw at him, but he'd already left. He really *was* dealing with this better than I was. Goddamnit.

Chapter Twenty-one

I waddled to the shower as soon as the coast was clear. I didn't know how men managed with something taking up so much room down there. And what the hell kind of design left a person's privates dangling loose in the air and changing sizes all the time?

The shock of freezing-cold, needle-fine spray against my chest made me yelp, but I stuck it out, shoulders hunched, determined. It pounded my head and neck and tattooed against my back, over the lines of thickened tissue just under the skin of Pritkin's left shoulder. I'd never asked him what had marked him like that, when all other injuries just seemed to disappear. And I guessed doing so now was out. I groaned. Even if I got us switched back, I was *never* going to live this down.

The water torture eventually helped with the whole thing-I-was-going-to-repress-with-a-vengeance, but the pull of wet body hair was still driving me nuts. I was addressing that when Billy popped back in. I ignored him, not wanting to add another cut to Pritkin's collection, and for a long moment, he was uncharacteristically silent.

"Uh, Cass?" Billy finally said, sounded a little odd."What are you doing?"

"I believe it's called manscaping."

"Why?"

"Because that is really, really disgusting," I said, pointing up and down wildly at all the hair on Pritkin's left leg. His right looked better. It was even kind of shapely, now that you could actually *see* it.

"You, uh, you don't think he might be a little . . . upset . . . about—"

"Oh, who are we kidding?" I paused to concentrate on the knee. That part was always tricky. "I don't know how to put him back, Billy. No clue. We could be stuck like this for days, weeks, *months* even—"

"I can get him back," Billy offered.

I almost took a chunk out of Pritkin's leg. "What?"

"Yeah. I was thinking about it last night. It's like when I helped you possess that dark mage that time. I pushed you out of your body and sent you flying into his. Well, the way I got it figured, you can do the same thing with Pritkin. You can move back to your own body and force him out."

"I know that," I said, resuming work. "I've always been able to go back. But there's no telling where his spirit will end up once it's on the loose."

"Yes, there is. Because spirits recognize their own form. It's like with ghosts and whatever we're haunting—it calls to us."

"You make it sound like we haunt our own bodies."

"In a way, you do. Your body feeds you, protects you, lets you move around. After death, if you want to keep doing all those things, you have to find something else for a power source. Like my talisman."

"I know. But—"

"And a soul separated from its power source is dragged back like metal to a magnet. It's why I'm able to find you sooner or later wherever you end up. I zero in on the talisman."

I rinsed the razor and put it down. Marsden had supplied it, along with a few other toiletries, probably assuming that I'd want to shave Pritkin's day-old beard. But it was probably too dull for that now.

I toweled off, crossed to the sink and brushed my teeth while Billy waited. "What if you're wrong?" I finally asked. "I could end up back home, safe and sound, and in the process kill Pritkin."

"That's why you have me. If the mage can't find his own

way home, I'll help. And if he blunders back into you, I'll inhabit his body until he's ready to try again."

Yeah. I could see myself explaining to Pritkin that he was about to have yet another houseguest. I sighed. "You know there's something wrong with a world where we're even having this conversation."

"I'm telling you, I can do it," Billy said stubbornly.

I stood over the sink, hands braced on the countertop. I grinned at my reflection, and my borrowed green eyes looked hopeful. It just couldn't be this easy. Could it?

"We can try," I said, my voice breaking the slightest fraction. God. To be back in my own body. It suddenly seemed like every other problem I had was surmountable, if I could only get that one thing right.

"What about the Senate?" I asked. "Did they mention where I am when they accused Marsden?"

"I don't know. It's a madhouse over at war mage central. They're trying to establish a new base in some warehouse out by Nellis, and it's not going so great. Nobody looks too happy."

"They're war mages. They're *never* happy."

"Anyway, if I were you, I'd assume they know. Which means that staying around here probably isn't healthy."

Crap.

I got dressed in record time despite the fact that none of the clothes fit. The blue polo strained over Pritkin's shoulders, the khakis were painfully tight in the thighs, and the waist was at least two sizes too big. But I tucked in the shirt, which helped a little, and ran barefoot down the stairs. Billy floated behind me, looking full of himself. I was going to owe him big for this.

I found them in the kitchen. Marsden was by the stove, turning sausages in a frying pan, while Pritkin was intent on a paper. The lurid title proclaimed it to be *Crystal Gazing,* which I hadn't known they had here. It was a pretty disreputable tabloid that didn't seem his style.

"Billy says the Circle knows I'm here. You may have more visitors soon," I told Marsden.

"Good morning, Cassie." His electrocuted hair was extra fluffy today, a bright halo around his head. It was kind of awesome. "What would you like for breakfast?"

"I'll skip it. We need to get out of here."

"The wards will hold," he said placidly. "Now, one egg or two?"

"I'll just have toast," I told him, hoping to hurry this along. I didn't have his confidence in the wards.

"She'll take two eggs, a side of sausage, mushrooms, potatoes and toast," Pritkin corrected.

"I can't eat all that!"

"You can and you will. You may starve your body, but you do not get to do it to mine."

"I don't starve my—" I broke off, getting a look at his plate. It had everything in the list he'd given Marsden, plus a side of what looked like baked beans. And an entire pot of syruplike coffee sat off to the side. "I thought you were a health nut!"

"You need to eat more," Pritkin said, taking a bite that appeared to have some of everything on it. "I almost cut myself on your shoulder blades this morning."

I ignored that. "We don't have time for breakfast, anyway. The Circle could be on the way here now!"

"Doubtful," Marsden said, looking unconcerned. "If Saunders is aware that we are in discussions, he will expect us to go to him and be preparing accordingly."

"We aren't in discussions! You brought me here against my will!"

"I'm sure you will have no difficulty explaining that to the Circle," the conniving old man said.

Pritkin looked up, scowling. "We're being railroaded!" I pointed out.

"Yes, but not by him." Pritkin pushed the paper toward me, and the screaming headline momentarily made me forget everything else.

CASSANDRA PALMER'S DARK PAST

"We knew it was only a matter of time," he said, as I snatched it out of his hands.

Pythia or Pretender?
While a successor to the recently deceased Lady Phemonoe has yet to be officially announced, sources

inside the Silver Circle allege that the power may have gone to obscure, noninitiate Cassandra Palmer. "If true, this would be a disaster," said a high-level source who asked not to be named. "Her background speaks for itself."

Indeed it does. *Crystal Gazing* has learned that her mother was Elizabeth O'Donnell, onetime heir to the Pythia's throne. This is the same initiate, it will be recalled, who was disgraced and dismissed after she eloped with Roger Palmer, a man in the employ of Antonio Gallina, the notorious Philadelphia crime boss. Her daughter is believed to have been brought up at Gallina's court, using her abilities to forward his nefarious activities. Since then, rumors have linked her name with that of Gallina's master, Vampire Senate member Mircea Basarab. The Senate had yet to comment on these allegations at press time.

Yeah, I bet the Senate was about as thrilled as I was to have my background splashed all over the press. Pritkin was right—I'd known it was coming—but it was still a blow. The article even included a picture. My own face stared up at me, not from a photograph—I hadn't had one of those taken in longer than I could remember—but from a composite sketch. My chin was too big and the artist had given me a better nose than I actually possessed, along with a sulky, hostile expression. But it was close enough.

I sat down because my knees felt a little weak. How was I supposed to go anywhere, do anything, now? If this had come out a day earlier, the pawnshop guy could have excused himself, placed a call and had a dozen war mages there in five minutes. I hadn't fully realized how much I'd relied on anonymity until I didn't have it anymore.

"The Circle leaked this on purpose."

"Very likely," Marsden agreed. "It's standard procedure before taking action that may be received negatively. A sort of preemptive public relations, if you will."

"The measure they're trying to prepare people for is my murder!"

He looked up at me, those blue eyes suddenly keen. "Which is why you need me, my dear."

I sighed. "Let me have it."

"Saunders won the last election by portraying me as a doddering old fool who was past his prime but was too stubborn to leave office. He promised a reenergized Circle, change, prosperity. What he failed to mention is that the prosperity was all going to him."

"What are you saying?" Pritkin was leaning over the table, his hawklike gaze fixed on Marsden.

"That he's been skimming, and very cleverly, too, ever since he took office. He's increased the rate of the tithe from all of us and pocketed the difference."

"That's impossible. Someone would have noticed!"

"Someone did notice. And it landed him in one of MAG-IC's cells."

"There's an oversight committee—"

"Staffed by Saunders' cronies. One of the first things he did after the election was to clean house. The only people in positions of authority today are those with an interest in keeping him there!"

"You realize I have no idea what you're talking about, right?" I asked.

"Have you seen the tattoo our mages wear?" Marsden asked, rolling up his sleeve.

"No. Pritkin doesn't have one." It wasn't like I could have missed it.

Marsden held out his arm. "It's a silver circle, for obvious reasons. It's used to link part of our power into a common fund to support such things as require a universal effort."

"Such as Artemis' spell," Pritkin explained.

"Okay, following you so far."

"The drain is supposed to be fixed at two percent of our magic—and no more. But Saunders quietly upped the percentage seven months ago—by almost half a point—and has been quietly selling the remainder."

"And that's illegal?"

"Highly! Not even the Council could approve such a thing. It would require the agreement of a majority of Circle members. And for that, he would need a better reason than lining his own pockets!"

"An extra half percent doesn't sound like enough to take that kind of a risk," I protested.

Marsden raised a bushy white eyebrow. It looked like a caterpillar crawling across his forehead. "Of one war mage's power, perhaps not. But of a quarter million?"

"A quarter *million*?"

"That is the approximate number of war mages currently in service."

I sat back in my chair. "Okay. That's a lot of power." I'd never realized exactly how strong the Circle was.

"That percentage could mean the difference between life and death for a mage in the field," Pritkin said.

"It's worst than that," Marsden told him. "Saunders' profitable sideline has warped his entire policy. He should have confirmed this child weeks ago. Instead he's had the Circle hunting her down when they should be fighting a war because he's afraid of what she knows or will soon discover through her clairvoyance."

"But what about Agnes' clairvoyance?" I asked. "She was still Pythia when he started this!"

"She was also frail and ill and preoccupied trying to locate her missing heir. The entire Pythian Court was bent on nothing else, leaving him a window of opportunity—which he seized."

"And wants to retain," Pritkin guessed.

"Yes. Having a Pythia over whom he exerts no influence come to power would not only mean the end of his profitable venture, but also very likely his exposure."

"That would explain why he hasn't wanted to meet," I said, feeling sick.

"A reasonable precaution. A clairvoyant is much more likely to see the truth when confronted with it face-to-face."

"What are you planning to do?" Pritkin asked grimly.

"To challenge him, of course."

"Jonas—"

"It's the only possible way, John. I could go public with my evidence, but Saunders controls the papers and has a stranglehold on the Council. The story would be hushed up and I would be silenced, either frozen in lockup like poor Peter or more permanently, given last night's example."

I looked back and forth between the two of them. "What's a challenge?"

"It's an old law but never rescinded. If a member of the ruling Council believes the Lord Protector is corrupt or dangerously incompetent, he can challenge him. And the fact that I lost the last election does not negate my appointment to the Council. I still have a month left on my last term, and I intend to use it!"

"I don't get it," I said as he set a pot of tea by my elbow. "Challenge him how?"

"To a duel," Pritkin said tightly.

Marsden nodded. "If he loses, the Circle will be without a leader, and the law says that in that case the most senior Council member will rule until such a time as an election can be held. And that would be me."

"Assuming you win," Pritkin pointed out.

Marsden shrugged. "Yes, but let me worry about that. All I want Cassandra to do is get me to him. And in return, I will personally see to it that she is confirmed as Pythia."

"And you're going to get the Circle to accept me. Just like that," I said.

He shrugged. "It really isn't up to them to accept or reject you."

"They seem to think otherwise!"

"Hmm. Yes. But it is difficult to support that case when they have nothing to do with the actual selection. The power chooses the Pythia. It has always been so, and I have yet to see it choose poorly." He flipped the edge of the scandal rag with a finger. "Your background notwithstanding, it *did* come to you. And there it ends."

"No. It ends when they kill me and hope that it goes to a nice, docile initiate Saunders can control."

"Something that will not happen once I return to power," he said calmly.

He slid a plate in front of me a moment later, and it actually looked pretty good. The potatoes were browned to a perfect crisp and the sausages were still sizzling. I dug in.

"What do you think I can do?" I asked between mouthfuls.

"Saunders rarely goes anywhere in public," he told me, filling a plate and joining us. "And when he does, he's so well guarded I can't get near him. But you can." He stopped to sip some deadly coffee. "Security has been maximized due to the war, and his location is a well-guarded secret."

Not tomorrow, I thought, shoveling in potatoes. Saunders would be at the reception for the consuls, waiting to meet with me. And I could get Marsden in. The question was, should I?

I knew Mircea was plotting something, or he wouldn't have agreed to another meeting with Saunders. But it seemed more than likely that Saunders was planning something, too, and I didn't think it was anything I'd like. If someone had told me yesterday that I'd seriously be considering a coup against the leader of the Circle, I'd have laughed. I wasn't laughing now.

But I also wasn't ready to join a coup. The problem wasn't just that it was insane. A much bigger obstacle was those damn visions. They had me so freaked out that I was hesitant to do anything in case I made the wrong decision. It wasn't a new feeling.

I'd spent the last month terrified of my position, sure that no human should have this kind of power. It had been reserved for a god, and even he hadn't done so great with it. It had felt like a choking noose of responsibility, in which one wrong decision could destroy a world. But the catch was, if I didn't act, I might destroy it anyway.

Maybe that was what the visions were trying to say: that if I didn't use my power, it was the same as if I didn't have it at all. And we couldn't win this war without a Pythia. Unfortunately for our side, I wasn't much of one.

I concentrated on eating for a few minutes, knowing that the draw Billy needed would wipe me out if I didn't. Everything was good, except for the sausage. It coated my tongue with grease and just seemed to get bigger the longer I chewed. I'd have spit it into a napkin if the cook hadn't been sitting right there.

"What is this?" I finally asked Marsden.

"My mother's recipe," he said absently. "Black pudding."

I poked at the remainder on my plate. It didn't look like pudding. It looked like a dark-colored sausage. "What's in it?"

"The usual," he said with a shrug. "Fat, onions, oatmeal—and pig's blood, of course."

I swallowed hard. Damn it, I knew I should have had
toast. I drank tea until the queasiness passed and stared
down at my likeness again. It really was pretty close. I guess
a few of the mages I'd battled in the last month had paid attention. At least I made the front page, I thought dismally,
flipping over to page two, where the story continued. And
stopped dead at the first line.

> Even more disturbing are rumors about Palmer's
> father.

Pritkin said something, but I didn't hear him. My brain
had frozen in its tracks, fixated on the word "father." Because I'd never known mine.

Tony had seen to that, engineering my parents' deaths
when I was four so he could monopolize my talents. As a
result, I'd grown up knowing almost nothing about them.
I'd recently discovered a little about my mother, but my
knowledge about my father had been confined to the single
fact that he had once been Tony's "favorite human."

My ignorance wasn't from a lack of trying. I'd asked everyone I could think of, but they hadn't known much or had
been under Tony's orders to say nothing. And since most of
them were his vampires, those orders were extremely hard
to disobey. I wondered now how hard they'd tried. Maybe
there was something that even those who were friendly toward me hadn't wanted me to know.

> Our source inside the Circle confirms that Roger
> Palmer was actually Ragnar Palmer, the infamous
> necromancer who was long thought to be part of the
> Black Circle's ruling elite. His sudden disappearance
> thirty years ago is attributed to infighting within the
> dark hierarchy, possibly due to an attempt by Palmer
> to take control of the whole for himself. It appears
> that Palmer did not die as supposed but instead went
> underground, changed his name and took service
> with another dark creature until such a time as his
> plans could come to fruition. Plans such as his daugh-
> ter becoming Pythia?
> When asked what steps the Circle was taking to

ensure that such an obviously unsuitable and dangerous candidate never be allowed to gain the Pythia's
throne, our source would only say that they are inves-
tigating their options. Meanwhile, they have offered
a substantial reward for information concerning Cassandra Palmer's whereabouts. Anyone seeing her is
urged to call the Circle at once. Names can be held
confidentially.

I threw the paper down in disgust. *Crystal Gazing* wasn't
exactly known for factual reporting, but this was stretching
things, even for them. The mages that Tony hired weren't
Black Circle. Most of them were barely competent to create a protection ward or to construct a basic glamourie. The
Black Circle were the elite of the magical underworld; they
had better things to do than run errands for a vampire.

"If they're going to spread rumors," I said angrily, "they
could at least think up decent ones."

"You didn't know." I'd been looking at Marsden, but the
comment hadn't come from him. I glanced at Pritkin and
did a double take. Despite the weirdness of seeing his expressions on my face, the truth was pretty hard to miss.

"Ah, *Crystal Gazing*. Always stirring up trouble of some
kind. I take it for the crosswords," Marsden said as Pritkin
and I stared at one another. "Excellent double acrostic."

I saw when it hit home, when Pritkin realized that he'd
done what the article never could have and made me believe it. With a single look he'd shaken my entire foundation.
He rearranged his features, but it was too late. Compared
to the vampires I knew, he was a lousy liar.

"You told me once that my line was tainted," I said, my
voice sounding oddly wooden, even to me. "But I thought
you meant my mother."

"Yes, your mother. Charming girl," Marsden said. "You
remind me of her." I stared at him as he calmly spread marmalade on his toast.

"You knew her?"

"Of course. She was always at the Pythian Court, whenever I had reason to visit."

"And my father?" The word tasted strange in my mouth.
"Is it true?"

"Hmm? Oh, yes. We had reason to believe that he was a leading member of the Black Circle for years. Part of their governing council, as it were."

"We don't know that!" Pritkin said. "The Black Circle doesn't publicize its inner workings! The people who spread those stories were criminals hoping for a deal. They'd have said anything—"

"John." Marsden looked at him severely over his glasses. "You aren't going to protect her by denying it. It isn't pleasant, I know, but if she's strong enough to be Pythia, she's strong enough to hear the truth."

I wanted to know and I didn't. Because some gossip rag's allegations would be a lot easier to shrug off than anything Marsden had to say. He'd headed the Circle for years, had their intelligence reports at his fingertips. But he was right: I needed to know. And it wasn't like anyone else had volunteered to tell me.

"What truth?" I asked, pushing away the sickness uncurling in my stomach.

"That your father was a powerful necromancer, capable of commanding ghosts to do his will," Marsden said matter-of-factly. "It's said he had a massive army of them, listening, prying, reporting to him about our activities. It's how the Black Circle always knew when we were planning a raid. His ghostly spies acted as a counterpart to the Pythian Court, giving the dark eyes and ears everywhere."

He munched toast, giving me a chance to absorb that. It was surprisingly easy. Mircea had told me once that my father had done something similar for Tony, although on a much smaller scale. I should have realized then—anyone with that kind of ability wasn't likely to be content as Tony's stooge. Information was power, even in the supernatural world. Maybe especially in our world, where glamouries and illusions so often helped to hide the truth.

Except from ghosts.

There had never been a ward invented that could keep a ghost out, not even that could detect one. Not to mention that Billy could slip inside people's skin for a little short-term possession whenever the urge struck. He didn't do it often, because it drained his power too quickly, and even when he did, he couldn't go sorting through people's thoughts, cherry-picking memories. But if they happened to think about a subject of interest when he was in residence, he would hear it. He'd done it before and reported back to me. And if someone had a hundred Billy Joes? A thousand?

But something didn't make sense. "How would they have met?" I demanded. "A dark mage and the Pythia's heir? It's crazy!"

"He didn't announce himself as a former Black Circle member," Marsden said dryly. "He was in Gallina's entourage when the vampire called on the Pythia."

"*Tony* went to see Agnes? Why?"

Marsden shrugged. "Throughout history, people facing a difficult decision have wanted a glimpse of the future. Norms go to palm readers; members of the supernatural community—those with any pull, at any rate—request an audience with the Pythia. What specifically he asked about we can't know. The records of the Pythian Court are confidential."

"You said my father was at court *once*. How long are we talking about here?"

"A little over a week. Usually, supplicants are sent away if the Pythia doesn't have an answer for them within a month, but Gallina received his fairly quickly. It was almost the only thing the court would tell us."

"And in something like eight days, my father persuaded my mother to elope with him?" I didn't bother to keep the skepticism out of my voice.

"Oh, no, I shouldn't think so. Your mother was a bright, level-headed young woman. If she had decided to give up her position, she could have chosen an easier, and much less flamboyant, path."

"Then why didn't she?"

Marsden shrugged. "We always assumed he put her under some kind of spell. Clairvoyant ability doesn't make someone proof against other forms of magic, after—" I don't know what was on my face, but he cut off abruptly.

There was a hard edge to Pritkin's voice when he spoke. "Could we have a moment, Jonas?"

"You know, I think I have a photograph of your mother around here somewhere," Marsden said, and hurried off.

I picked up the newspaper and slowly, systematically, ripped it to shreds. But it didn't help; pieces of sentences still shouted up at me: *infamous, dark, unstable, dangerous.* I swept them off the table in a sudden burst of anger.

"Why didn't you tell me?" I asked Pritkin.

"I showed you the paper—"

"I'm not talking about today! We've known each other more than a month." I had to work to keep my voice steady. "I admit, it's been a hell of a month, but there was never, oh, *five minutes*, when you might have mentioned—"

"I thought you knew," he said quietly. "You never spoke about your parents or your childhood. I assumed this was why. And you told me recently that you had reason to be ashamed of your father, of the things he had done—"

"As one of Tony's henchmen! Not as . . . as . . ." I couldn't even think of the words. Everyone talked about the Black Circle as if it was the locus of all evil. I'd seen vampires shudder at mention of it, guys who killed without a second thought, for money or for pride or just for sport—*they* thought the organization my father had helped to lead was wicked.

No wonder every war mage I met looked at me like I was about to sprout tentacles or start breathing fire.

"Hey, Cass." Billy floated over from beside the fridge, looking grave. "The mage is right—it could be exaggerated. You know what that paper is like—"

He reached for my hand and I flinched back, staring at him. I'd been able to see ghosts all my life and had never thought anything of it. Or of sending them on errands, asking them for information . . . The thought cut like a knife, giving me a quick stab with a twist for a good measure.

"Hey! It's me," Billy said, taking my hand anyway. The caress was as light as a kiss of wind against my wrist, soft, cloudlike and comfortingly familiar. "Faithful sidekick, remember?"

And my army of one, I thought sickly.

Everything had happened so fast, barely a month from some random clairvoyant trying to avoid Tony's wrath to someone who thought nothing of slipping through time, changing history, possessing people.... Was this how it started? Just trying to stay alive, to get through each day, not realizing how much you were changing until one day, you no longer recognized yourself?

Until one day, you woke up a monster?

Chapter Twenty-two

I ended up in the garden on a bench—I'm not sure how—with my mother's photo in one hand and a cooling mug of tea in the other. It was very un-British of him, but Marsden didn't use teacups. He preferred heavy stoneware that held about half a pot, along with a healthy dose of milk and a heaping teaspoon of sugar.

I stared at the photo blankly, my eyes taking a moment to focus on the right face. And even when they did, there wasn't much to see. The photo had been taken at the ceremony making her Agnes' heir. It was impossible to tell if we resembled each other in the face, because it was a wide-angle shot, showing her surrounded by other young women and a bunch of men who I assumed were war mages.

She was tall—something I hadn't expected—and she had straight dark hair, not strawberry blond curls. She was wearing a high-necked dress with long sleeves and she wasn't smiling. I ran my finger over the photo, a pit of loss opening behind my ribs. My hand tingled faintly where it rested on the surface. I was supposed to be a Seer, but I couldn't see her. I'd never been able to see her, except in the moment of her death.

Pritkin was yelling at Marsden about something inside the house, but the walls were thick and I couldn't hear him very well. Plus I'd fallen into a kind of weary numbness and didn't care. A beam of sunlight was flirting with some clouds overhead, sending down intermittent watery rays. It was nothing like the searing, bake-into-your-bones heat of Vegas, but nice anyway. It warmed my neck, light and soothing.

I closed my eyes and eventually the sunlight started to leach away my headache. I thought about going back to bed, because I was still kind of sleepy. Part of me didn't like that idea—it wanted to stay up and fret and worry and freak about what I'd just learned—but another part of me had had enough. That part wished Marsden had put up a hammock instead of the bench, because it thought a nap in the sun sounded really good about now.

The tea wasn't bad. I'd never taken milk in it before, but it made it creamier, heartier. I sipped it and stared at an overgrown rosebush that was in a battle to the death with some type of vine. The vine appeared to be winning, not surprisingly as its stalk was bigger around than my arm. It looked ancient, almost primeval, not like something that should be hanging around a quiet English garden.

It had flowed over an old sundial, eaten into the crumbling rock of the base, twined around the pedestal and almost obscured the top. "I only show the happy hours," it read. At least, I think that's what the worn bronze letters said. They would have been hard to read even without the leaves. The slow, steady pressure of the vine had cracked the face almost in two.

I hopped up, deciding that a walk might suit me better. Picking my way down the overgrown stone and moss pathway took up most of my attention, forcing me to concentrate on not twisting an ankle. There were puddles everywhere and the air smelled wet and green. But no raindrops disturbed the surface of the pools; it looked like the storm had decided to retreat for a while.

Pritkin caught me when I was halfway around the house, trying to figure out whether it was safe to wade through a patch of waist-high weeds that had set up a roadblock across the trail. "Saint Patrick ran off all the snakes, right?" I asked.

"That was Ireland. And I was never much of a gardener. I'd go around."

I decided to take his advice, stepping carefully through

a random but healthy-looking garden that flourished next to the encroaching jungle. I met him at the point where the path started around the other side of the house. "What do you mean, you've never been a gardener?"

"I think the term these days is 'black thumb.' I let the place go to rack and ruin, I'm afraid. Most of that"—he nodded at the dueling vegetables—"is Jonas' work."

"Wait a minute. This is *your* house?"

"For over a century."

"Then what's Marsden doing here?"

"He lived in an assigned residence during his tenure in office. Rather like your White House or our Ten Downing Street. But after the last election, he had to vacate it. And having held the title for more than sixty years, he no longer had a separate domicile." Pritkin glanced around at the genteel decay and a small smile tugged at his lips. "He decided he wanted to explore the bucolic life in his retirement and this was once a workable farm. I rented it to him a year and a half ago, when I transferred to the States."

He paused while we relocated to a bench safe from attacking flora. It had a chimney on one side, a small, scraggly patch of forget-me-nots on the other, and a nice view of the river. A butterfly sniffed a flower nearby, its feelers twitching excitedly.

"I wouldn't have left," I told him. "It's nice here."

Pritkin's mouth hardened for a heartbeat before relaxing once more. "I'm considering selling. It's too large for one person. And the reason it was acquired no longer exists."

I looked around. So this was the house he'd bought with his wife in mind. It suddenly became more interesting.

One of the few things Pritkin had told me about himself was his early—and, as far as I knew, only—attempt at the have-a-normal-life routine. Sometime in the nineteenth century, he'd met a girl and gotten married. Only no one had bothered to mention what might happen to a half incubus who took a wife. The result was the other side of his nature coming out on their first night together and draining the poor girl of life without Pritkin having any idea how to stop it. He'd had to watch, horror-struck, as she died because of him.

I could see him picking this place out in the months before the wedding. He'd probably expected years of quiet, happy normalcy. Only that so hadn't happened.

I could relate.

"Are you all right?" he finally asked.

"I'm fine," I said, because it took too much energy to explain all the ways I wasn't.

"You don't look fine."

"Sorry." I tried to relax against the hedge growing behind the bench, but its branches poked me like too-sharp fingernails. I couldn't get comfortable and sat up straight again.

"There is something you should know," he told me.

"Not now." My brain was already overstuffed with all the things I hadn't had a chance to think about, to accept, to find a place for in my self-image where they might not do too much damage.

"It isn't more bad news," he insisted.

I looked at him warily. He seemed sincere. "Okay," I said cautiously.

"Jonas overstated the situation regarding your father. What we know about him was gained from interrogations of minor figures in the magical underworld—the sort of people that the vampire who brought you up once employed. The Black Circle uses such people for errand runners and cannon fodder but limits considerably what they are told. And their information came years after your father's death. Much of it was likely not garnered from personal experience but from rumor and conjecture."

"You've never interrogated a single Black Circle member?"

"No."

"That doesn't seem possible. You guys have known about them for hundreds of years. You must have captured at least one—"

"It's a rare occurrence, but it does happen."

"And none of them ever talked?" I couldn't imagine anyone who did the kind of stuff that made vampires blanch having all that much loyalty to his partners-in-crime. It sounded more like he'd sell them out the first chance he got.

"They never lived long enough."

"I don't understand."

"The Black Circle has a similar tattoo to ours but with a more sinister purpose. Every Black Circle mage we've ever caught self-destructed within minutes. It's one reason most of them fight to the death. Capture, for them, is the same thing."

It was gruesome to contemplate, but it made a grim sort of sense. "I guess their tattoo doesn't come off, huh?"

"No. And as we have never captured one without it, I can only assume it is a requirement for admission."

"Isn't the Silver Circle's?"

"Yes—for most people."

"Why not for you?"

He smiled slightly. "Mixed-blood applicants need not apply. The Circle was pleased to have me around to hunt the more dangerous types of demons, but they preferred not to give me access to their power base."

"I don't get it. Wouldn't you have been donating, not taking?"

"Power drains can work both ways. It's the main reason the Circle cut off the connection to your pentagram—they were afraid you would reverse the flow."

"Marsden seems to trust you."

"Perhaps. But the Council as a whole decides most issues, with the head of the Council there to advise, to set up the meeting agenda and such. He has only one vote unless there is a tie, and on the subject of my joining the Circle as a full member, there was close to a consensus."

"Nice friends you have there."

"On such a matter, they were wise to be cautious. But we have strayed from the point. Necromancy is illegal. It is grouped with other prohibited manifestations of magical ability, such as those possessed by the children you are helping. But the mere fact of someone being a necromancer doesn't make them evil. The power can be misused, but the same is true for any magic."

"You seem to have a different take on it than the Circle."

"When I was young, the differences between dark and light magic were not as clear-cut as today. The only difference was the way power was acquired and the uses to which it was put. Magical energy is no different than any other—it can be perverted or it can be used for good."

"Well, my father's was perverted."

"You can't know that!"

"Yes, I really can." I rubbed my eyes. I didn't want to have to spell it out, but this was apparently face-up-to-crap day and no one had told me. Not to mention that the truth was pretty damn obvious. Pritkin wasn't stupid; he'd work it out for himself soon enough. I preferred that he heard it from me.

"Energy is the only coin of the ghost world," I said. "Once you're dead, money, the things it can buy, prestige—all that goes by the wayside. Ghosts are only really interested in two things: revenge, or whatever reason they hang around, and energy. Mostly energy, because without it, they'll fade away."

"Not fade," Pritkin corrected. "They transition to other realms."

"Yeah, only most don't want to go. And power is what they need to hang around. It can be generated by things like Billy's talisman or gleaned from places that have a significant psychic residue. People in serious distress shed life energy like skin cells, and in an old house or a grave-yard, there's often enough built up to sustain one or more ghosts. Graveyards are particularly popular because more distressed people show up all the time. It's kind of like a supernatural grocery store, always getting new deliveries."

"I don't understand what this has to do with your father."

"Everything. The only other way to get life energy once you're dead is to beg, borrow or steal it from someone who already has it. For a ghost, that means cannibalizing other spirits, which they do all the time, or getting it directly from a living donor. The latter is a lot more uncommon unless the spirit is really pissed off or unbalanced, because attack-ing a living body uses up more energy than it gains."

I stopped, having finished Ghost 101 and feeling strangely reluctant to go further. Intellectually, I knew that my father's crimes weren't mine, that I shouldn't feel any guilt over them. But emotionally, it felt like the taint of what he'd done had rubbed off on me, as if it was my fault somehow. I scrubbed my arms. The sun suddenly didn't feel all that warm anymore.

"So, like I said, life energy is hard to come by and highly prized. It's the only thing my father could have offered the spirits who worked for him."

"Jonas said he could command them," Pritkin reminded me. "They may have had no choice."

"I've never heard of anything like that, but I don't claim to be an expert on necromancy. Some people think that's what clairvoyants are—minor-level necromancers—but it isn't true. I can see ghosts and donate energy to the dead, but that's it. I can't bring anyone back to life—or any semblance of it. But I do know something about ghosts. And most spirits wouldn't have been able to go around gathering intelligence without a regular energy draw."

"Perhaps some are stronger than others."

I shook my head. "It doesn't work that way. Strong, weak, whatever you were in life—when you're dead, you're dead. And ghosts use up energy even faster than humans do. Their haunts normally only provide a subsistence. To do extra work, they need extra power. Like I give to Billy."

And for the first time, it struck me as perverse that I had such complete power over anyone. I'd always thought of our relationship as a fair trade—I gave something, Billy gave something, and we both benefited from the arrangement. Billy had saved my life dozens of times, just as I had helped to sustain his. Quid pro quo. Only now I wasn't so sure.

Was it really equal when one party could walk away from a deal, and the other couldn't? Billy could live without me. He survived for a century and a half before we met, because his necklace provided the same subsistence for him that most ghosts received from a house or graveyard. But that's all it was, a subsistence. Without regular donations from me, Billy couldn't go more than fifty miles away from the talisman, and even within that range, he couldn't do much.

What would it be like, I wondered, to be tied to an object that could end up anywhere, dragging you with it? To be too weak to do more than watch life go by—a life you no longer had? How had he lived for so many years with no companionship? Of course, he could talk to other ghosts, if he wanted to take the risk of being cannibalized. But even then, ghost conversation tended to be a little one-sided.

Like our relationship.

I decided that maybe I owed Billy an apology, although what I could do about the problem was debatable. He was a ghost; I couldn't change that. But maybe I could do a little more to show my appreciation for all he did for me. Maybe I could make a conscious effort not to take advantage of him.

Maybe I could try a little harder not to be like my father.

"Donating life energy is not a crime," Pritkin said, obviously still not following me.

"Depends on where you get it."

He frowned. "You use your own."

"Because I feed one ghost. Uno. And even then, there are times Billy has to rely on his necklace, because I don't have anything left to give." I saw comprehension begin to dawn in his eyes. I looked away before he hit revulsion. "So how much power would a ghost army need? There's no way one mage could supply dozens, much less hundreds, of hungry ghosts. Just no way."

"Dark mages are known to steal power from whomever they can," he murmured.

"And now we know one thing they use it for—or used to." I got up, suddenly finding the stone bench really uncomfortable. "And when a dark mage catches someone, correct me if I'm wrong here, but don't they usually drain them?"

"Yes," he said softly.

"And draining a magical human—"

"Kills them."

"So my father was a murderer. And if he supplied an army, he was a mass murderer." Not to mention kidnapper and probably rapist. I walked off a little way, the chimney suddenly getting a lot more interesting. "I'd say that's pretty dark, wouldn't you?"

It was really hard to imagine, because my only actual memory of him was a positive one. He'd been throwing a three- or four-year-old me into the air and hearing me squeal in glee. It was hard to reconcile that man with someone who could kill a person just for gain, for the coin that it would gain him in the spiritual world.

"If he was a member of the Black Circle," Pritkin said. "But we don't know that he was. The Circle chooses to believe the rumors at present because it suits their purpose."

"And if it is true?"

"It doesn't change anything," he said urgently.

"Except that my father was a monster." I'd never been under the illusion that he was some kind of saint—no one at Tony's was. But this . . . no. I hadn't really been prepared for this.

I felt hands on me, turning me around. The little dagger-shaped links of the bracelet around Pritkin's wrist slipped over my skin, feeling suddenly oily and strangely heavy.

I'd acquired it in a fight with a dark mage, when it deserted him for me. Ever since, it had clung to my wrist whether I liked it or not, defeating all attempts to remove it. At the time, I'd assumed that it had simply gravitated to the greater source of power, which due to my new position was me. But what if there had been another reason? What if it had been drawn to the greatest potential for evil?

"Cassie!" Pritkin's hands tightened on my shoulders, hard enough to be painful. I looked up, hurt and confused. "My father is a demon lord," he said crisply. "I win."

Pritkin isn't kind, exactly, or tactful at all, but he still sometimes manages to say the right thing at the right time. I guess if there was one thing he knew about, it was dysfunctional families. It didn't make things all right—I had a feeling nothing was going to do that for a long time. But it helped. Even with Rosier for a father, he'd turned out okay. Better than okay, I thought, smiling at him.

"Thanks."

He inclined his head. "No problem. But if you mention anything about getting in touch with my feminine side, I will shoot you."

And for the first time in days, I laughed.

"We have to discuss Jonas' offer eventually," Pritkin pointed out few minutes later.

And yes, we did. But I didn't have to like it.

We'd been sitting watching Marsden pick things out of

his overrun garden. He'd acquired a hat, I noticed, and squashed most of the hair underneath. He looked almost normal.

"I have a theory about war mages," I said. "The more powerful they are, the worse the hair."

"Cassie."

"You could make my day and tell me Saunders is bald."

"And you could make mine by facing up to this."

I scowled. "I can't believe I'm actually thinking about joining a coup."

"There no longer seems to be much choice."

"What happened to wait and see? A few hours ago—"

"A few hours ago, I hadn't heard Tremaine's evidence. A few hours ago, I hadn't seen the newspaper. Jonas is correct. Leaking that story is a clear-cut sign of the Circle's intentions. If Saunders had any plans to work with you, he would be suppressing unfavorable press, not assisting it."

Yeah. That was the way it looked to me, too. I sighed. "What do you know about Marsden?"

"He led the Circle ably for many years. He can be hidebound and intransigent on certain issues, he prefers to keep his own counsel—to the point of being secretive—and he is prickly and difficult at times—"

"In other words, a typical war mage."

"—but overall, he's a good man."

"Can he win?"

Pritkin was silent for a moment. "Had you asked me that question twenty years ago, I would have said yes. But now . . . I don't know."

"Your best guess, then."

"Jonas' knowledge is certainly greater, and he has more experience. But his power has waned in recent years. Of the two, Saunders is stronger."

"Then wouldn't it make more sense for someone else to issue challenge?"

"Only a Council member has the right. Anyone else would be summarily dispatched by Saunders' bodyguards. And that is assuming anyone could be found willing to take the risk. It is a duel to the death."

I swallowed. Wonderful. "So it's a long shot or no shot at all."

"Essentially."

I stared at the chimney and wished my head didn't hurt. "Saunders will be at a reception the Senate is giving tomorrow," I finally told him.

Pritkin's eyes narrowed. "How do you know that?"

"Because I'll be there, too. Mircea arranged it. The Senate has some plan to get me confirmed, only nobody's telling me what it is. I guess they think Saunders is less likely to try something in front of them."

"That could work," he said thoughtfully. "If Jonas challenges there, not only will Saunders' entourage hear it, the Senate will as well. There will be no way to refuse, and a cover-up will be impossible."

"Yeah." The only question was how the Senate would take having me bring a fight into the middle of their big party. Even if by some miracle this all worked out . . . I winced. It wasn't going to be pretty.

"You think the Senate will object to having us there?" Pritkin asked, watching me.

"Us?" I raised an eyebrow.

"You don't really think I would let you and Jonas go alone?"

"Afraid you'll miss out on some of the crazy?" He just looked at me. "I'll take care of the Senate," I told him. "They want this finished as badly as we do. You just keep the Circle from trying anything."

"Ah. The easy job, then."

"Pritkin, haven't you figured it out yet? We don't get the easy jobs."

Chapter Twenty-three

Marsden was elbow-deep in flour when we went back in, shaping homemade dough with a wooden rolling pin. "I'm making lasagna for lunch," he told us, "if you'd like to stay?" My borrowed stomach rumbled embarrassingly despite the fact that it had just finished breakfast. I stared down at it in annoyance and Marsden laughed. "I take it that's a yes?"

Pritkin went back upstairs for his weapons while I sat at the table and listened to Marsden's stories about Agnes. Highly unlikely stories. "She was messing with you," I told him. "She did *not* date Caesar."

"I admit, I found that one a little hard to swallow—"

"She couldn't have shifted that far back," I explained. "It would have killed her."

"Oh, I assure you, she could. She traveled even farther than that for us on more than one occasion."

"I don't see how. The farthest back I've gone was the sixteenth century, but that was in spirit. I don't know if I could make it that far with my body."

The rolling pin hit the table top as loudly as a gavel. "You've gone back in time *with your body*?" He looked outraged.

"Uh, yeah?"

"For what possible reason?"

"Because I can't stay anywhere long enough to get anything done when I'm in spirit form. I'm like a ghost with nothing to haunt—my energy gives out after a few hours and I have to shift back. Not to mention that trying to do anything without a body is really—"

"But you can have your pick of bodies! You're Pythia. You can possess anyone you choose! That is the reason you have that power, to make time shifting less perilous!"

I didn't reply, but I thought about Agnes' shoulder wound. It seemed like she hadn't told Marsden everything. She probably hadn't wanted to worry him, but obviously she'd taken her body along from time to time. Maybe there were missions where possessing someone was just too dangerous. Getting the person she was possessing shot might screw up the very time line she was trying to fix. Or maybe she hadn't liked possessions any more than I did.

"And how do you know that, Jonas?" Pritkin demanded from the stairway, his old coat draped over his arm.

"Lady Phemonoe mentioned it," Marsden said, grabbing a knife and cutting board and laying into some onions.

"Odd that she never told anyone else," Pritkin said, handing me his boots. I took them gratefully. Summer in Britain was a lot different than July in Nevada, and my toes were cold.

Marsden looked a little shifty. "Yes, well, we worked together a long time and . . . she trusted me."

Pritkin's eyes narrowed. "Enough to spill age-old secrets?"

"We didn't have in-depth discussions. It was just a . . . a slip of the tongue, here and there."

"A slip of the tongue?" Pritkin repeated, and something about the way he said it made Marsden go all pink.

"John!"

"Jonas, are you blushing?"

"It's hot in here!" Marsden said testily. "You might have installed some proper ventilation." He'd opened a window, but most of the fragrant steam had chosen to hang around.

"That's a bit tricky with stone walls," Pritkin said dryly. "And you're evading the issue."

Marsden glanced at me. "Do you know, I think I need more basil. Cassie, if you wouldn't mind?"

"Oh, I'd mind," I said, planting elbows on the table and looking at him expectantly.

He sighed and added the onions to a pot on the stove,

showing us his back in the process. "She was . . . we were . . . good friends, as well as colleagues."

Again, it wasn't so much what was said, as how he said it. "Wow." I was impressed. "You *and* Caesar—"

Marsden threw some mushrooms in a colander a little harder than necessary. "Yes. Well. As you say. But that isn't the point, is it? The point is that you've been doing it wrong, child."

"Yeah. Imagine that. And with all of thirty seconds' training, too."

"You're fortunate to still be alive!" he said sternly. "Do you have any idea how many diseases you could have encountered in the past? How many times you might have eaten foods that, while perfectly safe for the people of the time, would be deadly to you? And that is assuming the dark mage you are chasing doesn't kill you first!"

"Does that happen a lot?" I asked nervously. "Mages slipping through time?"

"It takes an extraordinary amount of power, and few are able to raise or to control so much. Most who try end up dead long before you need to worry about them. Leaving you free to deal with other responsibilities."

"Such as?"

Marsden went ninja on some garlic. "Any number of things. We've already discussed the petitioners who will expect you to see the future for them and give advice."

"Seeing the future is . . . problematic."

"Nonetheless, people will want you to try. Along with presiding over the Pythian Court and supervising the initiates, it is a Pythia's primary duty."

"I know I'm going to regret asking this, but the Pythian Court is what, exactly?"

"A court of mediation for high-level disputes among the supernatural community. For example, if the Clan Council of the Weres were to have a dispute with the vampire Senate that they could not work out themselves, they might bring it to you in an effort to avoid bloodshed. The Pythia can best judge these cases because she alone can see how the dispute will end if it is not resolved."

I swallowed. Great. Something else I didn't know how to do. Not that it made a difference in this case. Half the supernatural community wanted me dead and the other half thought I was their little pawn. Neither group was going to listen to a damn thing I had to say.

As for the initiates, I couldn't imagine a scenario that would have me seeking them out. Myra had been bad enough; I didn't need a whole court waiting for me to kick off. Or trying to help me do so.

I looked up to see Marsden staring at me suspiciously. "Please tell me this isn't the first you've heard of all this," he said.

"Okay, I won't tell you."

His knife thwacked into the cutting board hard enough to wedge there. He left it, glaring at Pritkin. "You should have brought her to me before this! She needs training!"

"I might have, if you had mentioned you could provide it."

"I would have, if *you* had mentioned that you were running about with the new Pythia! You used to keep me informed about such trifles!"

"Wait a minute." I grabbed Marsden's wrist, to keep him from trying to chop something else. "You can train me?"

"Not as Agnes could have, no. I can tell you what I saw and observed over a period of decades, but I don't have your power. I can't help you with things like possessions."

"I hate possessions."

"You seem to be holding up to this one fairly well."

"This is a body swap, not a possession."

"Semantics," he said offhand.

"No. It really isn't," I said flatly. "There's no one else inside my head and no one is getting hurt."

Marsden looked at me impatiently. "I'm sorry if you find the idea distasteful, but we're talking about your life!"

"No, we're talking about someone else's."

"This is exactly why you need training. The other initiates don't question the necessity for occasional unpleasant acts."

Yeah, I bet they didn't. The Circle liked to get them young and brainwash them from childhood. They'd probably walk into a fire if the Circle told them to and never even question it. But that wasn't my style. And if Marsden and I were going to work together, he had to understand that.

"I don't have the right to steal part of someone's life, put them in danger to protect myself and possibly traumatize them forever in the process," I told him quietly.

"That's overstating the issue," he said stubbornly. "And it's for the common good."

"Which makes perfect sense, unless you're the one getting screwed over for everyone else's good."

"It is not up to you to revise a system when you don't even know what it is!"

"But Apollo does know," Pritkin pointed out. He'd stayed quiet during our discussion, seated at a small table near the wall, systematically cleaning his weapons. But he'd apparently kept up, because his voice had a definite edge. "He'll be prepared for the status quo and have a plan of action for any move we make based on it. If we hope to best him, we must learn to think in new and different ways."

"Stay out of this, John!" Marsden snapped.

"Why?" I asked. "He's right."

Marsden looked at me in exasperation. "The rules are there for your protection—"

"They didn't protect Agnes."

For the first time, Marsden looked genuinely angry. I guess he wasn't used to people talking back to him. "She was poisoned because of the Circle's negligence! Of all the reasons I have to despise Saunders, that is by far the greatest! As long as I remained in office, she was properly guarded. As you will be once I return."

I put a hand on his shoulder. His muscles were knotted with strain, with grief. He misses her, I realized. He wanted to honor her memory by helping to fulfill her last wish—that I succeed her. But he wanted to do it on his terms.

I exchanged glances with Pritkin. "About that . . . ," I said.

"It's perfect!" Marsden announced when I'd finished explaining the plan. "Better than I dared to hope for!"

"Don't get too excited," I told him. "We don't have a deal yet. I can get you in, but I want a little more than confirmation in return."

"Namely?" The old man's expression didn't change, but his usually bleary blue eyes suddenly looked a lot sharper.

"There are some schools the Circle has been running. I want them closed. Permanently."

His forehead creased. "What schools?"

"The ones for kids with malfunctioning magic. The Circle has been locking people away for years who haven't done anything wrong, and that's including when you were in office. It has to stop."

Marsden was shaking his head before I even finished. "The schools you mention are an unfortunate necessity. I don't like them, either, but there simply is no other choice. We don't lock away the harmless sort, but some of those children have very dangerous gifts!"

"There has to be a better solution."

"If so, we've never found it. Unsupervised, they are a danger to themselves and everyone around them." It sounded final.

"How many have you met?"

"I beg your pardon?"

"It's a simple question. How many of them have you met? Because I've had nine hanging out at Dante's for a week now and the place has yet to burn down or blow up or suffer anything worse than elevators with doors that won't shut!"

"Then you've been very fortunate." His tone was dismissive, as if I couldn't possibly know what I was talking about.

"I also lived with a group of them for almost two years when I was a teenager. I'm not saying we never had a problem, but no one killed anyone or burned down any buildings. And the neighbors never noticed enough unusual stuff to bother calling the cops."

"Forgive me, Cassie, but I find that very difficult to believe." He sounded patient, and it pissed me off. I wasn't the one being stubborn here.

"Like I said, how many of them have you ever known?"

"None. However—"

"Don't you think it's time you met some?"

He looked at me for a long moment. "Perhaps. But you understand that I cannot promise you anything? To take such a step, the Council would have to approve, and while I once had a good deal of sway over that group, that is no longer true."

Oddly enough, I actually felt better that he hadn't automatically agreed to my demand. If he had, I'd have worried that it was only to get what he wanted, and that the kids would be forgotten if and when he came to power. But even so, I wanted something a little less vague.

"I understand. But I want the issue discussed—seriously discussed—in front of the Council. And I want a good faith gesture from you before then. On the day you return to power, you release to my custody the children the Circle kidnapped yesterday."

"I thought you had already retrieved them."

"Only some. I want the rest. There aren't many," I added, because his face was still stuck on no.

"I will release the children taken in this latest raid," he finally agreed. "And I will bring up the broader issue of the educational centers with the Council. But I cannot force their hand. The final decision will rest with them."

I didn't like it, but I respected him for refusing to promise more than he knew he could deliver. "Then it seems we have a deal."

There was only one thing left on the agenda, but Pritkin wasn't making it easy. "If you want this to happen, you have to drop your shields!" I told him, exasperated.

"You are certain this will work?" he asked for maybe the tenth time.

"Yes!" I put as much confidence into my voice as I could, but he didn't look convinced. "This was your idea, remember?"

Pritkin had vetoed the idea of Billy possessing his body, even for a moment, so we'd opted for Plan B. The idea was for Billy to slip inside my skin and nudge Pritkin out. And as Pritkin's body would be the only one in the room that wouldn't be shielded, his spirit should have no trouble finding its way home.

It ought to work. It *would* work. But not if Pritkin refused to lower the shields he'd placed around my body.

"He's afraid of opening himself up like that with a hungry ghost hanging around," Billy said with a grin. He was clearly enjoying this. "He's probably wishing he'd been nicer the last time we met."

"Billy!"

"What? What did he say?" Pritkin's head whipped around, his eyes wild. And, okay, maybe he wasn't taking this better than me after all.

"You remember," Billy said, "when we were in Faerie and I had a body and he slapped the crap out of me?" He was glowing with the power I'd loaned him and it was making him sassy.

"He didn't say anything," I told Pritkin.

"I mean, I could live with it if he'd punched me, but a *slap*—"

Pritkin broke and headed for the stairs. He'd have made it, but Marsden had been stationed there for just such an emergency and he blocked the way. "Drop your shields," I said soothingly, motioning Billy over as casually as possible. "It'll all be over in a second."

"That's what I'm afraid of," Pritkin muttered, glancing around. His voice held the little crack it got when he was really disturbed and trying to cover it, the one that made me want to duck because usually it involved someone shooting at us. I glanced around nervously, but no one was there.

Marsden punched Pritkin on the shoulder. "You're a war mage, man! Buck up!"

And to my surprise, after another moment, Pritkin did. Billy stepped inside and I breathed a sigh of relief. Maybe this would go okay, after all, I thought. Right before Pritkin started convulsing.

"John!" Marsden grabbed for him, but Pritkin jittered out of reach. A flailing fist took out one of the banister railings and knocked the phone off the wall before Marsden's hands managed to lock on his shoulders.

"Take it easy! You're in my body," I reminded him. He obviously didn't hear me. His eyes were unfocused, he was pale and sweating, and his knuckles were shining white where he'd dug his fingers into Marsden's arms.

I'd never seen him so out of control. Pritkin usually took things in stride that would send others into raging fits. "Billy—hurry up!"

"I can't do this if he keeps fighting me!" Billy said, sticking his head out of Pritkin's chest.

"He's fighting the possession," I told Marsden.

"John, listen to me!" Marsden shook him. "You have to let go!"

Pritkin didn't answer, just thrashed against his hold like a man possessed by something a lot scarier than a failed card shark. And he was doing more than struggling physically. Portions of Billy kept shooting out of him at odd places—a foot stuck out of a thigh, an arm poked out of his chest and Billy's head reemerged from a shoulder.

"Some help here," Billy gasped. "I'm losing him!"

"I can't leave this body until he's free!" I reminded him.

"If you don't he's not gonna *get* free. Distract him long enough for me to push him out, and then you can guide him back."

I didn't like the idea, but I didn't have a better one. And if we didn't do this now, I had a feeling it would be a very long time before we managed to talk Pritkin into another attempt. "We're changing the plan," I told Marsden. "I have to help Billy."

"I thought you said that John's body will die without a soul!"

"Not in a few seconds. And I'll return if it takes any longer than that." I stretched out on the floor so that Pritkin's body wouldn't collapse when I left. "Ready?" I asked Billy.

"And waiting!" he snapped, struggling to hang on.

My borrowed head fell back against the floor. I concentrated, and after a moment, my spirit glided up and the face on the body below me went slack. I'd gotten a little better at this sort of thing in the last month, meaning that I no longer rocketed around like an out-of-control comet. So it would have been easy enough to drift over to Pritkin, if he hadn't kneed Marsden somewhere sensitive and taken off for the stairs again. Damn it!

I floated after him and caught him as his foot hit the lowest step. But catching him and getting inside were totally different things. My body's shields were back up and operating at a level I hadn't known they could reach. I shield with fire, not water, but it was Pritkin's spirit projecting the mental barrier, and I splashed down into an endless ocean of gently undulating waves.

I surfaced, sputtering and coughing, but Billy was no-where in sight. And I didn't know how to get past armor this advanced. Unlike with most shields, there were no rips or tears—no chinks at all. Just blue, blue water spreading to the horizon in every direction.

Diving, I discovered, only made things worse: now I was in a featureless indigo world with no reference points. Hovering blindly in the dark, I could feel the crackle of my spirit's heat start to war with the ocean, churning up vast amounts of water that bubbled around me in a frothy tide. Then the ocean began swirling, a hard current took me and I rocketed back toward the surface in what I vaguely real-ized was a giant water spout. I tore through out into the open, thrust upward at a dizzying rate—and kept on going right back into the kitchen.

It took me a moment to realize that I'd just been exor-cised from my own body.

"Got him!" Billy said. And the next moment, the pale, glimmering form of a man was pushed out of my skin and into the kitchen.

Most new spirits are hopelessly confused for a few mo-ments at least, trying to depend on the senses of the body they no longer have to understand the world. And despite being half demon, it appeared that Pritkin was no different, hovering exposed and terrified in what probably felt like complete solitude. I tried to grab his insubstantial hand, but he shied back, horror passing over his hazy features.

He couldn't see me, I realized. He didn't know if the spirit who had touched him was that of a friend or a preda-tor. I tried to reach out with my senses, to let him know who I was, to tell him to follow me, and a feeling of *presence* slammed into me that left me shaking. But it wasn't coming from him.

Something was moving toward us, stirring up the spirit world with the force of a swift-moving storm. It shuddered across my awareness, filled with the spark of lightning and the hungry mutters of thunder. There were stray flickers at the edge of my vision, and a cold, brittle scent in the air.

A jolt of fear hit me like a punch. I froze, my entire form tightening in terror. Rakshasas. They had seen him, felt

him, and they were coming. We had to get out of here, get
of here *now*—

I grabbed for Pritkin, but his spirit form flitted off like a
leaf in the wind. I followed, knowing what would happen
if we didn't get back inside the protection of a body. But
before I could reach him, the tenuous membrane between
worlds shuddered around us and something stepped out.

My first glimpse was of a red-haired creature maybe six
feet tall that appeared suddenly out of the darkness at the
top of the stairs. He'd assumed the basic form of a man, but
the illusion wouldn't have fooled anybody who'd been able
to see it. Of course, anybody in that position wouldn't have
been hanging around for a second look.

Delicate bones underpinned a face with liquid black eyes
and an elegant Roman nose. It was difficult to tell more
than that because most of the features were hidden behind
a mask of blood. It also gleamed wetly on the powerful,
naked body, staining his golden skin in dark streaks, as if
the blood ran in never-ceasing streams over his flesh. Gore
was trapped under his nails, painted his lips and matted his
long, tangled hair. And the expression in those eyes wasn't
human, wasn't even animal. It was pure, ravenous hunger.

Another one appeared behind the leader's shoulder and
then four more in rapid succession. They were males and
females with human forms but the smiles of beasts, all of
them a nightmarish cross of wild beauty and absolute savagery. They spilled down the steps in a writhing tangle of
bloodstained skin, fanning out around me and cutting me
off from both my body and Pritkin's.

"Here's a pretty one," the leader crooned, reaching out
to me. A tender hand brushed across my cheek and I shuddered with revulsion. He smiled and his hand cupped my
nape, drawing me close to that terrible face.

"This one lives," one of the creatures purred. "I smell its
breath."

"Yes."

"Forbidden," another said. "Protected."

"No." The leader stroked a hand down my spirit form,
and a clawed nail sharp as a blade tore into me. For a moment, I felt nothing. Until a writhing agony ignited my spine

as every vein was traced with fire, burning and tearing and all-pervasive. "Like the traitor, this one is ours."

"We taste its blood." Parched voices cried from all sides. "We hunger. Give it to us. . . ."

"Mine first," the leader snarled. And I knew without asking that there would be no dealing with these things, no bribes accepted, no pleas heard. I had only one thing they wanted—and they were already taking it.

I looked down and saw that he'd ripped a gash in my spirit, and that something pale and completely unlike blood was starting to seep out. Power, I realized through the haze of pain. He was going to drain me.

The pack mewled hungrily but didn't move. The leader ran his tongue down my chest like a lover, licking at the spilled power. But it was the laughing hiss that followed that drove my panic beyond the bounds of reason. If I'd still had a body, it would have caused the adrenaline in my veins to congeal, turned my breath to ice in my lungs. As it was, I suddenly couldn't move, even when the leader tilted his head down, closed his lips over the wound he'd made and sucked.

It hurt, oh, God, it hurt, like acid on raw nerves, like barbed knives turning into bone. But more than the pain was the first bitter hint of loss. The knowledge that some part of me had been stolen, lost like a drop of water dissolving in a cold, dark sea. Forever gone.

The leader looked up at me and licked his bloody lips. "It tastes better alive," he said, and released the pack.

It felt exactly like having a body again as they bore me to the floor. The cold stone at my back only magnified the hot agony as they tore into me. I screamed at the grinding bites, twisting mindlessly, trying to claw out of their grasp, but everywhere I turned was another leering face. Within seconds faint curls of mist were coiling up from a dozen wounds. They seeped slowly outward, flowing away from my form to cling to the pack's hands and wind around their arms.

I watched, horror-struck, as they lapped it up, licking their fingers like kids with a half-melted ice cream. But it wasn't enough. They were starving, and this was only a taste. They wanted it all.

"She is not lawful prey!" I heard someone call and looked

up to see Pritkin stumbling into the middle of the feast, still half blind and probably extremely confused.

"Lord Rosier gave her to us," the leader said, crouched over me jealously. "As he did you."

Several creatures broke off the pack and started for Pritkin, but he avoided them and flung his flimsy, powerless form straight at the leader. For a split second, the pack forgot about me in the surprise of seeing someone running straight at death instead of cringing away. Then they released me to spring at Pritkin, and I threw myself backward, sending my consciousness crashing into his body lying so still on the floor.

Between one thought and the next, I was convulsing awake, my breath rasping in lungs gone tight and dry, starved for air. Red and violet spots exploded behind my tightly clenched lids, and I dragged in a ragged breath, coughing and gasping. Everything hurt. It was like the flu: no localized source of pain, just an all-over pervasive sense of illness.

For a second, I didn't understand what was wrong with me. I'd been gone for only a minute; Pritkin's body shouldn't have suffered any damage in that time. And then I remembered: spiritual attacks manifest on the body once you return to it. If those things savaged him badly enough, it wouldn't matter if we managed to get him back to his body. Because he'd die anyway.

Chapter Twenty-four

Marsden was there, helping me up, and he was saying something but I couldn't hear and didn't care. I threw him off and lurched for the table and the one chance Pritkin had: his potion belt. But once I had it, I realized that I could barely see the pack now, and if I missed even one . . .

My fingers fumbled on the belt, clumsy with adrenaline, my heart beating *no time, no time,* in a frantic pulse. In the end, I just threw everything as fast as I could shuck the little tubes out of their holders. My only concern was not to hit Billy, who was darting around the kitchen in my body, pursuing Pritkin's fleeting form.

The shadows retreated to the stairwell, waiting for me to run out of ammunition, which wouldn't take long. It was now or never, I realized, and threw myself at Pritkin. Billy had the same idea at the same time and lunged from the other side, causing us to crash into each other with Pritkin's spirit trapped between us.

For a split second, I couldn't tell which of us had him, or if either of us did. Then Pritkin stumbled into my body, I think by accident, but that was good enough. It grabbed him in a tight embrace and dragged him in despite his panicked efforts to get free. And just like that, we were back where we'd started.

"Cassandra! Is that you?" Marsden asked as Pritkin sank slowly to his knees. He was white and shaky looking, but he appeared to be in one piece. That was the important thing, I told myself.

"No, it didn't work," I said, bitterness staining my voice. Damn it! We'd been so close!

Marsden gripped my arm. "What happened?"

"Rakshasas."

"They aren't supposed to attack the living!"

"Tell them that." I knelt beside Pritkin and revised my earlier assessment. His pupils were dilated, his color was bad and he was breathing heavy—until he suddenly slumped over my legs, his body relaxing into an awful stillness.

"I'll get my medical kit," Marsden said.

A clock fell off the wall, shattering into a hundred pieces. My head whipped around. *"Now* what?"

"We're under siege."

"Since when?!"

"It began a few moments ago. It seems you were correct—the Circle is unwilling to wait for us to come to them."

"But you said they wouldn't attack you!"

"Those who served under me wouldn't. But Saunders sent Apprentices." Marsden's tone was bitter.

"Who?"

"Young mages still in the last phase of their training. They joined the Corps after I left office. Saunders is the only Lord Protector they've ever known."

"Let me guess. They'll follow his orders—whatever they are!"

"That is a distinct possibility."

"So now what? Because I can't shift!" At the moment, I was lucky to be vertical.

He put a hand on my shoulder. "One crisis at a time, child," he told me, and jogged upstairs.

He'd barely gone when Pritkin tensed subtly and his eyes snapped open. I bent over him and, before I could say anything, he grabbed me by the back of my head, dragged my mouth down and kissed me. *Kissed* me, with no drama and no explanation, like it was just something we did.

Knowing in a half-forgotten way that he kissed like a demon was one thing; experiencing it all over again was quite another. There was no refined seduction—Pritkin kissed openmouthed, hard and hungry, until I could hear nothing over the pounding of my heart, until I could taste my blood on his lips as his tongue thrust into me. My skin shivered helplessly, but my flesh wanted more, suddenly *starving* for this. . . .

My brain informed me that there was absolutely no reason to find the scent of my hair or the soft spot beneath my elbow the slightest bit erotic. It pointed out that I was, essentially, kissing myself, but Pritkin's body wasn't buying it. Soft little hands racked up my shirt, slid across my chest, tweaked a nipple and oh, *God*.

A breath of wind curled around me, an almost living prickle against my skin. It slid around my body sinuously, cool but not calming, not calming at all. I shuddered and the current shivered along with me. And a jagged cut on Pritkin's arm softened, faded and melted into the golden skin over his bicep. I blinked, and when I looked again, there wasn't even a scar. It was as if the wound had never even existed.

I was dazed and extremely confused when we broke apart. Pritkin lifted his head and his eyes were fever bright and slightly unfocused. He radiated a barely leashed violence that was strange and nearly alien—but also echoingly familiar.

I screamed and started scrambling away, but he caught me, holding me fast. "No! It's me! It's only me! Rosier isn't here!"

My own face coalesced in front of me and there was honest emotion in those striking eyes—worry, pain and a healthy dose of self-loathing. I stopped struggling. I was willing to bet Rosier had never had an honest emotion in his life.

"But I felt—"

"I'm wounded," Pritkin said, flushing slightly. "It's . . . something of an automatic reaction. I'm not going to hurt you."

"Automatic?" He didn't take time to explain, just levered himself to a standing position using the counter.

"Where do you think you're going?" I demanded.

"We need to get out of here," he said as another barrage hit.

"You can barely stand up, much less fight!"

"I'm perfectly fine," he said stubbornly.

"Not after attacking half a dozen demons on your own! What the hell did you think you were doing? You had no weapons, no shields, *nothing*."

"They would have killed you."

"So what did you think they were going to do to you?" He didn't say anything. "Or was that the idea? While they were busy *ripping you to shreds*, I'd have time to escape?"

"It was the only reasonable course of action."

The matter-of-fact tone had anger surging through me. "Reasonable? That was *my* idea—my stupid, stupid idea! If someone died for it, *it should have been me!*"

"Your plan would have worked, had you been with anyone else."

"What are you talking about? Those things—"

"Cannot normally attack the living. The demon lords made a covenant long ago not to ruin Earth—the hunting ground they all share—by overfeeding. Each race was limited to taking only one form of energy. In the case of the Rakshasas, they can only feed on whatever is left after death. But your body still lived; you should have been beyond their reach."

"So did yours. And that didn't seem to matter!"

"Rosier petitioned the Assembly of Lords to grant a special dispensation in my case." There was an odd light in his eyes, not sorrow or pain or regret but some terrible combination of the three, a kind of emptiness that made me want to shiver. "One it seems he has managed to extend to you."

"I don't understand."

Pritkin took a deep breath. "I have never explored the demon part of my nature. It's what Rosier wants, why he performed his obscene experiment in the first place. He hoped by incorporating Fey and human blood with his own, he would create a demon without the limitations of his kind. By refusing to investigate my nature, I've denied him the results."

"But you've also denied yourself. Don't you wonder what else you can do? What abilities you may have inherited?"

"I worry about that all the time."

"But that other side of you gave you immortality, didn't it? So it can't be all—"

"I'm not immortal, and my longer life span came from my mother's Fey ancestry," he snapped. "*Nothing* from my father's side is remotely positive! As he is currently demonstrating. I thwarted him, you humiliated him and he wants revenge."

"But Rakshasas can't hurt me when I'm in my body. So how does he—"

"You heard Jonas—you can't do your job safely without resorting to possessions. But they cause your spirit to become vulnerable, even if only for an instant. And with the Rakashasas, that will be enough."

"But my power as Pythia is supposed to be inexhaustible. Even if they attacked me—"

"You're confusing types of energy. Rakshasas feed off life energy, as do your vampires. Your magic doesn't interest them."

Marsden ran down the stairs with a basket draped over his arm but stopped short when he saw Pritkin on his feet. He nonetheless proffered a vial of viscous orange sludge that boiled with darker glints in it. Pritkin scowled but downed half of it anyway before I could ask what was in it.

"Energy potion," Marsden said, catching my eye. "It's harmless."

And foul, judging by Pritkin's expression. "If I take it, will it help me shift us out of here?" I asked as a ceramic water pitcher danced down a counter and crashed against the tiles.

"Oh, no. It isn't that strong. Just adds a bit of pep, so to speak. But not to worry; I have another way out."

Pritkin groaned. "Tell me you didn't bring that damn thing with you!"

Marsden looked affronted. "That damn thing won me six titles, I'll have you know!"

"And almost got you killed at least as many times!"

"A hazard of the sport."

Pritkin grabbed his coat and weapons while appliances rattled in their places and the dishes chimed together in the cupboard. One glance out the window showed why: bolt after bolt of energy was exploding against a bubble of protection that began just beyond the garden. None got through, but every hit shuddered the foundations of the house.

Marsden threw open the back door and led us quickly across the garden. Beyond the cultivated area was a patch of weeds surrounding a small brick structure. He flicked on the lights and dragged a tarp off what turned out to be a gleaming red convertible. It was obviously a classic, with a long, low frame, high fenders and an odd arrangement of three headlights.

"An Alfa Romeo Spider," he informed us, grinning. "Finest sports car ever made. Bought new in 1932." He slid behind the wheel, and Orion, the demon-possessed dog, jumped into the passenger seat. That was a little creepy since I hadn't even noticed him being there. "Get in, get in!" Marsden said impatiently.

"It only has two seats," I pointed out, and Orion's bulk pretty much filled his.

"We'll all fit," Marsden said with the confidence of a man who was already seated.

"You think we can outrun them?" I asked skeptically as Pritkin and I tried to squeeze two bodies into a negative amount of space.

"I know we can!" Marsden yelled, starting the engine.

And then the garage shuddered, and the door opened on a dozen mages all trying to fit through at once. Pritkin mumbled something, and I glimpsed several of them being plucked off their feet by vines as big around as my leg. But it didn't matter because the rest came for us even as we started moving—straight at the garage wall.

"Marsden!" I screamed, but he just floored it. And the old car jumped ahead with a growl that shook the frame, leaping straight for the very solid-looking brick wall.

But instead of hitting brick, we sailed straight into the middle of a pulsing beam of white light. It was blindingly bright, shedding a killing radiance that made the sunny day look dark by comparison. The garage disappeared behind us, winking out of sight with a pop.

I slid into the seat, pushing devil dog onto the floorboards between my legs. Pritkin found a perch behind me, his bottom on the trunk, his feet knotted into the seat belts to keep him from flying off. My eyes finally adjusted to the glow, allowing me to look out on a glimmering white landscape. Blazing but cold, it reflected diamond-brilliant off of the surface of the car.

We were in a ley line. But this one made the Chaco Canyon Line look like a backwoods road. I couldn't even see an end to it on either side. But I could see dark shapes behind us, like tiny clouds obscuring the sun.

"You know, I think this is where I came in," I said, trying to keep my voice from shaking.

"Don't worry!" Marsden told me, flooring the gas pedal. "I won three world titles in this car!"

"Jonas is a former champion racer," Pritkin explained.

"You race in the ley lines?"

"Used to. Gave it up a few years back."

"You mean they made you quit," Pritkin corrected.

"Why?" I asked fearfully.

"Jealousy," Marsden said, hitting the dashboard. "Pure and simple."

"Because it is fantastically dangerous, even with youthful reflexes," Pritkin amended. "No one wanted to see you explode."

"*Explode?*"

"It's nothing to worry about," Marsden assured me. "We're shielded."

And that's when I noticed the pale golden shield all around the car, flowing over us like an elongated soap bubble and about as sturdy looking. I'd seen something like this before, a magical ward that allowed craft carrying multiple passengers to navigate the lines. It made me feel a little better ... for about ten seconds. Until a jolt of power sizzled past us from the pursuing mages—the same ones who had just collapsed a much sturdier-looking shield around the house.

Pritkin twisted around, lying over the trunk of the car to fire a spell at them. "Do you remember what happened last time somebody did that?" I screeched, grabbing him by the waistband.

"The Belinus Line is perfectly stable!" he told me just as Marsden hit a patch of turbulence. If I hadn't been hanging on, Pritkin would have gone flying, taking my body with him. As it was, we both hit back down hard, while Orion howled and Marsden cackled like the madman he undoubtedly was.

Something smashed against the shield around us, almost rolling the car and threatening to give me whiplash. "Marsden!" I screamed. "They're gaining!"

"Not for long!" He jerked the wheel to the right, throwing me half out of the car. Pritkin grabbed me, pulling back hard enough that I almost kept my seat. We burst free of the line in a shower of silver-white fire—right into the middle of thin air.

It took me a second to realize what had happened, because piercing cold hit me like a fist, knocking the breath from my lungs. It felt like my body had been encased in a sheath of ice. I tried to move, but nothing happened. I decided that I should probably worry that it didn't feel like I had any legs, but I was too busy freaking out about the fact that I couldn't seem to breathe.

Most of my senses were useless: everything was utterly silent, and if there was any wind, I didn't feel it. I gazed around, but there wasn't much to see. The only clouds were miles below, leaving the sky an incredible, dazzling blue. . . .

It was the view from an airplane, I realized, except we weren't in one. We weren't even in the shield because it was designed only to operate within a ley line. We were thousands of feet above the ground in a car that had no business being there. I stared at the Earth, so ridiculously far below, but I couldn't get enough air in my lungs to scream.

And then I was thrown back against the seat as Marsden nose-dived straight for the ground. The wind caused by our sudden plummet hit my eyes and I couldn't see, couldn't breathe, couldn't think through the sheer terror of it. We were going to die, I thought blankly, we were all going to die—and then we hit another ley line head-on.

This one was tiny, barely large enough for the car, almost brushing us on either side of the newly re-formed bubble. In the few seconds we'd been outside, my eyebrows had frosted up, my skin had turned a vaguely purple shade of blue and I swear my eyes had iced over. I blinked them rapidly, trying to see, and finally managed it—just in time

to watch us slide straight down into a tunnel of leaping red
fire.

I'd gotten my breath back, so I used it to scream, but the
engine noise mostly drowned it out. I eventually trailed off,
my throat raw, and yet we kept falling. It was like being on
a roller-coaster ride with no bottom. The seat belt was cutting into my lap, threatening to bisect me; devil dog's hair
was floating straight up; and Pritkin was gripping the back
of the seat with both hands to keep from being thrown
against the top of the bubble. And still we dove.

Then the brilliant red suddenly shifted to crimson as we
plunged through some kind of border. The car went from
an almost perpendicular plummet to a steep slide, throwing me half out of the car. My arm flung out in an attempt
to grab something, anything, to steady me, and plunged
straight into freezing water.

Part of the car was outside the narrow confines of the
line, creating a hole in the shield. My arm had gone out the
hole and a flood of water was coming in. It hissed against
the line's energy, throwing a cloud of steam in my face.

"Get back in!" Marsden yelled. "I can't see!"

"I'll get right on that!" I snarled as the forward momentum did its best to rip my arm off.

Pritkin tried to drag me back. But with only my strength
to work with, it did no good. I turned, bracing my feet
against the side of the car, and *pulled*. My arm popped out
of the hole, the car swerved back into the line and devil dog
shook himself, spraying me in the face with waterlogged
fur.

"The Channel," Marsden yelled, looking perfectly normal except for the high energy in his eyes. "And I'd keep
your hands inside the car, if I were you. The energy of the
line tends to attract attention. Went a little offsides once
and next thing I knew, there was this great dolphin in the
passenger seat, flapping and writhing and thwacking me
with its tail. Took me forever to get it out. Cost me the
race."

I just stared at him until my attention was caught by the
huge, dark shape that coasted by outside the line. It was
indistinct through the jumping energy, but was easily as big
as a house. "Whale," Pritkin said from over my shoulder.

"Some animals can sense the lines; we've never determined quite how."

"Damn nuisances!" Marsden declared. "That's how Cavanaugh died, you know. Middle of the All Britain back in 'fifty-six, and this great blue decides to breach the line. Dove in right in front of him. Must have been daft."

"Then perhaps we should attempt to leave this one behind," Pritkin pointed out.

Marsden apparently agreed, because he floored it. We flew ahead along a twisting, perilous course, but the whale kept pace, ducking and diving and following the same crazy path from the outside. Until we suddenly shot up again, leaving the ocean behind along with the ley line.

I hung over the side of the car, staring down at the ocean and the huge head that bobbed for a moment among the iron-gray waves and then disappeared. We continued upward for another few seconds and then started to drop like the large hunk of steel we were. I kept waiting for another line to snatch us away, but nothing happened and the waves were close enough that I could see the foam cresting on them and—

We fell into a brilliant purple line and rocketed forward just over the top of the waves. "Can't we slow down?" I yelled.

Marsden shook his head, his wild white mane flowing out behind him. "Have to pick up speed. There's some skipping ahead."

Pritkin made a noise that sounded suspiciously like a whimper, and I clutched Marsden's shoulder. "Skipping?"

"Yes, like a rock over a pond. Ah, here we go," he said, and the next second we were sailing into thin air again. I was hit in the face with some spray before I could point out that iron cars *do not float*, and then we were crashing in another line—yellow—which we stayed in for barely a heartbeat before launching into the air and hitting a deep purple line. The whole thing had taken maybe fifteen seconds.

"You see, skipping," Marsden said happily.

I didn't say anything; I was afraid I was going to throw up.

We left the purple line at the bottom of a bank of cliffs, twisting and tumbling through a very startled flock of seagulls and the smoking spray of waves, before merging with a bright blue line. That one headed straight inland—thank God—and Marsden patted my leg. "Almost there now."

"Almost where?" I croaked as we leapt into thin air yet again.

I gazed dazedly at a rolling patchwork of yellow fields, and then we were dropping back into a silver-white ocean of the Belinus Line. But this time it was broken by the presence of a large dark mass extending almost completely across. "Barrier," Pritkin said a little shrilly.

"Yes, thank you, John," Marsden said, and spun the wheel. The car hit the side of the line, swooped up the side, and turned completely upside down. We skinned past the top of the barrier with maybe an inch to spare, and then we were rushing down the other side of the line, completing a graceful swoop that had my hands shaking and my stomach reeling. The barrier dissolved behind us as the mages hurried to catch up.

"How did they know we'd come back?" Pritkin asked as we hurtled ahead.

"One of them must be a racer," Marsden said, looking irritated. "I laid out that course myself some years ago, and a number of the young hopefuls are known to practice on it. I should have taken an alternate route, but not to worry. We'll lose them soon enough."

He pointed ahead. I turned from watching our pursuers and a wash of color exploded across my vision. A firestorm of light boiled ahead, like a curtain of fire stretched across the entire center of the line. It was almost impossible to look directly at it. The power surges threatened to sear my retinas, the glow leaking in even through the hand I had thrown over my eyes.

"We're taking a shortcut," Pritkin said.

"A shortcut?" Why didn't I like the sound of that?

"Yes. Try to relax, Cassie," Marsden advised. I stared at him, wondering if he was trying to be funny. Because despite the fact that he was gearing down, we appeared to be picking up speed as whatever that was pulled us in. And Marsden wasn't trying to avoid it, I realized; he'd cut back on his suicidal pace only to better handle the wicked currents being churned up by that thing.

"What is that?"

"A minor vortex," Pritkin informed me. He sounded tense.

"Minor?" The thing looked like a supernova. And then a more important thought intruded. "Wait. We're going *in there*?"

"Oh, no. That would kill us," Marsden said calmly. And then the phenomenon grabbed us and we were hurtling forward at what had to be a couple hundred miles an hour.

I screamed and grabbed Pritkin, who was trying to fire off spells even as we bucked and twisted and slingshotted around the outer edge of the phenomenon and then—

Dead calm. For a moment, we hung alongside the electric white hub of the vortex, energy pulsing around us like the heartbeat of some giant beast. And the next we were somewhere else entirely.

I'd had a shift go bad before, had the weight of time pressing down on me, stretching me, until it felt like my body spanned the width of the planet. This was nothing like that. There was no gravity pulling on me, no bones and cells warping, no anything. It was almost like being back inside the Shroud, except that that had just caused sensory deprivation. *This* was having no senses to deprive.

I tried to breathe through the panic that was threatening to overtake me, but I couldn't even tell if I had lungs anymore. I tried to reach out, desperate to feel, see, hear *something*, but if I had a hand it didn't connect with anything. For a long moment, I really thought I was dead—that something had gone terribly wrong and we would be left here, drowning in nothingness, forever.

Until I slammed back into the seat. I couldn't complain of a lack of sensation now. In an instant, I went from having no secure casing of flesh and bone to a body made of pain. It was everywhere, from my throbbing head to my bruised butt to the sharp pain radiating up from my lap where the seat belt was doing its best to cut me in two.

But the pain wasn't the main problem. I stared up in blank terror at a thousand lines of power crisscrossing all around us: vibrant greens and glowing golds, cold blues and rich silver, flowing ebony and shuddering, bloody reds. I could have traced the lines just as easily blind: the bronze clanging like a bell, the blue murmuring like a stream, the purple crackling like lightning, the reds screaming.

"We hopped over to Glastonbury Tor," Pritkin explained, looking a little pale. "The biggest vortex in Britain."

"Hopped?"

"For short trips, you take a ley line," Marsden said. "If one happens to be running where you want to go. For longer ones, you take a line to the nearest major vortex. All vortexes around the world are interconnected on the metaphysical plane, you see, with currents flowing between them. If you catch the right one, you can hop from one vortex to another."

I shook my head numbly.

"There is no space here," he said, trying again, "Only energy. Therefore distance is meaningless."

I stared around in awe at the streams of power running all around us, each threading through the middle of the massive vortex. This close, it was like a giant heart, the ley lines running in and out of it like brightly colored veins, energy pulsing around us with every strobing beat. Everywhere I looked, colors melted together, shimmering off everything, painting the car in a dozen hues. It looked like we were swimming in rainbow water.

If a small ley line sink could power MAGIC, what could something like this do? "Why doesn't somebody harvest all this energy?" I asked wonderingly. "It could power ... everything."

"Every generation has those who try," Marsden replied. "But no shield we've ever created can withstand the forces inside even a small vortex." He looked me over critically. "Have you recovered? Because I am afraid we have another jump ahead of us."

"Another one?" I said numbly. "Do they all *hurt* like that?"

"Not after you've done it a few times. The trick is to go limp." He snapped his fingers and devil dog demonstrated by collapsing against my leg, his long tongue hanging out. "You see?"

"This time we shouldn't have any pursuers, at least," Pritkin added. "Individual shields aren't strong enough to withstand the forces this close to the vortex. Our pursuers should not have been able to follow us—"

He didn't get to finish his sentence, because a dozen shapes popped out of nowhere, all huddled together in one big, dark blob.

"Unless they pooled their shields," Marsden finished sourly, and threw the car back into gear.

Luckily for us, the trainees looked about as rattled as I felt. It gave us a slight lead, although a glance behind showed that some of them were already starting after us. Marsden suddenly jerked the steering wheel to the right and we roared into the middle of an apple green line. He waited until the mages had followed us and then threw the car into reverse.

We were free and back in the nothingness in the corona of the vortex for a moment, before that awful free-falling sensation took us again. And Marsden had lied, the bastard. Going limp didn't help *at all*. And then we were racing through the middle of a world gone red. But it wasn't the red of a ley line; it was the blinding dazzle of miles of sun-baked sand.

We hit down onto a black snake of asphalt with a jolt, a squeal of tires and a burst of speed. The dark shapes of war mages tumbled out onto the roadway after us—four, no, five—who had managed to keep up with the crazy ride. But they were on foot and we had wheels. Marsden left them in the dust.

We'd hopped to the Chaco Canyon vortex in New Mexico while I'd had my eyes closed. Half an hour later, we jumped to the shimmering blue line that ran through to Nevada and Dante's. It didn't take long from there to notice a big black blob on the horizon. It looked somewhat like the barrier the mages had constructed, except that there were no gaps around this one. There were other things, though.

Ragged flutterings of light darted here and there around the edges of my vision. I could glimpse them out of the corner of my eyes but could no longer see them directly. But even so, the sheer number was staggering. They looked like a crystal kaleidoscope, constantly shifting and changing all around us.

I looked back at Pritkin, and the expression on his face was enough to let me know I was right. "Rakshasas," he murmured. I guess in that quantity, even my eyes could pick them out.

"Where?" Marsden demanded.

"Surrounding the ward. Thousands of them."

"How did they know we were coming?" I asked, trying to ignore the chills that had sprung to the surface of my skin.

"They didn't. And even if they had, two of us could never feed so many." Pritkin gazed around in awe. "This is like the gathering before a great battle. When they expect a harvest of thousands . . ."

"Well, as long as they stay on the outside of the ward, we won't have to worry about them much longer," Marsden said, diving straight for it.

"What are you doing?" I screeched as a wall of darkness towered above us.

"The ward is spelled to let you in, is it not?"

"I don't know!"

"We'll soon find out," he said as a swarm of black dots broke away from the base of the main structure. In a few seconds, they were close enough that I could identify them— war mages. It looked like Saunders' men had called ahead.

Some of them came straight for us, while others stayed at the base of the ward, waiting for us to try to land, I assumed. Pritkin threw a spell that scattered the ones directly in front of us, but they re-formed almost at once and rocked the car with half a dozen spells. Devil dog whined and I sunk my fingers into his fur, either comforting him or holding on, I'm not sure which.

"Jonas—" Pritkin began.

"We'll make it," Marsden said calmly.

"Not if they hit us with another combined spell!"

"Yes, but to do that, they'll have to catch us, won't they?" The car sprang ahead, headed right for the black tower and the swarm of mages in front of it.

I didn't care about them. At this speed, there wasn't going to be anything left for them to attack. We were going to be splattered all over Dante's ward like bugs on a windshield.

I clutched Marsden's arm with nerveless fingers, silently

begging him to turn around. He glanced at me and patted my hand fondly. "Where are you staying?"

"What?"

"Your room. Where is it?"

"The penthouse."

"Oh, good," he murmured, and we crashed straight into the wall of darkness.

I screamed, Pritkin swore and Marsden laughed, and then we were bursting out the other side, the ward dissolving like smoke in front of us.

It was still night at Dante's, the moon hanging heavy and marmalade orange over the casino. I could see the color because we soared out of the line for ten seconds, leaving our pursuers behind, before we plunged back into the maelstrom of electric blue. Marsden had succeeded in confusing the hell out of the pursuers—an even dozen whisked by us, going up as we were heading back down. He'd done a pretty good job on me, too. I stared around blankly, not even sure we were still right side up.

And then I caught sight of the building rushing straight at us.

"Slow down!" I shrieked. "We're going to crash!"

"Nonsense," he told me, and plunged into the middle of a forest of other craft riding the currents of the ley line.

The interior of the ward was like a parking lot. We ducked under a tall clipper ship, its sails furled inside its bubble of protection, slid past a modern luxury yacht with lounge chairs scattered about the shining wood deck and swooped past a familiar dragon-shaped barge. It was the personal conveyance of the Chinese consul. I assumed the others belonged to her counterparts, something that wouldn't have worried me except they were clustered around the wrong tower.

Mine.

"Oh, shit!"

"You can never get a parking space when you need one!" Marsden agreed just as a spell clipped our fender, spinning us straight at the balcony doors. I had a second to see a group of startled faces staring out at us, and then we were crashing through the windows, glass flying, bar stools soaring, couches splintering.

We slammed straight into the wall leading to the dining room but bounced off as if it had been made of rubber instead of wood and plaster. We spun back into the room, taking out a couple of potted plants and a cigar-store Indian in the process. The room was a blur of color and noise for a few confused seconds before we finally came to a stop beside the ruined sofas.

The antler chandelier swung wildly above us, slinging light everywhere. I clutched devil dog to my chest and glared at Marsden, who was grinning from ear to ear. "I thought you said we weren't going to crash!"

He clapped me on the shoulder and laughed. "Just a little crash. And I do so enjoy making an entrance!"

Chapter Twenty-five

Mircea reached us first, pushing a pile of expensive kindling out of the way, heedless of damage to his sleek black suit. He wrenched open the door and devil dog growled menacingly, but Marsden got hold of the collar and pulled him back. "Now, now, Orion. You remember the good senator, surely."

Mircea grabbed Pritkin and hauled him bodily out of the car, his eyes devouring Pritkin's face with a nearly desperate relief. I blinked, taking a moment to catch up. And then it hit: Pritkin was still in my body. And that was definitely not something I wanted to explain.

"Crap."

"If you find our company distasteful, Mage Pritkin, feel free to leave it!" Mircea said acidly.

Pritkin's hand curled into a fist and he glared at me over Mircea's shoulder as he was dragged into a bone-cracking embrace. I just shrugged. I thought he should have been grateful—at least Mircea hadn't kissed him.

Marlowe approached, wearing modern clothes for once—a black shirt and tie with a dark russet suit that brought out auburn glints in his hair. He was waving a bottle of whiskey. "Can I interest anyone in a drink?"

Marsden peered at the label. "Glenfiddich? Oh, yes, please." He climbed out, followed by devil dog, and surveyed the damage. "Not too bad," he said musingly. "A new coat of paint and a bit of drying out, and she'll be right as rain."

"You modified it," Pritkin accused.

"I added an external shield for landings that don't, er, go quite as planned. It's illegal in racing, but as I don't do that anymore—"

"Could have fooled me," I said shakily. I crawled out of the car and tried to take a couple of steps, but my balance was shot and the room swung crazily about me. My inner ears weren't convinced that we'd actually stopped.

I looked around, expecting to see a ring of ancient, disapproving eyes. I did, but not the ones I'd feared. Besides the five of us, the only other people in the room were Mircea's cold-eyed masters. It looked like the consuls had gone out for lunch.

One of the masters approached Mircea. "Sir, the representatives from the Circle have arrived."

"Stall them," he snapped, looking at Marsden.

The man bowed and exited, but Marsden just shook his head. "It's too late for that, I'm afraid."

"Cassie, may I see you a moment?" Mircea didn't wait for a reply, just hauled Pritkin into the hall leading to the bedrooms, I guess for privacy. Thoughts of how well that was likely to go had me scrambling after them until Marlowe blocked my path.

He smiled. "Are you sure you won't have a drink? You look like you could use it."

"Maybe later," I said, trying to hedge around.

He moved with me. "This is the last whole bottle left to us. I'd take advantage, if I were you."

There was a curse from the hallway, followed by a grunt and a thud. I winced as Pritkin ran back into the room, face flushed and eyes livid. "Actually, I think a drink sounds like a good idea," I said as Mircea followed.

"Cassie!" he hissed, his eyes on my face.

"Make that a double," I told Marlowe before an angry vampire had me by the shoulders, fingers digging into my flesh.

"It's not like we didn't try to switch back!" I said defensively.

"You're saying you can't reverse this?"

"No, no! We totally can," I promised quickly, because

Mircea was looking a little stressed. "It's just … well, the last time we tried, we sort of almost died and—"

Marlowe tried to hand me my drink, but Mircea took it instead and threw it back. "Ah," Marlowe said, looking back and forth between Pritkin and me. "This is … disturbing."

"Imagine how I feel," I said, which won me a dirty look from Pritkin. "What? You *like* wearing a bra?"

Mircea put a hand to his forehead and just stayed like that for a long moment. A small vein was beating in his jaw. It didn't look like the whiskey had helped much.

"Mircea," Marlowe put in quietly. "Saunders is downstairs demanding to see Cassie."

"He is in no position to demand anything, as you made clear in your communiqué. It appears thickheadedness is a requirement for Circle membership!"

"Perhaps, but he *is* here. She must greet him."

"She must do nothing of the kind," Pritkin spat. "He needs to be removed, not bargained with!"

"You don't know what we've learned about him," I added. "The man is completely—"

"Cassie, it is you who do not understand the situation!" Mircea told me.

"We understand it perfectly!" Pritkin snarled. "The man is a traitor to the Corps, putting its mages in danger to line his pockets—"

"How do you know that?" Marlowe demanded.

"One of the men Cassie released from the Circle's prison knew about his activities. He went to tell Jonas, who has decided to challenge."

We all looked at Marsden, who had commandeered a towel with which he was attempting to dry devil dog. He nodded and shrugged and then went back to clucking over his possessed pooch. Mircea shut his eyes briefly and Marlowe groaned. "Isn't that perfect!"

"What else is there to do?" I asked, confused. "He has to be removed."

"If we wanted him dead, we'd have arranged it before this!" Mircea informed me. "We want him controlled!"

"Controlled how? He's head of the Circle. It looks to me like he pretty much does whatever he wants!"

"A state of affairs that will end tonight!"

"I don't understand."

"The man you helped me release from the Circle's prison brokered the original deal for Saunders," Marlowe explained. "He was the liaison between the Circle and the final purchaser of their power. Saunders locked him away after the deal was finalized, to keep him quiet."

"Purchaser?" Pritkin's brow knotted. "You mean purchas*ers*. No one person could use that much power."

"The Black Circle could."

"The Black—" Pritkin stopped, apparently unable to process that.

Marlowe nodded, a grim smile settling over his features. "It's beautiful, isn't it? The collective energy of the Silver Circle was being sold to their fiercest rivals. Of course, according to Mr. Todd—the man you released for us, Cassie—Saunders never knew where it was going. But he didn't bother to find out, which makes him equally culpable. A point of view with which I'm sure the magical community would concur, were it to ever hear about this."

"*When* it hears!" Pritkin corrected.

"All you war mages are the same," Marlowe said dismissively. "Run at a problem full on and club it into submission! The finer points are lost on you."

I crossed my arms. "Then explain them to me."

Marlowe glanced at Mircea, who nodded tersely. "Saunders has been informed that we have Todd and his evidence. It would be enough not only to end his career, but to bury him if it ever came out—"

"Which it will!" Pritkin interrupted.

"Which it can't," Marlowe shot back. "Otherwise, whoever the Circle taps for his successor will put us back in the same quagmire in which we've been stuck for the last month!"

"You're talking about blackmail!" I said, catching up. "You stay silent about his activities and he confirms me as Pythia."

"And does any other little chore we may think up," he added with a slight smile.

"That is completely out of the question!" Pritkin's hands

kept clenching as if only the lack of a target was keeping him from pouncing on someone and beating them bloody. "The Senate does not control the Circle!"

"Does not control the Circle ... yet," Marlowe murmured, deliberately provocative. Pritkin's eyes latched onto him with an expression I didn't like, and Marlowe gave him a small smile. The temperature in the room escalated about ten degrees.

Mircea ignored them. "Cassie, if you want the recognition and cooperation you need to function, this is the only way."

"By leaving a felon in the most important position in the magical world? That doesn't sound like a great way to begin!"

"Better than not beginning at all," Marlowe said. "We haven't spent the last month looking for something to hold over that bastard's head to throw it aside now! Your scruples—"

"Are commendable," Mircea broke in, throwing him a look. "But of course, we will make it clear to Mage Saunders that his financial arrangement will have to be terminated, and that we will be keeping a very close watch on his future activities."

"You're forgetting one small matter," Pritkin said scornfully.

"And what is that?" Mircea demanded.

"Jonas intends to challenge—"

"Something that would not be the case had you not interfered!"

"—and indeed, I shouldn't wonder if he hasn't already done so."

We all looked around, but Marsden had disappeared. Marlowe swore and dove for the foyer. Mircea started to follow, but I grabbed his arm. "We're not done."

"This isn't the time, Cassie!"

"According to you, it's never time, not to tell me anything! You get angry with me for bringing in outside help—"

"I would hardly categorize Mage Marsden as help! The man was almost impossible to work with—"

"To dictate to, you mean," Pritkin put in.

"—not to mention that two days ago, you informed me

that you intended to swim, relax and perhaps do some shopping. Not to start a revolution!"

I stared at him. "Okay, let me make sure I understand. I'm supposed to vet everything I do with you—"

"If it involves aiding a coup, yes!"

"—but you don't have to tell me a damn thing in return. Not about Saunders, not about your girlfriend, not even about *my father*!"

That made him pause, if only for a second. "We have yet to confirm the rumors about your father," he told me more quietly. "I did not wish to upset you needlessly. We had no way of knowing that Saunders intended to spread them before half the world!" His forehead wrinkled. "And what girlfriend?"

I ignored him, so angry I was almost shaking. "Upset me? What am I, five years old? I'm Pythia, Mircea!"

"I have never questioned—"

"You question it all the time! Everyone does! The Senate is as bad as the Circle. They both want the Pythia's power but not what goes with it. They don't want someone who might make them do things they don't like or overrule them when they're being stupid. They want a dumb blonde who is going to do what she's told and stay locked away under a metric ton of guards the rest of the time!"

"For your protection, Cassandra! Or have you somehow failed to notice how many people wish you harm?"

"About the same number who are trying to assassinate the Consul, but she's not in hiding! Because she knows it isn't always possible to stay safe and get the job done!"

"Nor is it possible if you are dead! Do you have any idea how many plots against your life we have thwarted in the past month?"

"No! I don't know anything! That's my point! I need information to do my job—all of it, not whatever you think I can—"

"The Lord Protector and court," one of the masters intoned from the top of the stairs. I looked up to find a large party of mages staring at the destruction, trying not to let it show that the circle of gold-eyed vampires creeped them out.

Marlowe and Marsden were having a low-voiced conversation in the foyer. I couldn't hear them, but I assumed Marlowe was trying to persuade him to postpone his challenge. From the defiant jut of the old man's chin, it didn't look like he was having much luck.

A portly, balding man in an ill-fitting blue suit caught sight of us and stepped forward. "Miss Palmer, I assume?"

Pritkin just stood there for a moment before slowly stepping forward. "And you're Reginald Saunders."

I was grateful for the hint, because I never would have picked the guy out in a lineup. He looked more like a middle-management flunky than the leader of the most powerful magical association on Earth. But then, I didn't look much like a Pythia, either.

"Indeed." He held out a hand, but Pritkin made no move to take it. It was rude, but since we were about to get a lot ruder, I didn't guess it mattered. "I've been looking forward to this meeting."

"I'm surprised you didn't send another lieutenant in your place."

"Some things, it seems, it is best to do for oneself," he said mildly. Then the hand he still held out made an odd gesture. And Pritkin sailed off his feet, flew backward out the missing window and disappeared into the night sky.

I stared in disbelief at the spot where he'd just been for half a second and then I was scrambling across cowhide, running for the balcony. I hung over the railing, praying to see a shield bubble somewhere below, but there was nothing. The lights of the hotel extended only so far, and beyond them was only blackness.

I looked up to find Mircea beside me, scanning the darkness. His eyes were better than mine, but judging by the way the metal railing was squeezing up through his fingers like butter, he didn't see anything either. "Tell me he could manipulate your magic," he said, his voice expressionless.

"Normally, yes," I said breathlessly. "But we were attacked before we got here! He's pretty drained, and I don't know if—"

I didn't get the chance to finish the sentence. Mircea launched himself at Saunders, the crackle of his energy hitting the mage's shields like an out-of-control forest fire. It set the remains of the furniture alight, turning the center of the room into a bonfire, and threatened to scorch my skin even this far away. But Saunders acted like he couldn't even feel it.

"You have a reputation for sagacity, Lord Mircea," the man snapped. "Use it! The girl is dead. Even now, the power is passing to another Pythia—one I will control! The game is over."

Mircea didn't bother to respond, but someone else did. "Reginald! You worthless, spineless, murdering bastard! You couldn't control a TV with a remote! As a member of the Great Council, I challenge your right to lead the Circle!" Marsden came striding down the stairs, his mane of silver hair crackling with static.

Saunders ignored him. "Don't be a fool, Mircea! Did you think you were the only one to make preparations for this meeting? I have more than two hundred mages surrounding this building. It is time to renegotiate!"

"Renegotiate this!" The voice came from behind me. I turned, seeing nothing but darkness, until I looked down. The huge sailing ship hung suspended in midair, its prow dipping and rising, its rigging creaking lightly—and Pritkin hanging over the side. He threw a spell at Saunders that sent him slamming back against the wall, shields and all.

I don't think it hurt him, but the look on his face was priceless. For about a second, until his phalanx of bodyguards closed in, cutting off the view. Mircea's vampires moved to intercept them, and just that fast, things went to hell.

I helped Pritkin back over the railing while the ship just hung there, riding invisible currents. He must have ripped open the ley line to save himself, and fallen onto the ship. Like the Chinese barge, it appeared to be capable of levitating in real space in order to reach and descend from ley lines.

I looked back at the apartment to see Marsden calmly walking through the fray, spewing curses left and right, each of which landed like a hammer blow on Saunders' mages. I was beginning to wonder if Pritkin might not have underestimated him. Certainly none of the mages seemed all that eager to fight him.

One guy tried to hide behind a buddy, who shoved him away and scampered out of the line of fire. The first guy

stared at Marsden, who smiled gently back right before
hitting him with a curse so strong it knocked him clear
through the remaining balcony doors. He flew past us,
sailed over the railing and landed on the deck of the ship.
Only to be kicked off by a vampire in an old-fashioned
captain's outfit.

Once he'd cleaned off his deck, the captain barked an
order and the ship started moving away, out of the line of
fire. I didn't blame him. Spell after spell was flying out of
the apartment, exploding in the air like fireworks.

I ducked to avoid sparks from a near miss, and Pritkin
grabbed my arm. "You have to get out of here!"

"Me? What about you? You're in my body!"

"I'll be fine!"

"Yes, you will. Because you won't be here," Mircea said,
suddenly appearing beside us. His hair had come loose and
one of the ends was smoking slightly. I pinched the flame
out between my fingers, but considering the conflagration
going on behind us, that didn't make me feel any better.

Pritkin apparently had the same thought. "You're out-
numbered! You need the help!"

"And how much help do you think you would be in your
condition?" Mircea demanded, motioning the ship back toward us.

"More than you, vampire! The place is going up like an
inferno!"

"That is my concern. Yours is to get her to safety and
switch back as soon as—"

I never heard the rest of the sentence, because a spell
slammed into me, picking me up and hurling me into the
void. It happened so fast, I barely realized what was going
on until I was falling. The side of the building flashed by
all of three feet away, the windows blurring together into
a continual black line, the pavement rushing up at me at a
ridiculous pace. And then something snatched me, almost
cutting me in two.

I looked up to see the sailing ship above me, the prow
dipped low and Mircea hanging off the end of the wooden
figurehead. His fist was knotted in my waistband, which
explained why I couldn't breathe. Considering the alternative, I really didn't mind so much.

Even so, I was surprised his reflexes had been good enough to catch me. He looked kind of shocked himself. For a second, the reserved demeanor cracked open on something wild and fierce and compelling. Then he dragged me up, put a hand on either side of my face and kissed me full on the lips. From somewhere above, I heard Pritkin swear.

"I guess that whole blackmail thing didn't exactly work out like you planned, huh?" I gasped when Mircea released me.

"Saunders will die for this," he hissed, staring back up at the balcony.

"That might be kind of tricky," I pointed out as a swarm of mages burst out of the ley line and fell onto the deck behind us. It looked like Saunders hadn't been kidding; the vampires hadn't been the only ones making plans for this meeting.

Of course, plans don't always work out. The mages seemed to have assumed the ship would be level, because half of them slid down the rough planks before grasping some kind of handhold, and the other half went plummeting over the side. I stared after them for a second as a dozen little shield chutes bloomed against the night sky. Then Mircea dragged me against his side, vaulted over the railing and jumped—straight after them.

We didn't end up plummeting to our deaths but onto the surface of the yacht, which had quietly come around underneath. I grasped the railing, my heart still stuck on terror, but Mircea pried me off and we ran. The mages who had kept their balance followed us, and there seemed to be an awful lot of them.

"I can't believe they're trying this with the consuls here," I panted as we dodged deck chairs and little folding tables.

"The consuls aren't here. That's why I went to Washington State, to my court. I had to welcome them. They're there now, with the Senate."

"Something else you didn't mention!"

He grabbed me around the waist and tossed me over the side. I got a brief, dizzying view of the dark parking lot below before I was caught by a waiting vampire on the Chinese consul's barge. Mircea jumped the distance behind me, and as soon as we were aboard, it took off—only to be hit with a spell that shuddered it to a halt.

I looked behind us to see a dozen or more mages manipulating the biggest net spell I'd ever seen. It had enveloped the dragon's tail on the stern of the barge and was slowly drawing us back alongside the other ship.

"I couldn't very well tell you anything without being overheard," Mircea said, staring around.

"By whom?" I demanded. "The only people in the apartment were family!"

"Exactly." His neck craned upwards as he caught sight of something. I followed his gaze to see what looked like a wall of wood descending on us. It took me a moment to realize that it was the sailing ship's deck. The massive schooner had flipped upside down.

Mircea held me up and a vampire reached down and grabbed me by both arms, his legs enmeshed tightly in the rigging. Mircea jumped up beside him. "You don't trust your own family?" I gasped, holding on for dear life.

"I don't trust one of them. Someone tried to kill the Consul, if you recall."

"But you said you knew who that was!"

He shook his head. "The Bentley was serviced the day before MAGIC was destroyed, and the bomb would surely have been noticed at that time. So it was planted later, after the man to whom you're referring was already dead."

"Then why did you say—"

"To make the guilty party feel secure. Kit narrowed it down to eight suspects, five of whom belong to me. I had them transferred here as soon as I received his report and borrowed the consular ships to make it look like the Consuls were meeting here. If an attempt was made to disrupt the meeting, we would have our traitor."

"That's why you discussed their visit in the middle of the living room. You wanted everyone to hear!"

Mircea nodded as the clipper began to move away, putting some distance between us and the melee. But some of the mages had managed to get themselves untangled from the net spell in time to launch themselves at us. I thought things were about as bad as they could get, dangling upside down twenty stories up while the Circle's mages started swarming down the webbing toward us. And then the ship started to rotate.

I think the captain was trying to jiggle his stowaways loose, and he was doing a damn good job—on me. Mircea grabbed me as my grip started to slip and swung us over the side just as the rounded hull came into view. "No," I said, shaking my head vigorously. "You aren't suggesting—"

"I have you," he assured me, setting my feet down onto the very uneven planks of the hull. "Think of them as small steps."

"To where?"

"Up there," Mircea said as the ship slowly began to rise back toward the balcony.

"The people trying to kill us are up there!"

"They're down here, as well," he pointed out. "And we have more allies there."

"One of whom could be a traitor!"

"No. The suspects have been given the night off and instructed not to return before dawn. If one of them does, we'll have him."

We'd almost reached the keel, but the mages were right behind us and the balcony looked very far away. And unless I was imagining things, the rotation had picked up speed. "Wait. What if the traitor decided to go with a bomb instead?"

"We've checked. The apartment is perfectly safe."

"Yeah. It looks it!" I said, and then the flat deck was coming up at us again and there was suddenly nowhere to put my feet. Not that it mattered because the ship's rotation jerked to a halt, with my toes hanging off the edge. "Mircea!"

He didn't answer, just swept me up and jumped down to the mast, which was sticking out of the deck like a bridge. The mages had nowhere near good enough balance to follow along the curved, polished surface, and so they decided to start flinging spells instead. One of the furled sails went up in flames right beside us and then Mircea put on a burst of speed and we were suddenly out of mast and jumping.

"Did you *have* to carry her?" Pritkin demanded, as we landed back on the balcony.

Mircea ignored him, beckoning the Chinese barge closer. "Come with us!" I said, gripping his hand.

He shook his head. "If Saunders gets away tonight, he'll go into hiding. It may be months, even years, before we have him again."

"You don't have him now! He has you!"

The Chinese barge slid alongside, and Mircea picked Pritkin up and handed him over the side into the arms of the waiting captain. He said something in Mandarin, and the vamp nodded, setting Pritkin on his feet and reaching for me. I ended up over the side and on the deck before I quite realized it was happening.

"Mircea! Don't do this!"

It was like he didn't even hear. He turned and disappeared back into the thick, choking column of smoke that was now billowing out of the apartment. He didn't look back.

I turned to Pritkin as the barge slipped rapidly away. "We have to get him out of there!"

"I'd be a bit more worried about us, if I were you," he said as a large white ship appeared in the sky.

I knew it must have come from the ley line, but it had merged with real space so quickly that it looked like a magician's trick. That made sense, as there were a few hundred mages lined up along the railing—the ones Saunders had boasted about, I guessed. "Tell me again that they don't want us dead," I said as a fiery blast exploded out of the side of the vessel, passed a yard in front of us and hit the clipper broadsides.

The ship went up like a Roman candle. The explosion of burning wood, rope and sail hit us, causing our craft to swerve precariously in a wide arc. I held on to the railing and watched burning pieces of the clipper ship plummet to the parking lot below. They crashed onto the rows of employee cars, sending half a dozen somersaulting skyward and setting off a chorus of car alarms. I didn't see any of the crew make it off.

Even worse, the Lord Protector's ship was heading straight for the penthouse. If it got there with that number of reinforcements, Mircea was dead. There wasn't even a question.

I grabbed the captain by the collar. "Stop them!" He
didn't seem to understand, so I shook him and pointed at
the ship. "They can't be allowed to dock!"

He just pried my hands off his silk tunic. Not a word was
said, but the idea was conveyed anyway—he wasn't crazy.
Luckily, I was on board with someone who was—or at least
gave a fair impression of it most of the time.

"Hold on!" Pritkin told me, and threw his weight onto
the long rudder pole hanging off the back. Our course corrected with a lurch that sent me and the captain staggering
to the other side of the barge. The only reason we didn't fall
off was the railing, which was sturdier than it looked. And
then we were plowing straight into the side of Saunders'
ship.

Chapter Twenty-six

The impact slammed me into the railing and the reverbera-tion hit the inside of my skull like cannon fire, unbelievably loud and echoing. Saunders' ship tilted, sending a few mages overboard and making the rest very unhappy. The Chinese captain was screaming orders to his men as war mages swarmed over our deck. There were too many of them to fight, but the crazy staggering course of the conjoined ships was making that pretty much impossible anyway.

The initial impact had thrown us almost beyond Dante's property, but something seemed to be wrong with the navigation system, because the two ships had no sooner reached the highway than they lurched drunkenly back to-ward the building again. The captain was desperately try-ing to free his ship, but the dragon masthead had crashed through a porthole on Saunders' ship and it seemed to be stuck.

The weight was dragging down the other vessel, and tilt-ing it dangerously. "The other side! Get to the other side!" someone yelled, and a large number of mages ran to the opposite half of the ship, trying to compensate. But it was too late.

Dante's was rushing toward us, we were at least ten sto-ries up and there was nothing underneath but burning cars and asphalt. The captain took a final look at the situation, said something that sounded pretty profane and pulled a gigantic ax out of his belt. A second later, the massive dragon's neck was in two pieces and we were sliding away from the other ship.

The efforts Saunders' ship had been making to compensate for our weight backfired when we suddenly departed. The other ship flipped completely over, spilling mages across the parking lot like salt from a shaker. Shields bloomed everywhere and then Pritkin was yelling in my ear. "Brace for impact!"

He threw his shields around us, and a second later, while I was still looking down at the parking lot, we plowed into the side of Dante's.

The barge crashed through a window, into a bedroom, out into the corridor and through another wall separating the hall from a stairwell. We hadn't even stopped moving when Pritkin grabbed my hand, towed me off the side and down the stairs. Unfortunately, the mages had pretty good reflexes, too, and ten or more had still been on the barge when it took the plunge.

A spell sizzled overhead, slamming against the concrete wall directly in front of us. Pritkin still had shields up, but he couldn't maintain them long and no way could we fight so many. We hopped over the railing to the next level, and I spied a number six on the stairwell door.

"Get us to the fourth floor and I can get us out of this!" I told him as a spell evaporated his shields. He nodded, looking a little gray in the face, and we ran full out.

Two flights of stairs had never seemed so long. We didn't worry about safety, about bruised knees when we tripped or scraped flesh when we couldn't stop in time and slammed into a wall. We just kept going: past number five, dodge a spray of bullets, around the bend in the stairs, jump to the next flight to avoid being fried by a fireball, down another flight and finally through the door to four.

"This way!" I yelled, and we pelted down the corridor and into the tiki bar.

I hauled him through a side door and into the tiny storage room I'd been calling home. "Now what?" he demanded as feet pounded into the club.

"Now this," I said, and gave him a shove. He fell backward through the portal, and at the same moment, a mage flung open the door. He was young, with brown hair and glasses and a wash of freckles over his nose. He looked as surprised to see me as I was to see him, and for a moment, we just stared at each other. Then I jumped for the portal, he threw a spell and the world exploded in pain.

I tumbled out into the Old West saloon and rolled into Pritkin. I stared up at the out of order sign on the telephone and gasped in pain. My whole body was wracked with it, but my left leg felt like it was on fire.

The sound of clinking glasses, laughter and music drifted through the red velvet curtains, like there wasn't a war going on upstairs. Pritkin caught sight of my face. "What happened?"

I just stared at him, tears flooding my eyes, and shook my head. If I tried to speak, I was going to scream. But as bad as the pain was, we couldn't stay there. The mage had seen me disappear. He'd be right behind us.

Pritkin seemed to get the idea. He looped an arm under my shoulders and around my back, and he pulled me up. I put as much weight as possible on the good leg and we limped out into the club. People were everywhere, but thankfully the lighting was so dim, mostly from strings of lanterns overhead, that we didn't attract as much attention as our looks probably warranted. Of course, the vision onstage might have also had something to do with that.

Dee Licious was lying in the spotlight on a shiny black baby grand, her dress a blinding mass of skintight fuchsia sequins, complete with matching boa. She was belting out a Liza montage and flirting with the handsome pianist at the same time. We turned toward the street, putting the stage at our backs, only to see two war mages stroll by outside.

"This way," Pritkin said brusquely, pulling me back the other way. We hobbled through the forest of little tables toward the darkness at the side of the stage, where a red exit sign beckoned like a lifeline. We'd almost reached it when Pritkin stiffened. "What is it?" I asked.

"We have company."

I glanced over my shoulder to see a group of dark shapes spill out of the alcove, looking around blindly while their eyes adjusted. Then Pritkin threw us through a door beside the stage, closing it firmly. There was no lock, but considering who was chasing us, that was kind of irrelevant anyway.

Dee Sire paused in front of a lighted mirror to stare at us. It looked like this was the performers' dressing room. In addition to the table Dee was using as a vanity, there was a rack of colorful costumes in a corner and a towering pile of shoe boxes on a chair.

Dee smiled at me a lot sweeter than on our previous meeting. "Well, hello there." Then she caught sight of Pritkin. "Damn, girl. And I thought you couldn't look any worse than last time."

He glanced at me, but I just shook my head and fell onto a chair beside the door. There was no way to explain the fabulousness that was Dee Sire in a couple of words, and I wasn't up to any more. "Nice dress," I gasped.

It was about eighty acres of cheap white satin, cut low and short and festooned with a train covered in fat white roses. More were tied into a careless bundle on the dressing table and another pile adorned her towering wig—bright red this time—anchoring a frothy veil. A wedding dress, drag queen style.

"It's courtesy of that cow Licious," Dee said, turning back to her mirror. "She knows damn well *I* do Liza. But we drew for the opening spot, and what does she decide she just *has* to sing? Sticking me with the tired old 'Like a Virgin' shtick. Although I will admit, it's getting a little ridiculous at her age—"

"We, er, we're kind of in a bind," Pritkin said, cutting her off. "Is there a back way out?"

"Are you kidding? There's back, front, and sideways," Dee said, checking me out in the mirror while she slathered on the lipstick. "But your pretty friend there doesn't look like he's up to doing much running right now."

I stared back at her, agony racing up my leg to my spine, and had to agree. If we had to outrun anyone else, I was toast. Not to mention the fact my foot in Pritkin's boot was sliding on what felt like a lot of blood.

"Yes, well, there's no other option at present," Pritkin snapped.

Dee levered up her nine feet of satin and platforms. "There're always options, sugar," she said, and pushed him through the wall. "You, too," she told me, pulling me up and copping a feel of Pritkin's ass at the same time. "Ooh, nice," she said, and pushed.

I expected a portal, but ended up merely falling through a ward that had hidden a small room. It seemed to be used by security. It was dark except for the light from a bank of televisions lined the wall in front of a small desk. Most of them showed the street outside, but one was trained on the stage. There was only one chair, and I took it.

Dee followed us in and turned the sound up. Licious was still in the spotlight, but she wasn't singing. A handful of war mages had clustered around the stage and appeared to be trying to question her in front of the audience. Pritkin rolled his eyes. "Trainees," he muttered, tugging at my boot.

"What was that?" Licious asked, bending over to push the microphone into the nearest mage's face.

"I said, that sharp tongue of yours is going to get you in trouble one day!"

She laughed, a rich, full-throated purr. "Oh, but honey. It's not sharp. It's *flexible*."

The audience roared, causing the man to flush angrily. He looked her up and down contemptuously, taking in the towering black wig, the sequins and the chandelier earrings. "Are you gay?"

"That depends. Are you lonely?" The audience erupted in jeers and catcalls. The man's fellow mages jostled him out of harm's way while Licious rose to her usual towering height. She whispered something to her pianist. "In honor of my new young friend, my last number tonight will be 'I'm Coming Out,' by Miss Diana Ross. And, baby, if you can dump your jealous friends, call me!"

Dee turned the sound back down. "I'm on next. Don't worry; I'll tell the girls to say they saw you run out a couple minutes ago. If you'd like to show your appreciation, there's a charming pink number in Augustine's window that would look divine on me." She blew us a kiss and left.

"You have strange friends," Pritkin said, finally wrestling my boot off.

I expected to see half the calf gone, judging by the pain. The khakis were soaked red to the knee, and slick streams of brilliant blood cascaded over the flesh of my bare foot. But when he pulled a knife out of my belt and slit the fabric, the actual wound was an ugly gash extending from the knee halfway to the groin.

"It's a progressive curse," Pritkin said grimly. "If left untreated, it will literally consume you."

Consume him, he meant. "I'm sorry," I gasped. "I hesitated. A mage came in the door and I didn't jump in time—"

"You aren't battle trained," Pritkin said, dismissing it with a lot more composure than I'd have shown if the circumstances were reversed.

The wound was deep and bleeding heavily. He tried to hold it closed, causing me to bite the sleeve of his coat to keep from screaming. And it only caused more blood to well up between his fingers, the hot spatter soaking the front of his capris.

He stared at it for a long second, his hands gripping my thigh, and then looked up at me. "We have to switch back."

"Now?"

"Yes, now! My body can heal this, but you don't have the necessary knowledge and I don't have time to teach you!"

"Have you forgotten ... what's circling this hotel?" I gasped.

"No." He licked his lips. "But we have to risk it. You're losing too much blood."

I'd have preferred to wait until Billy Joe caught up with us, but that could be a while and I was already cold and shaky. I didn't think this body had a while. "I'll push you out," I panted. "Just ... don't panic."

Pritkin nodded, looking pale but relatively calm. I only hoped that lasted because as close as the Rakshasas were, we wouldn't have much time if anything went wrong. I closed my eyes and let my head fall back, and the next moment, I was sitting up with Pritkin's body beneath me.

I put a ghostly arm out and no shields were in evidence. My hand went right up to his chest, and a couple of insubstantial fingers slipped inside his skin. I felt him start at the intrusion, but he didn't shy away, although I could feel him trembling. I could feel something else, too.

Unlike most ghosts, his spirit was warm and almost solid against my hand. I'd never thought to ask Billy how ghosts feel to each other. But now that I thought about it, the times I'd possessed someone who was still in-house, so to speak, they hadn't felt like Billy Joe normally did. They'd been a warm, *solid* presence. Like Pritkin.

I started rummaging around in his chest, trying to get a grip, and he began to look very nervous. "Calm down. I have an idea," I told him.

"Whatever it is, can you *hurry up*?"

I nodded. This was either going to work or it wasn't, and hesitating could be fatal. I gripped his spirit as tight as I could, stepped into my body and thrust him back into his. The whole thing took a couple of seconds, and suddenly, we were home.

He blinked at me blankly for a moment and then winced as the pain hit. "That was it? That's all it took?"

"I guess," I said dizzily. The sudden absence of pain made me a little light-headed.

"Why didn't you just do that before?"

"Because I didn't know about it before!" I snapped, sticking my head through the ward over the door.

I borrowed the least sparkly thing I could find—a plain white cotton blouse—to rip up for a bandage and ducked back inside. A glance at the monitors showed that the mages had spread out, with a few left in the club to guard the portal and the others doing a systematic search of the street. I wondered how long it would be before they decided to retrace their steps.

"I'm going to owe Dee big-time," I said, shredding the cotton with the help of Pritkin's knife. "I just hope this was off the rack."

He didn't say anything, and he was sweating and trembling by the time I got a pad secured around his leg. It didn't look like it was doing much to staunch the flow. It didn't help that there were other wounds rending his flesh in several places that I hadn't even noticed; courtesy of the chase, I assumed. But the leg was what had chills running up my arms, making my hands clumsy, churning my stomach.

"Pritkin," I said carefully. "Why hasn't the bleeding stopped?"

Perspiration gleamed in the hollow of his throat as he breathed faster and more shallow than usual. But there wasn't a flicker of emotion in his voice when he spoke. "As soon as you are able, shift back to Jonas. Get him out of here and do not leave his side. You can protect each other until the issue with the Circle is—"

"What do you mean, when *I* shift back?" I demanded, the cold feeling in my stomach growing exponentially.

"Listen to me; we don't have much time—"

"Before what?"

"Stop asking questions for once and pay attention. Don't rely on the vampires to protect you from Saunders. There are too many tricks they don't know and won't be able to counter. And tell Jonas . . . tell Jonas he needs to—"

"Stop giving me orders!" I hissed, glaring at him.

That was less than satisfying since I couldn't see him very well. What little light there was in the room seemed to fall at an angle to him, skirting his edges. I moved in front of him so I could grab his arms, so I could get in his face.

"You said you could heal this. So do it!" He wouldn't look at me. "Stop the bleeding, Pritkin," I pleaded, my fingers digging into his arms. "Stop it and I'll do whatever you want."

He licked his lips. "My energy level is . . . lower than usual. Healing will take time."

Yeah. Time he didn't have. I stared at him in utter disbelief. "You tricked me! You wanted me to switch back because you knew—" I couldn't even say it.

I stared at him, unable to believe this was happening. That he could just disappear, along with everything rich and strange he'd brought into my life. Vanished, like magic.

"You can't do this," he said, finally meeting my eyes. And if I'd had any doubts that he was serious, that look would have dispelled them. "You can't tear yourself up every time you lose someone. War—"

"Don't give me some stupid lecture about war when the person we're talking about losing is you!" I said, surprised by the savagery in my tone. At least my voice didn't shake.

His face blurred and I tasted salt on my lips. It was warm,

warm like Pritkin's hands coming up and framing my face, his thumbs brushing over my eyelids, soft as his fingers in my hair. "One person is not so important in the scheme of things," he said, and his voice was gentle, gentle when it never was, and that almost broke me.

But you *are* important, I thought. And yet he couldn't see that. In Pritkin's mind, he was an experiment gone wrong, a child cast out, a man valued by his peers only for his ability to kill the things they feared. Just once, I wished he could see what I did.

"Then neither is this," I said, leaning in and pressing my mouth to his, the kiss lightened by desperation and weighted down by everything he meant to me.

His bloody fingers tightened on my face, but he kissed me back with a tenderness, a reined-in need that contrasted painfully with his passion in Marsden's kitchen. There was no spark of electricity this time, no cool breeze rolling up my body, ecstatic and draining, no—

No power loss.

I tore away and stared at him. "Wait. What was . . . You healed earlier—back in Marsden's kitchen. A scratch on your arm. I saw it!" Pritkin didn't say anything. "You're half incubus—you can feed from my power," I said, slowly catching up. His ability must be spiritual rather than physical, like my power. That was why I could still shift, even in his body.

Like he could still heal.

"You don't have any power to spare!" he told me.

"I have more than you!" I gripped his arms. "Pritkin, you can use my power to heal—" I stopped because he was wearing an expression that I'd never seen before. It looked a little like terror.

"This is precisely what happened last time!" he said harshly, his eyes skittering to the wall, the monitors, the wastebasket in the corner. Everywhere but my face. "You saw the house. It was even more isolated then, with nothing for miles but fields and water and forest. There was no one to help, no one to hear her scream!"

And it suddenly occurred to me that it wasn't his own death that had him looking like he wanted to bolt. It was mine. He drew in air, his face strained, and a flush darkened the skin of his neck. "You don't understand the risk," he said more calmly.

"Your father tried to kill me. Believe me, I understand." It had been added to my regular nightmare list, that horrible, sucking, draining sensation that had my flesh wanting to shudder off the bone. But that had been Rosier. Pritkin hadn't wanted to hurt anyone. He'd lost control with his wife because no one had warned him about what might happen. But he knew the risk now.

Which is why he wasn't going to take it.

It was written in the glint in his eyes, the flare of his nostrils, the jut of his chin. "I can't lose you!" I told him, feeling defiant and miserable and furious all at once.

"I promise—you won't. I'll follow you. But you and Jonas have to—"

"I didn't want to do this," I said, cutting through the obvious lie. "But you're not leaving me a lot of choice. This is my call and I'm making it. Do what you need to heal."

"Yours?" It was if he'd put all the frustration he felt into a single glare. "How precisely is it yours?"

"Oh. So suddenly I'm not Pythia?"

"That has nothing to do with this!"

"It has everything to do with it! You're a war mage sworn to my service who thinks he doesn't have to actually do anything I tell you! And yes," I said, as he opened his mouth, "I know you have a lot more knowledge and experience, which is why I listen to you most of the time. But you're wrong about this because you're too emotional to see that the risk has to be taken. So I'm making the decision—which, since *I'm Pythia* and it's *my body*, is my right."

I set my hand against his thigh, surprised by the heat of skin on skin. Pritkin twitched and looked at me, lips parted and eyes a little wild. "I warned you once before what someone looks like when an incubus has drained them completely. Do you truly want to risk that?"

"I'm a big fan of safe," I told him quietly. "I really prefer it to sorry. But in this case, yeah. I'm willing to risk it."

"I don't know that I am," he said thickly.

And I just couldn't take it anymore. I closed the distance between us, slammed him back against the chair and kissed him, holding his head still with both my hands buried in that stupid, stupid hair. I half expected more resistance, because Pritkin had never met an argument he didn't like. So it was a shock when he ran his hands down my sides, cupped my hips and slid us both to the floor.

"I'm going straight to hell for this," he muttered.

"At least you'll know a lot of people," I said breathlessly. And then I couldn't talk at all because his mouth had settled hot and fierce over mine.

I pulled his shirt off over his head and then let my hands wander. I wrapped one around his neck, running fingers into his hair. It was soft and silky—always a surprise— and slightly damp, like the skin below. I used the other to smooth down that powerful body, strong and filigreed with black ink and silver scars. It was almost as familiar as my own, and yet suddenly, it felt very different.

I followed a ripple of solid muscle over the hard chest to the flat belly, and then dropped to the light dusting of hair that pointed to even more interesting areas. But Pritkin intercepted my hand, pulling it away from him. "Don't," he said roughly.

"Why?"

"Because I have to remain in control, *Miss Palmer*, or this will go very bad, very quickly."

"If you call me that one more time," I said seriously, and then forgot where I was going with it when his mouth moved to my neck. His lips trailed a line down the side of my throat and along the curve of my shoulder before closing over a spot he liked and starting to suck.

I was quickly reminded of how determined Pritkin could be. Once he got his mind set on something, he was quite ... single-minded, and right then, he was focused on driving me crazy. He was doing a pretty good job, somehow managing to get my shirt off and my bra unhooked one-handed, a calloused thumb lightly brushing a nipple.

I returned the favor, raking my nails through the dark blond hair on his chest, finding a little nub that went hard under my fingertips. I played with it until he pushed that hand away, too. I gave a moan of frustration and moved on, my hands sliding over bare, hot skin, finding the smooth punctuation of scars, pressing fingers bruise-hard into muscle and bone. There was no softness anywhere, except the velvet of his skin, the touch of his mouth.

My lips slid down the edge of one of the old, pale scars on his shoulder, feeling the faint ridge under my tongue. "Please," Pritkin said hoarsely, and I smiled against his skin. "Don't," he added, and my patience broke.

"Pritkin! Sex pretty much requires losing control, at least a little!"

"This isn't sex."

I blinked. "Oh. Then what is it?"

"An emergency!"

I started to argue and then thought twice about it. Considering what Mircea would do to Pritkin if he ever found out about this . . . Yeah. Emergency sounded good.

But something I said must have gotten through, because hands, big and warm and rough, slowly slid down my sides. And something about their touch had changed. His fingers on my skin were as exquisite as a mouth, sizzling my nerves into overload, every touch sending spikes and waves of pleasure through me. I felt him strip away my capris and I didn't care.

A chill breeze swept through the windowless room and he groaned, low and deep in his throat, and started kissing a path up my body. My heart gave an odd little skip in time with the fear and longing that spiked behind my ribs. He kissed my knee and then a line up my inner leg, applying suction as he reached the crease between thigh and groin, and I shivered at the feel of stubble against delicate skin.

His technique was magic—which I totally should have expected, I thought, torn between tears and hysterical amusement. "Is it sex yet?" I asked unevenly right before a warm, wet mouth closed over me. The laughter died in my throat.

It was perfect, perfect, a slick hot tongue tracing patterns that might have been runes against the thin cotton, but I was already too far gone to tell. He painted me with his breath, alternating between sketching patterns with soft exhalations and tracing them with the very tip of his tongue. A moment with nothing but the whisper of air against me was followed by a delicate, moist stroke, over and over until my vision was blurring with tears and my panting breath was on the verge of sobs.

That barely there sensation had my heart racing and my skin flushed and my body craving *more* like a drug. Every movement sent spikes of pleasure arcing up my spine, turning my muscles soft and helpless. I barely noticed when the breeze intensified into a skin-tingling, hair-raising rush. But it was impossible to ignore when his skin went burning hot.

I slid a hand under the edge of his ruined khakis. My fingertips skidded over a crust of dried blood, but it flaked away when I brushed at it. And beneath, there was only soft skin and hard muscle that tightened under my touch. He'd healed, I realized, so relieved I was almost giddy.

"Pritkin! I think—"

A strong hand gripped the back of my neck, a thigh pressed hard between my own, and an unmistakable firmness pressed against me. I looked up to find myself staring into ravenous, alien eyes. Black and burning, there was only the thinnest rim of green around the pupil.

He kissed me, and on the surface, nothing had changed. The feel of his hair between my fingers was the same, cool, silky, irrepressible. The way he was so intent on the kiss that he forgot to breathe was the same, too, leaving us both gasping. But suddenly, what had been a breeze became a torrent, a freezing blast of power that swept over me, leaving my muscles weak as water behind it.

Unlike Rosier's horrible leeching presence, it didn't hurt, but it was a power drain nonetheless. A big one. Pritkin was still feeding.

Chapter Twenty-seven

For a heartbeat, I felt a blind panic constrict my throat, *knowing* what this meant in my bones. But before I could protest, everything stopped, fingers and mouth sliding abruptly away from me. I looked up to see Pritkin motionless above me, sweat running off his muscles, his thighs trembling with the effort of staying still. He drew in air, his lips pressed tight together as if fighting for control.

Those alien eyes met mine, and there was horror in them, but it was quickly being overtaken by something else—raw hunger. "Go!"

I didn't need to be told twice. I scrambled away from him, not even taking the time to get to my feet, just scuttling backwards on all fours through the ward. I fell down the small step and landed on the tile floor of Dee's dressing room, panting and panicking, because my capris had twisted around my thighs, momentarily trapping me. But Pritkin didn't come through the ward.

I wasn't sure if he was going to be okay, or if he was fighting to give me a head start. I really didn't want to find out what would happen if he totally lost control, but what was the alternative? Running into a casino full of war mages? Ones who no longer seemed all that concerned about capturing rather than killing me?

I was still fighting with my clothes and trying to think when the door opened and Dee came in. She paused when she saw me, and one painted eyebrow headed north. I felt a hot blush creeping up my neck. "It isn't what it looks like," I blurted.

"Relax, honey," she said, tugging her mile of rose-covered train inside the door. "We've all ended up with our panties around our ankles at some point."

"My panties are exactly where they should be!" I told her indignantly, trying to stand. But the capris tripped me up and I went sprawling, just as an announcement blared through the bar. "*Ladies and gentlemen, we regret to inform you that there has been a bomb threat against the hotel. For your safety, we are evacuating the premises while a team of experts evaluates the situation. Please exit in an orderly manner through the lobby to the street.*"

"They're looking for us," I told Dee, trying not to lose it. "If we leave with the crowd, we'll be spotted, and if we don't, a search won't take long to find us! Not in an empty hotel!"

Dee looked thoughtful, but she didn't demand any explanations. "Can your friend do a glamourie?"

"Yes, but they're war mages. They'd sense it!" Besides, I didn't think Pritkin was up to doing too many fancy spells right now.

"I may have an idea," she said. "Gimme a minute." She went back out into the club.

I sat in her abandoned chair and got my clothes rearranged, which was harder than usual with hands that kept wanting to shake. I'd barely managed it when she was back. "It's okay with the girls—they're pissed at the Circle for ruining opening night anyway. Now we just have to convince your friend."

"Convince him of what?"

Dee told me. I was still staring at her in shock when Pritkin emerged from the ward. His color was high, but otherwise, he looked fairly composed.

That didn't last long.

"No." He said it flatly, a muscle twitching in his cheek, when Dee had gone through it a second time.

"You absolutely have the body for it," she wheedled, holding a silver-spangled sheath in front of him.

"I am not wearing a dress!"

She pursed her lips, which were currently Day-Glo orange, and grabbed something flashy and purple from the rack behind her.

"There's always the catsuit. Of course, it's skin tight, so we'll have to hide the candy, but I can help with—"

I managed to grab Pritkin's arm before the catsuit ended up in pieces. "They know what you look like," I pointed out while pulling on my own disguise. "And even if they didn't, you're covered in blood. You can't go out there like that!"

"If I'm going to die tonight, I would prefer it to be with a little dignity!"

"I don't get you," I said, leaning against the wall for support. My five-inch, fire-engine-red, glitter-covered Mary Janes were just as hard on the ankles as they looked. "You just spent over a day in a woman's body—"

"Not by choice!"

"—and you're hundreds of years old. Didn't men once wear makeup and—"

"Court fops, perhaps. I wasn't one!"

"Then expand your horizons," I told him, throwing a boa around his neck. "And pick something."

Pritkin eyed the selection Dee had provided with loathing. She noticed and crossed her arms over her massive chest. "You're cute, but you're getting on my last gay nerve."

"I'm never going to live this down," Pritkin muttered, snatching up an opera-length cape made of a profusion of gold lamé ruffles. It must have been designed with platforms and towering wigs in mind, because it swept the floor after him and the hood covered his head and face. I decided it would do.

A few minutes later, three sequined and bejeweled visions glided out of the club and into the middle of the crush on Main Street. Dee was in front, providing distraction, her massive breasts jutting out in front of her like the prow on a ship. Pritkin and I followed behind. I was kind of short for a drag queen, even in the platforms, but the rainbow-sequined jumpsuit and towering Marilyn Monroe wig more than made up for it.

The mages were everywhere, their eyes scanning the exiting crowd. Yet most barely glanced at us, despite the spectacle we made. And those who did quickly looked away when Dee blew them kisses or flashed a little thigh.

It looked like hiding in plain sight might work after all. I'd barely had the thought when a vision crashed into me with all of the subtlety of a baseball bat to the head. It knocked the breath out of me and dropped me to my knees. It was like nothing I'd experienced before, vivid and crystal clear, and so solid that I couldn't even see the street anymore.

Vegas was burning, fire leaping into the sky, shedding sparks like shooting stars. It was impossible to recognize anyone in the darkness and chaos or to pick out a single voice among the panicked crowd. Just screams and faceless, running people.

Beyond, the desert sand was being consumed, mile after mile under a blackened sky. Long after all the scrub had burnt, it raged on. Like a forest fire without a forest, or what it was: a seemingly endless exclamation of wrath from a creature with power and rage and centuries of bottled resentment but no compassion. No compassion at all.

The world had remembered the healer, the lyre player, the golden god, but had forgotten the other stories. The ones that whispered of brutal punishments, of rape and murder and a beautiful face that laughed as it flayed its enemies alive. They remembered now, for an instant, before memory was wiped clear in a rain of blood.

The vision shattered as abruptly as it had come, leaving me gasping on all fours in the middle of the sidewalk. "—a little too much wine with dinner, you know how it is. Always was a drinker," Dee was saying to someone. She reached down and pinched my cheek. "Come on, love. Up you go. You can pass out at home."

She dragged me to my feet and I did my best to keep my head down when what I actually wanted was to run back up the street screaming. My dreams had been warning me all along, but I'd been blind to what they really meant. And now it might be too late.

A cold wire tightened around my heart. There was something wrong with my chest; I couldn't seem to get a deep breath. What had I done?

Dee and Pritkin started towing me back toward the lobby again. I gripped their arms. "We can't leave."

"Oh, yes, we can," Dee said. "I think I just ruined this dress. My heart can't take another scare like that!"

"We'll deal with whatever it is later," Pritkin told me, hurrying us along.

"Apollo's here."

He stopped abruptly, and we were almost run down by a harassed-looking woman with a kid in each hand. "Watch it!" she snapped, pulling the kids around. Pritkin dragged me over to the sidewalk.

"That's impossible!" he hissed. "The spell—"

"He got around it," I whispered. "I don't know how, but I Saw it. He's here!"

He was shaking his head in disbelief. "That spell has held for more than three thousand years. Yet he suddenly finds a way around it now?"

"I can't explain it. I just know what I Saw."

"It could be the future, the outcome of a civil war within the Circle. What could happen if we don't solve our internal—"

"No!" I looked around, rubbing my arms as chills broke out all over them. "I've been Seeing the same thing ever since MAGIC blew up. But only in pieces, like my usual visions. But this . . . He's here. I know it!"

"He can't be." Pritkin was adamant.

Dee had been looking at us out of the corner of her eye, and she'd started to edge away when I grabbed her wrist. "You told me once you can sense magic, right?"

"Maybe," she said warily.

"Can you sense anything unusual now?"

"Other than the battle raging upstairs?" she asked with understandable sarcasm.

"I mean a single source, stronger than all the others. Like . . . like a supernova."

"Maybe. But it don't matter because there's no way I'm going back in there! Not for—"

"A shopping spree at Augustine's? Ten minutes, anything you can grab?"

Her eyes narrowed and she looked me over. "You got that kind of cash?"

"I've got that kind of credit."

"I'd think you were lying, but you did have those shoes. . . ." She licked her lips. "Half an hour, take it or leave it."

A war mage walked up. "There's a mandatory evacuation," he told us. "You'll have to be moving on."

"I'll take it," I said.

"Shit. I knew you were going to say that," Dee told me, and slammed her gigantic purse into the mage's face. He went down, and may have also gotten stepped on as 250 pounds of satin-clad fashionista ran over him and headed back up the street.

We ran to catch up, battling the tide of humanity going the other way. Mages were converging on us from all sides—it wasn't like we were easy to miss. I grabbed Dee's train to keep it from getting trampled and she towed me along like a freight train, scattering tourists and roses everywhere.

We passed the fake feed store that marked the halfway point with most of the mages on the street after us, and plowed into a dozen more. They'd formed a half-moon shape in the street, forcing the crowd to surge around them and re-form. As soon as we ran out of tourists, we barreled straight into them.

Dee almost knocked a hole in the wall of leather coats, but they kept their feet. I looked behind us, but the mages had closed the circle, leaving us nowhere to run. And then one of the closest caught sight of me. "Cassandra Palmer."

The brown eyes searching my face still looked like they belonged to a mid-level flunky, but the snarl kind of ruined the effect. I didn't say anything, panic and exhaustion closing my throat. But Saunders didn't seem to expect an answer.

His gaze slid to Pritkin, who had stopped beside me. "Or is it?"

He looked Pritkin up and down, taking in the ruffled gold cape with a raised brow. "I've heard it whispered that the Pythia has more skills than she lets on. It would appear to be true. I've always been told that possession is impossible for humans, but either I accept that I was misinformed, or I have to believe that a slip of a girl threw me against a wall and almost shattered my shields. Which do you think I prefer?"

Pritkin didn't answer him, either. He fiddled with his cape instead, looking twitchy and almost nervous. Saunders smiled.

"Of course, I could solve the riddle by killing both of

you, but that would leave no one to put on trial. And the public does love the legal niceties," he said, taking a few steps back. He glanced around, but the crowd had thinned and the few remaining tourists were being hustled out of the way by the mages who had been following us.

At a nod, his men parted to either side, pulling Dee and me back, and leaving Saunders and Pritkin alone in the middle of the street. "On a count of three, I think?" he asked politely. "Wasn't that the way things were settled in the old—"

Pritkin threw out a hand and Saunders sailed off his feet, into the air and smashed against the side of a fake barn. Judging by the sound his skull made on impact, I didn't think he'd bothered with shields. He slid down the side, bounced off a wagon and was speared by the iron spike atop a menu sign.

I swallowed and looked away as his body began to spasm. No. Definitely no shields.

The mage holding my arm twisted it painfully behind me. I cried out and tried to pull away, but there was nowhere to go. There was another group of mages jogging down the street toward us, as if the other side needed reinforcements.

One of them, a tall African-American in a battered coat, pushed his way through the circle to me. "Hello, Cassie," he said somberly. He looked at the mage holding me. "Let her go, son."

"They just killed the Lord Protector!"

Caleb scanned the area until his eyes lit on Saunders' still quivering form. "Doesn't look dead to me. Don't you think you boys should maybe get him down?" I suddenly found myself released as the Apprentices rushed to aid their fallen leader.

"Caleb—" Pritkin began.

His onetime colleague raised a hand. "Jonas called us. Said he challenged and Saunders refused."

"Yes." Pritkin went very still.

Caleb exchanged glances with the mages he'd brought along. None of them looked young enough to be trainees. Several had gray hair, and one or two looked like they might even be Marsden's age. Their expressions ranged from sour to disgusted to war mage neutral.

"Well. I guess that makes him an outlaw."

"And us?"

Caleb smiled slightly. "Technically, there are still warrants out for both of you. The fact that the man who issued them is currently under suspicion himself doesn't negate that." I licked my lips and started to speak, but Pritkin's hand tightened on my arm. "So if I see you, I guess I'll have to arrest you."

Pritkin nodded.

"By the way, I liked the old coat better," Caleb said, and turned away.

Dee sidled off as soon as the group of mages parted in front of us, fanning herself with a hand. "I never thought I'd say this, but too much testosterone. We need to get out of here," she told me, heading for a bank of elevators.

"We need to find Apollo," I told her, catching her arm.

"Well, he ain't down here! We have to go up."

"You can sense him, then?"

"Oh, yeah. There's something up there, all right. Although I'm not getting a who so much as a what."

"He's . . . not exactly human," I explained, not having time to go into it all.

"I should have asked for an hour," she muttered, and then started for the elevators again.

Pritkin caught her arm. "We could get trapped that way. Saunders' supporters are all over the place, and it's going to take time to round them up."

She looked at him for a second, and then her eyes slid to the stairs. "You have got to be kidding."

He wasn't kidding. Of course, I thought savagely, Pritkin was wearing his usual boots. Dee and I were in platforms almost as high as the steps. Navigating even one flight in those ought to be an Olympic event. By the time we'd made it up five floors, I was drenched with sweat and had small explosions going off behind my eyelids.

I stopped in the stairwell, bent over and gasping, only my hand on the railing keeping me up. Pritkin just threw me over his shoulder and kept going, earning him a speculative look from Dee. "Don't even think about it," he told her. "I'm not carrying you."

"That wasn't what I was thinking," she cooed, and he

flushed. I guess there weren't any mages in the stairwell, because Dee's laugh could have been heard all the way down to the lobby.

By the time we got as far as the stairs would take us, Dee was no longer laughing. "I think I hate you," she told Pritkin, who had all but run her up the stairs. She looked like hell. Her roses had mostly been lost on the street and the rest had fallen off on the stairs. Her wig was askew, her makeup had sweated off and a huge fake eyelash had come unglued and was clinging tenuously to one cheek.

"Good for the figure," he said, putting me down. He was also hot and sweaty after our marathon, with damp tendrils of hair stuck to his forehead and neck. His lashes had gone spiky dark, turning his eyes emerald. Grungy was a surprisingly good look for him.

I didn't know what I looked like. I preferred it that way. If it was anywhere near as bad as I felt, I'd scare off any mages we encountered before they could shoot me.

"This is where I get off," Dee said, sitting on a step to rub her arches. "The power is coming from the next floor up."

I looked at Pritkin. "The penthouse."

I didn't have a key card, but Pritkin convinced the elevator to take us up anyway. The doors opened onto a deathly quiet foyer that looked a little worse for the wear. The gold flocked wallpaper had a big hole through it, the bronze sculpture had half melted into a Dalí-esque mess and the cow skin rug was covered in dirty boot prints. But the John Wayne posters had survived without a scratch.

We walked into the living room. Wind through the broken balcony doors was blowing the curtains inward in a billowing mass that, for a moment, made me think someone was there. But nothing else moved, except for the chandelier swinging gently overhead, no longer spilling light onto the roadster still parked below.

"Where did they all go?" I asked, looking around at the carnage. At least Casanova wouldn't need to gut the place. The mages had pretty much done it for him.

I breathed a slight sigh of relief. Dee had been wrong. There was no one here.

Pritkin shrugged. "They took the fight elsewhere," he said,

crossing the lumber and glass obstacle course to the balcony. I followed, having to concentrate not to break my neck.

Outside was a wreck of destroyed patio furniture, shattered glass and a pool filled with flotsam. And a body, I saw sickly. Someone wearing a war mage coat was bobbing gently on the surface. Pritkin fished him out, and then I almost wished he hadn't because the face was mostly gone.

I bit my lip and looked around. I wanted to check the rest of the apartment, but what if I found Rafe's body? Had they gotten him out in time? What if I found—

"We need to check the place for survivors," I said, cutting my thoughts off. I wouldn't think that way. I wouldn't think at all. I'd just go look because I couldn't stand not knowing.

We didn't have a flashlight, but the casino's light through the windows was enough to see by, once our eyes adjusted. We found three more bodies in the dining room, none of them vampires. There was something to be said for masters, after all, I thought with relief. And then I wondered if they'd leave much of a corpse, with some of the spells the mages could throw. My stomach sank back down to my toes.

I'd turned to move on to the kitchen when Pritkin caught my arm. He put a finger to his lips, and the next moment, I heard it—a shuffling sound, like someone walking through the debris and not bothering to be quiet. We reentered the darkened living room to see a shape outlined against the expanse of windows leading out to the patio. It took me a second to recognize it.

"Sal!"

She turned slowly, obviously not surprised to see us. Of course, with vampire hearing, she'd probably known we were there all along. "Cassie? Do you know what happened? Where is everyone?"

"You just got back?" I asked, already knowing the answer. She hadn't been here when everything went to hell. I imagined that it would be a little bit of a shock to come back to this. It was shocking to me, and I knew how it had gotten this way.

"A few minutes ago. I didn't want to interrupt if the meeting was—"

She broke off at the sound of the front door opening. A moment later, Marco stepped into the room. Like Sal, he took a moment to survey the damage. "Well, I guess anything would have been an improvement," he said, coming down the stairs.

Sal moved a few yards back, keeping her eyes glued to Marco. "It looks like we'll have to find somewhere else to sleep. It's almost daylight."

He shook his head. "Won't do, Sal," he said quietly. "The master ordered five of you to stay away until just before dawn. And only you came back."

"And you," Sal snapped. She looked him up and down contemptuously. "You can ape Mircea all you like, but the finest clothes in the world will never give you his power. And everyone knows how much you hate him for that!"

It took me a second to realize what they were talking about. With everything else, I'd almost forgotten the trap Mircea had laid for the traitor. I looked at Marco, suddenly tense again, but his eyes never left Sal.

"Hate's a little strong," Marco demurred. "But you're right. I like power. I just got limits on what I'll do for it."

Sal kept her eyes on Marco, but she spoke to me. "Cassie, think about it. Mircea told us the kind of person they've been looking for. Someone close to a senator, someone trusted, someone with resentment Myra might have been able to use!"

"He did say that," I agreed, as Pritkin shifted next to me. He was trying to keep Marco and Sal both in sight as she started backing up. I don't know why; the only thing behind her was the balcony, and we were twenty floors up.

"And Marco said it himself—I'm just a hick," Sal reminded me. "Just like you. A nobody from a court so far out in the sticks, most people never even heard of it!"

"Making you too powerless for Myra to have bothered about," Marco agreed.

I blinked at him, confused. "Are you confessing?" I demanded.

He looked slightly amused. "Would that surprise you?"

"Hell, yes! Mircea made you my bodyguard! And he didn't trade you out, even after he got Marlowe's list of suspects. He would never have done that if . . ." I trailed off, belatedly realizing what I'd just said.

"Sounds like she's voting for you, too, Sal," Marco murmured.

"Just tell me where the Consuls are, Cassie," Sal said, ignoring him. "We need to warn them that there could be trouble."

I was in too much in shock to reply, not that Marco gave me a chance. "Of course, there's an easy way to settle this," he told her. "We'll just wait until the master gets back and ask him."

"He's not *my* master," she hissed.

"He might have been, in time. He's a good one, as masters go," Marco said with a slight twist to his lips.

"I wouldn't know," Sal said bitterly.

He shrugged. "Master's been busy. You should have been patient."

"Right," she said contemptuously. "I should spend my time shopping, maybe getting my nails done, while the war comes closer every day. All Mircea knows how to do is talk! Rafe ending up like that . . . It could be any of us next! Tony may be a worm, but at least he knows how to act!"

I'd been looking back and forth, trying to keep up, but finally something made sense. "Oh, God. Mircea never broke your bond. Tony is still your master."

"And still giving me little tasks to perform, all the way from Faerie."

I was hearing it, but I couldn't believe it. Sal wasn't some superspy. She wasn't a traitor. She was just Sal. I'd known her all my life.

"You told me once you'd kill him if you ever saw him again!" I accused. "How can you take orders from him?"

"Because I don't have a choice," she spat. "I practically begged Mircea to break my bond, but all he did was talk: *soon, soon*. Well, it wasn't soon enough!"

"But . . . Alphonse is fifty years younger than you!" I protested. "And he's been able to ignore Tony's orders for years! You don't have to—"

She cut me off with a laugh. "Yeah. And he's an idiot, you know? I taught him everything—how to talk, how to act, what to do to impress the boss. He'd be nothing without me. But power doesn't care how smart you are. Doesn't even care how old you are. Some people never reach master status, and others do it in a matter of decades! And I've never been strong. Why do you think I put up with Alphonse? He was the only way I had any position at all."

"That's why we couldn't catch you," Marco said, lighting a cigarette. "It was pretty clever. Everyone was looking for the traitor among the old masters, the guys close enough to a Senate member for Myra to have wasted her time trying to turn them."

"Which is why Tony decided to use me."

"The Consuls aren't here, as you can see," Pritkin said, watching her narrowly. "Whatever your master ordered you to do, you've failed. Mircea can still break your bond. You have no reason to—"

He broke off at the identical expressions of disgust Sal and Marco were sending him. "Why the hell do you hang around this guy?" Marco asked me.

Pritkin looked at me, and I shook my head. "It doesn't work that way," I told him numbly.

"Why not? If she is truly under a compulsion—"

"Vampire law doesn't care about the why. It only cares about the result. Or in this case, the intended result. And Sal came back here intending to kill the leaders of the six vampire senates. It doesn't get any worse than that."

"Close, but no cigar," Sal told me, sounding awfully unconcerned for someone facing certain death. "I'm just the doorman, you might say." She held out her hand, and a shaft of light through the balcony doors lit up something on her open palm.

"My pentagram," I said, recognizing it even from this distance. "You said you'd get it fixed."

"Yeah. Only it's a lot more useful broken."

"I don't get it."

She laughed. "You know, I used to think it was ludicrous— you with Lord Mircea. I figured he was just using you, like everyone said. But lately, I've begun to think you two deserve each other. You're just as clueless as he is!"

Marco tensed. "Give it to me," he told her.

"Or what? You'll kill me?" she asked incredulously. "You don't have a lot of threats left, Marco."

"Oh, I don't know. Mircea didn't specify how the traitor was to die, just told me to take care of it if anybody showed up. I got a lot of leeway here, Sal. Give me a reason to make it quick."

"Oh, yeah. That's tempting. Or I could follow Tony's orders, and when his side wins, I not only *don't die*, I get the position I always deserved. How about that instead?"

"Your side isn't going to win," Pritkin told her.

Sal ignored him. It looked like she was having fun. I was beginning to wonder how hard she had tried to resist Tony.

"Remember MAGIC?" she asked me. "Because this is gonna make that look like a sideshow."

"What are you talking about?" I demanded. "It's just a ward. It can't—"

"A ward that channels your power—or used to," she corrected. "Lately, it's been channeling something else instead. You know, that damn wardsmith gave me a fright. I thought for sure one of you would figure it out. You survived direct contact with the ley line even though you couldn't access your power. Yet even when he told you your ward was feeding off the Circle, you still didn't get it!"

"Get what?"

Pritkin drew in air, and Sal grinned at him. "Dumb as a rock, isn't she?" Her gaze returned to me. "Let me spell it out. Tony and company figured out a way around Artemis' spell. It acts like a lock on a door, but a door isn't much help when the wall of the house is split open. To get Apollo back, they needed to rip apart the space between worlds. They needed to crack open a ley line."

"But nobody on Earth has that kind of power," I protested. "That was the problem all along, trying to figure out who . . ." I stopped, a really horrible idea surfacing.

Sal saw my expression and grinned. "Yeah, that was the best part, hearing everybody say, over and over, that no one had that kind of power. When it was right under their noses, all the time. *You* had it. Apollo gave part of his power to the Pythias. All we had to figure out was how to access it."

And suddenly, I caught up. I looked at Pritkin. "You said the Circle wouldn't give you one of their tattoos, because power drains work both ways. They've been draining me, haven't they?"

He nodded slowly. "It's possible."

Sal snorted. "Hell, it was easy. Richardson—our guy on the inside—just opened the conduit to your ward again. The Circle had closed it off, thinking you might try to drain power from them. Instead, we opened it up to do the same thing to you. Then Richardson got it to our allies by bundling it with the percentage Saunders was selling to fund his early retirement."

"You used my power to weaken the ley line," I said, still not quite believing it.

"Yeah. We almost had it porous enough to get Apollo and his army through, but Richardson just had to pull his little stunt with you. He hated you so much, he was afraid someone else would get to kill you. And then the battle broke out and ripped a huge-ass gash in the ley line, screwing everything up!"

"But why didn't Apollo come through then?" I asked, confused.

Sal just stared at me. "Don't you get it yet? He's been here since MAGIC fell! But it wasn't supposed to happen then, and it took everyone by surprise. The breach was supposed to take place over Vegas and to have to run all the way to the ley line sink at MAGIC before it was sealed. That would have given him time to get his whole army through."

"But it hit MAGIC and sealed almost instantly," I said, remembering that awesome funnel of power disappearing over the hill. I suddenly remembered something else, too.

My vision at MAGIC had shown me a ruined Dante's. I finally understood why. If I had gone back and changed time, ensuring that MAGIC never fell, I would have handed Apollo everything he wanted. In that case, the original plan would have been carried out and he and his whole army would be here. And by now, the magical community would be well on its way to extinction.

My other visions were starting to make sense, too. The second had shown me the route the ley line's destruction was meant to take on its way from Vegas to MAGIC. It was trying to do more than warn me about Rafe; it was telling me that the danger was still there. The third vision had reinforced that once again and showed me at the center of it all.

Because it was my power that would give our enemies a victory.

Chapter Twenty-eight

"Apollo got through," Sal told me, "but the rest of his forces didn't. He was back, but he'd been severely weakened when the line exploded around him, and he was stuck in a world with a quarter million war mages, any fraction of whom could banish him again. He realized that he needed to bring through his army before he threw down with the Circle."

"But contact with the ley line fried my ward. You can't get any more power!" I pointed out.

She shook her head. "As long as the ward was on your body, it continued to pull from you, but instead of transmitting the power to us, it stored it. It's been building up the amount we need ever since the breach."

So that was what Dee had sensed. Not Apollo, but my pentagram. And Sal, waiting for her master.

"Now we have enough," Sal said cheerfully.

"Because the line is still weak," I murmured. Mircea had said that it would take a couple of days to calm back down.

"Yeah, that's why we have to do it now, before the line starts to strengthen again. Of course, Apollo thought it was a bonus that the consuls were also meeting here tonight. Destroy the leaders and everyone else would fall that much easier." She grinned at me. "But you know, I really think he'll settle for you."

The sky flared red beyond the balcony doors. Crimson

streaks that were nothing like a sunrise crackled across the heavens, shedding a killing radiance that made the hotel's electric lights look feeble by comparison. Something was coming.

The whole time she talked, Sal had been slowly backing up, edging closer to the balcony. No one had tried to stop her. After all, even a vampire was unlikely to survive a fall like that. But now she could toss the pentagram over the edge anytime she chose, and we'd never find it. Not before her master did.

"Give me the pentagram, Sal," Marco said again. He suddenly sounded deadly serious.

"Are you still trying that? When you have nothing to offer me but a quick death?" She sneered. "Don't expect me to be so generous with you!"

The wind picked up as the light grew brighter. It looked like dawn was coming early. Or the sun anyway, I thought dizzily.

And then, faster than my eyes could track, Marco moved. I blinked and Sal was still standing there, but the hand clutching my ward was flying through the air—straight at me. She twisted, a snarl overtaking her face, and the next second Marco was staggering back, a sliver of the ruined couch frame sticking out of his chest.

I didn't get a chance to see if it got his heart. Because Sal's severed hand hit me and the impact jarred my ward loose. It went flying, I dove after it and Sal dove after me.

And then, just as suddenly, she was gone.

I felt a breath of wind pass me and looked up in time to see Nicu come out of nowhere and tackle Sal by the waist. I don't know if he didn't realize that she was as close to the edge as she was, or if he thought the railing would catch them. But it had taken as much abuse as the rest of the apartment and gave way under their combined weight. I saw bright gold eyes staring at me for an instant before they fell, and then they were gone.

Something bit into my palm. I looked down to see that I'd clutched my ward so tight, it was digging into my flesh. I pried it loose and looked up, only to realize that I wasn't likely to keep it long.

Light spilled over the balcony, bright as the noonday sun. I couldn't make out what I was looking at, at first. Until it came closer, and then it was nothing like I'd expected.

I'd met Apollo, at least in a metaphysical sense, a number of times before. But he hadn't been in this world then and couldn't reveal himself in anything other than mental impressions. And since my brain had interpreted them, he had always been in a form I could understand. This wasn't.

A glowing tangle of light hovered in the sky, every color and no color, transparent like water, huge and abstract. If anything, it looked like a fractal on a computer screen, constantly changing into new patterns. None of them were particularly menacing, but the power radiating off the creature was enough to scorch my skin even this far away.

Apollo had once told me that I wouldn't be able to withstand him in person, but I hadn't known what he meant. I did now. Frozen in place, I stared into the fiery center of a creature my mind couldn't even comprehend, pitifully aware of my own insignificance, and wondered how I could ever have thought I could fight something like this.

The bands of light thickened, swirling around a central point, and formed themselves into a monstrous head rising clear and fluid against the heavens. Faint points of light glittered in the huge skull, like savage eyes cold and measuring. My breath stuttered in my chest, out of rhythm with the sudden mad pace of my heart. Swaying on my feet, I clasped my hands together so the shaking wouldn't show.

"Cassandra Palmer." The voice was surprisingly soft, like a breath of wind. "We finally meet in the flesh. So to speak."

"Apollo."

"If you like. This world once had many names for me. Ra, Sol, Surya, Marduk, Inti . . . It has forgotten them all. It will be reminded." The god's intense gaze was fixed on me with almost affectionate mockery. I didn't know if his anger had burnt itself out, or if he was merely savoring the moment now that I was finally trapped.

"I've seen it," I said dully. "The city in ruins . . ."

"I've decided to leave it as a monument to your failure. The former seat of the blind Pythia." He laughed. "You know, even your namesake did better. She understood what was coming but could not convince others. You, on the other hand, have been wandering about as foolishly as everyone else. It has been most entertaining."

The wind picked up, stinging my eyes. "And I put the power to bring your army here into Sal's hand. I gave it to you."

The great face didn't change, but the air around me shimmered with laughter. "Yes, that is the very best part. I won't destroy your friends, your world, Cassandra. *You* will. I wanted to be sure you knew that, before the end."

The voice remained soft, but the light patterns suddenly changed. The huge face had been almost clear, but now dense blue-black boiled up from the bottom, filling the form like ink in water. No, I thought, staring up in blank terror. It didn't look like his anger had faded, at all.

I heard the sound of a car engine start behind me. Before I could turn around, an arm reached out of nowhere, grabbed the front of my shirt and dragged me into the seat of Marsden's roadster. My legs were hanging over the side, my butt still in the air, as we drove straight off the balcony.

"You're wasting your time, Cassandra!" Apollo thundered. "Where do you think you can hide?"

I was too busy screaming to reply. I grabbed the seat belt in both fists as my legs floated up behind me. I looked down at the concrete speeding up at us and saw no bubble of protection, no jumping blue fire. And then the air tore open around us and we were swept into the middle of the line.

I slammed back down, my legs landing painfully on the trunk as we suddenly leveled off. Pritkin was in the driver's seat, frantically shifting gears, as I began to slide off the side. He hauled me into the seat with one hand while steering around a very surprised war mage with the other. The ley line was alive with activity. Ships and men were everywhere, still fighting a battle that no longer mattered.

"You do know how to drive one of these, right?" I asked nervously. The car had a lot of weird buttons and gears I hadn't noticed before. And none were labeled.

"In theory."

"In theory?"

"I've been with Jonas a few times."

"How many is a few?"

"Counting today?"

"Yes!"

"Er, that would be . . . twice then."

I bit my lip on a retort and instead twisted around to stare behind us. Apollo wasn't there. He was right—in a world he controlled, there would be nowhere to hide. I might be able to stay ahead of him for a little while, but he'd find me eventually. I doubted I'd care very much at that point, after he finished destroying everything I loved.

"Turn around," I told Pritkin.

"What?"

I grabbed the wheel and swerved. A war mage shot by us and out of the line, as we banked at an angle that almost had us both plummeting along with him. Pritkin cursed and wrestled the car back into the middle of the stream. "Don't touch that! And why the hell do you want to go back?"

"Apollo isn't following us. I'm not sure he realizes I have the ward. I never had a chance to tell him."

"You *want* him to follow us?"

"Yes."

I didn't get a chance to explain. The wind pushed my hair out of my face, allowing me to see a cloud of pure energy barreling right for us. "I think he knows," Pritkin said, swerving violently and sending us careening toward the outer edge of the line.

"Back! Back!" I screamed as my half of the car was pushed completely out of the line. I could see Pritkin silhouetted inside all that jumping energy, while on the other side of me the parking lot was racing up at us at breathtaking speed. "No, pull up, pull up!" I screeched as we headed straight for a group of tourists who had just come out of the casino doors.

"Would you make up your mind?" he demanded, fighting with the car. I just stared at the tourists, who were now pointing at us with awed expressions, watching them get nearer and nearer, and— Pritkin suddenly swerved upward, maybe two feet above their heads.

"Building!" I yelled as one of Dante's towers loomed straight in front of us. Pritkin could sail right on through in the non-space of the line. But I was about to be vertical roadkill if he didn't—

Pritkin swerved sharply and the building slid by, close enough that I could have reached out and touched it. A couple in bed stared out at us from a third-floor window, openmouthed, and then Pritkin jerked the wheel again. Suddenly I was back inside the line, lying against the seat, panting.

Apollo was right on our tail. The energy lines ran slower at the outer edges of the line, and we'd lost most of our lead. I reached over and jerked the steering wheel hard to the left. "Do not touch the wheel!" Pritkin snarled.

"We have to stay in the center, or he'll catch us for sure!"

"And if you keep attempting to drive, we're both going to be—" He stopped, staring behind us.

I twisted around, but other than an angry god, I didn't see anything. "What now?"

"Rakshasas. They're following us."

"How many?"

"Many."

I was thrown back against my seat as Pritkin floored it. "We need to get him as far away from populated regions as possible," he told me. "Jonas can rally the Circle. However that creature got in, we can banish him again—"

"You told me that spell takes thousands of mages! There's no time for that."

"Do you have a better idea?"

"I have an idea," I hedged. I wasn't taking any bets on how good it was. "Just get us some distance ahead."

We left the city behind, speeding into an area of high rounded hills and smooth, empty valleys. The ley line twisted and turned among them, and sometimes through them, and that seemed to give Pritkin an idea. "Hold on," he told me, and raced straight for the very top of the line.

We left the line, sailing into the vast and brilliant canopy above. So many stars, jeweled and burning bright. A meteor slid eastward. Beautiful, I thought dazedly, as a roar split the air behind us.

I turned in time to see the world go briefly monochrome in a tremendous flash of light, the hills jumping up at me against the terrible whiteness behind. Then we plunged back into the line, and a cloud of dirt and rubble incinerated all around us, throwing burning bits against the car's shield. "What was that?"

"Slowed him down!" Pritkin said with a little of Marsden's mania in his eyes. "He took off half the hill trying to follow us. But it wasn't enough. We need bigger mountains!"

He jumped again just as the line curved around another hill. We went one way and Apollo went the other, taking out the hilltop along with him. But I didn't care because the ground was racing up at us and there was no line to catch us and—

The line curved around the other side of the hill and caught us.

"You knew that was there, right?" I asked, shaken.

Pritkin swallowed. "Of course."

I shut my eyes. "Can we make it as far as Chaco Canyon?"

"Even if we could, he would simply hop with us! He can follow us wherever we go!"

"But can we *get* there?"

"No," he said tersely. "My weapons aren't designed for fighting a god, and I'm running out of tricks."

I opened my eyes and stared at the dashboard. "Then maybe Marsden has a few." There was a panel of buttons by the steering wheel that didn't look like standard equipment. "What do those do?"

"I don't know. Some of Jonas' meddling. And don't—"

I punched a green one and we rocketed forward. We were going fast enough to throw me back against the seat and to flatten my cheeks to my face. I couldn't see. The pressure was too great for me to even catch a breath, too great for me to so much as move. The ley line looked like an almost solid tube around us, the flashes and flares streaming together into one long line of color.

"—touch anything," Pritkin finished as we shuddered back to normal speed.

I drew in a gasping breath, my lungs feeling flattened in my chest, and leaned forward against the dash. I groaned when I had enough breath, feeling every pain, every bruise. But when I raised my head, the vortex was shining like a small star in the distance.

We made it there ahead of Apollo, but only just. We

jumped from the dazzling energy of the line into the non-space pooling around the vortex with maybe a ten-second lead. Pritkin was desperately searching for the correct current that would allow us to hop to the next vortex, so he didn't see Apollo enter. But it was all I could see.

This time, it seemed, Apollo was done talking. The boiling energy ball never even slowed down. Neither did the huge flock of demons that poured in after him. The faint glimmers of thousands of Rakshasas were visible even to my eyes as they wheeled around us like a colony of bats.

I grabbed the wheel and jerked it straight at the vortex. "We've got to get closer in!"

"Closer to what?" Pritkin snarled, fighting the current to keep us from doing exactly that.

"The vortex!"

"Are you mad?"

"You said we need a weapon to use against a god." I pointed at the Rakshasas. "I think we've found one!"

Pritkin's head jerked up, watching the long arc of demons flowing around the vortex. I saw when he realized the same thing I had—they weren't following us. Every single one of them was clustered on Apollo's tail, like dust following a comet.

"Apollo is an energy being," he said slowly.

"*Life* energy," I corrected. The very kind the Rakshasas fed on.

"And he isn't from Earth. So the prohibition doesn't apply."

I nodded. "But he's shielded. If he gets close enough to the vortex, it may weaken his protection enough for them to get at him."

"And it may do the same to us!"

"Do you have a better idea?" I demanded as the black cloud caught up with us.

"No," he said, and swerved straight for the heart of the vortex. It had been my plan, but I screamed anyway, staring into the face of oblivion. Then Pritkin threw on the brakes and bumped across three currents before sliding to a halt on an inner one. It had a shorter orbit and whipped us around the phenomenon at a crazy pace.

We came rushing back around the vortex, Pritkin fighting the current to keep us from falling in, the car groaning and shaking in protest. And then we had to duck as Apollo came rocketing by in front of us. He must have gotten a lot closer to the phenomenon than we had, because his shields were virtually gone.

The Rakshasas realized it the same time I did and dove as one entity straight for him. We passed out of sight once more, and by the time we zoomed back around, the cloud of raw energy had been savaged. It looked like the Rakshasas didn't have much reverence for gods of any sort.

Apollo broke and ran, but they pursued him over and around the vortex, weaving easily through the lines of energy. The massive battle churned up the currents, tossing us around like a ship on the high seas, and for a few moments, I couldn't see anything. I finally caught sight of a much reduced energy sphere edging closer to the pulsing heart of the vortex.

That may have been deliberate—Apollo might have thought that the energy it was giving off would hurt the demons badly enough that they would give up the chase. But it didn't seem to affect them much that I could see, possibly because they weren't entirely in this world. Maybe that's why they were able to pull back when he got a little too close and the vortex sucked him in.

The death of a god caused barely a ripple on the surface of the massive ley line sink at the heart of the vortex. But an energy wave radiated outward, picking up our small bubble of protection and throwing it completely out of the lines. Pritkin cursed, grabbed me around the waist and jumped clear.

We started to drift slowly downward in a chute formed from Pritkin's shields, just as the star-filled sky above bled into golden dawn. The crash of Marsden's car was barely audible so far below. But Pritkin winced as it smacked down and immediately went up in a ball of flame.

"We got out of this alive!" I reminded him, hardly able to believe it.

"*You* did," he said, staring at the burning pile of metal far below. "Jonas is going to kill me."

"Explain again why I am paying for this . . . *this*?" Mircea asked, indicating with a gesture the cackling drag queen who was all but dismantling Augustine's shop. The great man himself was standing by the door, wincing at the carnage and fingering my AmEx. He still detested me, but it seemed my money was okay.

"I'm paying for it, or I will be," I assured him. "Jonas says I have a month's back salary coming." Of course, at Augustine's prices, that meant I might be able to pay Mircea off in a decade or so.

He sighed and laid his head back against the nice Louis XIV striped satin chair that Augustine had rushed to bring up for him. I'd had to fetch my own. I shifted uncomfortably. Everything hurt.

Mircea noticed and opened an eye to look at me. "You are going to give me a stroke," he said flatly, with none of his usual charm. "I sent you away to keep you safe. Instead, you kill the Lord Protector—"

"That was Pritkin, and Saunders isn't actually dead," I corrected. "Jonas is circulating the rumor that he was tragically wounded while bravely battling Apollo's forces."

"Apollo didn't have any forces."

"Yes, but nobody knows that." Luckily very few mages had witnessed what really occurred, and they'd mostly been Apprentices. Apprentices who currently had bad headaches from having their memories altered.

Marsden had decided that it was better to get his rival out of the way diplomatically rather than risk civil war when we could least afford it. He'd managed to convince the Senate, but Mircea didn't appear pleased to have the former head of the Circle still with us. I had a sneaking suspicion that Saunders' recovery wasn't going to go well.

"And for an encore, you kill a god!" Mircea accused.

"Technically, the demons did that. Or maybe the ley line. We're not completely—"

"So your argument is that you did *nothing*?"

"Isn't that what you wanted me to do? Swim, read, maybe do a little shopping?"

"Yes! I would vastly prefer that you spend your days doing exactly that rather than come back to me covered in blood!"

"At least I came back."

"This time."

"Mircea . . ."

"Yes, you have a job to do, or so you keep informing me. I understand that—intellectually. Do not expect me to like it."

"But no more handcuffs?"

He gave me one of his slow smiles, the first sign of good humor I'd seen. "Not unless you request them."

I swallowed. "About that . . ."

He sighed and laid his head back again. "Why do I doubt that this is going to be a request for one in every color?"

"They come in colors?" He smiled without opening his eyes. "No! No, I mean, I've been thinking. We knew each other when I was a child, but now . . . there's just so much I don't know about you."

"You know me," he said, his forehead wrinkling. "Better than most."

"But it doesn't feel that way. I've never even been to your court!"

"That's easily remedied. Indeed, you may visit sooner than you think. Mage Marsden is proposing to have your inauguration there. A goodwill gesture to the Senate after the unpleasantness with his predecessor."

"Will the consuls still be there?" I asked nervously.

"Probably." Mircea opened his eyes to frown at the ceiling. "The negotiations are dragging somewhat. The Consuls are currently asking why they should agree to an alliance when our chief adversary is dead."

"They can't be serious! We have a major war brewing in Faerie, Tony's group is still on the loose and plotting who knows what, and we have no idea how Apollo's fellow gods are going to take his untimely demise!"

"All valid points. Whether they will be enough to override centuries of suspicion and dislike is yet to be seen. The Consul believes they will, and I sincerely hope she is correct. I do not relish the idea of proceeding into Faerie on our own. But Antonio is hardly going to come out and face us after this."

"So we have to go in and get him." The thought didn't make me any happier than it did Mircea. I'd been to Faerie once. I hadn't enjoyed the experience.

"Yes, but that can wait for another day. To more important matters." He looked at me severely. "Are you attempting to break up with me?"

"No! It's not . . . That isn't what I . . . I'd like to date," I blurted out.

He raised an eyebrow. "By vampire law, we are already married."

"But I'm not a vampire, Mircea! And I wasn't exactly asked about the marriage thing!"

"You wish I had not claimed you?" His face shifted to the closed expression vampires use when they're being especially guarded. Great. This was going about as well as I'd expected.

"No, that isn't what I'm saying."

I stopped and gathered my thoughts, trying to put what I felt into words. "I always viewed not having any attachments as a strength. I thought I was better off, not getting too close to people I'd probably just end up hurting. Sometimes, I still feel that way. I'm more of a target than before, more of a liability in some ways than I ever was. But I always will be now. And I can't live the rest of my life closed off from everyone. . . ."

"*Dulceață*," Mircea said patiently. "I am a target independently of anything you will ever do. And I assure you, I can take care of myself."

I shook my head. "Nobody can be sure of that, not anymore. We almost lost Rafe; we did lose Sal—"

His eyes closed, and a flicker of something crossed his face. "If I had broken her bond as she asked, Tony would not have been able to use her."

"He would have found someone else. We were vulnerable because of the problems within our alliance. He exploited it."

"Nonetheless, I will blame myself for that, always. And for Nicu's death."

I swallowed. I was still trying to deal with that myself. He'd died to protect me, and I'd barely even known him. And the only times I had talked to him, I'd mostly been yelling. Marco was right—there was a lot about vamps I still didn't understand.

"At least Marco's okay," I said, thinking about the last time I'd seen him. He'd been assigned a bed in the clinic, while the penthouse was being remodeled. He'd looked surprisingly cheerful for a guy who'd been staked through the heart. That would have killed anyone below master status, but Sal hadn't lived long enough to take his head, too, so Marco would recover.

"But it looks like I'm off guard duty for a while," he'd informed me, and then he'd made a noise that sounded suspiciously like a giggle. I'd just stared. I'd never seen him so happy.

"I have been too busy of late," Mircea said, watching Dee strip a pink negligee off a mannequin while a valiant salesman tried to shove her size fourteen foot into a maybe size eight shoe.

"I don't think it's going to fit," the sweating salesman gasped.

"If I had a nickel for every time I've heard that," she muttered, and shoved it home.

"You've done the best you could," I told Mircea. "That's all any of us can do. And that's ... I think that's what I've come to realize. I can't keep the people I care about safe by distancing myself. They're at risk anyway; they're always going to be. I just have to love them now, while I can. Now is all we have."

"I am afraid I am not following your reasoning, *dulceaţă*," Mircea said gently. "You want closer relationships, yet you push me away?"

"I'm not putting this very well," I said, frustrated. "What I'm trying to say is that the *geis* we were under gave us feelings for each other. But they were feelings we might never have had otherwise. I need to find out if what I feel is based on something more permanent than a spell gone awry. I want to get to know you. I want you to get to know me."

"You wish to be courted?"

"If that's what you want to call it. Yeah, I guess." He looked thoughtful. I took a breath and almost did it— almost asked about the mysterious brunette. But then I let it out again without saying anything. Screw it. I'd had an awful week; I deserved a break. Besides, if I was going to his court, I'd have plenty of time to ask around. And if he did have a mistress ...

"Is there a reason you are looking at me like that, *dulceaţă*?"

"Like what?"

"The last time I recall seeing something similar was on the battlefield—from an adversary."

"I'm not your adversary, Mircea. I just want to know you better."

"And you cannot get to know me as we've been?"

"Not and keep a clear head, no!"

He smiled at that, and then his gaze shifted to a spot over my shoulder and it faded. "These doubts wouldn't have anything to do with the company you're keeping of late, would they?"

I didn't get a chance to answer before the shop door was thrown open and a furious war mage stomped in. Pritkin spotted me and his eyes narrowed.

"You shaved my legs?!"

Mircea looked at me and folded his arms across his chest. I looked from one unhappy face to the other and suddenly remembered that I had somewhere else to be. "You know, Jonas said something about lessons," I said quickly. And shifted.

EMBRACE THE NIGHT

by Karen Chance

Cassandra Palmer may be the world's chief clairvoyant, but she's still magically bound to a master vampire. Only an ancient book called the *Codex Merlini* possesses the incantation to free Cassie—but harnessing its limitless power could endanger the world...

Available wherever books are sold or at penguin.com

CLAIMED BY SHADOW

by Karen Chance

Clairvoyant Cassie Plamer has inherited new magical powers—including the ability to travel through time. But it's a whole lot of responsibility she'd rather not have. Now she's the most popular girl in town, as an assortment of vamps, fey, and mages try to convince, force, or seduce her—and her magic—over to their side. But one particular master vampire didn't ask what Cassie wanted before putting a claim on her. He had a spell cast that binds her to him, and now she doesn't know if what she feels for him is real—or imagined...

Available wherever books are sold or at
penguin.com

TOUCH THE DARK

by Karen Chance

Can you ever really trust a vampire?

Cassandra Palmer can see the future and communicate with spirits—talents that make her attractive to the dead and the undead. The ghosts of the dead aren't usually dangerous; they just like to talk…a lot.

The undead are another matter.

Like any sensible girl, Cassie tries to avoid vampires. But when the bloodsucking mafioso she escaped three years ago finds Cassie again with vengeance on his mind, she's forced to turn to the vampire Senate for protection.

The undead senators won't help her for nothing, and Cassie finds herself working with one of their most powerful members, a dangerously seductive master vampire—and the price he demands may be more than Cassie is willing to pay…

Available wherever books are sold or at
penguin.com